Praise for Jane Healey and *The Ophelia Girls*

"No one writes more beautifully than Jar
—Natalie Jenner, internatic
of

"Set over the course of two stifling British summers, *The Ophelia Girls* is a dreamy exploration of the interior life of teenage girls and the tangled relationship between mothers and daughters. In her hypnotic prose Jane Healey captures the slipperiness of the adolescent experience, the thirst young women have for independence, and the sometimes perilous ways they attempt to define themselves. A siren song of a novel, *The Ophelia Girls* seduces as much as it disturbs."
—Ellie Eaton, author of *The Divines*

"*The Ophelia Girls* is a novel saturated with beauty, menace, longing, secrets—and with passions deep enough to drown in. It's a sinister, suspenseful page-turner that gripped me tightly and still hasn't fully let go."
—Clare Beams, author of *The Illness Lesson*

"Sensual and lush, *The Ophelia Girls* captures the dangerous power of approaching the world with an artist's eye, of seeing others and being truly seen in turn. Jane Healey's prose holds the haunting beauty of Pre-Raphaelite paintings, paired with a page-turning exploration of girlhood, secrets, desire, and art."
—Sara Flannery Murphy, author of *The Possessions*

"A lush, seductive portrait of desire."   —*Publishers Weekly*

"Deliciously atmospheric and brilliantly constructed, *The Ophelia Girls* tugs at the reader from the very first page until its satisfying finish. Engrossing and rich in imagery . . . Jane Healey writes the way dreams feel. I loved it."
—Elissa R. Sloan, author of *The Unraveling of Cassidy Holmes*

"A knowingly put-together page-turner; a potent blend of art, beauty, awakening desire, and mortality that seduces the reader."   —*Daily Mail*

"There's a feverish intensity to *The Ophelia Girls* that mirrors the drama of adolescence . . . Healey's second book is a compelling meditation on what it means to be a girl, and a woman, in a world that often wants to define that in a narrow way."

—*Book Reporter*

"A bruising and beautiful novel about girlhood and desire. Set over two heady summers, *The Ophelia Girls* perfectly captures the power and vulnerability of being a teenage girl. Within its flower-strewn pages, girls float carelessly down rivers and fall in love with devastating consequences. It's an immersive and intoxicating summer read with the long-lasting feel of a classic. I was captivated by it."

—Molly Aitken, author of *The Island Child*

"An atmospheric, haunting story that alternates between two summers and two teenage girls—mother and daughter—and explores the 'perils and power of being a young woman.' This is a challenging and memorable read that combines beautiful writing and creeping unease."

—*Book Riot*

"This novel has a sinewy, enchanting style that draws us into the reverie-like world of the river and its dangers and, like the characters it has so bewitched, never lets us go: it's powerful stuff."

—*Big Issue*

"Healey uses the art of photography as a means to view mother and daughter. As they are captured by different lenses, their lives become perfect representations of the secrets that threaten to destroy us until we live fully, and honestly, our own lives."

—*Portland Book Review*

"Those seeking stories of female coming-of-age and how experiences of sexuality and death can shape teenage girls into the women they later become will find much to explore in *The Ophelia Girls*."

—*Booklist*

THE OPHELIA GIRLS

THE OPHELIA GIRLS

A Novel

Jane Healey

MARINER BOOKS

Boston   New York

THE OPHELIA GIRLS. Copyright © 2021 by Jane Healey. Discussion Guide copyright © 2021 by Houghton Mifflin Harcourt. Excerpt from THE ANIMALS AT LOCKWOOD MANOR copyright © 2020 by Jane Healey. Note from the Author copyright © 2021 by Jane Healey. All rights reserved. Printed in the United States of America. No part of this book may be used or reproduced in any manner whatsoever without written permission except in the case of brief quotations embodied in critical articles and reviews. For information, address HarperCollins Publishers, 195 Broadway, New York, NY 10007.

HarperCollins books may be purchased for educational, business, or sales promotional use. For information, please email the Special Markets Department at SPsales@harpercollins.com.

A hardcover edition of this book was published in 2021 by Houghton Mifflin Harcourt.

FIRST MARINER BOOKS PAPERBACK EDITION PUBLISHED 2022.

The Library of Congress has catalogued the hardcover edition of this book as follows:
Names: Healey, Jane, 1986– author.
Title: The Ophelia girls / Jane Healey.
Description: Boston : Houghton Mifflin Harcourt, 2021.
Identifiers: LCCN 2021007263 (print) | LCCN 2021007264 (ebook) |
ISBN 9780358106418 (hardcover) | ISBN 9780358449829 |
ISBN 9780358449898 | ISBN 9780358105268 (ebook)
Classification: LCC PR6108.E118 O64 2021 (print) |
LCC PR6108.E118 (ebook) | DDC 823/.92—dc23
LC record available at https://lccn.loc.gov/2021007263
LC ebook record available at https://lccn.loc.gov/2021007264

ISBN 978-0-358-69743-5 (pbk.)

22 23 24 25 26 LSC 10 9 8 7 6 5 4 3 2 1

So much of my girlhood was fictive. I lived in my mind. I made up the girl I thought I was.

— Jenny Zhang

When we define the Photograph as a motionless image, this does not mean only that the figures it represents do not move; it means [...] they are anaesthetized and fastened down, like butterflies.

— Roland Barthes

Prologue

That summer of '73 they called us the Ophelia girls because we dressed up like Shakespeare's ill-fated heroine, or our own teenage versions of her, in silk slips from jumble sales and long floral dresses we ran up with our mother's sewing machines, and lay out in the frigid waters of the river in the woods, taking turns to stand on the mossy bank and take photos of each other looking beautiful and tragic.

We liked the way we looked and the way we felt in the water, our bodies held up and cradled, skin sharp with the cold; the stones under our backs shifting with the current. We would take the deepest section of the river, sometimes wade over to help each other into the right positions or to plait hair, rearrange the way our dresses lay to make us look as beautiful as possible. Sometimes we would sink a little further under the surface, until the lip of the water met over the end of our noses, and hold our breaths until our cheeks ached. Eyes open or closed, arms curled or stretched, we left our platform shoes, our sandals, on the riverbank.

We were fifteen, sixteen, seventeen then, and our families were summering at the cottages in the hamlet on the hill above the woods in the English countryside. Our parents had been bemused at first with our obsession, the armfuls of flowers we

picked or stole from gardens, begged from the startled boy
working at the florist, the outfits we sewed feverishly into the
night, the damp clothes left in heaps on our floors. But then
they grew concerned. We were obsessed, they said, foolish,
even hysterical. We laughed at them, at the name they had
given us, when we tripped up through the fields after dark
with our blue knees and shivering, coltish limbs, our sodden
dresses leaving a sticky trail behind us in the dry grass, petals
crushed underfoot. We smiled when we huddled together under
the shade of a tree to open the packets of developed photographs or watch our bodies bud and bloom on Polaroids held
in sweating hands. We quivered with a giddy kind of joy when
we lay out in the river, our dresses waterborne, lace and satin
and polyester moulding to our skin, rings tugged loose by the
gentle current, hair like weeds, flowers slipping from our grasp
and floating downstream.

I have run from that summer, tried to forget its hazy pleasures
and its tragedies, how it ended, how things fell apart. I have
trusted the years to fade my memories and destroyed those
photographs, never to be looked at again. But now, twenty-four
years later, back in my childhood home in that same hamlet
above the woods, and now a mother myself, the memories
keep returning, like driftwood washed ashore.

And though I have never since walked far enough through
the woods to reach the river, nor stood on its placid banks
while the willow trees whisper in the breeze above me, each
night I find myself waking gasping for air as if I am breaching
its surface, remembering the tug of the waters on my limbs
and the loamy smell that lingered for hours afterwards, my
chest slicked with a sweat that chills me to the bone.

Chapter One

Maeve is on her bedroom floor remembering what it was like to die. She has arranged her body in a slump, like she has fallen in a faint, and is listening to the muffled noises of the other occupants of the house – her mother corralling her two younger siblings, the six-year-old twins, who are talking loudly about their day at a petting farm, and her father, home early from work. She wonders how long it will take for someone to walk past her door and find her, and whether they will be concerned, whether they will rush to her with a cry and try to wake her, or know that she is only pretending. She would prefer the first, and feels guilty for that, guilty enough to eventually sit up, her hip sore from the thin carpet, her eyes adjusting to the light of the summer afternoon as if she has been buried underground.

This is her first summer free of hospital for many years, her first summer being *well* after the infections and complications from her bone marrow transplant two years ago. She is an ordinary seventeen-year-old girl now, not a sickly creature bound to bed, not punctured by needles and ports, not observed and watched and studied.

It is sick of her to miss it sometimes, her sickness, to miss the attention, the love, the care, the doting. Perhaps she came back wrong when they brought her back from the brink that day, perhaps the core of her is spoiled, like a book that fell in the bath whose pages are swollen and gummed together.

Death makes you glad to be alive, makes you take stock of all the things you have, the blessings, her father said a few months ago, after her grandfather's funeral, when he had slumped three glasses of wine down at the kitchen table in the poky flat in London where Maeve's family had lived so she could be closer to the hospital, the one they left for her grandfather's house in the countryside and its twenty-seven rooms and rambling gardens. But death didn't do that for Maeve, it only made life feel more fragile, tenuous. Every death scene in every film and show she had watched and book she had read, where the dying said their piece, where they felt comforted by the loved ones around them, where they fought the coming darkness, was replaced by a whirl of noise and pain and confusion that tumbled into an anonymous nothingness, a welcoming blackness. It frightened her how easy it was to die, and she kept wanting to return to that day in the hospital bed, her body weak from the cancers, her lungs liquid with pneumonia, and do it differently, feel something more than tiredness, than a body coming to its conclusion. How was she supposed to face the world now, or look forward to her future when she knew how it would one day end?

A summer here will be good for you, her father had said, when he helped unpack her belongings in the bedroom at the back of the house with the bay window looking out over the walled garden, the fields beyond and, in the distance, the woods down below in the valley. *You'll get colour in your cheeks – you'll remember what it's like to live again, to be wild and free like a teenager should be,* he added with a wink, before hurrying to his phone to answer a work call.

A week into said summer and Maeve is unconvinced, as she stares sombrely at her reflection in the mirror on her dressing table: her mother's old chipped dressing table in her mother's old room, with the fading rose-printed sixties wallpaper behind her. She makes herself smile, rearranges the mass of red curls around her shoulders, noticing all the imperfections of her skin, her face, in the streaming sunlight. In some ways she looks like how she feels inside, *peaky*, like one of those sickly Victorian characters from her favourite childhood books, but in others – the flush on her cheeks, her lips sucked red – she looks healthy and sometimes she hates that, looking well again like everything is fine. She taps her bitten nails against the tabletop, poses her head like one of those languid models in *Vogue* or *Elle*, tired and surly in their beauty. But a sudden cry in the house makes her freeze, her eyes wide in her reflection, and she stands up and hurries on unsteady legs towards the sound.

'Don't baby him, Maeve,' her mother says from the hob, as Maeve holds the squirmy mass of her little brother in her lap in the den connected to the kitchen. 'He's fine, there isn't even a bump.'

'He was crying,' Maeve replies, and her mother sighs.

Maeve can't bear it when children cry, when they wail, even if the reason is something trivial, like a biscuit snapped in two, or a cat running away. She knows how it is to feel wretched, inconsolable, and how the world can be so bright and painful. She understands the need to be spoiled and petted. And besides, her brother saved her life with the transplant of his bone marrow, so if she's going to baby anyone it will be him.

Michael – not Mike, never *Mike*, he corrects new adults of

his acquaintance with a scowl – is staring up at her beatifically as she strokes his hot head.

'Am I brave?' he asks her, in a small-boy voice.

'The bravest,' she declares. 'So brave that Mum will give you an extra chocolate mousse after dinner.'

'Maeve,' her mother says.

'You said he needed fattening up,' she replies, as Michael wriggles free and runs across the kitchen tiles towards his sister, Iza – never Isabella – to show off his newest war-wound. 'Why are we having chocolate mousse anyway?' she asks, with a nod to the fridge. Pudding is normally ice cream, or bourbon biscuits from the tin; her mother never likes spending too much time in the kitchen.

'We've got guests coming, did your father not tell you?' her mother says with a slight frown, and then winces as she burns her finger on the tray she takes out of the Aga. *That bloody Aga*, her mother has already taken to calling it.

'No.'

Her mother is running her finger under the cold tap, staring out at the garden vacantly. She's lost in her head so much these days.

'Guests?'

'Judy and her husband, the Shaws, Mrs Quinn from down the lane, and Stuart.'

'Who's Stuart?' she asks, fearing that someone might be bringing their horrible teenage son that Maeve will have to entertain. She'd rather miss the dinner entirely and hide in her room.

'Stuart's an old friend,' her mother says, turning off the tap. 'He lived with your dad and me at university, and I knew him growing up. His father was the gardener for the hamlet, back when the old Abbey estate still owned all the buildings except for this house and rented them out, the barn and oast house and all the cottages. Stuart used to spend his summers here.'

'Here, in Grandad's house?'

'No,' her mother looks bemused, 'in the cottage where his father lived. Although he was hardly there really – he spent most of his time outside, we all did.'

Maeve keeps forgetting that her mother had a whole life here before she left for London, before she was a mother. And the idea that both of them, Maeve and her mother, are spending their adolescence in the same place, that those neat slices of life might be held up and compared to one another, makes her uneasy. Her mother looks so wholesome in photos from her youth, her smile natural, and whenever she's mentioned those years there's been such a vast cast of characters that Maeve feels like a sad loner in comparison. It's not easy to make friends when you're in and out of hospital, when you're too tired to keep up the pretence that you care about so-and-so getting off with so-and-so, or so-and-so getting caught smuggling vodka into school.

'I hadn't seen him for years before we crossed paths this spring, neither of us had, because he was off abroad,' her mother continues. 'He was a war photographer, that was how he made his name, but he doesn't do that any more; he takes other pictures, for magazines. He might stay in the annexe here for a month or so,' she adds distractedly now, looking out of the window. 'He's doing a project across the south-east.'

'Do I have to come to dinner?'

'For a little bit at least, yes,' Ruth says, hurrying to the oven again. 'But I'm sorry there's no one your age coming tonight. Next time we'll invite the Langfords over, or maybe one of the girls from your new school?'

For so long, school to Maeve meant hospital school, the two

cramped rooms at the far end of one wing, their walls plastered with colourful posters about history and maths that were childish and yet a welcome break from the posters of medical information, the cartoons and fake fairytale forests and jungles painted on the walls of the children's wards.

But hospital school makes her think of so many things – the smell of disinfectant, the squeaky shuffle of nurses' shoes down corridors, the bleep of monitors that bled into fitful dreams – that she doesn't want to remember. So she hurriedly offers to help with dinner, hoping that the warm glow of her mother's appreciation might cover up the sick tremble inside her chest, as she cuts the fleshy roasted peppers into slices and plucks slippery olives from their cold brine.

The dining table has been moved to the large front lawn. The wasps hover lazily over the plates and the shade of the umbrella shifts away in the early evening sun. It's always awkward meeting her parents' friends, and it only seems to be more awkward as she gets older. They look nervous when they make half-hearted jokes at how grown-up she looks, as if she has muscled her way out of her proper place, as if she is some strange interloper. It makes her want to hunch her shoulders, it makes her want to scowl, but, having been a patient for so many years, she is good at being still, placid, pleasant, as they eat the starter of too-tart gazpacho and she helps the twins with the heavy silver spoons that her mother has brought out for company.

Stuart is late to dinner. They watch his car speed down the drive that curves around the lawn, and when he gets out, he folds his sunglasses on the collar of his t-shirt and walks over with a bottle of white wine in one fist, waving the other hand.

He looks younger, cooler, than the other guests despite the grey flecks in his dark hair, and not grizzled as she thought a war photographer should look. He looks interesting, she thinks, pulling her hair over her shoulder.

When he spots Maeve, his easy smile drops. *Poleaxed*, she thinks, as he looks at her with shock, her toes curling in her sandals, a twisting cramp of delight in her stomach.

She watches the nervous swipe of his tongue across his lip and then she glances down at her plate, blushing, and he greets her parents with affable apologies for being late.

He accompanies her father, who has placed an eager arm around his shoulder, into the house with his bottle of wine as Maeve watches their backs and wonders at what just happened, at his reaction. She glances at her mother to see if she noticed, but she's busy waving flies away and laughing at something Mrs Quinn – whose advanced age belies her dirty jokes – has said.

Maybe it was nothing, Maeve thinks as dinner continues, as Stuart barely looks at her after the first brief introduction from her parents, as she studies him. Maybe it was just the sun in his eyes, her own wishful thinking.

'God, it's been an age since I've been back here,' he says, leaning an elbow over the back of his seat as he surveys the house and the lawn, the pampas grass lining its edges, the trees that hide the house next door.

Sometimes when he talks his mouth quirks to the side, and when he blinks it's slow, thoughtful. His voice is softer than she first thought, his movements – the swing of his head, the twitch of his wrist on his knife – less confident. She's fascinated.

'Tell us about Ruth as a girl then,' Mr Shaw says.

'Oh, she was wild,' Stuart drawls, with a hint of something that makes her father laugh.

'I was perfectly proper,' her mother insists. Her cheeks are ruddy with wine and her blonde bob is sticking up on one side where she's tucked it behind her ear.

'Well, we were all wild back in those days,' Judy's husband says with a snort, and when he catches Maeve's eye he looks suddenly embarrassed.

They should really have these dinners with adults only, Maeve thinks, as she waves away his awkward offer of wine. Iza and Michael are busy with a game of their own invention, whispering sleepily to one another as they share the same bench on the end, but Maeve feels like she's just in the way, like the adults are children and she's the parent looking down on their fun.

'It was paradise here, really,' Stuart says, smiling down at his plate.

'Paradise,' her mother repeats, and lifts her glass so fast it clips her teeth.

Later, as the fabled chocolate mousses are brought out, sweating in their crystal bowls, and the twins are dozing off on a rug in the long shadows of the trees, her mother rests a hot hand on Maeve's shoulder.

'Can you take Mrs Quinn's flowers back inside, darling? I think they're drooping out here in the heat.' Her mother is using the voice she uses in company; posher, warmer, with a slight quiver at the end of sentences that Maeve thinks she's the only one who notices.

Maeve takes the large porcelain vase in her arms, clutching it to her middle, and walks carefully across the lawn towards the shingle path to the front door. When she's back at the table she'll say she wants to go to bed, that she's tired. No one has mentioned her illness, beyond an initial comment from a couple of the guests to her parents that she's *looking well*. If she says she's tired, her mother's face might drop, she might apologize, or she might just wave her off to bed.

Stuart has paused on his way back from the kitchen, the chilled bottle of wine at his foot as he crouches over the lavender bush, bruising purple flowers between his fingers. When he sees her coming, he puts his hands in his pockets.

'You don't have a lighter, do you?' he asks, taking out a cigarette from a battered pack.

'No.' Her face brushes against the flowers, a petal smearing across her chin. She wishes she did have a lighter, that she could pass it over to him and he could nod a thanks around the cigarette, that she could watch his stubbled cheeks suck in with the first sharp inhale. 'My dad might have one, although he's not supposed to.' Her father gave up smoking when she was born, but the stress of her time in hospital turned him back to the habit. Another thing to feel guilty for.

'A terrible example to make,' Stuart teases. He folds the cigarette into his palm. 'You know, you look just like a Pre-Raphaelite painting, with the flowers and your hair,' he says, and she feels dazed, thrilled, and hopes it doesn't show on her face.

He blinks and looks down at his feet like he might be secretly shy. 'I'm sorry,' he says, 'I bet that comparison gets old.'

'No,' she says, her body hot now as if it's midday. No one has ever noticed the resemblance except her, gazing at the postcards of paintings pinned to her wall, the girls with their ruddy red hair and plaintive expressions.

'Like the Lady of Shalott. Or Ophelia,' he says, eyes meeting hers again, a small smile on his lips as his voice trails off.

The vase is getting heavier, like her arms are being tugged

out of their sockets, but she doesn't want to leave. She doesn't want Stuart to go back to the table either. Then someone calls for the wine and he bends to pick it up.

'I think I'll stay inside now, can you tell my mother?' she says, feeling embarrassed by that word, *mother*.

'Sure. But you're all right?' he checks, looking at her carefully.

No, she thinks of saying. 'I'm fine.'

In the cool of the house, which is always dark, no matter the weather or the time of day outside, the wood a dark Victorian stain, the wallpaper in the hall a faded striped yellow, her foot slips on the worn-down tiles. Water slops on her feet from the vase and she wants to cry.

Chapter Two

Even dosed with wine, I still wake up from another nightmare, my t-shirt stuck to my chest with sweat, the feeling of watery weeds slipping over my ankles making me kick at the covers with a panicked moan.

Sheets shoved down to my hips, I stare at the ceiling as my breathing slows, trying to think of something other than water, than the river.

Alex is still asleep, his body ripe, his dreams peaceful. He's never woken easily. I used to have to plonk the twins right on him to get him to help them settle when they were crying and I was despairing of not having enough arms or leaking breasts or motherly reserves left to care for them. *Twins*. I love them but I would never do that again, I'm not sure now how I even survived those first years. If Maeve had been sick in that first year, and not later when they could be farmed out to nurseries for a portion of the day, I might well have gone mad.

Now that I'm awake, I can hear it. A drip somewhere in the house, soft and echoing. I picture a pool forming in a basin, picture it rising and rising and slipping over the edge onto the floor below, crawling out towards other rooms, wet and thick.

This house has five bathrooms. Our ensuite, the upstairs family bathroom, the smaller guest bathroom, the downstairs loo, and the outside toilet which the gardener used to use. Five bathrooms with leaky taps, with mildewed tiles and splotches of rusty mould, with ageing groaning pipes that need to be replaced as a matter of urgency. Alex sees the excesses of this house – all the rooms that a family of five don't actually *need* – as something to be proud of, to revel in. I see them as extra work, as caverns where money will get flung and lost in an attempt to keep this old house, my father's house, from crumbling.

I go in search of the sound, pausing outside my children's rooms, waiting to hear their easy breaths. I always feel a low panic that something might have happened to them, that they might have slipped away as I slept. When Maeve was sick and home from hospital, it wasn't enough to stand outside her door; I used to crouch by her bed and watch her, note the shadows under her eyes and her laboured breaths. Sometimes Alex found me there in the morning, slumped on the floor in a restless doze. *You'll tire yourself out*, he used to say, *she's fine*.

She's fine – a phrase meant to comfort but one that only ever made me want to protest that she's not, she's not fine, and I didn't notice it when it first began, I didn't listen when she said she was tired and breathless. I called it growing pains and told her *she was fine*.

The leaking tap is in the guest bathroom, the one so narrow that you can sit on the toilet and reach the sink and the bath at the same time. Now, as I stand in front of the sink in the dark, I cup a hand under each tap to find the culprit, or as if I am waiting for some kind of blessing, I think. For a moment, nothing, and then a cold drop in my right palm that rolls down the inside of my wrist.

In the shadowed mirror, I am ageless, unrecognizable. I could be her, my teen self, awake at night with giddy thoughts, restless with sadness, wishing to be anywhere but here. It could be the start of that summer, and I might be able to stop it happening before it did.

I was the one who took the first photograph of a girl in the river, and sometimes I think this means I am to blame for everything. It was a picture of Joan Summers. Joan Summers, with her straight black hair and watery blue eyes that looked eerie and old in some of the washed-out photographs.

She used to wear a particular stripy halterneck dress she'd bought on the King's Road that she had shrunk in a hot wash to show off her knickers, and had a reputation for being a good-time girl. If my mother had been alive, she might have called her 'trouble'; although maybe she wouldn't – not having any memories of my mother, not even the press of my baby cheek against her woollen jumper, or the touch of her soft palm on my forehead, I do not know what she was really like.

Joan's parents were drama teachers and later we would use their theatre programmes, the covers and illustrations in their books on *Hamlet*, along with the reproductions of Millais's *Ophelia* in my art books, to align our own visions with that of Shakespeare's heroine, but before that our inspiration had been more primal, innate, as if a drowning girl lived inside each of us waiting to be discovered.

It was me and Joan and one of the other girls that day – though who exactly I forget, maybe because by the end of our time in the river we became in some ways interchangeable, as if the water had softened the delineations between us – and we were walking along the riverbank in the sun, singing a James Taylor song with drooping daisy chains around our thin wrists. We threw sticks in the river to race, and when hers got stuck under a mossy root, I dared Joan to go in and get it. That day she was wearing a white, frothy peasant's blouse, and as she swore at us and clambered into the water to get to the other side of the river, the water made it billow out, turned it see-through so we could see the much-envied lacy brassiere she wore underneath.

I had a camera with me. I remember thinking that that year was important, worth recording, as if our small teenage lives could be set against the whirlwind happening in London, New York, San Francisco, Vietnam.

She turned around triumphantly when she had retrieved the stick and saw me unclipping the camera case.

Take a picture of this! she called. *Of me drowning in the river.* And then she swooned back with a laugh, with a theatrical wave of her arm, and I thought, *Yes, yes, this*, and something inside me trembled, bloomed. I crouched on the bank and Joan tipped her head back, stick forgotten and floating further downstream, her blouse borne up around her, her legs pale in the glittering green waters, the daisy chain joined by a fern frond that tangled around her throat.

Afterwards, I pushed the camera into Joan's hands to take my turn. And oh, that first step into the river, the cold of the water, the stones sore on my toes – could anything ever be sweeter than that?

It looked calm from the bank but a river isn't like a swimming pool, you don't slip easily into it and then lie placid; there's a current that wants to nudge you onwards, weeds and leaves and flotsam, stones and rocks underneath you, branches and roots like outstretched arms reaching towards you. The light on river water on a hot summer's day is blinding, brilliant in its patterns, the branches of the willows above dizzying in their detail as the lip of the water dances across your skin and the gurgling underwater world washes into your ears.

It was then, I think, that I understood baptism, and it was then that my body first felt alive, my own.

We didn't leave the river until we started chattering with the cold, until the sky grew dark with heavy clouds, and as we clambered through the woods, our clothes slapping against our prickling skin, we felt washed ashore on some strange new land. And when the photos were developed, when I cycled back from the village with the sealed packet, and the four of us sat underneath a tree with our mouths sticky from toffees twisted out of shiny wrappers, our legs criss-crossed over one another's, and we saw ourselves transformed by the lens and the film, the leaking light of the old camera like the golden light in the painting of a saint, like the summer sun blinding us, we felt a new thrum of power, of possibility.

Where did that possibility go? I think now, my hand aching as I try in vain to turn the cold tap tighter to stop the drip, as if fixing this one thing will prove I have some small modicum of control over this house. Where did the hopes and dreams of that girl go, the one who swore she wouldn't do what was expected of her, that she would live a life free of the shackles of marriage and children, that she would travel and make art, and leave these dark stifling rooms behind and never return?

I don't regret the children, not when they hold a piece of my heart inside them, but I would do anything not to be here, surrounded by my father's belongings, by my memories. There are no new answers to be found from this house, from the fields, the woods and the river, even if my dreams are searching for them. Only regrets, I think, as the sound of the dripping tap, a mocking metronome, follows me back to bed.

Chapter Three

The next day, Maeve takes longer than usual standing in front of her wardrobe, dissatisfied with every top, skirt, dress she has. She doesn't remember the last time she went shopping; she hasn't had the energy for it, nor the mental fortitude to deal with packs of teenagers roaming the aisles of Topshop and Miss Selfridge, so she's just been wearing her hospital clothes – soft and shapeless – or ordered from catalogues. She's slim but not too thin any more, she thinks, as she lifts up the large t-shirt she sleeps in, glancing nervously to the closed door of her bedroom and the curtains drawn across her bay window before she looks at herself in the mirror, eyes tripping from scar to scar. Her periods might have come late and still be irregular, but she looks like a woman: breasts, hips, dip of her waist above the hipbones that jut out of her skin like buried pottery shards.

Last night she wore a short-sleeved gypsy blouse and knee-length skirt, both made of cheap, stretchy fabric. Today what she wants is a slip dress, slinky, silken, in some pastel shade. But she'll have to settle for a denim skirt and a plain purple top with a peasant neckline, the one she hasn't worn before because it shows off the thumb-sized raised scar from the port below her left collarbone.

'You look nice today, darling,' her mother says at breakfast, and Maeve shrugs awkwardly.

Her mother is wearing a large sleeveless shirt and a pair of corduroy shorts that look mannish on her athletic build.

'We haven't talked much about the summer,' she continues, watching Maeve as she circles a spoon in the half-eaten Ricicles gone soggy.

Her mother used to worry about what she ate, used to stare at each spoonful Maeve lifted to her mouth as if it were the only thing that stood between her and death. Appetite was a marker in hospital, a small triumph remarked upon by nurses and doctors and other parents. *Oh, she's getting her appetite back now*, they'd say with knowing pleasure, with a jangling kind of relief.

'I'll get some strawberries in tomorrow,' her mother murmurs, and rinses out her own coffee cup. 'Summer,' she begins again. 'Have you thought about what you might like to do? There's some courses at the village. Art, music. Or we could get a tutor to come here if you like, if you're worried about catching up with school. And your father and I talked about taking you lot on a proper holiday, down south maybe. What do you think?' she asks, with a look of such tender hope it makes something inside Maeve squish, like stepping on a too-ripe fruit.

She winces, scrapes her spoon against the curve of the bowl. 'I just want to rest.'

'Of course,' her mother says, and rests a hand on her shoulder. 'But let me know if you change your mind. We could visit a historical house, or go to London and see a show, whatever you want.'

After breakfast Maeve returns to her room and lies on her bed, feeling her stomach gurgle. She turns her head to look at the wall of posters and postcards she put up in a brief manic burst her first week here because the tiny pattern of the old wallpaper was making her dizzy, because she wanted to make this space hers and not her mother's. She might have continued and plastered the other walls too, but her mother had said, *Oh, that looks nice*, when she came into the room the next day, and it had soured the whole thing.

Now, Maeve's eyes trace the fashion editorials as slow bass beats throb through her head from her Discman. A woman in a dress with a long train, sitting on a rearing horse. A woman lying on a pile of pastel mattresses, a modern Sleeping Beauty. Two women in white summer dresses, in a field blanched yellow with light. A glamorous girl slumped next to a large perfume bottle with a man in a sharp suit frowning at her, his hand curled tightly around her upper arm. The pictures of actors and actresses cut out of magazines, the handful of photos of a young childhood that seems so far away: her on her father's shoulders, her with a toothy smile holding the twins in her lap, her in a too-large tourist t-shirt frowning at the beach. And lastly, the images that have been on her mind recently, the postcards of paintings, mostly of women: Impressionist, Pre-Raphaelite, Renaissance.

She bought the postcards on the trips the hospital school took to galleries. When her mother had taken her round art galleries as a child, she had been bored, bought only pencils and colourful rubbers in the gift shop with the usual proffered 50p. But her trips with the raggle-taggle group of sick kids – with their headwraps and wheelchairs and oxygen canisters and shuffling feet – had been glorious. There was something slyly enjoyable about being part of such a group, about the pity and curiosity they created amongst the other gallerygoers.

Here is your sick youth, Georgia, her best friend, murmured gleefully in her ear once as a woman gawped at them. *Here*

*are the ghouls and ghosties you hide away. You too might get sick
and die!* she declared, making her thin arm shake as she pointed
at an elderly man, and Maeve muffled a laugh that hurt her
chest.

Sitting in front of the paintings then – at the Tate, at the
National Gallery – or the sculptures and statues in the British
Museum and the V&A, Maeve had an appreciation of their
beauty that was agonizingly sincere. She had felt the contrast
of her daily life – the fluorescent halls of the ward, the thick
plastic bars of her bed, the ache in her body – set against the
cool, marble-floored buildings with ceilings that soared like a
cathedral, the rich gold of the frames and the wonders they
encased: seascapes and picturesque ruins, women in every era
of costume, Eden-like gardens, sunsets and sunrises, gods and
goddesses, dresses of silk and lace and fur and samite. She
had fallen a little in love too with the guides their teacher had
arranged, in their tweed jackets, their black sheath dresses or
old-fashioned cardigans; the way their eyes glimmered with
worship when they looked at the art they were describing, the
point when they ran out of words and shrugged with a wry
smile as if to say, *I know I'll never be able to explain fully, I
know our language isn't good enough, but just look.*

She tries to summon that feeling now as she looks at her
postcards, tries to breathe her way into the memory. The warm
wooden bench under her; Georgia beside her saying *wow* under
her breath and meaning it; the haziness of her painkillers
dropping away for a moment of pure searing pleasure that had
nothing to do with her broken body, nothing to do with herself
at all.

But here, now, her leg is itchy and her stomach aches; the
pictures have the sheen of printed paper obscuring their
surfaces; and she is alone. Her heart flutters with a single

shake of panic, and she tugs out her earphones and sits up, rakes a hand through her hair.

At dinner on the patio in the back garden, the twins are fractious, whining and tired from a day of too much sun. Her mother sighs as she tries to get them to sit up straight, to eat their dinner, and her dad's jokes fall flat, Iza turning up her nose as if she is some rich old lady watching a terrible play, her curls frizzy around her face as though they have been set in rollers. Iza has the same dirty blonde hair as her father, and so does Michael. Maeve used to, but when her hair grew back from the chemo it was red like her mother's was as a girl.

Maeve is sitting at the other end of the table to her father, her usual favourite spot, but today, with Stuart there at dinner, she feels exposed, awkward, her eyes stuck on the dry wood of the table, grey with so many summers' exposure.

The house phone next to her father's elbow rings and he answers it quickly, striding back inside to his office. After a hastily served yoghurt, uneaten by the twins, her mother declares tightly that it's bedtime and guides her youngest back into the house.

Stuart smiles politely at Maeve. She should say something, she thinks, mouth sour with yoghurt, she should make the most out of these minutes when it's just her and him.

'Shall we take some of this stuff inside then?' he offers, stretching his arms over his head and running his hand through the waves of his hair.

Maeve nods, the scrape of her chair wincingly loud as she stands up. She counts the objects on the table, thinking about how many trips four hands will need to clear everything.

In the kitchen, she quickly decants the Greek salad into a

container, biting into a cherry tomato as Stuart heads back outside. She watches him through the low kitchen window as he bends over the table to reach something. She likes his belt, the way the brown stands out against the pale denim of his jeans and matches his worn suede shoes.

She rinses a cloth and carries it back out, the water cold on her fingers, drips darkening the patio slate before her. Stuart passes with an armful of plates, glasses, spoons. On the table there are two glasses left and a stack of placemats. She sweeps the surface with the cloth, feeling the hem of her skirt press against her thighs.

Stuart wanders out, unhurried, sipping at a fresh glass of water. She sees him glance at the port scar above the neckline of her top, and then he takes a seat on one of the loungers with murky green-yellow cushions at the edge of the patio. When she has finished wiping the table and stacking the two glasses on top of the placemats, she takes the lounger next to him, perches on the seat as if only pausing for a brief moment, as if she is so tired from wiping the table that it's only natural to sit down there.

The sun is setting, the colours in the sky like a painting. 'It's beautiful,' she remarks.

He nods, twirls his lighter in his hand, and then leans his head back against the seat. 'I heard about you being ill. Well, more than ill,' he corrects himself, looking pained as his eyes flicker to her scar again. 'It must be difficult now, to get over something like that.'

Her body softens in the seat. 'Yeah,' she says, and folds her top lip over her bottom. 'I stopped breathing once,' she confesses quickly, 'they had to revive me.'

He blows out a breath, raises his eyebrows. 'Shit.'

'Yeah,' she says again. Her knee is shaking, there's so much she wants to say. Her parents blanch when she tries to bring it up; her father has used the words *dwell* and *unhealthy*. It hurts them as parents to remember, she knows that, she's not that selfish. It's just that it hurts her too, all the time.

'That's heavy. Well, I'm glad you survived.' His smile is a little sad. She's pleased he doesn't say something like her father did, about death making you all the more glad to be alive. 'It must be hard,' he repeats, rubbing the side of his thumb against his bottom lip.

'It is.' She holds his gaze, soaks in his concern.

He rubs his dry palms together. 'I better get an early night, I've got a long drive tomorrow.'

She's up and reaching for the stack on the table when he says, 'Wait, I have something for you. Wait here and I'll get it from the annexe.'

'OK,' she says, and watches him lope across the back garden towards the gate that will lead him to the courtyard and then the old dairy, the annexe. It's a studio technically, a long one-storey building with whitewashed walls and a jumble of odd furniture rejected from the main house. When they moved here her father joked, in the way she knew wasn't a joke, about it being a hangout for her, that she could have friends to stay there, get up to all the teenage shenanigans she had missed being ill. She imagines herself inside the annexe, lolling on the worn corduroy sofa, holding a vodka bottle in her fist, a tinny house music beat working its quick way through her.

Maeve lingers on the patio. The light in the garden is now a purpling blue, the birds chittering in the trees, the breeze making her skin prickle. But she's worried she'll be found there, waiting, and will have to say why, so she starts making her way across the lawn. After last week's rain the grass is soft under her feet, the perfume of the flowers musty.

The gate creaks as he opens it. He doesn't seem surprised to find her in the middle of the garden, hidden from the house by the rosebushes. He has a lit cigarette in his mouth now, which he takes out to speak. 'Here,' he says, blowing smoke at an angle away from her, a small motion of consideration that feels achingly chivalrous. 'For your wall,' he says, as he gives her two postcards a little worn at the edges, like they've been jostled in a bag, or held in a hot hand for too long.

'Your dad was giving me the tour of the house,' he explains, answering a question she didn't ask, 'and I saw your wall from the door. Do you have them already?'

'No.'

'This is the Millais, of course.' He comes closer so that the sleeve of his t-shirt touches her arm, so that she can feel the heat his body gives out. 'And this is Waterhouse, the one from 1889. He painted three Ophelias, slightly differently each time.' The light has dropped now and she can't make out the details of the background of the images, just pale faces and the white of Waterhouse's swooning heroine.

'I've seen this one in the Tate,' she says, and looks up from the postcard to see him smile.

'I'm glad. The Waterhouse is in a private collection,' he adds, tapping the corner that sticks out, his finger brushing over her finger, making her knees twitch. 'Lucky fucker to get to gaze at that over breakfast every day. Although knowing the rich, he's probably got it in storage somewhere – it's criminal.'

The light of his cigarette is like a firefly in the air.

'Anyway, I thought you would like them.'

'I do, thank you,' she says, trying to imbue that phrase with a deeper gratitude.

'Goodnight then,' he says, with a brush of his hand on her shoulder.

'Night,' she murmurs, as the gate swings open and closed behind him.

Back in the house, she stands shivering in the middle of the dark kitchen before reaching for her father's fleece and pulling it around her, wrapping her arms around herself too. The postcards are in one hand, the surface cool against her palm, and when she hears a sound in the hall, she hides them behind her.

'What are you doing in the dark, darling,' her mother says in a teasing tone. 'Where is everyone?' she adds, as she turns on the tap and the pipes groan.

'Gone to bed,' Maeve says.

'Who was that on the phone?' she asks Alex as he joins them.

'Someone from work, some fuss in the Madrid office. That colour looks good on you, Maeve,' he says of his navy fleece. 'Are our two troublemakers asleep?' he asks Ruth, as he kisses her on the cheek and opens the fridge.

'Finally.'

'It's lucky you were such an easy child, Maeve, or we might not have had any more.'

'Lucky that you had them before I got ill, you mean,' she says, taking off the fleece.

'Hey, don't say that.' Her father frowns.

'I'm tired,' she says and leaves the room, climbs the stairs, pausing on the top of the landing, the place where you can hear almost everything in the house.

'Sometimes I feel like she blames us,' she hears her father say.

'Well, aren't we to blame?'

'I'm not going to dignify that with an answer. Are you sure you don't want to talk to someone?'

'About what?'

'About everything. Your dad—'

'I'm fine.'

'Fine.'

In bed, with the new postcards carefully pinned to her wall, Maeve thinks of the walled garden. She thinks of the rose-bushes, of the sliver of moon, the way the air on a hot summer evening feels thick with possibility. There used to be a pond near the back of the garden. She remembers crouching beside it as a child on one of her few visits to see her grandfather, staring at a pond skater and an autumn leaf twirling in its wake; she remembers the pain in her elbow when her mother snatched her back away from the edge. It was filled in with earth and flowers the next time she visited. But she imagines it wasn't. Pictures herself there tonight, waiting among the lilies and dragonflies, her skirt heavy with water, the tremble of her breath rippling concentric rings in its surface.

Chapter Four

We are in the upstairs room that my father used to store junk, the air hazy with warm summer light and the dust our movements have kicked up. Michael, Iza, me, and the window man Alex had invited round to give a quote without telling me, so that earlier I had left the downstairs loo while still zipping up my shorts to see a strange man in the dark of the hallway beyond the open front door.

He taps a pane with one finger. 'This window frame is rotten.'

'Is it?' I reply briskly. All of the windows are rotten and leaking, the paint of the frames peeling in extravagant ribbons and shards that make me glad the twins are not young enough to put things like that in their mouths. As we tour the rooms, so many of them a jumble of boxes old and new, the man's declarations of the windows' poor state, the suck of his teeth, the scratch of his head, have taken on a satisfied tone, as if he had judged this house falling apart from the outside and is pleased to be proven right.

'Have you tried opening this?'

'That one, no.'

'Mm, I wouldn't. When they're in a bad state, you can knock the whole thing out if you open it.'

'I'll keep that in mind.'

Iza is balancing on an old wooden chair, and I tug her back by her waistband as it wobbles when she reaches for a battered hat on top of the wardrobe. The twins haven't been allowed in here before and ignored my polite request that they go and play downstairs, or join Maeve who is wisely slumped in front of the TV.

Michael is jimmying open a drawer of the filing cabinet with loud screeches, and the window man looks over at him and then at me. Something on top of the filing cabinet falls with a thump and rolls towards the man, who coughs pointedly.

I'm not interested in my parenting being judged along with the rotten windows and the state of the house, and by someone I never actually invited around. 'Are you finished with your survey?' I ask.

'Well, almost—'

'I've looked at the windows myself,' I say, picking up the offending missile, a dusty cricket ball. 'They're all in a bad state, so just extrapolate, and call my husband when you have a quote.'

When I've led him to his car, I turn back to the house, ball still in hand. My thumb runs over the rough string, slides across the apple-red leather.

My father loved cricket. Sometimes he would bowl to me on the front lawn, calling out which ball he was throwing as I heaved his giant cricket bat towards it. I used to sit on the floor of his office on a rare Sunday when he was at home, listening to crackling test matches over the radio with the tang of pipe smoke and sherry in the air, hanging on his every wry comment. But he stopped playing cricket with me when I was nine or ten and stopped leaving the door to his office open, would switch off the radio when I knocked and entered, saying, *Yes? Did you need something, Ruth?*

I was too old to be a tomboy, to be treated as such by him, but he didn't seem to know what to do with me as a girl either. It was as though he assumed that the next part should be up to my mother, only she wasn't here. Most of my parenting had been done by the housekeeper and my teachers at school because he worked long days in London and went to events afterwards, sat on local boards, and disappeared on Saturdays for golf and lunches and more trips to the city; but that precious extra time with him faded away as I got older. He grew colder with me too, as if I was disappointing him, but left it up to me to work out why.

Stuart was welcome in his office though, in the last two summers before he went to university, and I had been jealous of him, though not as jealous as I would have been if he was being bowled to, perhaps, because I found everything about my father's job in business law boring. Stuart wanted to work in law too – though not in business or family law but to fight against corporations and governments, to take the people's side – and my father let him sit in on calls and discuss cases with him, quiz him on the knowledge inside the weighty tomes that looked desperately dull to my eyes.

Now, as I pass through the hall, I remember one summer afternoon when I had loitered there in the dark listening to the muffled voices in his office – my father's crisp consonants and then the silences where Stuart's softer voice fell. I remember that the empty house behind me had felt lonely, but that I couldn't muster the energy to leave it for the bright outdoors either. My feet had been cold on the tile floor, my hair gnarled at the nape of my neck after waking from another airless night.

I heard a creak but couldn't move fast enough as the door opened.

'I look forward to hearing your thoughts,' my father was saying, and I was close enough to see the warmth on his face as he looked at Stuart and then the twist in his mouth when he saw me.

I flushed.

'Hello, Ruth,' Stuart said with boyish delight.

At least someone was pleased to see me.

'Did you want . . . ?' He held the office door open for me.

My father was looking down at his desk now, scribbling notes in the illegible handwriting that made me feel bad for his secretaries.

'No, I was just passing by.'

Stuart closed the door and the hall was dark again. 'I don't know what you're doing inside on such a lovely day,' he teased, and I followed him out towards the front door. He paused on the threshold, squinting at the sun.

I had met Stuart for the first time about six years before, when I was walking along the lane of the hamlet and found a boy with dark curls and a sideways smile sitting in a tree. His father had just moved into the groundskeeper cottage, and Stuart was to spend his summers with him and away from his mother in London. *They're going to get divorced*, he told me confidently that first day, as we shared sudden intimacies in the way children sometimes do, placing story upon story on imaginary scales to see if we might measure up. I didn't see him between summers, or even think of him much, busy with my girlfriends from school, but whenever we met again we would slip back into a welcome closeness. Boys could be funny about being friends with girls, I had learned, but it seemed natural to Stuart.

'Are you coming to the field later?' I asked that summer day, as he pushed a curl behind his ear. There were three other teenagers staying with families in the holiday cottages, and we liked to hang out in the field near my house with the record player.

Stuart shook his head. His father made him work for him – mowing the lawns, shimmying up tree trunks, carrying garden waste to the compost or the bonfire, cleaning his tools. *It's not a holiday, boy*, Stuart would recite with a guttural voice and a hint of a sneer, when he did an impression of him. The rare times I saw them standing near one another, I was endlessly surprised that they were even related: father red-cheeked and large-bellied – mean – son sallow, slim, always smiling.

'How's the law going?'

'I'm learning a lot, being pushed. He knows so much.' His voice dipped as he looked back at the house wistfully.

'He's *my* father, you know, you can't have him,' I said, trying to make a petulant joke.

'I don't want him. Don't worry, I like you best,' he said, putting an arm around my shoulder and squeezing it.

I shook him off and stuck out my tongue, ran across the lawn knowing that he would follow me. He caught me halfway with a laughing tug on my arm. I bent over to catch my breath, and to hide my pleased smile.

'You don't mind him tutoring me, do you?' he checked.

'It's fine.'

'Not all of us were born with a silver spoon, you know, Ruth, I need every bit of help I can get.'

'Oh, yeah, we're rolling in money,' I said.

I remember that now, the solipsism of my youth, how I thought that because we didn't have nice cars and fancy holidays and fistfuls of cash, my father and I weren't comfortable, well off, compared to others, to Stuart. I think of it now that I know how expensive it is to keep a house like this one going, as my eyes skim across the patch of damp by the base of the stairs and the bulge of the flaky window pane at the top, before returning to the junk room.

The piles of boxes, the sheer weight of my father's belongings crowding out the room, make me angry. Why should I be the one to have to clear it out, why couldn't he have done it? I hadn't expected to be left the house and its responsibilities – we were estranged after all – but when I told Alex this, he only said quizzically, *Well, who else would he have left it to?*

Alex is a fan of logic, of things that make sense, and estrangement doesn't make sense. He doesn't like to have the neat rules of his world upset. When Maeve had first been diagnosed, he had sat there frowning at the doctor as if she were a schoolchild who had made a mistake with her algebra.

I'm in the garden when Alex gets home, drinking a gin and tonic with gin pilfered from my father's healthy stash of dusty bottles in the cellar, and an old tonic from the fridge gone almost flat.

'I saw Paige at the station,' Alex says, as he walks up to where I've dragged a chair, facing the rosebushes.

'Who's Paige?'

'The market stall. The woman who sells honey from her bees?'

'Oh, yes.' Alex has discovered the Saturday market in the village and comes back from his trips laden with farm goods of varying quality, gossip, and a wholesome glow. The things he buys are extras; he doesn't have to do the twice-weekly shop or drive in and out to the village, to the pharmacy and the doctor's and the library, with the twins arguing in the back. He still has to drive to and from the station in the other direction though, so perhaps I'm being unfair.

'Have a good day?'

'You didn't tell me the window man was coming.'

'Did I not?'

I stand up and shield my eyes from the sun. 'I'm not a housekeeper, Alex.'

'Hey, where's this coming from?' He puts a hand on my arm. 'You know they needed doing. I'm sorry if I forgot to tell you. If you let me know your schedule—'

'We don't always have one. You can't expect that I'll be waiting around here.'

'That's not fair—'

'We can't even afford the windows done.'

'I wanted to check, to be thorough.'

Stuart has arrived home now and is walking towards us. 'I brought some rosé, do you two want some now?'

'I'll get the glasses,' Alex says, and I watch him go.

'Alex thinks I'm pissed at him.'

'How come?' Stuart gets a penknife from his pocket and hinges open the corkscrew. He's so boyish, Stuart, so the same as he was as a teenager. Puckish, earnest, sly, with that core of gentle sadness that had a line of girls at his door in halls, never laughing off every hint of vulnerability like other young men could. I've missed him.

'Oh, I don't know. He scheduled someone to look round the house and I didn't know they were coming.'

'Wow, that does sound bad,' Stuart teases sarcastically. 'I'd be on the gin and tonic too.'

'Yeah, I know, even our arguments are thrilling here in Middle England,' I sigh. 'How did you know what I'm drinking?'

'Your dad used to use that glass for his G&Ts too.'

'I don't remember that.' I tap my nails on the crystal.

We head to the patio, and the twins spill out of the door with ice lollies that will no doubt ruin their appetite for dinner.

'You ask him,' Alex is saying to Michael, with a nod towards Stuart.

Michael puts his hands behind his back and looks at Stuart sceptically. 'Have you ever used a gun?' he asks him.

'Alex,' I reprimand.

'No, it's fine,' Stuart says. 'No, Michael, I've never used a gun.'

Michael sighs disappointedly and joins his sister.

I remember seeing Stuart's pictures of the atrocities in Bosnia in a weekend magazine once, with a hollow-cheeked photo of him, his eyes smudges of black, at the end looking a world away from the carefree boy he had been. He had always wanted to be a lawyer but sometime after university, in those busy couple of years when Alex and I were finding jobs in London, getting married and then getting pregnant much earlier than I had ever planned, Stuart drifted away from us, and then left the country completely and stopped answering letters or calls. The first I'd seen of him since had been at my father's funeral, which he had heard about from an old university friend, and then Alex and I had gone for lunch with him a few weeks later and he'd mentioned he was looking for somewhere to stay in the summer.

'Actually, that's a lie,' Stuart tells us. 'I've never shot one, but sometimes when you meet with rebel leaders they like to show their guns off, want you to pose with them. If they had asked me to fire it at a target, a painted one, I would have probably agreed. We'd do anything for access, to get that one photograph.'

'And now you're here in boring Kent,' Alex says, clasping his shoulder. 'No shootouts and rebel leaders here. You'll have to make do with us this summer.'

'How does it feel to be back?' I ask. After he left for university I don't think he ever came back to the hamlet, and his father had left the area himself a few years afterwards following a heart attack.

'It's strange, strange but good.' Stuart sets his pack of cigarettes and lighter on the table and stretches out his arms. 'This old farmhouse,' he adds, his eyes cutting to me.

'What's that?' Alex asks.

'Don't you remember at the beginning of uni when Ruth used to tell people that she grew up on *a farmhouse*, as if she lived in a two-room cottage with a dirt floor and a pigsty?'

'I remember you teasing her about it. I think it was before I met you both.'

'It wasn't quite like that,' I protest but know he was right, feeling the second-hand wash of embarrassment. It was the era of counterculture and my home, my upbringing here with a distant father and a housekeeper, felt so strangely Victorian that I was ashamed of it. Stuart had introduced himself as the groundskeeper's son of 'Ruth's estate' a few times at parties that he, a cool second-year, took me to in my first term at university reading literature, and I hated it – although this being Cambridge, no one batted an eye at the idea of someone having an estate. I had followed in my father's footsteps at Cambridge, not that he seemed to be all that proud of me – for that or anything else – and I'm pretty sure he had used his connections to put in a good word for Stuart too.

'It is a gorgeous house though,' Stuart says, looking back at it, 'I always loved the colour of the bricks against the ivy.'

The ivy that is crumbling the mortar, I think, brushing a wasp from my shoulder. And the roof shale that is leaking and needs to be fixed before the autumn – but with what money? – the dodgy plumbing, the Aga that eats up so much oil, the damp in the basement leaching upwards, the peeling wallpaper, the patch of black mould I found yesterday in the utility room, the ancient wiring that keeps blowing out the fuses. Alex won't listen when I ask him what we should do, tell him we can't afford this house and the upkeep it will need, alongside paying for the twins to go to the local private school because of the terrible Ofsted reports for the state primary; to him all that matters is that it's ours, mortgage-free after the negative equity disaster of our flat in London.

'It's not quite grand enough for my project though, you're right,' Stuart continues.

'What is it again?' Alex asks.

'It's called "English Ruins". I take photos of English stately homes and their owners in their pearls and hunting jackets in their finest rooms, the ones with family portraits in gilded frames and antique tables topped by chinless busts and oriental clocks. And then I take photos of the staff behind the scenes in the poky backrooms and crumbling attics, but with the same large-format camera, the same composition and light. It's a comment on class and decay, on the edifice of old Britannia crumbling.' His fingers make the shape of rain in the air.

'And the owners let you?'

'I'm upfront with them – maybe not about the mission statement, but they know what I'm taking pictures of. I think they think people will feel sorry for them, like they're posing for an article in the *Mail* to drum up sympathy and funds for their houses. It's a far more bucolic assignment than some of my previous projects.'

'You know, I always thought you were going to be a lawyer.'

'Plans change,' he shrugs, 'and I'm not sure we really know what's good for us as young people, teenagers, do we?'

As a teenager I wanted to stay in that river forever, I wanted to never leave. To stay in a watery world of fantasy and sister-hood.

A shout from Iza has me gladly leaving the conversation and its invitation to ruminate more over the past. As I walk through the thick grass towards the filled-in pond where Iza has hidden herself between the blue hydrangea and the purple buddleia, my neck feels hot, as if Stuart might be watching me, Stuart who was staying with his father that summer of '73 too, who knows at least some of what happened then. But when I glance at him, his head is tilted back and he is studying the house instead.

Chapter Five

The only places in the house that you can see the annexe from are the drawing room and the tiny glass room next to it that her mother said was called the flower room. It is only large enough for three people to stand inside shoulder to shoulder and has a tiny bench and a shelf, and it sits between two sets of narrow double glass doors with the original curving handles, one set leading to the overgrown former vegetable patch with the dairy courtyard beyond.

That rainy afternoon, as Maeve sits on the antique tufted armchair in the drawing room, its fabric worn to a roughness like horse hide, she studies the flower room from a distance. Was it for flowers to be grown in? Or for flowers to be arranged, their stalks snipped and lower leaves discarded in a heap before the neat vase of blooms was carried into the rest of the house? Did some servant work there, between its narrow glass doors, sweating on hot days, feeling like a beetle pinned under glass? Or was it the daughter of the house who tended to her plants there, breathing in the hot smell of vegetation, imagining herself striding through some jungle landscape, free from the watchful eye of her mother in the room next door? Would she touch the petals of a miniature rose and sigh at their velvety softness, feeling her ribcage ache at the press of her corset like the grip of a large pair of firm hands?

Maeve opens her eyes, watches water overflowing from the gutter pour down the outer doors of the flower room, a river of it occluding the green outside and the roof of the dairy beyond.

The drawing room is still full of her grandfather's things. She drifts from table to shelf to chair, studying them, rubbing her fingertips through dust and old wax. She remembers little about her grandfather, and what she does might only come from photographs. They – she and her parents – used to make trips here when Maeve was little, but never overnight, even though, she thinks now, there would have been so many empty rooms waiting for them. There are photos in their family album of Maeve on the front lawn holding her grandfather's hand, in the kitchen stirring cake batter in a bowl next to her mother, and here in the drawing room, sitting on her grandfather's lap behind his desk.

Perhaps she can recall cigar smoke, a deep voice, thinning grey hair. Or perhaps not, she thinks as she runs a hand along his desk, and then crouches before one of the dark wood cabinets to either side of the fireplace. She searches through a stack of dusty yellowing folders and boxes, empty photo frames whose loose glass is still sharp, antiques wrapped in crinkled old newspaper – tarnished candleholders and napkin rings, an ivory wine screw, two small glass bottles. There's a watch in a case lined with velvet, the leather of its strap stiff when she tries to put it around her own thin wrist. She imagines Stuart wearing it, imagines fastening it around his arm for him, feeling the bend and snap of the tendons underneath his skin.

Tanned skin, older skin, feels different to the touch. She remembers a doctor who examined her once, his meaty hands like a boxer, the scrape of a callus on his knuckle against her belly making the hairs on her body stand on end. *Sorry, my hands are cold*, he had apologized, but she could tell by his glance that he knew just why she'd shivered, even with the nurse there and a chaperone. No one had ever touched her inappropriately, but sometimes now she wished they had. A sick wish, and a sick thing to be doing, trawling through her grandfather's belongings looking for secrets. But it's raining, her father is at work, her mother busy with the twins, and Stuart is out taking photographs of other people somewhere else. She's bored, but she knows that word covers up a tremulous well of other feelings.

There's a photo right at the back of the cupboard, jammed behind the shelf. Two photos, she corrects, peeling them apart and bringing them out into the light. On one of them, yellowed by time, teenagers sit in the grass, squinting at the sun, laughing. It's mostly girls, in short dresses and earth colours, seventies fashions, with hair lying lank on their shoulders. She searches for her mother in their faces but it's hard because they're all bleached by time. There are three boys too, their hair long and legs bared by short shorts or encased in tight flares.

Is that Stuart? she thinks, leaning closer, pressing down on the photo as if it might make the image clearer. The boy has dark hair and a familiar smile, and is resting back on his elbows, ankles crossed over one another. He isn't holding hands with any of the girls, nor leaning cosily on their shoulder, and she is relieved.

The second photo doesn't contain any people. *The river*, the caption on the back says, in handwriting that might be a younger version of her mother's. *Which river?* Maeve ponders, fingers tracing the silver glimmer of its surface. *Is there one nearby? In the woods, maybe?* She hasn't ventured in there yet.

In the other cupboard under a stack of old law journals she finds a shoebox with her name written on it. She glances to the open door and then pulls the box out.

Her parents don't really talk about her grandfather; there were no pictures of him displayed at any of their London flats, nor cards from him for the children's birthdays and Christmas. Grandparents are supposed to do that, to send gifts, Maeve remembers telling her mother, serious in the way only an aggrieved child can be, and how Ruth had said she was sorry that she couldn't give Maeve a better grandfather. Her mother and he were not close, she has gathered over the years, and she never heard her cry when he died, but then her mother seems to pride herself on her strength, on never saying she is tired, fed up, that she's had enough, on always staying on her feet.

Lifting the lid of the box, Maeve finds a fistful of cards, named again in her grandfather's old-fashioned scrawl, and two wrapped presents, their paper faded and dull.

The thundering noise of the twins set free from their cartoons and running through the house, followed by the call of her mother, has Maeve shoving her finds back inside the cupboard, brushing her clothes of dust and sitting back on the tufted chair.

She closes her eyes as two sets of footsteps hurry inside the room.

'Don't run around in there, you'll knock something over,' her mother says from the hallway.

Maeve hears noisy breathing next to her, the inscrutable whisper of twin to twin. 'What are you doing?' Iza asks.

'Sleeping,' Maeve replies.

'Don't lie, you're pretending,' Michael says. 'You're smiling.'

'Am I?'

'Yes,' Iza says, and Maeve opens her eyes with a gasp, making them jump and laugh.

She wriggles her hands in their sides so they giggle and squirm away from her.

Once they're gone, she takes the cards upstairs, hiding them under her top in case she's seen.

The contents of the envelopes – birthday cards for her tenth to sixteenth birthdays and a couple of Christmas cards – are mundane and don't reveal any secrets beyond the one that makes her eyes hurt: that her grandfather had written her letters, that he had thought of her. *To my granddaughter Maeve,* he writes in the last, *I hope you have a wonderful birthday. I'm sorry that I can't join you for cake, I hope you will forgive me. I can't believe how old you are now, I remember when I could hold you in the crook of my arm.*

Why did he never send these to her? Did he just forget? Why did he and her parents fall out? She doesn't know who to blame for their estrangement but she wants to blame someone, because now she feels like she's missed out on knowing him, on being loved by him, and it's too late because he's dead.

Later, the rain has stopped and the sun is steaming it from the earth and from the leaves, drying the grass beneath Maeve's feet as she sits on the bench in the far corner of the garden next to the lavender bush, wanting to escape from the house and her twisting sadness. Branches of one of the apple trees outside the garden droop over the top of the crumbling brick and fuchsia is bright at her side, its petals reminding her of the dress of the flower fairy in one of her favourite childhood books. If she slits her eyes open she can see the whorl of the iron of the gate, and is thus perfectly positioned to see Stuart come into view half an hour after she first sat down, pausing with his hand on the gate as he looks at her.

'Enjoying the sun?' he asks.

'Yeah.' She holds her hand above her eyes like it's him who is too bright to look at as he walks closer. 'How was your trip?'

'Bit boring,' he says with a shrug.

He's standing in front of her now, throwing his shadow over her. 'How was your day?'

'Bit boring,' she shrugs and he laughs. She wants to tell him about what she found, but doesn't know how to explain why silly childhood birthday cards made her feel so upset.

'Can I tell you a secret?' he says, sitting next to her on the bench, setting his camera bag carefully down at his feet.

'Of course.'

'I'd rather be working on my other project, not taking photos of boring rich people and their fancy houses.'

'What project?'

He has the keys to the annexe in his fist still, is wearing his usual belt and leather shoes, sunglasses hooked on the neck of his faded shirt, plain watch on his wrist and a braided leather bracelet beside it. His wallet is peeking out of his pocket, and she sees the shape of his silver lighter in the other, assumes he has a pack of cigarettes in his back pocket as well. Maeve is wearing only a sundress. She likes the contrast between them, likes that he has so much *stuff*.

He leans forward, rests his arms on his legs. 'I have this idea to remake old paintings in modern settings, in photograph form. Like those postcards I gave you. Paintings that reference myths or cultural icons. I want to try and translate them into the modern world.' He squints and looks up at her. 'Does that sound stupid?'

'No, I think it sounds amazing.'

He smiles. 'I'm glad you approve.'

Will he ask to take her photo? Surely he will, she thinks. He told her she looked like Ophelia, he gave her those post-cards. But maybe he has proper models in mind, willowy creatures without scars or round cheeks. Maybe he's just being nice to her, friendly like an adult to the daughter of his friend. Maybe she's an idiot.

'Are you all right?' he asks.

'I'm fine.'

He studies her like he doesn't believe her. 'Are you still in pain?' He looks pained himself, as though it hurts him to think of her suffering, as though it's unimaginable, and she loves him for it.

'No. I mean, there was some pain but it was mostly exhaustion, you know. Bone-weary tiredness.'

'I've never been seriously ill. I have scars, I've been injured, but not sick, touch wood. And some of those injuries were my own fault. Like the time I bruised my coccyx and broke my wrist.'

'What do you mean?'

He looks down and she notices the fan of his dark eyelashes.

'Oh, I was doing something stupid as usual. I was on assignment in Sarajevo during the siege,' he says with a scrub of his fist through his hair, 'and I was just trying to observe the horror, you know, the devastation of it all. Neighbour becoming enemy, death arriving at the corner where your children used to play, dodging marksmen as you walked to the shops. I still have these dreams—'

He makes a sound in his throat and she touches his arm. She wants to be the one to comfort him, she wants to reach him wherever he's gone.

'Anyway,' he continues, catching her wrist gently and turning her arm as she tries not to make her own sound. 'I saw this shape in the street and I thought it was a young child. The others were trying to call me back but I was feeling heroic and stupid, and I slipped on rubble and broke the bones here,' he says, stroking across the thin skin of her inner wrist, making her stomach clench. For a moment, she feels the same queasy flush as she did when a gloved nurse searched for a vein, a zap going through her blood vessels, before he slides his grip to the base of her hand, before she breathes in the smell of his aftershave.

He studies her palm. Her fingers have reflexively curled in, like the petals of a flower in a rainstorm. He brushes a fingertip along the inside of her index finger to straighten it out, a twitch of movement at the corner of his mouth.

'What happened to the child?' she asks.

'Oh, it was only a coat or something,' he says, meeting her eyes now and relaxing his grip on her wrist so she has no choice but to take her arm back. 'I was an idiot.'

'How can you be an idiot for trying to help someone?'

'You're not meant to get involved as a photographer, you're meant to be an impartial observer.' The keys in his other fist jostle. 'But we're not robots, you know. Everyone reaches their limit,' he says, looking at her as the sun heats her legs to molten warmth, turns the top of her head hot like a halo; the flowers bright against the green around them, the grass tickling her feet.

'Did you know my grandfather?' she asks.

'I did.' He looks away from her.

'What was he like?'

'Clever, self-contained, old-fashioned.'

None of those descriptions help her much.

'He was mentoring me, as the Americans would say. I wanted to be a lawyer, and the last two summers I was here I spent a lot of time in his office, or the drawing room as he called it, listening as he recited letters and documents to his secretary over the phone, discussing law with him and other things, history, philosophy.'

'I'm jealous of you, I don't remember him at all.'

'Really?'

She shakes her head. 'We didn't see him at all after the twins were born.'

'That's strange.'

'Yeah. I was looking through his things today and found these birthday cards from him but he never sent them.'

'I was at your christening, you know.' He rubs his fingers across his mouth, smiles wryly. 'I arrived late, once you were already down for a nap, but everyone there talked about how proud he was, how he had carried you around the garden of the hall.'

'I wish I could remember.'

'Well, you were only tiny then, no one remembers that far back. He would have been a good grandfather to you, I think. You should ask your parents what happened.'

'You think they're to blame.' She's never had a conversation like this with an adult who wasn't a teacher or a doctor, whose care she wasn't under.

'I didn't say that.' He smiles as he gathers his bag and stands up.

'Hmm,' she says, narrowing her eyes playfully. 'I think you know something. Just you wait, I'll wear you down.'

'I bet you will,' he says, head tipped to the side.

When he's left her, she replays the look on his face, the tone of his last words. She's not just imagining it, she's sure.

Chapter Six

In the garden, I pin laundry to the line, wrestling with the clothes pegs and the slack line, missing the cosy rumbling space of the laundromat in London, the familiar faces I used to see, the daytime television that we watched and commented upon as we waited for our loads to finish, the air fusty with fabric conditioner.

It's the company I miss from London, from my working years in offices and then afterwards when I was a mother full-time; the mostly anonymous kind, the press of other people's lives that made mine seem smaller and more manageable. Like those little moments of grace in the hospital waiting room amongst so much fear and horror – a mother taking her own mother's wrinkled hand, a child's cries halting after the fifth iteration of a mumbled nursery rhyme from a tired father who barked a hysterical laugh that almost set him going again, or the lost teenage visitor who plucked up the courage to ask the receptionist where he was as the waiting room silently cheered him on. I don't like the quiet here. The open, lonely spaces.

As I turn to the sun I sigh and close my tired eyes, feel the animal pleasure of warmth on my face, see the blush of my eyelid, the threads of capillaries. I imagine that when I open them again I will see the dry earth of the path through the field towards the woods and be holding a hot fistful of corn-flowers. Breathing in the warm smell of the grass, I picture Sarah Lithlingow on the path beside me, fumbling the French words of a song she had once seen Bowie sing, her chin rising and falling with the slide of notes from high to low, holding the long skirt of her coveted Laura Ashley dress with its tiny blue flowers above her knees so she could hop from patch to patch of grass.

Sarah was my second favourite photo subject. A curvy girl who shrugged at the era's lust for trimness, looking bemused any time dieting was brought up in conversation. Where did that inner confidence come from, that absolute ease with her body? And is she still like that, or have the years changed her? I hope not.

'I want to look homespun,' she said, that day at the beginning of the second week of summer as we entered the woods on our way to the river. 'Like I'm on the American prairies, like I've been waiting for my soldier beau to come home. Like there's a river nearby where I go to sit and feel anguished.'

'Are there rivers in the prairie?' I asked, clambering over the branch of a fallen tree.

'There are rivers everywhere, Ruth.'

'We should get a photo of you standing on the bank then, and one with the water at your knees before you swoon into it, overcome by the letter that says he's never coming back—'

'Because he's died in the war. Oh, or he's wedded someone else.' She clutched a hand to the ruffles on her chest. 'Or maybe I could be a milkmaid . . .'

'Is it a cow she mourns then? One gifted by her sweetheart?'

She pushed at me and laughed, and we tumbled into the clearing by the river where Joan and Linda Harvey were waiting.

Linda was the oldest of us at seventeen and would be off

to university after the summer. She ringed her eyes with heavy mascara that melted in the river, making dark tears smear down her cheeks that looked all the more tragic on film. Her hair always started off straight but when she emerged from the water it would curl and puff up as it dried, while she used a hand mirror that flashed the sun's light in a neat searing circle to reapply an orangey lipstick worn almost to the nub.

'Did you bring the camera?' she asked.

I lifted it up. It was a Pentax with an adjustable lens and a black and silver casing that shone in the sun. I had borrowed it from my father – without asking him because I thought it likely he would say no.

'I brought the flowers,' Linda said, nodding towards the pile of foliage as she inhaled the last of her cigarette. 'Some from the meadow, some from our garden. My dad said, if he knew spending the summer in the countryside would get me flower arranging, he would have done it earlier.' She rolled her eyes.

I crouched by the flowers, snapping thinner stems to make them shorter, sawing with the golden sewing scissors I had brought with me, which were really not sharp enough to deal with tough fibrous stems. My fingers were soon sore and sticky with sap. Joan had borrowed Linda's mirror and was frowning at a blemish on her chin.

Camille entered the clearing then, waving with that shy dip of her head, her battered satchel thumping against her bare thighs. With her presence, the five Ophelia girls were complete. Camille Prudence, a swot who probably wouldn't have been friends with girls like Joan and Linda at school but who had been welcomed into their confidence here on summer holiday, and here at the river.

'I got distracted,' she said, sitting down cross-legged.

'By a boy?' Linda asked.

'By books.' She nudged her satchel.

'*Books*,' Linda replied with a put-upon sigh. 'Are you going first then, Sarah?' she called out.

Sarah kicked off her shoes and edged down the riverbank, her breath punching out at the cold of the water. She laughed when she waded further in, showing us how the water had made her dress billow out like a circus tent around her. 'Glamorous enough?' she asked, posing a hand by her head like a model.

'You make an excellent milkmaid,' I told her, snapping a photo of her as she was.

She stuck her finger up at me and I took a photo of that too.

When she sank back into the water, her giddiness turned into something quieter. Her face creasing with that now-familiar fusion of ecstasy and pain at the cold and the concentration needed to float and not be pulled away down the river, the concentration to look serene. When you're that close to the surface of the water, it can blind you if you don't pick something to stare at – the blue of the sky, the willow trees, a camera lens.

'She's forgotten the flowers,' Camille said by my side, with a touch to my waist that made me twitch. 'Here.' She passed them to me. She had tied them into a neat bouquet with string.

'Thanks.'

She sat next to me on the bank, the both of our feet trailing in the water. Perhaps it was wrong to describe Camille as shy; it was more that she often seemed in her own world, that she was quiet.

Sarah rearranged her own hair and the flowers, and her dress whose volume and weight were difficult to control. She kneeled on the riverbed and frowned.

'Wait,' I said, 'just like that,' and I took a photo of her. Her head was above the surface, ropes of her hair pulled taut around her as if she were holding the weight of the water, the reflection of the sun making her face golden, and the billow of her dress underneath her pale and ghostly.

Then she turned onto her back and rolled over and over in the water, laughing, her body churning up silt, the skirt of her dress hoisting up around her waist as her legs kicked. I took a photo of her then too, and I remember that when it was developed the only thing you could see amidst the maelstrom of choppy water and bright sun was a pale arm grasping upwards.

Afterwards, once Sarah had taken photos of Joan and Linda of Camille, we sat in a circle in the sun, the clink of Joan's bangles joining the sparkling sound of the river behind us, passing around a flask of sun-warm water as if it were a libation.

'Geoff asked what we've been doing, at dinner last night,' Sarah said, speaking of one of the two teenage boys who were also staying with their families at the cottages. I wasn't a fan of Geoff – he was brash and had, I thought, the makings of a bully, especially when compared to someone innately considerate like Stuart.

Most of the families had dinner together, with the wives taking it in turn to cook. It would have been convenient, no doubt, for us to use the long table in the garden of my house and not the three odd tables that were shoved together near the chestnut tree in the cottage Joan's family took. But my father, when he was not busy at work, did not socialize with the *temporary residents*, as he once called them. I think he was disappointed that the previous owner of our house hadn't been able to buy the rest of the estate at the same time, that he wished he owned the whole hamlet, although he would hardly have been able to afford all of the different buildings just on a lawyer's salary. But if he had an opinion on my taking dinner with the guests, he didn't share it; as a child I ate dinner with the housekeeper before he got home, and the pattern continued when I was a teenager.

'What did you tell him?'

'I said we were doing girl things, and he sneered and said, *oh, women's lib nonsense?*'

'Geoff is a twat,' Linda pronounced.

'I told Stuart we were doing an art project,' I said. 'I think he must have seen me looking at the photos.'

I had wanted desperately to be an artist back then, and to study art at university, but I hadn't worked my way up to telling my father that yet. My bedroom had been full of sketchbooks and large art tomes from the library, the inside doors of my wardrobe pinned with collages I had made using magazines and newspapers. I had spent the previous summer outside with watercolours, trying and mostly failing to paint the fields and the valley. If Van Gogh could make a field something spectacular then so could I, I told myself stubbornly, but the yellow of the rapeseed always came out jarring, as though it had been painted by a toddler who didn't know his colours. Now I was starting to think that photography might be my thing, and portraiture.

'It *is* an art project,' Joan said. 'And they wouldn't understand, would they?' She looked around the circle.

'I think they'd just laugh,' I said.

'Or want to see our clothes go see-through.' Joan rolled her eyes. 'Let's take a vote then. Should we let the boys join us, let them watch?'

'No way,' I said, surprising myself with the vehemence of my reply.

'Agreed,' Joan said. 'Sarah?'

'Agreed.'

'Oh, me too, I agree,' Camille said quickly when Joan looked at her, as if she had not expected to be given a vote.

'Linda?' Joan asked.

'Agreed,' Linda said, combing out her hair with her sky-blue fingernails.

We returned to the river, the cold lick of water on our skin like an oath, unaware that this rule, this promise, would be broken before the end of the summer on the same night our world splintered and fell apart.

This afternoon, in the domestic present, I'm in the living room with a headache, two baskets of laundry to be put away at my feet, and a lapful of post from the last fortnight that I've mustered the courage to sort through. Bills and stray condolence letters, all the admin that needs to take place after a person dies. There's dozens of memberships to professional organizations and golf clubs and members' clubs that I need to cancel, all with their own particular idiosyncratic cancellation processes and unnamed secretaries to write to. I wonder how many widows or children let their dead fathers stay members, how many dead men pay fees to still belong to old boys' clubs, to have newspapers ironed and set out for them, crisp invitations to Captains' Dinners and drinks at the House of Lords arrive through letterboxes and lie unopened on the mat.

The world goes on. On the television in front of me, fire-bombs are lighting up the streets of Northern Ireland, police huddle behind riot shields, masked men stand on corners of brown streets holding guns.

'I kept thinking it would be over each time I came back from an assignment,' Stuart remarks, standing in the doorway. 'But look at this shit.'

'*Language*,' I murmur, because I know it will amuse him.

'You don't even say "shit" in this house?' he asks sotto voce, coming to sit beside me.

'Not when the twins are around. We try anyway.'

'Wow,' he says, 'Ruth Sinclair as a mother, who would have believed it.'

'Ruth *Hawkins*.'

'Mea culpa.' He holds up his hands.

'Should I take offence at that?' I ask, turning to face him. When he was young his face was narrow and fey, but with age it's broadened to be handsome. I always think that unfair; that men are supposed to get better-looking with age and women lose their bloom.

'Well, you were always saying you didn't want to be a mother.'

'Mum,' a voice calls from the hall, 'where's my—'

Maeve pauses in the doorway. There's something accusatory about the way she looks at us – because she doesn't like my attention not being on her and the twins, or because she thinks I look too cosy with Stuart? There's a proprietariness to my children that I don't remember ever having for my father. Maybe I would have had it for my mother. Maybe, I thought often, with bruising self-recrimination, I didn't know how to be a parent at all, that being motherless had made me defective.

'Where's your what?' I ask.

'Never mind,' she says, and turns on her heel.

'I'm not sure I ever pictured myself as a mother to a teenager, that's true,' I tell Stuart.

'Yeah?' he says, but his attention has drifted to the television. I can't compete with firebombs, with the nervy commentator and his clipped consonants.

'I worry about her – Maeve. She's had all our attention and I think it's an adjustment for her to be a normal teenager,' I say, watching the side of his face and glancing at the cityscape of Hong Kong on the screen as the news continues. 'One of her doctors said it was important not to smother her now, to let her be. It's hard though, not to worry about her every minute of every day.'

'She seems well adjusted from what I've seen,' he says, reaching for the TV controller and turning it off, focusing on me with a concern that reminds me of how he was when he was a boy. Back then, I knew that I could say something offhand about anything bothering me, pretending it didn't mean anything, and have him catch my hand and say, *Hey, what did you mean*, or, *Are you all right, what can I do to help?* There had been something intoxicating about his friendship then, almost devotional.

'She's probably far more sensible than we were at her age,' he adds, as if he too is reminiscing.

'She'll be off to university before I know it. It's mad. Where the hell have the years gone?'

'Don't tell me that,' he groans, rubbing a hand over his chin.

At university the three of us – Alex, Stuart and I – had been thick as thieves in our shared student digs, with late-night conversations about politics fuelled by alcohol and, if we could scrounge it up, pot, where everything felt so urgent and vital, as if we could solve the world's problems at 3 a.m. in a Cambridge bedsit, and lazy hungover mornings when we sprawled in the kitchen listening to the tinny sounds of the radio, making fry-ups with cheap squashed vegetables from the market and laughing at the gossip of our circle. I know friendships come and go at that age, that people change as they get older, but I had been friends with him since we were children and had thought he would always be there in the background of my life. Then he vanished soon after Maeve was born – at least that's what it felt like. He went abroad and gave no forwarding details, never replied to any letters or calls. To have him back, to have him look at me with kindness, have him joke across the dinner table on a warm summer evening, feels like I have been forgiven for some crime I did not know I had committed.

'It's good to spend time with you again,' I say.

'Likewise. I'm really grateful to you and Alex for letting me stay here, especially after so long. It would be a nightmare to drive from London every day to my shoots.'

It had been Alex who had said, *Why don't you stay with us?* at lunch that day when Stuart had said he was looking for a summer bolthole. *That's all right, right, Ruth?* Alex had continued and I had had the mean thought that it was all very well for Alex to offer, but it was me who was going to have to actually do the hosting.

'It's no bother. It's good for Alex to have someone to drag on his cycle rides.'

'Good old Alex,' Stuart says, chin on the heel of his hand. 'You know, you've done good, you two. Most of our contemporaries are divorced.'

'Thanks, I think.'

'Are you going to ask, then?' he says, settling back in his seat.

'Ask what?'

'The usual. Have you been married, have you been almost married, has someone broken your heart?'

A classic Stuart manoeuvre, undercutting your questions before you can ask them yourself. 'Actually, I want to ask about your work, your art.'

'My art,' he repeats. 'You mean my work out there or the glossy stuff since I've been back?'

'Both, either.'

'I struggle with it, to be honest. With being back, not being in the thick of it. I took my role as witness seriously. I can't say that the kudos wasn't part of it – the awards, and the thrill – but it meant something, you know.'

'Why did you come back?'

'It's a young man's game and it was getting hard to earn enough as a photographer. If I was a cameraman I might have lasted. What about you, you ever take photos any more?'

'Not really, no,' I answer carefully.

There's no way Stuart can stay here for the summer without the topic of the Ophelia girls being brought up, and maybe that's why I agreed to it. Maybe it's like when you have a scab on your knee you know you're going to pick off just so you can feel the cold wet slide of blood down your shin. Or maybe I was just eager to have a friend; maybe the past is the past and we're all adults now.

'That's a shame,' he says. 'But you still draw though?'

'No. When would I have the time?' I say, lifting my knees so that the mountain of correspondence on my lap shifts with a small earthquake.

'Can I help with anything?'

'It's fine, I'm just feeling sorry for myself.'

'Well, let me know if I can help with anything this summer, keep the twins busy while you draw or something. Seriously, Ruth.'

'I will,' I say, although the idea of picking up a pencil with the headspace free to draw sounds impossible, which is galling. I used to have the excuse of Maeve, of time filled with appointments and childcare and worry, but now the only thing in the way of one of my supposed passions is me.

He stands up and stretches. 'Will you and Alex be doing the house up then?'

'Eventually.' Just keeping the house standing is the priority, but I'm not going to reveal that. 'We started clearing things out but it feels like an endless task.'

'You find anything interesting?' He looks around the room; at the heavy mirror above the fireplace, the paisley patterned curtains and their faded fringe. He touches the dusty edge of some shelves and looks back at me. 'Anything surprising?'

'Just antiques, schoolboy relics. And endless prints.' Almost every wall of the house used to have them, black and grey and a murky kind of white. Prints of houses and stately buildings, scenes from old plays and staid drawings of fussy classical statues.

'Gloomy things,' he says. 'Do you remember there was one of Hamlet meeting his father's ghost on the wall in here? You told me that it frightened you and you didn't like to be in here alone with it.'

'I did? I don't remember that. I mean, I remember being scared of it, but not telling you.'

'We told each other lots of things,' he says with a small smile. He glances at the family photos Michael decided should be placed on the shelf in here. 'There weren't many photos of you back then though.'

A sore point. I shrug. 'And none of my mother. Not on display at least. Did he ever talk about her, with you?'

'Not really.'

'I remember that I heard the housekeeper—'

'Helen?'

I nod, remembering how Stuart had been Helen's favourite too, that I used to roll my eyes at his flirting with her for extra biscuits – *I'm not flirting*, he had insisted, *I'm just being nice*. 'I heard Helen talking to someone once, in the kitchen during a dinner, saying that my father was devoted to her, to the memory of my mother. That he loved her too much to ever marry again. And I remember the way she said that word, *devoted*, like it was something out of the ordinary.' This feels too personal to talk about with someone I haven't seen in so many years. But there's something about this house and its uneasy familiarity, about Stuart standing there as if he never left. 'I don't know,' I say, smoothing a thumb across my father's name on an envelope. 'Widowers usually marry again quickly, don't they? I suppose she was frozen at that age for him, forever young.' Is that why I had disappointed him? Because I couldn't live up to her perfect memory?

Stuart winces, touching a finger to his inner lip like he's just found a sore. 'You would know him better than me. But first loves are always like that, aren't they?' He sucks his teeth. 'They imprint on you, they're formative.'

I look down and the papers in my lap crinkle. Outside, a bird calls across the garden.

'I better head out now,' he says. 'I need to pick up something from the village. You need anything?'

'I'm fine, thanks.'

As he passes, I glance at the black mirror of the television, my face smoothed of features by its murky depths.

Chapter Seven

This is to be the summer of dinner parties then, Maeve thinks, as she hears the sounds of her mother downstairs swearing at the oven and dropping something on the floor with a clang.

'You'll be good for your mother tonight, won't you,' her father is telling the twins as he sits in the upstairs hallway, and they show off their forward rolls with a *thud-thud-thud* on the floor. 'It's stressful for her, cooking.'

'Why don't you help with it then?' Maeve asks, emerging from her bedroom.

'Maeve,' he reprimands. If she was younger he would have told her not to be so cheeky. Now she's just rude.

Lately, she has started to feel a curdle of dislike for her father, noticing for the first time what he is like as a man, a husband, and the friction between her mother and him, the gendered expectations upon her. But then her feelings for her mother are complicated too.

Maeve had opened the two unsent birthday presents from her grandfather, an antique copy of an Enid Blyton book that she wasn't much interested in, and a small wooden jewellery box which opened to reveal a ballerina spinning to a *Swan Lake* tune that she knew her younger self would have adored.

Her mother had caught the sound through the closed door of Maeve's bedroom and called out, *That's nice music, what is it?*

Something on the radio, Maeve had replied, wishing, not for the first time that summer, that her mother wasn't hovering in the house, that she could have a few hours just to herself. That she could talk to Stuart without worrying about them being seen.

Maeve ordered new clothes at the beginning of the week and she's going to wear a new top to dinner tonight. It's made of grey mesh with a thin silky strappy top underneath, and on its surface there are flowers embroidered in reds and greens and pinks and whites. She leaves her hair loose, tries to neaten her curls by wrapping them tightly around her index finger, tight enough to make her fingertips throb as she looks in the mirror, considering her reflection. She can't wear much make-up; her parents would notice and comment – positively, but it would still rankle – so mascara and concealer for her dark circles will have to do. She's seen girls in period dramas pinch their cheeks to make them blush, and she does that now and then gets embarrassed, annoyed with herself for acting like a schoolgirl with a crush.

You are *a schoolgirl with a crush*, she hears Georgia say in her head. Georgia would approve of what she's doing, would tell her to be daring, but Georgia would also have hated Stuart because she always declared that she hated all men out of principle. She had made the teacher at the hospital school cry once when she went on a righteous rant about why they had to study so many *great* men in history lessons when they were *colonialists at best*. She had a certainty about her, an iron will, that Maeve couldn't imagine having herself. *I know what I'm doing*, the mulish set of Georgia's jaw seemed to say, even when the nurses thought she was self-sabotaging her recovery.

I don't know what I'm *doing*, Maeve thinks, sitting at the dressing table and peering at the back garden over the mirror, the twins wheeling about the grass as her father practises his cricket bowling, his hand cupped around air.

She decides the minute Stuart's eyes glance over her in the kitchen where he sits on the kitchen table that her outfit was a mistake, and wishes she could run upstairs and change without that looking worse. He's chatting to her mother and greets her with a casual *hullo* to match her mother's greeting, and then he continues his conversation, something about an art exhibition in London. Maeve makes a note of various references – the YBAs, Hirst and Emin – as she stands at the fridge with the door open, hoping the chill will stop her cheeks from going naturally pink with shame.

'Excuse me, darling,' her mother says, touching her at the waist as she flinches from her. 'I need to put the salad in here so it doesn't wilt. You can't help me pick some mint for the tabbouleh, can you? I need to get changed for dinner.' Her mother doesn't look excited about the prospect.

'Sure.'

'Oh, and wash it well,' she says, hand on the doorframe.

'I'll help,' Stuart offers, and her mother gives him a grateful smile.

Maeve walks outside first, the touch of her bare foot on the hot stone of the patio like a branding. 'Shit,' she says, 'it's hot.'

'That's why you should wear shoes,' he says. She looks at his feet with her eyebrows raised. 'I'm used to it, they're tough as elephant's hide. Although I still wouldn't attempt to walk barefoot in a desert again.'

'That does sound stupid,' she retorts, pleased with his quirk of a smile.

'I told you last time we spoke that I do stupid things.'

She'd like to think he's been turning over every small encounter they've had in his head like she has, but it's enough that he remembers anything at all.

'So, *mint*,' he says, putting his hands on his hips as he stands before the overgrown bush that reaches beyond the windowsill. He's standing like he's about to wrestle an animal to the ground and she laughs. 'It's a serious task, Maeve, no laughing.'

'I won't laugh,' she says, and then does just that, the tension of only two minutes ago turning into a giddy relief.

'Mint is one of the worst things you can grow in a garden, you know that? It spreads like a weed and is impossible to get rid of.'

'I'm sure there are *worse* things, like poisonous plants or ones that smell awful,' she says, as he brushes the crown of the bush with his palm, searching for the best leaves to pick.

'Touché.'

She tries to pluck a few individual leaves but they tear in her hands. Stuart has more luck, twisting a bouquet from the stem.

'I've been thinking about what we were talking about last time. About your illness,' he says, voice quieter now as he spins the leaves with forefinger and thumb.

'Yeah?' she says, digging her nails into the soft flesh of a stalk to pull off a grouping of three leaves.

'I don't know if this is a strange question . . . but was there something you thought of that helped you back then, like a daydream you could disappear into? Like, I don't know, a tropical beach somewhere, or a story you imagined yourself inside?'

'A daydream . . .' *Is this not one now?* she thinks as he looks at her, the air hazy with mint and the hot sun on the back of her neck. 'When it was bad,' she says, looking down at the topography of the patio stone, 'there was nothing I could think of, I just blacked out. I went into nothingness.'

'I suppose that's the mind's way of protecting us, forgetting past pain. Memory is a funny thing anyway. Sometimes we remember what we wish we didn't and forget things we wish we hadn't.'

Her father's shape appearing in the kitchen through the window draws their conversation to a close.

'Here, I'll take yours.' Stuart holds out his hands.

The three leaves are wilted and crushed by now but she still gives them to him, feeling the catch of his rough skin against hers, and then glancing up to see if her father noticed. But he's busy with the corkscrew, his happy hum drifting through the door Stuart enters.

'Oh, we've got you gardening already, have we? Got to earn your keep, I suppose,' her father says in greeting.

Maeve leaves the patio for the garden, not wanting her mood to be punctured. She takes the gate on the left wall and walks along the outside, reaching for the puffs of yellow flowers from overgrown weeds, feeling the hard ground underneath her feet. Once she's through the natural archway between two banks of trees and bushes, she stops with her elbows on the splintery wood of the fence at the top of their field and looks across the valley. The roll of fields in the distance, in shades of yellow and green, the line of trees at the top of the far hill that hides the road, and the speck of other houses surrounded by their own greenery. The field they own slopes sharply down before her, more meadow than pasture, with the woods that cut through the middle of the valley beyond. Out there she wouldn't be bothered, she thinks, wouldn't have her mother keeping an eye on her, but Maeve hasn't ventured much further than the garden yet.

At dinner Maeve is sitting at a diagonal from Stuart. There are three couples this time, and the husbands of two of them work with her dad. One of them has brought along their nineteen-year-old daughter. *Back from backpacking*, they announced with warm pride, glancing at Maeve as if to check that their daughter does indeed look the most healthy, the best travelled. Still, as if to show Stuart that she isn't a moody loner, Maeve asks the girl, whose name she didn't catch, about Peru and the Nazca Lines, and listens politely to her answers. At one point the girl says, *My parents said you've been ill*, and the intonation of how she says that word makes Maeve want to grimace.

Luckily, the girl is too busy enjoying the food – and intoning about its differences from that of South American cuisine to the table at large and the proud looks of her parents – to monopolize Maeve's time. She can still luxuriate in watching Stuart while she sips the glass of white wine she accepted from her pleased father. Having rarely had crushes on anyone who wasn't an actor or a singer, Maeve revels in the opportunity to study Stuart in person, to learn what he looks like from every angle. When he smiles his eyes get slightly hooded, and when he argues he often drops his gaze with some combination of bashfulness and sly confidence. She wonders if it's this facial expression, the thick lashes on Stuart's cheek looking almost feminine, that seems to rile the older man at the end of the table, or the way Stuart is so good at undercutting him while getting the rest of the table to laugh. Stuart has barely glanced at the backpacker and her bronzed skin, her blonde ponytail, and Maeve is viciously pleased. The backpacker can keep all the other men that are no doubt attracted to her, and she can have Stuart. Maeve has finished her glass of wine and, rarely having ever drunk alcohol, is admittedly a little tipsy.

'There's been a bit of a disaster with the meringue,' her mother announces after the table has been cleared of the main course. Maeve hates the way Ruth's voice has taken on a higher pitched anxiety, that though her mother is so confident else-where, something about cooking seems to defeat her. 'So if you'd like to have a wander round the garden while I try and remedy things?'

The backpacker and her mother follow her into the kitchen to help, another wife goes to retrieve something from her car, one of the couples pours more wine and settles deeper into their chairs, and Alex leads two of the men to the shed to show off his newly inherited golf clubs. Stuart heads into the garden. Maeve follows him.

It's dusk again, and the outdoor light near the annexe must have been left on because there's a glow above the right wall of the garden that spills yellow onto the dark leaves of the rhododendrons where she finds him, hands in pockets.

'Ophelia,' he greets her, his eyes dancing from flower to flower across her upper body.

'I thought you would approve,' she risks.

'I do,' he says, and tugs at the flounced hem of her top, his knuckles grazing her stomach.

Chapter Eight

'So,' Nick says at dinner, pointing his glass of wine at Stuart, 'what's your story? What do you do?' Nick is an old schoolfriend of Alex's I haven't met before because he rarely strays from the south-west. I knew the minute he arrived tonight that I disliked him. Something about the way his eyes studied me with a quick flick, something about the popped collar of his shirt and the way the ice-blue shade highlighted the ruddiness of his neck.

We used to have cultured friends, I think, as Nick and his wife talk of their latest holiday – the size of the pool, the tennis provision, anecdotes about various disasters at the buffet. At university we talked about politics and art and philosophy; in London our friends were pooled from many different walks of life; but now I seem to have emerged from a decade's childcare into a world I don't recognize. Or is it just the meanness of the white wine talking? Because surely out of everyone tonight, I might have the most boring topics of conversation at my disposal – how to wash jam stains out of children's socks, for instance, or how to clean mould from bathroom walls, how to muster up a fancy-dress costume out of an old sheet. Stuart is the only interesting one here, the one whose company I want.

'I'm a photographer,' he answers Nick.

'Oh,' Nick says, with a rounding of his mouth.

'A celebrated war photographer, actually,' Alex corrects. I try to catch his eye, see if he is as bored as I am by Nick, but he's looking at Stuart.

'I wouldn't have pegged you for that,' Nick says.

'Why?'

'Well, you look normal.'

'Normal?'

'It just seems a little ghoulish, that's all, standing at the sidelines of all that death and famine. Observing from a distance.'

'And how do you think the civilized western world hears of wars, Nick?'

'Touché,' he replies.

'He does art photography now – is that what they call it, Stuart?' Alex says. 'And fashion photography, editorials.'

'Fashion photography, that sounds glamorous,' one of the wives says, adjusting the large pendant of her necklace.

'It certainly pays well,' Stuart says.

'What do you think about the problems with it? With the glorification of anorexia and heroin chic?' Nick's daughter, the bronzed backpacker, asks with scholarly concern.

'What do you think about it?' Stuart asks.

'I think it's wrong, obviously. That sickness is supposed to be glamorous, that *heroin* is. I saw the devastation of the drug trade on my travels and I can't see how a fashion magazine could condone that, I think it's sick.'

'You visited the Colombian cocaine fields? Wow, that's definitely off the beaten track,' Stuart says.

Oh dear, I think.

'No, I mean, I saw the knock-on effects,' the girl backtracks.

'As for the glorification of sickness, of pain, of suffering,' Stuart says, tilting the bottle of white wine, rubbing a thumb over the condensation, 'I don't know about glorification, but I don't see why images of those things can't be beautiful in a dark kind of way. My images of war have graced gallery walls. Dead bodies, blown-up buildings. Someone still calls them art.'

'I rest my case,' Nick says with a hearty laugh.

Stuart smiles as he picks at the wine label.

'Can you pass the bread?' one of the men asks, and I watch as his wife returns the heated look Nick throws at her.

Suddenly I am remembering another dinner party twenty-four years ago. The families summering at the cottages, the Ophelia girls among them, and the wasps circling the three tables shoved together underneath the chestnut tree, the younger children playing on a plaid rug and the air thick with smoke.

I say dinner party, but it was in the afternoon with the sun still blazing – a late lunch, an early dinner; as the summer went on the normal strictures melted away. Children left to get sticky and hungry and flushed with sun; mothers giving up on bras, on make-up and shoes; fathers growing out patchy beards and waving around thick joints as early as breakfast. The fathers were all teachers from London or the commuter belt and the mothers were housewives or teachers too; the owner of the cottages liked to advertise to schools so he could hire them out for the whole six weeks, and so they were all mostly liberal, but not so liberal as to not sneer at hippies, while doing their best, I thought then, to take on all their affectations.

I remember that meal because it was when the flirting of some of the parents went beyond what the children might expect to grin and bear. When, four wine bottles down as the light lengthened, Joan's mother sat herself on Sarah's father's lap and kissed his bristly cheek, and when Joan's father asked which woman he would have in compensation and Linda's mother sauntered around the table and kissed him full on the mouth to cheers and rounds of applause, sitting back with a flush and an arch of her back that made him whisper something in her ear and her smile grow rich and pleased.

We left them then, the Ophelia girls and the three teenage boys, who peeled off to the fields with a bottle of wine when Joan told them not to follow us to the woods with a viciousness that brooked no argument.

There was no argument between us girls about which one would enter the water first either, as Joan fumbled down the bank and sank right under the surface, the bubbles of her furious breaths – her screams? – emerging before her head did.

'Well, go on then,' she said to us, her jaw tight, silver water caught in her collarbones, 'take a photo.'

I handed the camera to Camille who did as asked, crouching on the bank as Joan sculled her hands, her feet sometimes kicking sharply as if knocking away weeds, her harsh breath visible even with the ripple of the water around her. She tipped her head back, groaned at the sky, and then turned onto her front and floated, and I heard the shutter click as Camille took a photo of that too. An inversion of the classical paintings of Ophelia, a drowning girl refusing to show her face in all its loveliness to the camera, her jeans and blouse plastered dark to her skin as she lay motionless.

'All right,' Joan said, when she had turned onto her back again, panting. She stood up and her blouse made a sucking noise that made her grimace. 'Jesus.' She clambered onto dry land. 'I'm not doing this in jeans again.'

The jeans had been tight before they got wet, and when she struggled to get them off, Linda and I took a leg each, peeled them off her chilled blue limbs as she wriggled around on the ground, bellowing and complaining. And then she was free; her white knickers gone see-through, her blouse tugged over her head too as I looked away from her braless top half in a flush of embarrassment. We had all seen each other half naked by now, but I still found it hard to know where to look. Presumably, I thought, because I hadn't grown up with any mother or sisters.

She lay out in the sun, her eyes closed. 'If I catch them fucking,' she said, the word sounding obscene in her mouth, 'or if she forgets to take her pill . . .' She shook her head like her ears were blocked with water.

'At their age,' Linda remarked, with a jaded knowingness and a sighing stretch of her arms. 'My mother's done it before though, slept with other men. She thinks we're best friends and she can tell me everything, like I'd be happy that she's sleeping with the P.E. teacher. Like she and I are on one side against my father. Well, when I leave for uni she's on her own. She can come up with her own lies.'

'It's bacchanalian,' Camille said then. She was plaiting stems of flowers together in her lap. 'The wine and the heat. All they need now is some animal sacrifice.'

'I wouldn't put it past them,' Joan said.

The light was growing yellow with the waning day, the river mostly shadowed by the trees. Sarah had been quiet, and the four of us kept glancing over to her and then at each other.

'You want to go in next, Sarah?' Linda asked.

'Sure,' she said, brushing dust off the blue skirt of her dress and looking carefully at the ground as each footstep brought her closer to the river's edge. She gasped when she entered and it sounded like the beginning of a cry, but when she turned back to look at us, she was smiling. She shivered at the chill of the water and then waded out further. She had a large patterned shawl around her shoulders, and as she dipped down and splayed back in the water, it spread out like a blanket between her and the hard stones of the riverbed.

I came closer to take her picture, sitting on the bank, my own feet submerged in the tug of the current, the slip of mossy weeds stroking past.

When she turned her head to look at me, her smile had faded. She stroked her hands through the water, picked a strand of hair out of her mouth, and kept staring. As I adjusted the lens, I felt the weight of trying to record her as she was, beautiful, sad, aching; of trying to capture what she was trying to say, words that could not be spoken or heard or understood.

Soon it was too dark for my camera, the water of the river darker still, the bluish light of dusk around us.

'We'll have to bring candles next time,' one girl said.

'Have our own bacchanal,' Linda added, nodding at Camille.

By some unspoken invitation, we stripped to our knickers and entered the river together, swimming and floating, grasping onto each other's legs and arms, kicking against the pebbles of the riverbed. There was something so thrilling about it, our bodies there in the dark together, the shriek of fear at the touch of another person's fingers on your side and then the shiver of pleasure when that same hand smoothed down a shoulder in apology. You had to be close to see anyone's face, had to tread water or hook your legs around hers to try and catch the shape of a mouth moving, the glint of moonlight on dark eyes, as you said something that seemed vital at the time.

'It's like this,' Sarah began.

'What if there's a creature in here with us?' Linda joked.

'Is it even water, what we're swimming in, and how would we know?'

Sarah, clasping my hand, 'I think this is what witches did, all those tales of secret rites in the woods.'

When we lay exhausted on our backs and stared at the sky through the willow trees, we could see one or two stars, could hear the night's breeze flee through the woods towards us.

'How long do you think it would take for someone to come looking for us if we stayed here forever?' Camille wondered out loud, as I floated next to her.

'Weeks,' Sarah said. 'Or until my mum gets sick of looking after my siblings and wants me to take over.'

'I know how to make a shelter with wood and leaves, I learned it in a book,' Camille offered.

'Of course you did,' Linda said.

While the other girls usually sunbathed on the riverbank, tipping their faces to the sky, Camille always lay on her front, reading one of her books, her hair a curtain shielding her eyes from the summer light.

'I can hunt,' Sarah said. 'Well, make traps for foxes.'

'And we can drink the river, it's freshwater,' I said.

'Well, there you are then. We can stay here all summer,' Joan declared. 'Our own little witchy commune.'

But it was too cold to stay in the river and too cold to stay on its banks with our chilled limbs and cotton dresses. So, eventually, we made our way through the quiet woods and then up through the fields with the moon to guide our way.

Two days later our second lot of developed photos arrived, five whole rolls of them, and we gathered under the tree on my front lawn to look through them.

Some of the photos weren't focused right, or the light reflecting off the river had been too bright, and in those it was hard to tell the identity of the girl, faces and bodies a smudge of silvery yellow, the banks and the trees a whirl of green and brown and orange.

But the ones where you could see details – the shape of a lifted hand, parted lips, toes emerging from the surface, the swirl of a dress floating around its wearer, sad eyes looking back at the viewer – were beautiful. They made my chest ache, made me want to cry.

'We need to get serious about this,' Joan said with a bossiness we didn't mind, once we had all taken our turns looking through the photos, passing them gingerly by their edges as if our fingertips might blur the ink. At dinner the night before, Joan's mother and Sarah's father had continued their flirting, had gone off giggling together and emerged rumpled from the garden, and we could sense Joan's need for control of this at least, for a concentrated distraction. 'We need better dresses and clothes. Better flowers.'

'There's a jumble sale at the village church today,' I said.

'And my mum brought her sewing machine with her,' Sarah said, resting her head on her arms, looking peaceful like a dozing cat in the sun.

'I could probably find some of my mother's old dresses.'

'And my dad has some Shakespeare stuff, programmes and books with him. If we're doing Ophelia properly.'

'What about the library, for art books?' Camille suggested.

'I'll go with you and carry them back,' I offered. 'We can go this afternoon.' There was something intriguing about Camille. I told myself it was only that she was so quiet, that I already knew so much about the other girls compared to her and wanted to balance things out.

She smiled. There was a graze on her knee from when she had tripped over a root in the woods in the dark yesterday, landing on the hard ground with a punched-out breath.

'As for the flowers,' Linda said, 'maybe I'll steal a few more from gardens. Or beg some from the florist. How much do flowers cost anyway?'

She looked at me. We didn't talk about money much at the river, or our families' wealth, but still I was aware that while the other parents were on well-earned holidays in small cottages that had once been for the estate's workers, I was a daughter of the big house.

'I've never bought any. I have some pocket money to spare though, I'll get some today. I mean, not lots, but some,' I said, voice stumbling as I tried not to be awkward.

'Or you could just ask the gardener's son,' Joan said as we watched Stuart come past, his arms full of newspapers and books and his battered leather journal as he left my house. 'You know he's in love with you.'

'He is not,' I said, and then he looked up at us, at me, and waved, and I waved back as Linda sniggered.

'Hullo, Loverboy!' Joan shouted out as I grabbed the sleeve of her top.

'Hi, girls,' he called, sweeping his curls from his face as the others poked me and I swatted them away, rolling my eyes.

Now, back in the present, as I clean up the mess from the pavlova that took forty-five minutes longer to make than it should have, I watch Stuart make his way inside from the dining table, carrying an armful of plates.

'Alex can still pick 'em, can't he?' he says, lifting an eyebrow.

It had been a running joke between Stuart and me that Alex

had terrible taste in friends, because he was forever turning up at college parties with the most boring young men from his sports clubs and maths tutorials. *If I have terrible taste in friends then you two are included in that*, he retorted when we told him once, laughing drunkenly around a narrow table in a student pub. *We're the exception*, Stuart had declared, smacking a kiss on his cheek. Alex liked Stuart because he pushed him out of his staid comfort zone – encouraging him to climb the roof of the chapel at 3 a.m. one night or signing the both of them up to be in a raucous college pantomime – and I think I probably liked Stuart because I trusted him more than the other boys, or girls at that. Having him here for the summer is one bright spot of being back in this house.

'You sure I can't do that for you?' Stuart offers, as I scrape a spoon along some of the unfamiliar fine china I unearthed last week from the back of a cupboard, still in its original box and aged tissue paper.

'You know, I think this is my parents' wedding crockery,' I say, realizing only now and setting the plate down. 'I thought it was just one of Dad's antique collections. That he might roll in his grave to see me use it instead of preserving it. And for what? What's the point of all these old things you can't use, that he didn't even display?' I wipe the back of a soapy hand across my forehead.

'Let me do the others.' He nudges me out of the way and rinses the next plate, as I rest a hip against the counter.

I pull the last piece of meringue off the cooking tray before he dunks it in water. It's so chewy it hurts my jaw. 'I think my mother would have been a better hostess than me,' I say. 'I just have this mental picture of her in pearls and full skirts with a perfect hostess smile.'

'You never used to talk about her, your mother.'

'I didn't really have anything to say. I know so little about her, really.'

The fact of her death eclipses all the other meagre things I might have ferreted out of those who knew her. Her death leaving me alone, tiny and vulnerable, on the same day she brought me into the world. It spooks me to think of it, to not know, after so many years of estrangement and coldness before that, quite how to imagine my infanthood, my father holding me as a baby. And if I think of my mother I feel either a low hum of grief, or a nothingness that then turns to a queasiness, as if I judge myself for not remembering her with great emotion. Would I have been happier if I had grown up with a mother, would I have made fewer mistakes?

'My mum had all the makings of a great hostess,' Stuart says, wiping his hands on his jeans. 'She was a good cook. She could rustle up a gourmet feast from three squashed tomatoes and a hard loaf. She made friends easily, she loved a party, she was beautiful.' He looks down as he takes out his pack of cigarettes and lighter. He still has those long lashes, Stuart, the ones any girl would have died for.

'Can you not smoke inside, please? And I wish I could have met her.' His mother had died in his first year of university. I was in my last year of school, and I can't remember if I sent him a letter, or if we talked on the phone about it.

'You would have liked her, everyone did, even when she was a drunken mess. But they didn't have to clear up after her, to wrestle her out of her vomit-soaked clothes and put her to bed.' He sighs. 'When she had friends round for dinner she would put on a record and dance around, and I'd watch her do her make-up in the mirror and sing along and she'd say, *I'll just have one glass now to get me warm*, but one glass always turned into two and three and four, and she'd be on the floor by the time the guests arrived, and I had to finish the cooking and open the door for them. *Tasha's little helper*, they'd call me, and ruffle my hair.' He puts a cigarette in the corner of his mouth.

'Those will kill you, you know.'

My father died of lung cancer. When I saw Stuart at the funeral, a face from the past whose sudden reappearance felt only right in that church full of other faces from my family's history, I had hugged him and breathed in the smell of tobacco and found it hard to let go, to take my face from his jacket. If he found the way I clung to him odd, he hadn't said, only murmured, *I'm so sorry, Ruth, so sorry.*

'Tell Alex that,' he replies archly.

'Oh, Alex knows how I feel about his smoking.'

'But you forgive him anyway.'

'Well, I married him, I'm kind of stuck with him.'

'I envy you, you know,' he says. 'Your family, this house full of life.'

'You could have that too, surely,' I say, instead of saying, *If you think my life is something to envy then you are quite mistaken.*

'I suppose.' He clicks his lighter and a flame ignites and then dies, ignites and dies. 'I just feel I've missed my chance.'

'You haven't. And you shouldn't— You shouldn't let memories of your mother stop you, shouldn't think it would be the same,' I say, perhaps too boldly. What do I really know about him now, seventeen years on?

'Oh, I'm not sure that's why. I think I'm just picky, I want to be swept off my feet.' He smiles and I laugh.

Alex enters the kitchen then, hair curling at the heat, mouth red with wine. 'My two favourite people,' he says. 'What are you talking about?'

'About the past,' Stuart says, cutting a glance to me, 'and bad fashion choices.'

'Oh, Jesus,' Alex says. 'I wore that cape *once* in the seventies, and you've never let me live it down. Like you fared any better with your silly hair, Stuart.'

'I never wore a cape,' he retorts.

'It was more of a jacket, really,' Alex argues, running the tap and bending down to drink from it.

What I remember most about the first time I met Alex, on the college lawn in the April sun, was his easy physicality, how comfortable he seemed in the world. A golden boy with a direct smile and a firm handshake. If I had only felt at home in the river, he felt at home everywhere.

'You OK?' he asks me as he puts an arm round my shoulder, kisses me on the cheek.

'I'm fine,' I say, wondering what Stuart sees when he looks at us, if we resemble a happy couple, if he can see the cracks.

That night I dream of them, I dream of her, of Camille. We are in the river, and I am arranging her honey-brown hair over her shoulders as she watches me, the lip of the water moving up her chin and meeting her own lips as she smiles at me, as the petals of the bouquet she holds bob up and down with the movement of her floating body.

How do I look? she asks.

Perfect.

Perfectly tragic? she says in that stilted way of hers. She tilts her head back; the water slips over her forehead and into her eyes before I catch her head and lift her to the surface again. She laughs and then looks sad. Her eyelashes are beaded gold in the sun; the frills of her dress tickle my legs.

There, I say, *stay just like that*, and I wade backwards through the river, my feet slipping on unseen pebbles because I don't want to look away from her.

On the riverbank, I wipe my hands on the dry grass and pick up my camera as a breeze travels down the river towards us, lifting leaves, rippling the surface of the water. In the viewfinder I see her come into focus. I see the kick of her foot as she adjusts her position. I see her turn her head to look at me, her lips parting as if she is about to tell me something. I take the picture. With the click of the shutter, she disappears.

Chapter Nine

'Are you enjoying dinner?' Stuart asks Maeve. Muted laughter sounds from the table near the house and then the garden quietens again, the breeze ruffling the plants around them, the creak of a tree branch shifting outside its walls. Maeve wonders how long they will have this time, imagines the bushes around them pushing out new shoots, leaves unfurling black in the dark and hiding them from anyone searching.

'I'm enjoying the wine,' she says.

'I'm glad. You deserve to have fun, to be happy.'

Do I? she thinks.

'You're frowning – you don't think so?'

She wishes he hadn't taken his hand back, wishes he was still touching her. Her body feels too heavy to carry alone, too light to stand in place without floating away.

'Have you ever slept out here, in the garden?' he asks.

'I don't think I've slept outside anywhere.'

'You should try it. You'd see the foxes and the cats and the other night-time creatures. Sometimes if you sleep outside, you'll see things you won't believe the next day, and you'll wonder if they were a dream or not.'

'Like what?'

He looks down, rocks on his heels. 'I saw a bride once, in

Bosnia, just before dawn. She was dressed in white with a red waistcoat, a belt made of golden circles, and I saw her pick her lonely way through the rubble, the trail of her dress tattered, staring ahead as if she was sleepwalking. We were at someone's house, sharing bottles of smuggled spirits, and I had gone out to the courtyard for air and lain down on a wall. But when I clambered out, she was gone.'

'I lied earlier,' Maeve says, swaying closer to him, feeling the fuzz of the wine like prickling dots in the dark air. 'I do – I did have daydreams.'

His hand cups her elbow; she feels the brush of his shirt.

'But they're stupid, childish things.' *I am a child, don't blame me for that*, she means. *I am a child, you have to know that, don't expect me to be a woman and worldly-wise. If you want me, want me for who I am right now.*

'You don't have to tell me.' A squeeze of her elbow.

'But I want to,' she says. 'I used to – to imagine I was something like Sleeping Beauty, that I was only waiting. That someone would heal me with a touch and carry me out of there, carry me and never put me down. I prayed sometimes,' she says, with an embarrassed puff of breath, 'tried to make bargains with God, but it never worked. When I was younger, before I ever got ill, I used to wish I was some prince's pampered pet, locked up in a tower.'

'That's not such a strange wish,' he says, thumb circling a rose embroidered on her upper arm. 'When I was a child and arguing with my mother's boyfriends in our small flat, I used to dream of houses – cottages from fairy tales, huts in the wood, snowy palaces.' He smiles at his past self. 'And then, when I was abroad, it was art, paintings. I used to picture myself walking through a gallery, imagining myself stepping through the frames into the worlds beyond.' He pauses. 'Will you let me take your photo, Maeve?'

'Yes.' More sigh than word.

'We could start Monday?'

'Sure,' she says, while her mind hums with that word, *start*, which promises more than an hour's quick posing, that promises a project, of her and him and his camera alone.

'I need to grab something from the annexe now but you should head back,' he motions with his head, 'before they declare you missing and send out a search party.'

He doesn't want them to walk back together and have it look suspicious, she thinks, just as she knows that neither of them is planning on telling her parents about the photos he wants to take of her.

On Monday morning, she heads to meet Stuart in the field, so awkward in her body she feels like a jerking marionette, like he will take one look at her and say that he's changed his mind. Yesterday he told her in passing that she should come just as she was, wear a dress maybe but whatever she felt comfortable in, and there was no need to do any make-up. She had nodded as if she had had her photo taken many times before, like, *Sure, of course.*

Her mother is taking the twins to the village and her father is at work, and there's no one to question her when she slips out of the house in a pale floral sundress.

She sees him before he sees her, standing halfway down the hill looking towards the valley. The grass hasn't been cut for years and is waist-high and flecked with yellow rattle, tall daisies and purple knapweed as she walks through in her sandals, feeling the dry blades of grass sharp on her bare legs, hearing the creak of hidden crickets.

He waves when he turns round, and she concentrates so

hard on walking towards him that she worries she'll stumble. Once you start thinking about parts of your body – knees, feet, hips – it's difficult to stop. Like when the scans had shown her blood was wrong inside her, like when the needles punctured her bones to get to the rotten marrow inside.

'There you are,' Stuart says, his eyes a little wide and his smile warm. He's holding a bunch of the meadow flowers in his hand. 'These are for you,' he says, and she takes them from him as he opens up his camera bag.

'Thank you,' she says, mouth dry, pleased that she can busy herself with studying the flowers, touching their petals in between quick glances at Stuart's face, brown in the sun, and his concentrated frown as he fiddles with the dials and the settings on his large black camera.

'I thought we could start with this painting.' He hands her a postcard with another Pre-Raphaelite image, a woman with wild brown hair wearing a white dress and lying down in a field with white and yellow meadow flowers around her, one arm swooning above her head. 'Waterhouses's Ophelia from 1889.'

'It's beautiful.' She squints at the small face of the painted woman and wonders how she will match up to it.

'I don't want to do a straight copy, more of an "inspired by",' he says, 'and besides, I think the colour of your hair will look better than hers.'

His manner is more impersonal than it has been when they've talked in the garden but she can tell it's because he's in his working mode and she likes it, that he's taking this seriously. That he's not going to get her to pose for five minutes and then laugh it off.

'How should I . . .'

'I think we'll start with you standing, with the valley and the hills in the background, and then depending on the light, I'll get the slope of the field behind you next. Then we'll try with you lying down. Is that all right? Sorry, I get quite a narrow focus when I'm working. You've never done this before, right?'

'No.' The last time a man photographed her, it was a nurse performing a chest x-ray as she stood shivering and vulnerable behind a screen.

'That's better, you'll be a natural,' he says, hand on her bare shoulder bringing a sudden prickle to her skin. 'But tell me if you have any questions, or if you want to stop, or if you don't feel comfortable.'

'I don't really know how to pose,' she admits. Or what to do with her face.

'Don't worry, I'll tell you exactly how I want you.'

'And what if I do odd things with my face?'

He laughs. 'Don't worry about that either, I'll take a whole bunch, try and capture you in between the odd faces. I've got a lot of film to work through.' He pats his bag and she thinks of how many film canisters he can fit inside it, of her tiny self repeated in a long line of negatives that spool around and around.

He directs her to stand and then backs up a few steps to get the background into the shot. She bites her lip and then stops. She shifts on her feet and feels her shoulders swing, flexes her hand around the flowers. *Hold your hair back*, he says, *and look over my shoulder. Good*, he says, *that's good, hold the flowers loose at your hip. Now look to your right, further, there, and lift your chin, too much, there, that's good. Hold that.* She feels her eyes start to water with the sun. *How are you doing?* he asks. *Fine*, she says, turning towards him and shielding her eyes with her hand. *Oh, that's perfect, stay like that*, he says, as she looks at him, staring at the lens of his camera with a shiver of daring, thinking about him staring at her from behind the camera, their eyes meeting with only the blink of the shutter between. *Now, look to your left, hold your skirts with the same hand as the flowers, can you do that?* he says. She nods without looking at him.

There's barely a breeze today; the bright heat of the sun and the yellowing grass make her feel out of time again, as if she's slipped into some other long summer. She thinks of that painting, of the girl who modelled for it. Who was she? What was she thinking as she posed for months and months and the painter studied her, watching her every small movement?

Stuart walks a wide circle around her, changing the background of his shot, taking pictures of her from different angles as she feels her cheeks ache, her chin twitch. She wishes he'd tell her what her expression is supposed to be, direct her to smile or look serious. She worries that she's only going to be frowning in these photos, squinting at the sun.

'Do you need a break?' he asks, coming closer as he loads a new film in his camera.

'I'm fine. But if you need one?'

'This is a holiday compared to dodging bullets or risking frostbite in my fingers in Moscow. You're doing really well, Maeve, I know posing can be tiring. We'll do the lying down ones now, I think.'

'OK,' she says, 'here?'

He nods and she awkwardly sinks to the ground, feeling the grass flatten around her and the hidden landscape of the earth underneath – dry beads of soil, small hummocks, the cool freshness of leaves hidden from the heat of the sun.

'I want the grass to rise up around you, so it looks like it's hiding you,' he says as he crouches down at her side. She feels her limbs twitch, feels the strangeness of lying down in front of someone else that she always did when being ushered towards couches in doctors' rooms.

'I think it will look better without your sandals,' he says, and she sits up to reach the buckle but it gets stuck beneath her fingers. 'Here, I'll help. Models shouldn't be in charge of dressing themselves too, not when they're sun-blind,' he adds with a smile.

She wants to make a noise, a gasp, when he lifts her foot onto his legs to untie her sandal, when she feels the warm grip of his hand around her ankle. She wonders whether he can see up her skirt where the hem rests on her knees.

'There.' He sets her bare feet back on the grass. 'OK, so what I'm thinking this time, is for this hand to lie like this . . .' She gives him her right hand and he places it at her side, curls her fingers inwards to make it look relaxed. 'With the flowers on the ground nearby, and the other holding some of your hair over your head, like the painting, do you remember?'

She does as she's asked, and then he leans over to adjust strands of hair caught on her face as she feels a throb in her stomach. The ground is hard underneath her, the grass shifting with her minute movements, tickling her bare legs, her neck.

'Perfect,' he says, kneeling by her side, staring at her as she looks back.

Right now, she feels viciously glad that he's a photographer because she can't think of any other situation where it would be possible for the two of them to spend so long looking at each other, to be crouched down in a hollow of grass, a meadow bower. To have his hands adjust her body and her dress, smooth a wrinkle from her waist, tug the hem slightly lower down her knees, brush a piece of hair away from her blinking eyes with a dry thumb.

What does the camera see, what will it record? she thinks, as he moves around her with one hand adjusting the lens, stepping back and forward, standing up, crouching down, the cool shadow of his body morphing with his position. When he develops these photos, will he see how much she wants him, will he stop and think, *I can't do this again, I can't lead her on,* or will his eye be only artistic, will he see the shadows in a small patch of grass or the crook of her elbow and frown, ask her for a redo so he can fix the balance of colours and her proportion in the picture?

Under his gaze and that of his camera, she's thinking of herself as something beautiful, not as a medical specimen, or as a child in her parents' family photos. She's picturing what she looks like to him, seeing herself from the outside.

'Right.' He stands up with a groan and a press of his hand to his back. 'I think I've got what I wanted to today.'

'Yeah?' She coughs at the pollen as she bends forward to buckle her sandals back on. It feels like hours have passed but also like the sun hasn't moved at all.

'You were great,' he says. 'Will you do this again, model for me?'

'Yeah, sure,' she says, trying to sound casual, trying not to sound like she'd do anything to do this again.

'And we haven't talked payment,' he says with a teasing note, as he hoists his bag up on his shoulder. 'I'll think about that too.'

The blood rushes to her head when she stands. 'My going rate is a thousand an hour.'

He laughs and then squints over her shoulder. 'I guess if I deposit a cheque in your account someone might see that.'

Her fingers twitch against the soft seed heads of the meadow as she tries to parse his tone. Is this photoshoot an inconsequential secret to keep for him, like he's sneaked a beer to a teenage daughter of his friends at a party, or is it something more, something personal?

'Maybe I'll save it for your next birthday,' he adds.

Her next birthday. To be able to think of that, of getting older, living another year, feels dizzying. She doesn't want to be a proper adult yet, responsible for herself. But maybe if she's older, he will treat her differently, let himself think of her as more than a child.

'I'll take the flowers as a down payment for now.' She'll put them in water in her room, say she picked them herself.

They start walking up through the field, long grass parting and closing behind them. Will the hollow where she lay this morning stay there, she thinks, or will the plants rise up towards the sun again and hide the impression of her body?

'I'll think of something,' he says. 'And of course we'll need to find water at some point, to take a proper Ophelia portrait. You can swim, right?'

'Yes.' She shoves him playfully.

'Well, that's good, we don't want life to imitate art.'

He puts his arm around her shoulder and she wishes the field could stretch on forever, that the weeks of his visit could lengthen, this summer never end.

She feels both of them slow down before the gate and the line of trees and bushes, while they're still hidden from the front lawn. 'What were you like when you were younger?' she asks. She's been thinking of that photo she found in her grandfather's office.

'You mean when I stayed here?' he asks.

'Yeah.'

'Hmm.' He has a rueful smile. 'A dreamer and a bit of a fool. I had principles then, I was idealistic.'

'And now you're not?' she asks, shading her eyes from the sun.

'Now I'm not. But you should be.'

'I'm not sure I can be, not any more.' Not with what she knows now, about how easily the body decays and meets its end, about pain and suffering.

'OK, but a dreamer then,' he says, stroking a finger down her arm. 'You should be a dreamer. You shouldn't hurry to grow up and leave that behind.'

If he says she shouldn't grow up, does that mean he only thinks of her as a child? That he's letting her down kindly? Are the photos of her the only thing he wants?

Chapter Ten

Michael woke us up in the middle of the night and Iza wasn't far behind. Normally I can get them to go back to sleep in their own beds but Michael was inconsolable, hot-cheeked and sobbing as he described his nightmare of being in hospital. It was Michael whose bone marrow transplant saved Maeve's life; his was the closest match and, after consultations with the doctors and the team at the hospital, and a conversation in terms that a three-year-old might be able to understand, we had given our permission for the operation. The ethical argument is that the minor pain of a low-risk operation is less than the pain of losing a sibling, of a family imploding, and I accept that, and I wouldn't have made any other choice, but I still feel so guilty.

But what's one more piece of guilt to all the rest? I thought last night, as Michael wriggled and poked me with his sharp feet.

They are both too tired to get up to much mischief today so I have left them in front of a video, with two fondant fancies each, and have retreated to the attic, my eyes and mouth dry and sore with exhaustion.

Why try and sort through the attic when I still have the junk room, two bedrooms and many cupboards to work through? Because I had the thought earlier, seeing Michael lying there beside me in the white light of the morning, that maybe I could find something of my mother's up here.

But, in the first box I open after clambering over the insulation and beams, it is my history I find and not hers. The soft slide of a silk slip through my fingers and the memory of visiting the village jumble sale with Camille to buy it.

What did I know about Camille at that point? That the ends of her hair looked neat and thick as a brush, that she liked to read, that she seemed like the kind of girl who should wear glasses but that I had never seen her squint, that all her clothes looked handmade; that, though she was quiet, there was a rootedness to the way she held herself and moved through the world that intrigued me. That sometimes she looked sad and I wanted to be the one who made her smile.

We went to the library first, and stuffed both the wicker basket I had brought and her satchel with heavy art books. Her well-worn satchel had belonged to her favourite teacher who had given it to her after the shopping bag she was using for her schoolwork fell apart in his class, she told me, looking at me side-on, uncertainly, as though I would tease her.

In the village I noticed passersby turn to look at us in the way they did with young women in youthful fashions. Leering, fascinated, judgemental. But while I felt my face scowl, Camille gave no indication she had noticed them looking.

'Do you go to church?' I asked her, as we walked through the graveyard to the village church.

'Only at school. Do you?'

'The same,' I said, holding out the door for her as we entered the cool of the nave, blinking at the change in light.

'My mother was raised a Catholic,' she said softly. 'French Catholic.' Her placid expression had changed on entering the church, become troubled as she looked towards the crucifix.

Do you still believe in it, in God? I wanted to ask, but it wasn't the sort of thing you could say when there were nosy church ladies leaning over their stalls of bric-a-brac. 'So is that where your name comes from?'

'I think so.' She shrugged, seemed to come back to herself.

There was a table full of old metal tins and signs, their edges rusted, and a box of miscellaneous tools; another of cakes and dry biscuits, the dregs of last year's bitter jams. On the table underneath a church plaque to the fallen of the First World War, there was a pile of knitted baby clothes, booties and hats and cardigans, in soft yellows and greens and pinks. We found what we were looking for near the back, a rack of second-hand dresses and coats and a cardboard box of Victorian underthings – faded camisoles, bloomers and slips.

I tried not to show how excited I was so that the hawkish woman manning the stall didn't overcharge us, and acted as if I didn't really want the mauve slip with the delicate lace edging, or the ivory camisole with its ribbon hem and slender straps.

'They're beautiful,' Camille whispered at my shoulder as we looked through the rack. She glanced back at the box and its silken treasures. This close to her I could see a single white hair growing from her widow's peak.

'Are you going to get this?' I asked, touching the tea dress with its delicate floral print that she had been studying intensely.

'Oh, no, I don't have any money,' she said.

When I asked the stallholder how much the slip and cami-sole were, Camille pointed out that the slip had been dyed mauve at a later date, that Edwardian silk didn't come in that shade, and the price duly dropped. I bought a lace shawl too and a roll of floral fabric, and when I unhooked the tea dress from the rack and placed it on the pile, I felt Camille grow still beside me.

'And this too,' I said.

'You didn't have to do that,' Camille said, as we walked home with our bounty. She had asked the stallholder for tissue paper to fold her dress in, slid it carefully between the library books.

'If you went back later someone else might have bought it.'

'I can't pay you back,' she said, looking away from me as she hoisted the strap of her bag higher.

'It was a gift, it's fine. You make most of your own clothes, right?' I said, to change the subject.

She nodded. 'I sew them by hand,' she said, as if it were a secret. 'I haven't saved up for a sewing machine yet.'

The idea that a sewing machine might be beyond someone's reach surprised me, made me think I had really been living in a bubble.

'Even zips? That's impressive.'

'Buttons are cheaper.'

'I let our housekeeper take my hems up,' I said, feeling chastened. I should be as self-sufficient, as clever as Camille was. Both she and Stuart were studying hard, they were thinking seriously of their futures, while I was still hedging bets or avoiding thoughts of choosing a university subject. I vowed that I would tell my father I wanted to study art, or at least art history.

That evening, my father found me in the room our housekeeper called the scullery, hand-washing the slips and the floral fabric along with the two dresses I had been using to pose in the river. It was rather pointless to wash them when they would just be getting wet again, but the things from the church smelled like fusty old woman's perfume, and I'd noticed that my dresses from the river, which I usually hung to dry hooked over my wardrobe, were making my room smell of mud.

I looked up when he entered holding a tin of boot polish and felt embarrassed, wishing he would turn back before he saw what I was doing.

'It's good to see you wearing dresses again,' he said. He looked at the plain shorts and t-shirt I was wearing, a marked contrast with the dress dripping dry next to me. *You look like an urchin,* he would sometimes say of my corduroy trousers and jumble sale woollen jumpers, *like a grubby boy.*

'It's just a costume,' I said.

'For what?'

'The girls were talking about putting on a play.'

'A play?'

'It probably won't happen. It's just a game.'

'Well, you should think about looking smart, being ladylike.' He seemed a touch embarrassed by that word. 'You're not a child any more, you have to think about the future, your future.'

What dresses had to do with my future, I didn't know, I thought sourly. He would have liked an elegant daughter, a feminine one – although how was I supposed to know what ladylike was when the only female company at home was the housekeeper, and the teachers at the village school were mumsy and plain? It wasn't that I didn't like dresses or skirts; it was that I liked them just for me, that I didn't want to be put inside a box labelled 'girl' and have all the expectations that came with it placed upon me. But in the river I could pretend to be some tragic heroine, some beautiful creature outside time and space, with only other girls who knew what I meant to see me. In the river I was in control.

I remembered my earlier decision. 'I've been thinking about applying for art history, at university,' I said. My hands were itching as they dried, as they clutched the edge of the sink.

'Art history,' he repeated.

'You can go on to work in auction houses afterwards, in antique appraisal,' I said, trying to appeal to his interests. But I should have known that though he might be interested in buying old prints and gilded letter-openers, jewelled snuff boxes and marble figurines, the idea of his own daughter being involved in anything to do with sales was unsatisfactory.

'What's wrong with English or History, or Classics?'

'Nothing,' I said.

He placed the boot polish onto the shelf next to the brushes. I could tell by his mannerisms, by his stiffness, that he was disappointed in me, that my idea was to him ridiculous. My face was hot.

'Art history,' he repeated again. 'Is that even a proper subject?'

'It's a new department at Cambridge.'

'You only get one shot at university, Ruth,' he said. He wasn't looking at me; he was looking at the dress dripping onto the draining board.

'It was just an idea,' I said.

'If you need more money for clothes, let me know,' he said and left the room.

I plunged my hand into the water of the sink and fumbled for the plug, watching the water ebb down and down, listening to the creaking suck of the pipes and imagining my shame gurgling away too.

After dinner, we retreated to Linda's cottage bedroom with two bottles of wine, the sewing machine and our finds – shawls, fabric, a lace curtain and an old floral bedsheet. It was stifling even with the small window open, and when we stood to dance and pose and sing along with my record player, we had to duck under the beams of the ceiling, catch ourselves on the narrow walls with our hands as we spun.

'What do you think?' Linda asked, smearing eyeliner down her cheeks. 'Do I look sad enough?'

'Pretty enough,' Sarah said, kissing her cheek as Linda swatted her away laughing.

Joan had got me to lie down on the floor swathed in a sheet, arms crossed over my chest. Camille was crouching over me applying blusher, her swaying motions betraying her drunkenness.

'Well?' I asked with my eyes closed, trying to look serene. 'Do I make a pretty corpse?'

'A suntanned one maybe,' Linda said with a snort, and I tried to kick her.

'Or a vampire,' Camille said, looking down at me, her small hands on my hot cheeks.

'I'd need blood-red lipstick for that,' I said, thinking of how she might tilt my chin up and apply it slowly and carefully, concentrating as if she were reading a book. But Sarah declared that it was her turn with the sheet and I was pulled up and unwound like a mummy, four pairs of hands tugging and twisting until I was free.

Linda's father looked in on us at midnight, his smile indulgent, and declared we were all mad. But when we didn't laugh in response, when Joan, in her froth of lace and a veil made from a curtain covering her face, bowed and said, *Thank you, good sir*, he looked for a moment deeply unnerved.

*

In the night, I wake slick with sweat, shivering, a cry caught in my mouth. I stumble out of the bed – in the bedroom that used to belong to my father, to him and my mother before she died – and away from Alex who sleeps on oblivious.

Switching on the light of the hall bathroom, I wince and peel my nightie away from my damp chest. In the hot shower I glance down the pale flesh of my body, watching rivulets of water, the drops that fall from my chin to the floor; I try to grasp the liquid edges of my nightmare, try to cup it in my thoughts. I was drowning, and it wasn't for show. I was somewhere narrow, dark, and the water was rising up from my toes. Someone else was there – in the water? Outside it?

Tipping my head up, I let the water beat hard on my face. I know already that although the imagery of my dream is fading, the sensation will stay with me for the day at least, and maybe longer.

The sudden screech of the shower door opening has me yelping, my feet slipping before a hand catches my arm.

'That hurts,' I hiss with embarrassment, wiping the water out of my eyes as Alex lets me go.

'I was only trying to stop you from braining yourself,' he says, bemused, his voice creaky with sleep. 'Are you all right?'

'I'm fine, just a bad dream, sorry,' I say as I turn off the shower.

I step out, wind a towel around me as he drinks from the tap. One morning, not long after the twins were born, I was so sleep-deprived that the sound of the tap running, his quiet gulps, was enough to sear me with fury, and I remember shouting, *Why don't you ever bring a glass to bed like a normal person!* and then bursting into tears as he led me back to bed and took the baby monitor with him to the living room.

Back in bed, my hair wet on the pillow but the night warm now, my legs and arms throbbing with heat, I feel Alex turn his head towards me.

'Was it the hospital?'

'Was what?'

'Your dream?' he asks.

'No, I can't remember what it was.'

'You're sure you don't want to see someone again?'

'One nightmare doesn't require a course of therapy.'

'I just don't want it to get like it was before, when you weren't sleeping, when you were running yourself ragged.'

'It won't, I'm fine. Maeve is better now.' I push my heels into the bed, flex my knees until they ache. I lie so easily to him and it's horrible. I've never told him about the girls and what happened that summer. By some mutual unspoken agreement, Stuart never brought it up at university either.

'That night in London,' Alex says, 'when you vanished, when I found you outside in the rain . . .' His hand strokes my shoulder.

'I'm sorry I scared you.'

'It was a scary time. But we got through it.' He turns on his back. 'And we'll get through the next thing,' he says sleepily.

Alex slept with someone else once, while Maeve was hospitalized. He was on a business trip, had had too many sambucas on an empty stomach after a day in the blazing sun; as he explained to me later, penitent, cheeks red with shame. He had called me crying right afterwards, incoherent, in the middle of the night, and I remember my only fury being that I had thought it was the hospital ringing to say that she was dead, that I had had to put the phone to my ear knowing that my daughter was dead, that this was it, that the world had shattered apart. That it was only my husband having sex with a woman whose face and identity he couldn't even recall felt so much less painful, important, compared to that.

Later I wondered if I hadn't deserved it. I haven't been fair to Alex, I haven't been the easy uncomplicated wife he could have had. And could I judge him for how he dealt with everything, after what I did a few months after that phone call?

It was the rain that hid my sins that night in London when he found me in the communal gardens of our flat, because if it hadn't started bucketing down I would have had to explain why I was soaked to the skin, why I smelled of silt and pond-water, why there were weeds still caught in my hair.

Chapter Eleven

Maeve has felt in a daze since her morning with Stuart in the field. It is as if, she thinks as she lies on the sofa in the sitting room one afternoon, her legs dangling over the arm, her head tipped so far back she can feel the pulse in her neck, she has walked into the world of his camera and has yet to return.

Stuart is away shooting at one of his stately homes, but he promised her he would have the photos to show her soon. She hopes that the spell won't be broken when she sees her image, that it won't ruin her memories of those perfect hours in the middle of the grasses with the tick of crickets throbbing, the heat of the sun warming every inch of her, Stuart's unblinking focus on her.

'Nothing on TV?' her father asks and she sits up quickly, embarrassed to be lying like that, languid and wanting.

'Nope,' she says, looking at the black screen in the corner of the room as he sits beside her.

He tugs one of her curls, and she drops her shoulder so his hand doesn't brush against it. Suddenly it feels wrong to have him touch her like he usually does – not because he's doing something wrong, but because she is— No, that isn't right, she hasn't done anything wrong either, not really, she just feels

– she feels that right now she only wants to be touched by one person and him alone.

'Are you OK? You've been quiet lately,' her father asks.

'Am I usually gregarious?'

'You can be, with the twins.'

'That's because I feel outnumbered.'

He shifts in his seat and her eyes glance over the familiar contours of his face. Sometimes, when her mother was her only company at the hospital, besides the doctors and nurses and the other kids, Maeve used to ache with longing for her father and his face and his arms around her. She said it sometimes when pain, or even boredom, made her cruel, said she'd rather have him here instead of Ruth. Once her mother flinched as if hit but the other times she only said, *I know, darling*, and stroked her hair back from her head or lifted a glass for her to drink.

'I imagine it might be hard for you sometimes, the attention they need from us. But you know, when you were ill, they missed out on a lot too.'

'I know that, I *know*.'

'Of course you do.' He puts his hand over her hand and now she can't take hers back without it seeming weird. 'Actually, your mother and I spoke to someone about it, family dynamics, getting things back to normal now that you're well.'

Maeve feels a sudden rush of anger like the chill of a drip through her veins. 'Why wasn't I there for this conversation? I'm seventeen, I'm an adult.'

'You're right.' He nods, looking down at his feet as he flexes them. 'That's what I wanted to talk to you about actually, you being an adult. University,' he declares, with a pat of his thighs, 'have you thought about what subject you're interested in? There's not long until you apply.'

I'm not one of your employees, Maeve thinks, stuck on the

image of her parents talking to someone about how to handle her. Her father has always liked problems to be solved swiftly, for solutions to be found. Thus his difficulties with her illness, the way he seemed to find ways to keep busy, and sometimes avoided her eyes as if she didn't fit in with what he wanted the world to be. 'No, I haven't.'

'No ideas at all? You don't have to decide about a career now, of course, unless it's something like medicine, or sciences.'

The word 'career' makes her feel viscerally tired, like she wants to slump down right now and never get up again. Isn't it enough that she's alive, that she's living and well? Picturing herself in an office somewhere is like picturing herself hiking a mountain; wearying, impossible.

'I mean, you must have some idea about subjects you enjoy studying,' he presses, looking at her as if she is being ridiculous. Perhaps she is.

'All of them?' she offers. 'Except maths.'

'There you go, the Humanities.'

'What if I don't go to university at all?'

'Well, what else are you going to do?' He has an open look on his face, is doing his best to hide his frustration with her.

Why don't you ask the therapist you saw? she wants to reply, but her jaw aches with fatigue, her head too heavy on her neck for bitter comebacks. 'I don't know.'

'That's why university will be good, it'll give you time to decide. And you'll have fun, Maeve. God knows your mother and I did. You might even meet someone there.'

She picks at the edge of her thumbnail, drawing the sharp pain of a shard tugged from too far down. 'Stuart was at your university too, wasn't he?'

'He was, probably one of my best friends there.' Her father smiles. 'We all lived together when we left halls.'

'Is he the same as you remember?'

'Yes, I think so. Maybe he's less political, but we all are.'

'Political?'

'He went to all the protests, wrote letters, fundraised for radical groups, you know. He was good at it too, at getting people to understand. Sometimes I'd lose him at a party and find him holding court, talking about Ireland and Vietnam, about how we were the generation who could change things.'

'Is he disappointed then, that you work in chemicals, that you used to work in oil?'

'What? No, of course not. We grew up, like everyone does. And Labour are in power now, things are heading in the right direction.'

Her father had made them all stay up, her and the twins, to watch Blair be elected, to watch the landslide. *What did I tell you*, he had said, turning to Maeve, *this year is a good year*. As if her remission had been somehow connected to the political health of the country too.

'Dad, why did we stop visiting Grandad? Why didn't we ever come here after the twins were born?'

'Did we not?' His face is guileless but she doesn't believe him. Why is it that he can question her about her plans for university but she can't ask this one question about their family history?

'No. Did you fall out with him?'

He touches his thumb to his jaw, finding the same patch of missed stubble he always does. 'Your mum had a difficult relationship with him, he was a complicated man.'

'What do you mean?'

'You'll need to ask her.'

Iza shrieks from somewhere else in the house.

'So, you'll think about it, university choices?' her father says, standing up.

He's in his summer uniform of large faded t-shirt with stretched-out collar and old shiny shorts, and she wants to tell him that he looks ridiculous. 'Sure,' she lies.

Maeve waits in the cool dark of the hall, sitting on the stairs, the carpet itchy under her thighs. Opposite her is a large mirror with a gold frame in which she studies her face, her flat expression, the nervous biting of her nails. The house is empty and feels emptier still but she doesn't want to wait out front for him – there's too little shelter with the long open lawn – and if she waited in the back garden he might not think to come and find her.

She should have brought her Discman, she thinks, looking at her pale legs in the mirror, but she doesn't want to walk the few metres upstairs in case she misses him, in case her standing up breaks the spell.

There. The sound of a car.

She stands up too quickly, feels the rush of blood, her reflection darkening so she can't do one final check.

She's at the front door as Stuart emerges from his car, camera bag on his shoulder, battered leather holdall in one hand and folder tucked in the other.

He smiles when he sees her. 'I got the photos back. Do you want to come see them?' He motions his head towards the old dairy courtyard and the annexe.

'Yeah,' she says, stepping out onto the gravel with bare feet, feeling the bite of each stone.

He glances at her feet. 'I would carry you, but my arms are sort of full right now.'

'That's OK.'

'It's amazing the amount of stuff I manage to carry with me

for one trip to the home counties, when I managed with nothing but my camera abroad,' he groans at the door to the annexe, fumbling for his key.

She has the brief thought that she should offer to get it out of his pocket for him, and then imagines the opposite, of him sliding his hand into any of the pockets of her shorts.

'After you,' he says and she brushes past him, feeling the bulk of his bag against her side, smelling his aftershave. 'Can I get you some tea?' he asks, as he sets down his things and turns on the kettle.

'I don't drink it.' Her hands hover on one of the mismatched chairs at the round table serving as dining table and workspace both. She's trying not to study the space, to note his belongings, trying to act casual with being a guest in a room where the bed he sleeps on, and its ruffled sheets, are only a few steps away.

He leans back against the sideboard and crosses his arms. 'No tea? Your mother has raised a heathen.'

'Too bitter.'

'I'll have to get hot chocolate for next time, the good stuff with cream. In the meantime,' he says, as the kettle boils and he makes his cup with practised ease, 'the photos.'

He sets his tea on the table to one side of her and then places an envelope on the table to her other side, shoulder brushing against hers. His hand rests on top of the envelope. 'Ready?' he asks.

She turns to look at him. He's close enough that she can see the texture of his skin, the wrinkles around his eyes. 'Are you pleased with them?'

'I am, yes. Here.' He opens the envelope and fans the photos out on the chipped polish of the table.

Her eyes can't focus immediately; she sees a wash of flaxen

grass-green, a splash of cream, her dress, then the red of her hair, and then, as she picks one up, her face. She inhales sharply, feels her eyes smart. She knows he's looking at her but she can't look at him, embarrassed about how much it means to her to look like this. Beautiful. Beautiful and sad and sullen, hopeful, wanting, languid. He seems to have caught so much, even in the ones where he's furthest away, where she is shading her face with her hand.

'Verdict?' he asks, voice soft, reaching across her to take his tea.

'Amazing,' she says and touches his arm. 'Thank you.'

'I should be the one thanking you, Maeve.' He picks up a few of the photos to show her, commenting on what he likes about the light, or the shapes of the grass and her body in its hollow, the colour of her hair.

She didn't remember baring so much skin but her legs and arms seem to merge with the pale dress. There is a vulnerability to her in these images, she sees, and thus an innate feeling of trust towards the photographer, towards him. Noticing that now makes those feelings stronger.

'I know we were going for Ophelia, but I think some of these look more Persephone,' he says. 'You know the myth?'

She nods.

He slides the photos around. 'I'm still surprised at what a camera can pick up that the eye doesn't. Something can be beautiful in real life but the lens transforms it into something more, gives it meaning.' He holds up a photo in which her face fills half the image, the focus fuzzy around the edges, blades of grass softening her jaw, hair curling across her fore-head as her head lolls to the side. 'There's something ancient about your expression here.'

'Are you saying I look old?'

The children in the hospital looked old, especially the sickest ones, *like little wizened gods who have seen the world's horrors*, Georgia said once, shivering like they gave her the creeps.

'Your expression, not your face or your eyes,' he drawls, 'I don't see any cataracts, any clouding in those baby-blues of yours.'

'You're the one with the blue eyes.'

Holding his gaze is unbearable, but in a good way, like jumping on a swing seat made boiling hot by the sun.

'I stand corrected,' he says, 'your eyes aren't blue, they're greeny blue, they're cyan, teal.'

'Those are all different colours.'

'Well, I'll have to study them closer.'

Stuart's eyes are always blue – blue like the bottom of a deep swimming pool.

'So, I had an idea for our next shoot. Come here, let's sit down.'

She follows him to the old corduroy sofa below the skylight, settles by one of the armrests.

'Do I smell bad or something?'

'Well, you have been driving all day.'

He laughs, and she turns her hips towards him and puts her legs up on the seat, feet awkwardly hanging off the edge. He clasps her ankles, puts her heels on his thighs. She's wearing shorts today and spent a long time in the shower making sure her legs were perfectly smooth.

He keeps a hand on her ankle as he retrieves his tea from the floor.

'What's your idea then?' she asks, to cover up the twitch of her leg.

'Have you been out back?' he nods. 'In that overgrown patch.

I found a bath there, of all things. It's a little weather-worn and full of soil, but I'm going to clean it up today. I want to riff off the origin of Millais's Ophelia, how Lizzie Siddal lay in a bath while he drew studies of her. Did you hear that story?'

'She caught pneumonia,' Maeve says, remembering what the guide had told her in the Tate gallery. 'Pneumonia is what I almost died from.'

'Oh, shit, I didn't know. We'll do something else.'

'No, it'll be fine. I mean, it's a viral infection, you don't get it because you're cold.'

He squeezes her foot. 'I'll fill it with warm water.'

She wants to go there now, wants to slip under the water to cool her face, wants to lie back with her head on the lip of the bath as the sun beats down on her.

'I'll need to pick up some more flowers too, I can't rip up your whole garden.'

'Friday?' she offers. 'My mum's taking the twins to a fair all day.'

'That sounds perfect. Do you mind if I smoke in here? I'm lazy.'

'Sure,' she shrugs, feeling her legs lift up as he retrieves the pack from his back pocket.

He watches her as he lights one. 'You looked upset when I got back today, is everything all right?'

She scrapes a fingernail down a groove of corduroy. 'It's just my dad, he's been stressing me out about university.'

'Why? You won't be applying until the winter, will you?'

'Yeah, I know, but he wants me to choose a subject.' She drops her head on the back of the sofa, breathes a heavy sigh. She wonders if Stuart's eyes are roaming her body while she's not looking.

'I would have assumed you'd have a gap year or something,'

he says, thumb pressing into the arch of her foot. 'Although maybe not an expedition to Peru like Miss Adventurer.'

She snorts, lifts her head again.

'But you still need to rest and recover, surely.' He leans over to tap his cigarette into his mug and she sees the black band of his boxers above his jeans.

'What would I do for a year?' she asks, flexing her foot in his hand. She hasn't put nail varnish on this summer but she doesn't care now.

He shrugs. 'Interrail, visit Italy, stay in a tiny room in a picturesque loggia, tour the galleries. Stay here, read books, take photos, expand your musical education beyond the Spice Girls—'

She kicks him. 'I don't like the Spice Girls.'

'OK, then. But really, you can do anything. You don't have to *do* anything either, just rest and see what comes your way. If you don't know what you're interested in yet then what's the point in applying for university?'

'That's what I thought. What did you study?'

'PPE.'

'Not law?'

'No, I changed my mind.' He stubs the cigarette out. 'I'm not sure I've used any of it since though, except to impress those who tried to underestimate me. Saying you went to Oxbridge is a good passport sometimes when trying to gain an audience with a despot or hitch a ride on a helicopter, but I could have lied all the same.'

'Did you always want to be a photographer?' she asks, and then reaches to pick up a small squat book on a pile, which says *The Photography Book*. Underneath it is a similar-sized volume called *The Art Book*.

'Those two were actually gag gifts, but it turns out it's rather useful to have the entirety of western art history at your finger-tips for quick reference. When I was a boy, sometimes I used to see paintings in black-and-white reproductions before I ever saw them in colour. You want to borrow them?'

'Yes, please,' she says, hoping to have something of Stuart's to keep her company in the hours she's apart from him.

'So polite,' he teases.

'I should probably get back to the house.'

'Do your parents keep tabs on you?' he asks, circling her anklebone with his thumb.

'Not as much as they used to. I guess they want me to be a normal teenager now.' She feels awkward saying that word, but then she's decided she's not going to lie and try to pretend she's older for him.

'Drink and drugs and all that?'

And sex, she fills in, in her head. 'Is that what you were like?'

'Do your parents ever talk about their university days?'

'Not really.'

'They ever tell you they smoked weed sometimes?'

'No.' She feels a sudden rising of anxiety. There's something unnerving about discovering the secret pasts of your parents, perhaps because it means you don't know them at all, or because it reminds you that their existence isn't reliant on you as yours is on them.

'I suppose parents don't share that kind of stuff because they don't want to be a bad influence. You won't tell them I told you, will you?'

'Of course not.'

He slides her feet off his lap so they can stand up.

'Can I have one of the photos?' she asks. 'I'll keep it safe.' *I'll hide it*, is what she means.

'Be my guest. I'm curious to see which one you'll choose,' he says, rounding the table as she leans over it.

She can feel his body behind her even though he isn't touching her, and her back spasms. 'This one,' she says.

'I like that one too.'

She holds it up and it catches the light. A swooning girl with a floral bouquet abandoned at her side; the dark shadow of a photographer almost touching her feet. Persephone waiting for her Hades.

Chapter Twelve

Joan's mother didn't want her to go to the river any more. She had seen the photos, Joan told us early one morning as we walked down through the fields, sharing a sticky stack of toast and marmalade that Sarah, as the self-proclaimed mother of the group, had brought with her so we *wouldn't starve*.

'She thought it was morbid,' Joan said, with a kick at a clump of grass, 'to keep doing it, to keep *drowning*.'

'So what did you say?'

'I asked her if she would prefer me spending time with the boys and getting into trouble.'

'Do you have a boyfriend back home?' I asked.

'No.' She shrugged and then looked puckish. 'But Linda does.'

'You've kept that quiet,' Sarah teased.

'It's nothing serious,' Linda said with a flick of her hair. The ends were frizzled from the sun, and she would scratch them together and complain how dry they were before slathering on conditioner that she washed out in the river.

'But you have, *you know*, right?' Sarah asked, as we entered the dappled shade of the woods.

'What?'

'Don't play dumb.' Joan rolled her eyes.

'No, I haven't.'

'Well, I have,' Sarah said. 'And it wasn't like it usually is – I was the one who wanted it.'

'Didn't you worry what might happen?' I asked.

'I started praying again until my period arrived. *Dear Lord,*' she recited, clasping her hands together, closing her eyes so that I had to pull her out of the way of a nearby tree, '*I swear I'll be good, I swear I'll never do it again.*' She laughed and opened her eyes. 'And then I did it again anyway.'

'Are you going to marry him?' Camille asked.

'I don't know.'

'She doesn't have to,' Linda declared with a snort. 'You don't have to tie yourself to the first boy you sleep with.'

'Why haven't you had sex then yet?'

'Because I haven't been impressed with the calibre of my offers,' she said with a sniff.

'Would you sleep with Stuart?' Joan asked me, looking sly.

'No way.'

'You two looked awfully cosy last night.'

Before dinner, as the families congregated in the garden of Sarah's cottage, Stuart had sat beside me on the grass as I flicked through a book of Pre-Raphaelite paintings. They were all in black and white except for two pages in the middle. *You look like her,* he had said, pointing at Ophelia.

It's just the hair, I replied, ignoring the soft way he was looking at me.

I think it's great what you're doing, you girls, he said.

You do?

It's art, isn't it. And recreating paintings in photos, making it modern, I think it's groovy.

Thanks, I said, nudging his knee with mine.

His smile was sweet.

I haven't seen you much this summer, I said. He was too busy with my father, with his books. I resented the time he spent in my father's office. I wanted Stuart's attention even though I didn't return his romantic interest. I wanted to be admired, desired; what girl doesn't?

I've been studying. And you've been busy with the girls.

There was a cry then, one of the children who had fallen over, but when no parent came running, Sarah walked over and picked the little girl up, singing to her, rocking her from side to side.

I don't think I ever want to be a mother, I said suddenly.

Then don't be, Stuart replied easily.

Just like that.

Just like that. He leaned back on his elbows. He was so much more comfortable in his body than I was, I thought, looking at him then, lithe in his tight flares and form-fitting collared top, the furthest thing from a stumbling child.

You know, if you're going to apply to art school, you'll need more than photographs and watercolours, he said.

Who said I was applying to art school?

Do they do life drawing at your school?

No. Still lifes.

He was right. I knew that any drawing of a vase filled with dry flowers or a bowl of pale apples was unlikely to light any fires in the admissions department. But then, my father wouldn't let me go to art school anyway.

I humbly put myself forward for your model then, he said, just as one of the fathers clapped his hands together and announced dinner was ready.

What, naked? I hissed as we stood up.

He looked embarrassed. *Not necessarily. I mean, you can just draw me in my shorts.*

We reached the table before I could answer, but as I sat in between Sarah and Camille and ate that night's lentil stew, my only thought was, *Why would I draw him when I could draw one of the girls instead?*

When we arrived at the river the next day, the weather was already changing, the clouds growing darker and a wind picking up.

Linda cupped her hands around her cigarette to light it, passing it to Sarah after she had taken a drag.

'Can I?' Camille asked.

'Sure.'

I watched as she tilted her head, as her cheeks sucked in and eyes narrowed. Was it just because I knew she was part French that she looked so cool smoking?

'So who are we today?' Sarah asked, nodding to the river.

The water was darker than the sky, murky, green. And yet still so inviting. Maybe even more so.

'Ophelia, of course,' I declared, standing up.

I pulled my jumper over my head, leaving me in only the vintage slip.

Linda wolf-whistled.

Stepping into the river, I could see the surface prickled by raindrops. I was cold and the water felt sharp, the stones on the riverbed painful on my feet, but the discomfort, the chill I dipped down into, felt welcome, thrilling.

'You need flowers in your hair,' Sarah called out after she had taken a few photographs. I wondered if you would even be able to see me on film in today's dim light or if I would melt into the river.

Camille clambered into the water, clutching a few branches

of white sweet peas. I could feel her approach by the wave she pushed before her, the crest of it breaking over my side.

I stood up, my slip plastering to me and the hairs on my skin standing up at the chill. The rain was still falling, sparse thick drops on the top of my head as Camille wove the flowers into my hair, her mouth crowded with pins to fix them in place, a hand steadying me when I found myself slipping on a large smooth stone.

I thought about what we might look like if someone was taking a photo right now, and flinched from her hands.

'You OK?' she asked.

She was looking at me intently. It felt like something had changed between us since I bought her that dress.

'Fine,' I said, a cold wash trickling through my arms and legs. I wanted Camille to step away from me, to ignore me. I wanted the other girls to leave Camille and me here alone.

The rain was getting harder now, the leaves of the trees around the river shaking and twitching, the girls holding arms and scarves above them.

I lay down in the water, pushed my arms back and forth, feeling the strength in my muscles, imagining I could swim for miles down the river and find myself somewhere new. I had never lain on my back and stared up at a raining sky, and as I blinked and jerked with each drop on my eyes and the delicate skin beneath them, I gasped. And when the rain lashed down in sheets, I let out a kind of scream, delighted, deranged, feeling as if I was lying in the middle of a storm, surrounded on all sides by nature's fury.

I heard voices calling for me and half swam, half crawled towards the bank.

'You're crazy,' Linda said, holding out her hand for me to climb onto the grass.

'Did you get any photos?' I asked, out of breath, swiping the rain from my face as the flowers from my hair stuck to my skin.

Sarah nodded. 'Before we hid the camera from the rain.'

'Are we going to stick it out here?' I asked the group, carefully avoiding looking at Camille although I could feel her looking at me.

The rain was slicking my arms and legs, coming down hard through the leaves and trees across the clearing where we sheltered. We were all drenched. Then there was a bright flash of light and I blinked, the negative image of the trees seared into my eyelids, white and blazing.

'Is it better to stay in a forest with trees or be out in the fields when it thunders?' Linda asked Camille, her voice rising as the thunder rolled its way through the woods.

'I don't know,' she replied.

'I think we go back,' Sarah said after another lightning strike.

'We'll be sitting ducks!' I called out as she gathered her scarf around her head and fled, Linda following and then Joan, who let out a gleeful scream at the next clap of thunder.

'Fine,' I said, and then ran after them too.

My bare feet were unsteady on the wet ground, my sodden slip hobbling me until I hiked it up my thighs. I could hear Camille right behind me, could hear both of our breaths, the slap of our feet on earth and fallen leaves.

Another lightning strike cracked down and a roar of wind came straight towards us, every branch creaking and the leaves heaving like rough seas.

Camille gasped as the thunder hit, but she didn't sound afraid. I looked back, stumbling over a root. She had stopped and was looking up at the sky through the tumultuous treetops, her eyes shining wildly.

'Come on,' I called, 'we need to get back.'

She gave no sign that she had heard me. Her chest was heaving like she was taking breaths before diving into deep water.

I grabbed for her hand and tugged, feeling the taut resistance of her muscles, thinking in the panic of the storm that she wasn't going to move, that I couldn't get her to leave and the storm would take her. Then she met my eyes and gave in. Her fingers were slippery and cold, and as we left the boundary of the woods for the open fields, the rain driving in sheets across them, I held tighter.

We used the stile to cross into my father's field and bent low towards the hill as we climbed through the long grass. The storm was further away now, the sky a lighter grey, and I could see the tiny figures of the other girls waiting in the shelter of the barrier of trees.

I let go of her hand and sped up, holding my slip down so it wouldn't ride up above my knickers. I felt burning cold now; the thrill of the storm was bleeding away and the image of Camille standing still in the maelstrom, wild and beautiful, was left in its wake.

'I have your jumper,' she said when we came to a stop.

'Thanks.' I bent over, catching my breath. My chilled feet were flecked by grass and dirt.

'We thought we lost you two,' Linda said. 'Thought you'd drowned in the storm for real.'

Their clothes, meagre as they were, were plastered to the skin, translucent or slipping off shoulders, skin flushed from the run and beaded with water. Here, out of the shade of the trees, all I could see was our – their – nakedness.

I pulled the jumper over my head.

'Tea at mine?' Sarah offered.

'I'm going back to the house,' I said, feeling exposed, as though the rain had washed away some barrier of protection and bared some secret held deep in my body.

The gravel of the pathway hurt as I ran along it away from the girls, and I thought it was good that it hurt, that my cold skin felt sore, my ribs aching with a stitch.

Back in my bedroom, I stripped without looking at myself, putting on a different jumper and pyjama trousers, and burrowed under the blankets of my bed, pulling them around my head so that the air I breathed became wet and thin.

Maybe Stuart was right, I thought, maybe I *should* draw him. Maybe spending so much time with the girls, photographing them, considering their bodies and mine, was confusing me.

*

I'm staring down at the white of the ceramic sink in the kitchen, at the way the water of the tap eddies over the teaspoons I dropped in, their brown coffee residue smearing towards the plughole.

The stairs creak and I pick up the sponge to wipe the spoons clean.

'Raspberries?' I offer, turning to see Maeve enter the room. Maeve who looks both lethargic and wary, her shoulders raised.

She shrugs.

'More for me then. What have you been up to today?'

'Just resting.'

'That's good.' I open the fridge and look at nothing. I used to know everything she did, and now I don't know how to reach her, what tone to use, what to say. 'Dad said you've been thinking about university.'

'No,' she says sharply.

'No?'

'Dad brought it up, I wasn't thinking about it. I'm too tired.'

'Are you having any symptoms?' I check, picking up raspberries one by one from the plastic carton.

'No. I'm just tired.'

'They said exercise might help to build energy. If you ever want company for a longer walk—'

'*Mum*, I've just said I'm tired.'

'I know, darling. I just don't want you to get stuck.' *I don't want you to step away from the world before your life has even begun.* 'I'm sure some summer sun will do the trick.'

Her quick smile is fleeting as a hummingbird.

It's when she passes me towards the back door that I smell it. 'Have you been smoking?'

'No.'

'I can smell smoke.'

'I was wearing Dad's fleece earlier – I was cold – it must have transferred from that.' She looks betrayed.

'That must be it,' I say, and she slinks off and I know I have lost even more of her goodwill.

The light switch in the pantry blows a fuse, and as I climb the rickety ladder to the fuse box under the stairs, I think that Maeve and I were so close when she was ill. I knew what every shift of her body, every twitch of her face meant. I knew, because she told me, the catalogue of her body's pain and discomfort.

I knock on her bedroom door and wait, hearing a shuffle – the sound of something being put away? – and then her voice, slow in the way only a teenager's can be. 'Yeah?'

'It's me, can I come in?'

Another pause. 'OK.'

She's sitting on her bed, hands clutched in the sheets to

either side of her. The wallpaper is still the same, the one I
used to stare at as I lay on my floor listening to records. I
could blink and the other girls would be here too, painting
their nails, sewing beads and sequins onto the hems of skirts.

'I just wanted to come and say hi,' I say.

She looks at me balefully.

'Are you worried about next week?'

'Next week?'

'Hospital, the check-up.'

'Oh.'

I sit next to her gingerly, reach out to brush her hair back
over her shoulder. 'Were you trying on perfumes?' I ask. There's
a strange smell in here, like perfumes or flowers.

'Mum,' she says.

'Am I only going to get one-word answers from you this
summer?' I tease.

She blows out a breath. 'I don't want to think about hospital.'

'I'm sure it'll go fine.'

She gives me a look as if to say, *How can you know, don't you
remember that I wasn't fine?* But it's my role as parent to lie
optimistically, to tell my children that their futures are only rosy.

At the door I step over two pink petals lying on the carpet.

Later, trailing the twins around the back garden, I try to
find the plant she must have picked the petals from but I can't
remember the shade. None of the flowers here are really all
that pink.

After that summer, I had never looked at bouquets of flowers
the same way again. When Alex once bought me a bunch of
roses at university, in a fumbling attempt at high romance, I
had to tell him that I was a girl who didn't like flowers, that
they had always reminded me of funerals.

Chapter Thirteen

The wait for the next photoshoot with Stuart feels torturous. Maeve tries to roam the gardens, to read books in the sun and pluck tiny petals from the lavish blooms of the hydrangeas, to sit on the grass making daisy chains. But she can't settle out there, can't relax with the echoing voices of the twins playing near the patio, so she gives up and retreats to her room with its locked door, where she can listen to CDs on loop as she lies on her bed with her feet propped up on the wall; where she can try all her clothes on and study herself in her mirror.

When she looks at her reflection now, after seeing the photos he took, she looks different. The angles of her face, the plush give of her mouth, the freckles across her cheeks. Like she has been made something new, transformed by his camera.

On Friday, she ventures down for breakfast and sits at the kitchen table, peeling an orange slowly and watching the clock. 'It's good to see you up and about so early for once,' her mother says, as she attempts to corral the twins out for the day. When they're finally ready to leave, Maeve stands at the door to wave them off so she can be sure they've gone.

The door to the annexe is open when she arrives there, ready to become Ophelia for him.

'I've filled the bath with a hose,' Stuart says, his warm smile making up for her wait. 'I wouldn't drink from it, but aside from that I'd say it's safe.' He winks. 'Oh, and I hope you don't mind, but I've got a dress for you.'

She glances down at the dress she's currently wearing, the same pale one from the field photoshoot. The rest of her clothes are too modern to pretend to be some Pre-Raphaelite heroine; it would be a strange kind of horrible to wear a t-shirt and a denim skirt in a bath and be photographed like that, as if she had just been dumped in it.

'What do you think?' he asks, bringing it out from a bag. 'I got it from a vintage shop although I don't know if it is actually all that old.'

'Oh, it's gorgeous.' The dress has two layers – a cream-coloured silk slip underneath a gauzy short-sleeved overlayer embroidered with lace and tiny beads, and with pearl buttons from the waist to the neckline. It has something of Victorian underthings about it, she thinks, or the faded glamour of an opera house.

The silk and the lace might be see-through in the water but that isn't a surprise. Deciding what underwear to put on beneath a wet dress has been a decision that took many hours, which was embarrassing perhaps, but she had realized halfway through, as she flung an old bra down at her feet, that thinking about the photoshoots, and Stuart, means she has hardly had a chance to think about her future, nor to feel the deadening weight of her past.

'I'll check the bath if you get changed,' he says, and then slips out of the Dutch door to the old vegetable patch.

She peels her own dress over her head, and steps across the room to pick up his gift in her white lace bra and knickers which are pink and frilled and were part of her Christmas present from her mother, along with a pack of thongs which made her feel awkward, as if she were somehow pushing Maeve to be a proper teenager, to have someone – a teenage boy naturally – to show them to, because she certainly couldn't wear them to hospital.

The slip feels almost wet against her legs, the pearl of the buttons hard little nubs underneath her fingertips. She feels a similar nervous flutter in her stomach that she did before each operation, until she steps outside and feels the warmth of the sun on her body.

'Oh my God,' she breathes when she reaches the scene, 'it looks incredible'. Stuart has brought in bunches and bunches of meadow flowers – sweet peas, dahlias, cornflowers, zinnias, foxgloves, lavender – and placed them in troughs and pots propped on bricks and stools so that the bath seems to float in the middle of a lush flower garden.

'You look even more incredible.' He has the sleeves of his shirt rolled above his elbows and there is something black and coiled in his hand. 'I think the florist thought I was buying them for a wedding. Oh, and the vintage shop said a ribbon would look good around your waist.'

She stands in front of him as he loops a black velvet ribbon high over her ribcage, tying a bow at the front, the whisper of his fingers there making her shiver. 'The water should be warm, but you'll tell me if you get cold?'

She nods.

'Your bath awaits, madam.' He holds out a hand so that she can clamber in.

Her foot slips on the bottom and she laughs nervously. The water is as warm as he'd promised, almost body temperature. Standing in the raised-up bath she is just taller than him.

'Hi,' he smiles, and she smiles back.

'Do you want my hair to get wet right away?'

'Maybe put it over the side first,' he says as she sinks down, one hand holding her hair up, the other on the lip of the bath, its rust rough to the touch. She feels the water soak up into her dress and make the fabric heavy, plaster it to her body as Stuart watches.

'Will I do?' she jokes, but it isn't really a joke.

'Perfect.'

The water is cradling her, rocking with every shift as if she is in a shallow sea. He hands her a bouquet to hold and then lifts his camera. He's closer than in the field and this time she can hear the sound of the shutter, and the clicking sound of one of his wrists – the one that had broken? – as he works.

At first she poses with her neck on the lip of the bath, but then he has her slip further down so that the water reaches her collarbones. He directs her to splay the fingers of her empty hand over the edge and then by her side, then above her head. The bouquet rests on her middle; her feet meet the end of the long bath. He circles around her, squeezing past flowers, changing lenses, checking the light with a separate light meter.

The sky is blue today with the occasional small fluffy cloud; the sun is hot on her face. When parts of her emerge from the surface of the water, she feels a prickle as they dry. Glancing down, she can just see the shape of her bra through the dress and the points of her nipples, but can't see past the bouquet to see if her knickers are also visible. She thinks they are.

He talks to her more this time, directing her, praising her, narrating what he's doing. *Look at me*, he says, *now look away. Stay like that, perfect. Relax your mouth, tilt your head.*

When his voice is soft there's a burr, a hum to it, like the pleasurable disorientation of putting your head against a car window, like the deep throb of an MRI, like the right note in a song. She wants to lay her head on his chest and hear, feel, his words travel through her.

'I want the light to glisten on the water but not blind the lens,' he is saying, 'and for the paleness of your skin not to get lost against the white of the bath.'

Some of the flowers that made up the bouquet are loose around her now; they bob and sink, stick to the sides of the bath and her limbs. He adjusts their position at intervals, and her hair which, wet and darker, lies in strands across her shoulders.

The water is cooling now too; she feels it against her legs, her arms, her sides when she shifts, feels the slip of it down the inner channel of her ribcage when she breathes, the way it pools in the space between the tendons of her neck and collarbone.

'What are you thinking about?' he asks. His elbows are propped up on the edge of the bath and the sun is just above him, searing bright.

'Nothing.'

'It doesn't look like nothing.'

She shrugs, creating a wash of water back and forth. She feels drunk, dizzy, with his gaze. *Remember this moment*, she tells herself. This: her half-naked and wet, him fully clothed and watching, directing.

'I'm struggling to get the right angle of you – I think I'm going to have to join you in there,' he says.

'OK,' she replies, without quite understanding what he means.

He rolls up his jeans and then steps into the bath by her feet. He stands either side of her calves, his ankles pressing hard against her skin in the cramped space, and holds the camera above her, looking down.

Her head is floating in the water now, her ears bobbing under the surface where she can hear the strange clicks and gurgles of her body, the squeak of skin against the ceramic. He told her not to drink the water but it keeps running across her cheek and past her lips, brackish.

'Lift your head up,' he says, motioning with his chin.

She rests the crown of her head against the bath, tries to focus on that hard point of pressure so that she doesn't float away, so her eyes don't close. He crouches down and she stares into the black circle of his lens. He is so close she can see a reflection of herself there, distorted, curved.

'I never asked,' he murmurs, 'do you have a boyfriend?'

'No.'

'Good.'

It feels as though his words, his breath, are rippling the water around her, but maybe that's just her trembling.

'Are you cold?' he asks.

'No.'

'Are you lying to me?'

'Yes.'

His eyes are hidden by his camera but she can see his smile as the shutter *click-click-click*s in swift succession. 'Don't lie to me, Maeve.'

'OK, so I'm cold,' she says, and lets herself slip right under the water, closing her eyes, holding her breath.

It feels loud under there; the sounds of her body, maybe even her heart, the muffled thump of her knee knocking against the side. She opens her eyes. The world above is blurry, bright, silver like a mirror, the black smudge of his camera in front of his face. Her chest hurts and she breaches the surface with a gasp, at the same moment his hand curves under her neck to help her.

'Almost lost you there,' he says and wipes water from her
eyes, a callus on his thumb sharp on the delicate skin.

He leads her, shivering, back to the annexe, telling her to
shower, to get herself warm and he'll make her some of the
hot chocolate he got for her.

In the bathroom her chilled fingers, their tips furrowed by
the water, fumble on the first button. She pauses. She could
unbutton herself; it would take a little time but she could
do it.

She opens the bathroom door and his head turns sharply
towards her.

'I'm having trouble with the buttons,' she says, and only
realizes how childish that might sound after she's said it and
he's come towards her. Although she doesn't have a child's
body, does she, she thinks, as his eyes flick down to her breasts.

'They are fiddly things,' he says, starting at the top. 'You're
covered with goosebumps. If I've given you a chill—'

'There's no such thing as a chill. There's hypothermia, but
I don't think I have that.'

'Strangely, that doesn't make me feel any better.'

'Are you worried about me?'

'Always,' he confesses, and she feels his answer like a sweet
stab in her gut. 'Lift your arms,' he says and she does as asked.

'It's attached to the slip with thread,' she says, when the top
part gets caught over her head.

'Oh.'

She waits, vision distorted by sodden lace, and then bites
her tongue when his hands meet her hips. He tugs the slip
up her skin and then her sides, drags it over her head, and
she's finally free.

She stands still as he studies her.

He touches a finger to her port scar. 'It's crazy that with all you went through, you only really have one scar.' He turns to put his palm over it. It would take the merest shrug to shift his hand further down. What is he waiting for?

She thinks about what might come next, what it would feel like, what it would look like, the two of them together, his weathered skin against her pale. Her body twitches.

'You really will get a cold now, get into the shower,' he insists. 'And I'll finish making that hot chocolate.' He shuts the door of the bathroom behind him. She cranes to look into the small mirror above the sink to see what he saw, to know what she looked like to him. Bedraggled, damp, her bare skin stark under the lightbulb of the windowless room, her eyes feverish. In the shower, she runs a finger across the horrible scar that has been made something lovely by his touch.

She can hear him on the phone outside the studio when she emerges. She left the dress where it lay in a sodden pile so that, she hopes, it might remind him of her when she's gone.

She picks up the hot drink he left her, tastes it briefly before setting it back down. There is a pile of contact sheets on the table, and she peers closer at the tiny faces of lords and ladies emerging from grand rooms of ruby and emerald, so many busts and paintings and polished furniture pieces that at this scale it is almost a puzzle game to find the living. Next to that pile are two black-and-white photography books. His books, she sees, reading his name. The image on the cover of the smaller one is the silhouette of a tree. The other, titled *Witness*, is heavy when she lifts it up. A man is crying on the cover, the bayonet of a gun a sharp line above him, a small shoe at his knee, and a skeletal ruin cutting off half the sky behind him.

She opens the book at random, turns the page quickly when the heaped shape on it becomes a pile of bodies. On the next page a soldier laughs, pale cigarettes tucked into each strap of his armour, behind his ears, fisted in his hands. On the next, a group of people in work clothes stand in front of a pockmarked building, staring at something behind the camera, their bodies tensed to flee. She flicks forward and pauses, turning the book around. A black-and-white image, a woman of indeterminate age lying on a dark ground surrounded by pools of light from recent rain. It is difficult to tell if she is alive or dead; her left arm lies outstretched, hand cupped. Fabric of some kind, maybe plastic, is caught on a pile of rubble behind her, lending the image a painterly feel, like the rich folds of a silk dress belonging to a Georgian noblewoman.

'How's the chocolate?' Stuart asks, entering and setting down his mobile phone.

She closes the book quickly. 'It's good.' She feels the slide of the cover of the book under her hand. 'I hadn't seen any of your war photographs. My mum said you'd won awards.'

'You asked your mother about me?'

'Just about your work.'

'What do you think?' He looks at the book.

'I wouldn't know how to judge them.' She feels stupid for bringing in the topic of war photography now, of souring such a glorious day. He's standing over on the other side of the room and she can't read his face.

'What makes a photograph *good* is a question that some of the best theorists have tried, but mostly failed, to answer,' he states. 'It's a gut feeling a lot of the time. You can learn all about light and perspective and shape and the golden ratio, but often it comes down to feeling. People talk about truth a lot with photography, especially reportage. Does this image show the *truth*? How much is manipulated by the biases, unconscious and otherwise, of the photographer?' He moves to her side. 'The images in that book. People have asked me, are they real, are they posed, did that really happen? They want me to say no, it's fake, it's not real, things like this don't happen anywhere in the world and certainly not here in Britain.' There is a bitterness in his voice, something sardonic.

'When you look at each photo do you remember taking them?'

'Not all of them. But sometimes, yes. I remember the exact aperture, the shutter speed, the film I had just loaded with a fumbling hand while crouching behind a tank. And the mayhem, the noise and the gunshots and my breath always so loud as I ran, my throat tight from smoke and fire. Sorry,' he says and touches her arm, 'I shouldn't talk about this.'

'I want to hear, you can tell me anything.'

'Can I tell you that you're beautiful, Maeve?' he says, hand rising to cradle the back of her head. She's disorientated by the sudden shift in mood. 'And that sometimes it makes me sad.'

'Sad?'

He follows a lock of her hair down the side of her face to her shoulder. 'Isn't beauty always a little sad? How fleeting it is?'

'You mean I'll grow out of it soon, I'll get old.'

'No, the other way around. I'll get old, I am old. And you'll always be younger than me.'

Is that his excuse, she thinks, for not taking things further? Is her image the only thing he wants, an untouchable kind of beauty?

'I don't think you're too old.'

'I'm as old as your dad,' he says in a pointed kind of way.

His eyes are kind but she doesn't want that kind of pitying kindness.

She breaks his soft grip, feeling a sharp spike of loathing for her father, for ruining this with his friendship with Stuart.

'Maeve—'

'What do you want from me?' she asks, hating that it comes out plaintive.

'Nothing.'

If she were someone else she would make a move on him, she would kiss him. But she doesn't want to, she wants him to want *her*, to be a beautiful object in his hands.

'You don't want to take my photo?'

'That's not what I meant,' he says. 'And taking photos is safe.'

'Is it?' She thinks of him standing over her in the bath, her dress see-through, thinks of lying there under the water as he took photos of her about to drown. A mean part of her thinks about how she might coerce him – *I'll show someone else the pictures, I'll tell my parents* – but that would only make him run away and she doesn't want that.

Her eyes are burning.

'I don't want to hurt you, when you've already been hurt so much,' he says, pained. 'I only want good things for you, Maeve.'

'And you're not good?'

Maybe Maeve isn't good either, maybe that's why they fit so well together, she thinks, staring up at him as his eyes fall to her mouth.

'Maeve,' he says again, but it sounds apologetic, and so she leaves him and the annexe and runs back across the sharp gravel to her house.

––––––––––

That night she can't sleep. She feels hot, reckless. Not reckless enough to do what she should do, to knock on Stuart's door and push her way inside, but enough to leave her bedroom and walk along the dark hall, to touch the black line of the banister as she slowly walks downstairs, breath tight, listening to the creaks her footsteps make, the settling of the house, the rumble of her father's snoring.

There's something terrifying about being awake alone in a dark house, something thrilling. No one watching you but the walls and the empty rooms and the pictures, the mirrors reflecting a shadowy second self.

She leaves the house by the front door. The night air feels soft and damp on her skin. When she looks back at the open door she thinks it looks like a mouth, like a dark cavern. She skirts the annexe, the security light not switching on like it should, as if she isn't here at all, as if she's truly invisible. The flowers aren't arranged around the bath any more; they're stacked in a heap by a wall and she has to search for them by smell, by feel, because the colours are bleached by the night. Would her mother think anything if she found them here, question Stuart? Or would he just say they were for his house project? Maeve doesn't have a neat lie to use – her mother would be curious, or might offer to buy her more if she liked them, which would be horrible. It's not the flowers Maeve wants, she thinks, plucking the blossoms from some of them, creating a pile of silk-soft petals at her feet – it's the memory of Stuart and her, of being watched and desired, being beautiful.

Maeve gathers her bounty up in her arms, her bare feet damp from the dew, and walks over to the bath through the scrub and weeds. She has the strange thought, brought on by the strangeness of lurking in the gardens alone in the middle of the velvet night, that there might be a girl still there now, some ghostly version of her, like an after-image, but when she leans over she finds nothing but a shallow pool of water and the trembling reflection of the moon.

Chapter Fourteen

The day after the rainstorm, I delayed my journey to the river by stopping at the village florist. I had some thought that the moment I came upon the girls, they would know – know the name of the slippery feelings inside me, how I was different from other girls, the thoughts I sometimes had when I looked at them.

People knew me by sight in the village and I disliked it immensely. I walked along the street that morning telling myself like a mantra, *Soon. Soon I'll be gone, I'll be far away where no one knows me, where I can start again with no watchful eyes and no expectations.*

There was a strange sound above the usual noise of the bell of the shop doors opening and closing, the hawk of a market trader, or the bark of a dog being tugged away from the butcher's, and when the path in front of me on the pavement cleared, I saw where it was coming from. A man with long hair, wearing a waistcoat beaded with mirrors and pale trousers that looked like long johns, sitting on the kerb. He was hitting a tambourine and warbling along with the beat in a thin voice, his face beatific with a vicious kind of joy, as mothers hurried their children quickly by and men sneered. This wasn't San Francisco, I saw them think, and

there was nothing for this man here, surely, no hippie deni-
zens to join.

A woman crouched down next to him and said hello and
he paused, turning his smile on her.

It was Camille's mother, her dark hair pinned up loosely, a row
of necklaces heavy down the front of her thin dress. She was
smoking and she passed him her cigarette with an artful hand.

I had the sudden horrifying thought that she might invite
this man to dinner. That he might play his stupid tambourine
and get all of us to sing and dance round the table. Camille's
parents only came to our meals sometimes; they were usually
off on drives through the countryside, visiting antique bookshops and ruins and castles, Camille had told us when we
asked where they were. Maybe they would take this man with
them on one of those trips, I thought as I walked past.

It was a different apprentice florist today, a girl around my
age, with thick glasses and a long blonde plait. She smiled at
me encouragingly when I entered and I soon realized why as
I watched the man at the counter lean over towards her, heard
his chuckle, his overfamiliar tone.

'Will you be long?' I said, looking at the apprentice as the
man turned around.

I could feel his annoyance like a fleshy thing between us.

'That's quite a rude question to ask, young lady,' he said.

I looked at him and smiled, copying the look of the man
outside, a mad kind of cheeriness. 'Oh, I'm sorry.'

He had a moustache that shadowed his mouth and he
smelled of beer.

'I'm done actually,' the girl piped up, sliding the three red
roses in their paper wrap towards him.

He duly paid, but paused at the door to say he'd be in 'next
week, same time, my dear.'

'What a creep,' I said.

'He asks me my favourite flower each week,' she murmured, 'and he forgets each time so I just choose the most expensive.' Her eyes were bright with mischief, but her movements as she prepared the bunch of chrysanthemums and baby's breath that I asked for had the jerkiness of adrenaline.

'This is for your pictures, right?' she asked, ringing it up on the till. 'You and the other girls.'

I didn't like the thought of people talking about us, of the gaze of the village turning to the woods and the river.

She leaned her elbows on the counter, curious. 'One of the boys from the cottages – Geoff, I think his name was – was at the hall on Saturday night talking about you lot, said you called yourselves the Ophelia girls.'

I felt a wash of cold, a twitch in my chin. 'These flowers are for my mother's gravestone,' I said.

Her smile dropped. 'My condolences.'

'She drowned,' I lied. I was shaken by the protective barrier of our woodland idyll breaking. It was one thing for the parents to talk about us and another for us to be the subject of broader gossip. 'They found her body on the shore, bloated and blue,' I found myself saying, mean and cold. I could feel my face go hot.

'That sounds horrible,' she said. She meant that I was horrible as much as the words of my story were.

I left her then, my mouth sour, feeling a nasty bitterness that made me want to kick at stones on the pavement and throw my flowers into a bin.

There was a chunk of flesh taken from her calf where a fish nibbled, I imagined myself continuing, as I broke into a stumbling jog along the path out of the village, *and a row of kelp around her waist so tight it could have stopped her breathing again. She was buried with sand still in her hair and tiny pebbles between her toes, her skin so tight with salt that it crackled to the touch, that it crumbled like dust.*

I stopped when I entered the wood, leaning against a tree gasping for breath.

My mother died when I was born, but somehow when I was young and didn't know for sure how things like giving birth worked, how a baby could emerge from a woman's body, I had heard the term *waters broken* and imagined that my birth had somehow turned her flesh to water, that I had brought a flood with me that drowned her.

Children are stupid creatures, I thought, wiping my face and weaving in and out of the trees to get to the river.

'There you are!' Linda called out when she saw me, and Camille turned around with a start.

'I brought these.' I held up my flowers, bedraggled and hot from my run.

'Perfect,' Joan said, standing up. She was wearing a white dress and the lace veil thrown back over her head. 'I need a wedding bouquet.'

'Who are you then?' I asked.

'A jilted bride, of course. My prince has taken off with another.'

'I don't know why, when you look so lovely.'

'Oh, you,' Joan said, but I could tell she was pleased.

That's one thing about girlhood I forget: how hungry, desperate we were to be told we were beautiful, lovely, pretty; as if we almost doubted we existed at all without that confirmation.

'If I was a jilted bride it would be the *groom* who would drown, not me,' Linda drawled, smoke furling from her lipsticked mouth. 'I'd do it with my bare hands.'

'Maybe I didn't want to marry him anyway,' Joan said, wading out through the river, 'but now I'm spoiled goods, aren't I? Maybe that's what I'm mourning.'

It was difficult to know if she meant what she was saying or if it was just part of the game.

'You know, the abandoned women in folk songs and myths, the coded way they're described and the iconography in paintings of them, like the choice of flowers – it usually means that they were pregnant,' Camille said.

'Luckily, I'm on the blob right now,' Joan said, sinking down until only her head remained above water.

I looked towards Camille, and though I had been expecting to feel repulsed today, to feel terrified, I was only fond, wanting, as she stood there in her own little world, frowning and biting her lip. When she noticed me looking she smiled shyly and it made me feel warm. She was beautiful that day, flowers in a ringlet around her head and wearing the dress I had bought her. I wanted to buy her more things, I thought, I wanted to dress her like a doll.

'You all right?' she asked, dropping down beside me.

'Fine.' I nudged her with my shoulder.

'Guess who I am?' she asked.

When I first met her I had thought her shy, but now when we talked she would hold my gaze and barely blink. Maybe it wasn't that she was shy, but that she was waiting for something, for someone, to focus on. *I shouldn't find that flattering*, I thought, *I shouldn't be encouraging whatever this is.*

'Ophelia?'

'No.'

'Eve?' I ventured.

'Hardly, in these clothes.'

'A princess? A lady of the manor? A Roman goddess?'

'Close. I'm Persephone. Who are you today?'

'I don't know,' I said, dragging my fingers along the dry ground until a small pebble caught under my nail and I winced.

'What did you do?' she asked, catching my hand.

'It's just a stone.'

She took a pin from her hair and the flower garland drooped down one side of her face. 'There,' she said, scooping the pebble out before I could use my teeth to do it.

'Thanks,' I said, as she re-pinned her garland. 'What are you reading at the moment?' I still felt I knew so little about her.

'A book of classical myths.'

'Hence Persephone.'

'Exactly.'

'You don't read modern novels?'

'Not usually. The older the better, I think.'

Linda was in the river now with Joan, crooning and sprinkling petals around her as she lay there, a blur of white.

'Why?'

She twisted a piece of her hair and frowned thoughtfully. 'Older stories can be more dramatic, I think. Everything is fraught and terrible and wonderful. Everything *means* something. Modern stuff feels so quiet and dull, so lazy, so ironic. When I read a poem or a play or a tragedy I want to feel my heart race, I want to cry and ache. That probably sounds stupid,' she added quickly.

My own heart was racing now. 'I don't think it does.'

'This, what we're doing now,' she nodded her head towards the river, the girl on the bank with a camera, 'it's wonderful.' Her voice was hushed as if she were telling a secret; her big eyes sheened bright like she might cry. 'It feels like we're making something that might last beyond us, you know? Or that we're snatching a summer of beauty from the world, stealing it. It's like living in a dream. You won't laugh at me for saying that?'

'Never, I'll never laugh at you,' I swore.

'At school the other girls call me a swot, they say I'm boring, but they don't know me really.' She tugged a flower loose from her garland, studied it. 'They don't know my secrets,' she said and caught my eye.

Tell me your secrets, I thought, even though I was pretty sure I knew what they were, that she and I shared the same one.

'And they see me quietly reading,' she said, 'but they don't know that in my head I'm dancing with satyrs or following Achilles on the battlefield as he cuts down men left and right in violent revenge for Patroclus, or that I'm the Sphinx in Thebes demanding Oedipus answer my riddles.'

'I wish reading was like that for me.'

'But your art is, isn't it?'

'Yes.' I nodded and we shared a sympathetic smile.

Sarah called out that the roll of film had ended, holding up the camera, and Joan clambered out of the river. She was laughing under her veil, weighed down by her sodden wedding dress that bled its own small tributaries on the hard summer ground.

Home from the river before dinner I searched through my wardrobe for a dress or a top, for something I could give Camille, who seemed to have only brought three summer outfits with her to wear, unlike her mother who had a rainbow of scarves and dresses.

Nothing in my wardrobe was right; it was too babyish or too current. What I wanted to give Camille was a faded velvet gown, a real 1920s slip, something to go with her timelessness, to match her interest in history. I imagined myself sewing her something through the small hours by the light of a lamp, my fingertips raw from the prick of a needle, but I knew I wasn't the kind of person who could do that. Instead, I went up to the attic, where my mother's things were kept in trunks and boxes.

She was a stranger to me, my mother; I only had a few pictures and the taciturn memories of others. My father did not speak of her at all. No *your mother would have done this,* or *you looked just like your mother then,* or *have I ever told you how we met?*

She was beautiful, I knew that from the photos, but of her inner self, of who she was besides her looks, I knew so little. I had trawled through her things before once, when I was around eight years old, searching for the letter I just knew she would have written to me before she died, a foolish thought indeed, but the objects in the boxes – the silver brush set, the old-fashioned perfume bottles, the *shoes* – made me so sad that I never returned to them.

That afternoon, at sixteen years old and presuming that I had more mental fortitude, that I was no longer a child (and with the burning motivation to make Camille happy, to have her smile at me), I opened the dusty boxes again.

I lifted out the stack of children's books – from her childhood and presumably saved for mine too – without stopping to study them, holding my breath as if I could catch tears from their musty smell. I lifted the pile of records and shifted aside a hat box, a silver filigree pen dropping to the floor with a clink. She had a fine wooden jewellery box that still smelled of polish, its insides a blood-red velvet. I pressed my finger into the sharp gem of a ring that sat in a row with others, until I could feel it make a mark in my skin. I rubbed a thumb along the links of a bracelet. But I didn't dare pick any of them up nor try them on.

There weren't many of her clothes – someone must have thrown them out; my father? one of her relatives? – a cashmere jumper, a pair of trousers, a tartan skirt, and a black tulle dress that I didn't want to take out of its tissue paper. There was a lone sock too in the corner of one box that made me want to weep, and a silky pale peach nightgown trimmed with lace.

I picked up the nightgown, standing up to hold it against me. It had cap sleeves and the frilled hem reached my shins. It smelled of the attic, of close air and old boxes. No other perfume remained when I put it to my nose.

I pulled it on over my t-shirt, feeling the zip of static in my hair from the silk, feeling a shiver at the cool catch of it on my bare arms. I twisted from side to side to watch the hem billow and swirl. There was no mirror up here so I left the attic, scaling the steep steps carefully in case I tripped on the fabric.

It was a Saturday but I was in the haze of summer and didn't realize that, watching the way the skirt floated and hid my feet, not until I was halfway to my bedroom and noticed my father in front of the hall window, looking out over the lawn.

He startled as I did. 'Ruth,' he said, and his face looked pinched.

Look, I'm wearing a dress, I thought of saying spitefully, but I felt utterly ridiculous all of a sudden, in a way I never did at the river with the girls. Like a child play-acting at being a woman.

'That's nice,' he said of my outfit, glancing out of the window again and then back.

'It's Mum's,' I said, because I wanted to push for more of a response, even if it was a negative one, to have him *care*. It was like I was a ghost, I thought, some unwelcome spirit haunting his house.

'Where did you get it?' he asked, voice clipped.

'In the attic.'

'You shouldn't be up there,' he said. 'And you shouldn't be messing around with those things.'

I took the disappointment I had asked for, read the reminder that I couldn't hope to measure up to her, for him, for anyone.

'Why not? She was my mother. Don't I get them now?' She was my mother and these were the only things I had left of her. *He* had memories, he knew what her voice sounded like, what her hand felt like in his, he had been loved by her.

'You'll put it back where you found it,' he stated.

'Yes. I'm sorry, Dad,' I said, voice breaking then, not because he was being harsh but because his face was blank, his voice cold.

He walked away. I listened to his heavy footsteps going down the stairs and then the sharp closing of his office door.

I went into my bedroom and stripped off the dress in front of the mirror, watching myself cry, feeling sadder for it, like an endless loop. Why was it that sometimes it wasn't enough to be sad – you had to *see* yourself be sad too, to wallow in it?

I folded the nightdress into a tight wad.

Instead of returning it to the attic, I hid it under the sheets of my bed. I would give it to Camille. My mother's attic boxes were thick with dust, untouched, and he would never know it was gone.

———

Camille was as pleased with the gift as I had imagined, her eyes filmy, stroking a reverent hand down the silk of the nightgown.

Joan was jealous. 'Why does she get it?' she joked.

'I can share, it's fine,' Camille said.

'No, it's yours. But I bagsie the next one Ruth finds lying around.'

Was there an undertone in what she was saying? My smile grew strained. Did she see my preference for Camille and think it meant something more?

Linda arrived then carrying the newest developed photos, and we spread out around her on the grass handling each photo carefully. We laughed at the ones with strange facial expressions, a frozen sneeze or yawn, and called out ones we liked – but only of the other girls and not ourselves. The photos of ourselves we scrutinized, tilting them in the light, not quite knowing which of our internal opinions to trust – that we were beautiful, or that we weren't. We praised each other as we could not often praise ourselves. *You look amazing here, like an actress*, we'd say, and the other girl would say, *Really? You're sure?* And we would insist, press our certainty on her and wait for it to be returned. *Well, you look really pretty here*, they'd say. It was best when we spread them all out on the grass, when we could see how we looked together, like a bouquet of flowers rather than a spindly bloom on its own.

'The Ophelia girls,' Sarah said that day, hands on her hips, as we looked at what we had created.

There was a breeze, the willow trees quivering above us, the river surface ridged.

'Beautiful and tragic and ever-young,' Linda declared, tapping her foot next to the close-up picture of her upper half, the silver of the water and the blue of the reflected sky dazzling, her eyes shut as if she was in pain.

'Waterlogged and damp and smelling of mud,' I added.

'We'll never be this beautiful again, will we?' Camille said ruefully.

She touched my arm and I felt my face go hot. My eyes tripped across the pictures of her that I knew I had taken, the ones where she wasn't looking at the camera and the ones where she was, her searching gaze preserved, the ghost of mine there in the framing.

'I need to go help my father with something,' I said suddenly. 'Here, take the camera.' I pushed it into Sarah's hands. 'I'll see you at dinner.'

I left without looking at Camille, or answering the muffled question Linda called out.

The housekeeper had left a plate of shortbread on the kitchen table. I ate two without tasting them, the grit of sugar scraping the top of my mouth. I could hear my father's low murmur from the drawing room. I stared through the kitchen doorway at the dark hall beyond and the front door, my eyes unfocused, thinking of the river, of the girls, wishing I was there and not here in this dark, close house.

A well-oiled door opened, a wry dismissal sounded, and then a shadow filled the hall.

'Hi,' Stuart said.

'Hi,' I replied, my heart pulsing fast.

He leaned against the doorway. He had a couple of heavy law tomes in his arms. 'You all right?' he asked, studying me closely.

'I'm fine.' My voice was gummy. I poured two glasses of water and handed him one of them.

We faced the back garden. I gulped the entirety of the glass, turning when he nudged my shoulder so I could see him copy me.

'You been at the river with the girls?' he asked, wiping his mouth with his arm.

My eyes followed the blue line of the vein down his inner arm. 'Yeah. Came up here for a break.'

'And have you given my proposal any thought?' He dipped his head, smiled that sideways smile.

'I have. It would be good, it would help with my applications. If you still want to?'

'Of course. Where should we go?'

'The old dairy,' I decided. 'Wait here, I'll get paper and pencils.'

The dairy back then hadn't been made fit for living; it was only a storehouse with crumbling whitewashed walls and a smell of must and mould. But the light was bright through the windows on a summer's day, and no one would come looking there and find us.

'How do you want me then?' Stuart asked, sitting on an old armchair he had dragged in front of a wall. He was bracketed by rusting farm equipment on one side and two cannibalized bicycles on the other.

I sat on a narrow stool, my pad of cheap paper held awkwardly in my lap.

Stuart took his shirt off, pulled it up with his arms crossed over like men did, his back arching. He had a faint line of dark hair from his navel to his trousers, the first button of which was undone.

I dropped my pencil, picked it up. He leaned his arm on the back of the chair. 'So?'

'Like that is fine to start,' I said. I straightened the paper, made a mark in the corner to check the pencil and then rubbed it out, brushing away the rubbings with the back of my hand. I felt more confident now, pencil in hand, canvas at the ready. 'You're all right to stay still for a bit?'

'Yes,' he said, nodding and then stopping his movement sharply.

I was in control, I told myself. In control of him as my model, of the scene, and of the portrait, of my pencil.

I began to sketch, glancing up at him and then down at the page, measuring the angles with a thumb on my pencil and one eye closed. My movements sped up and I sank into the zone of drawing, somewhere deeper than thought, seeing shadow and line and colour and light and shade. My eyes skimming across the planes of his muscles, noting the ridges of veins and tendons, the flecks of hair.

'Am I doing good?' he asked.

He had chosen to look just over my shoulder, so that when I looked down and saw him from my periphery it seemed he was looking right at me. But I was barely conscious of that, I was only thinking of the shape emerging from my white page.

'Perfect,' I said, rubbing a finger along a line to smudge it, to soften the line, to quicken the image into life.

*

In the afternoon, I can't find Maeve. She isn't in her room or the bathroom, the drawing room or the kitchen, and she isn't with the twins where I've left them sprawled in front of a video in the living room.

I take the folded laundry up to our bedroom and put it away in the chest of drawers, glancing out across the front lawn.

Alex knocks on the doorframe as he enters, an old habit, and I realize with a start that it's another Saturday.

'The lawn needs cutting,' I say.

I hate that as parents our greetings to one another have become lists of things to do, which contain within them pleas for help or admonishments, passive-aggressive digs or expressions of absolute weariness, of I-cannot-do-this-I-cannot-keep-going. Like the first time the both of us were back at the flat after Maeve's pneumonia and her near miss with death, and how I had said, *The fridge needs clearing out,* and he had said, *The bins smell,* and we had looked at each other with a bewildered, astonished hurt.

'I'll do it later,' he says.

'And I can't find Maeve, I don't think she's in the house.'

'She'll be out in the gardens, I'm sure she's fine. We have to let her be, remember. Not hover over her.'

'I'm trying. I'm worried about her.'

'Try not to worry,' he says, putting his hands on my shoulders.

Does he have any suggestions for how to do that beyond the platitude? I wonder tiredly.

'Summer's treating you well.' He touches the freckles on my shoulder.

The house is quiet, the sun a warm glow outside. Alex kisses me. I clutch the front of his t-shirt as a way to keep some space between us.

'I need to make dinner.' I move my head away.

'We don't have any guests tonight, it's just us.'

'The twins have been too quiet, they'll be up to something.'

When Maeve was an inpatient, and the twins were good nappers, Alex and I would sometimes have sex with the curtains open, move so harshly in a delirium of frustration and grief that I would get carpet burns on my knees, that his wrists would bruise. That's the way we've always done it since the first few months of playful exploration at university when we were both young and sweet – him on his back and me on top, holding him down with my weight or with the grip of my hands, and sometimes saying, *What if someone could see us, you, like this,* to make him groan. I like control, I guess, and he likes to give it up, at least in the bedroom. I used to think I was lucky to find a man like that, that our preferences fitted, but now the thought of touching him, or worse, of him touching me, leaves me cold.

'You know, you could just say that you don't want to,' he says, with a hurt smile. The cruelty of knowing someone so well, of us being married so long, I sometimes think, is how easy it is to hurt one another.

'My head just isn't there.'

'When will it be? I'm sorry, but it's been months. I didn't press you before with your dad's funeral and everything, I'm not a monster.'

'I know you're not. I'm just tired, honestly, truly. I keep having these dreams.'

'Then see someone.'

'I'm not a machine to be fixed. I don't imagine everything up here,' I tap my temple, 'will get fixed with a few sessions of talking to some insipid counsellor. And where would I find one out here in the sticks anyway?'

He turns his back to me, opens his bedside drawer as if he's looking for something. 'At least it's nice to have Stuart here.'

'What does that mean?'

'Nothing.'

I stare at the open door once he's left the room, screwing up my face with something like scorn.

The twins have an early dinner today and Maeve leaves the table halfway through, complaining of a headache. I watch her go: the awkwardness of her movements as she steps through the back door, the way she clicks the fingers of one hand against one another in a nervous tic. It seems that now she is well, she is accelerating through her lost teen years, moody and sullen. I feel for her, especially with the hospital trip tomorrow. Maybe I can make her a chocolate torte afterwards, like the one I did for her last birthday, when she told me it was the best cake she'd ever eaten and looked at me like I'd hung the moon. I used to listen to other mothers talk about their prickly daughters and think that I had got so lucky, that somehow I, a mother who had been motherless herself, had miraculously done a good job with her. But now I can see it was her illness that caused her to cleave so strongly to me, to us as a family. That she had no reserves left to bond with the rest of the world, no energy to differentiate herself from her kin as teenagers are supposed to do. If you face death every day, a part of you stays childish, clings to a motherly figure as if you're an infant again. That's not to say there were never any arguments, that Maeve was never rude or sullen or mean, it's just that those moods never lasted all that long – she'd say something cruel, then reach out for my hand and clutch it desperately, and say she was sorry.

Stuart is watching me when I turn my attention back to the table.

'Is she OK?' he asks.

'Just worried about tomorrow, I think. She's going for some tests at the hospital, just a check-up.'

'I bet you're both sick of hospitals by now.'

'Just a bit,' Alex replies, tipping up his wine glass.

It's late and we've lit four assorted candles on the table, old ones we found in the back of a cupboard.

Stuart dips his fingers into the wax of the one between us,

lifts them out and watches the wax harden pale as Alex scoffs at him.

'I was thinking about drawing you,' I say to Stuart.

'I'd be up for that, a revisitation.'

'I meant in the past,' I correct, 'I was remembering drawing you—'

'So I'm too old now? My body too weathered?' He pouts. 'Ruth used to draw me,' he tells Alex. 'Life drawings, you know, she was going to apply to art school.'

'You were? I don't remember that.' Alex reaches for the second bottle of wine.

Did I never mention that to him at university? So much of those years is a haze. I wouldn't have brought it up often, not wanting to be reminded of the girls and my photography, but not to mention it even once is impressive. Or perhaps he just doesn't remember. I'm sure it was the same for him, anyway, that Alex has kept secrets too, whether inconsequential or not.

'I wasn't *totally* naked, I hasten to add.' Stuart holds up his hands, looking anything but contrite.

'You should take him up on his offer, Ruth,' Alex says.

I look at him but there doesn't seem to be anything more to his words, even with his odd conversation change earlier. 'I wouldn't be any good. It's decades since I've drawn anything.'

'You won't get better unless you try.'

'Well, I can't argue with that logic.' I get up from my seat, gather the plates and cutlery, the fat of the lamb chops congealed in smears in the grooves of the plate rim. I feel like I've been pressured into doing something I didn't even want. But then maybe they can see how stifled I am by the house, maybe it's just a nudge for me to do something for myself for once.

I take the opportunity to go upstairs and check on Maeve.

Her door is closed but there's no light leaking from the bottom when I switch off the light in the hall, no radio playing.

'Maeve?' I ask softly, but she doesn't answer.

I think of when she was critically ill in hospital, how I could simply watch the monitors to know how her heart was, how much oxygen she had. How she could press a button to call a nurse or a doctor who would know what to do to stop her pain, while I stood helpless beside her bed.

Chapter Fifteen

It was hot when they left the house but in the car to the station, Maeve feels cold. She stares out at the countryside; yellow fields of rapeseed, hedges and trees whipping past. She wishes that Stuart could have somehow come with them, or that he could have just taken her. Her mother's voice is too bright today, her smile too nervous, and Maeve keeps catching the movement of her blonde bob as she glances over at her.

On the train the wind of the open window tugs past Maeve's face; the carpet seat itches even through her jeans as her eyes skim the newspaper her mother handed over – the latest opinion pieces on Diana, arguments between Britpop bands, and an artist's impression of the lander on the fiery barren surface of Mars.

The hospital is familiar, horrifyingly so, and there are familiar faces too, nurses and receptionists, parents of other patients, who say hi to her, who tell her she looks good. It's the look of the parents that's the worst, their tremulous hope, their eyes running over her for some sign of health they might be able to find in their own child if they only search carefully.

Usually her mother comes with her for tests but she tells her, and the nurse who comes to escort them, that she'd rather be on her own today. When Maeve looks back as she's led away, her mother's strained smile, her clutch on her handbag, feel like a physical hurt.

She changes into a robe first and can't help comparing it to changing into the beautiful dress for Stuart, soft and lovely, not draughty and scratchy. She feels vulnerable as she steps on the scale in the nurse's office and then stands with her back against the wall so she can record her height, as she puts the cold thermometer under her tongue, as she sits on the chair and the blood pressure cuff bites into her upper arm.

'Good,' the nurse repeats. The kind of good that means Maeve did well following instructions, that she is being a good patient.

Next, blood is taken. Maeve watches it fill up the plastic tubes, one after the other. *Do you want all of it?* she wants to say. *Will you leave me anything for myself?*

She sits on the couch in a different room and the doctor, an old man with white wisps of hair and thin hands, searches her body for any signs the leukaemia might have returned, asking her to move the neck of her gown so he can hear her heart. She lies back as he presses his hands into her abdomen, the hinge of her jaw, asking if she is tender anywhere, if it hurts.

It hurts everywhere, she wants to say, even though it doesn't.

The last test she has is a chest x-ray, shuffling into the room that always has a strange appearance of abandonment. She clutches the handles as she's told, holds a breath as the disembodied voices tell her that she's doing well, instructing her to turn and breathe in again.

She dresses and returns to the doctor's office, and her mother joins her.

'OK?' she asks, and Maeve nods.

'We'll get the results of the blood test within the week,' the doctor says, 'and order a bone marrow sample if needed then, but I can't see any physical symptoms at the moment so there's no need to be concerned. You look a bit peaky, but I'm sure that's just being a teenager and spending all your time inside,' he adds to Maeve.

'She's fatigued sometimes,' her mother says, placing a hand on her shoulder.

'She will be, after what she went through. The body needs time to recover. But no symptoms beyond that?'

Maeve shakes her head.

'That's us then,' he says.

He shakes her mother's hand and then Maeve's. His skin is papery and dry. 'Now promise me you won't go home and worry about it until the tests come back in,' he says, 'you look like a worrier.'

He's a new doctor, he's inherited her case from her last who has gone on maternity leave. *If you had almost died, you would worry too*, she wants to tell him. But she is a good patient, quiet, polite, easy to handle.

'That wasn't so bad, was it,' her mother says, as they leave the hospital and walk to the tube station.

'Maybe for you.'

'Maeve,' she says, her face creasing in pain.

'Sorry. I'm just tired. All those fluorescent lights.'

'We'll stop off at the bakery at Charing Cross, get you a pastry.'

A treat, just like the countless small offerings she was given by her parents during her illness. She's seen the younger children at the hospital perform elaborate charades thanking their giftees, knowing even at their tender age that the present was more for them – parents, relatives – than the patient. That sweets and toys and books were small tokens of control, of guilt and penitence.

'Only if you get something too,' Maeve says.

Her taste buds were changed by the chemotherapy, just like her hair, and now everything sweet tastes fuzzy and wrong. So she chooses a cheese pastry, the filling hot and oozing when they sit down in their seats. But she still feels cold. And as the train rolls dizzyingly fast past power lines and trees, stations and houses, she thinks of the symptoms she didn't bother mentioning to the doctor. That she's tired, that she bruises, that she gets headaches. That last week her left elbow hurt all day even though she didn't remember hitting it on anything. That she finds it hard to sleep, that in her dreams she keeps choking, drowning.

It's only when the car turns into the long drive through the fields to the hamlet that Maeve realizes a part of her had thought they were returning to the flat in London, the one with the tiny bedroom painted pink and the shelves that her dad built her, the comforting yellow glow of the city sneaking under the too-short curtains and the consoling sound of life being lived outside the cocoon of her room. Her parents spoke of nature when they said they were moving out here, of the greenness, the *life*, but if there is anything living here besides the bees and wasps and the occasional soaring bird, besides the mute grass and hedges and trees, then Maeve hasn't found it.

The front of the house, grey stone and ivy such a dark green the depths appear black, looks austere, as cold as she feels inside, and when she looks at it she thinks that the moment they go inside her mother will disappear off to another room and Maeve will be left alone in the quiet.

'Will you be all right on your own for a bit until Dad gets home?' her mother asks, as they round the lawn and park in front of the house. 'I'll walk to pick up the twins from Mrs Quinn's and I want to stay for a coffee to chat, pick her brain about house stuff. Stuart is here,' she nods to Stuart's car, a battered silver, too small to be a family car, 'so you can knock on the annexe door if you need anything.'

'I'm fine, Mum. I'm not a baby,' Maeve says, her voice pitched sullen even though her heart is racing.

'Well done today,' her mother says again as Maeve leaves the car, leaning over the passenger seat so that she catches Maeve's eye. 'I mean it. You're so much more put together than I was at your age. Stronger. There's good things for you to come, Maeve, I know it. The world owes you.'

'Thanks, Mum.'

As her mother walks back along the path to their front gate, Maeve unlocks the front door, screwing up her face against a sudden wave of tears. How is she stronger than any other girl? she thinks. And why is it that her mother's love, these tender hopeful moments of honesty and admiration from her, seems to hurt so much?

In the house she only stops to strip from her jeans and top, trying to change so quickly that she stumbles, that she swears at herself. Back in a summer dress, and without a bra, she runs back downstairs and out the front, sharp quick steps across the gravel to his door.

She knocks and he opens it as if he's been waiting for her.

'Hi,' he says.

'Hi. Can I come in? My mum's over at the neighbour's.'

'Of course.'

In her bedroom as she changed she had imagined they wouldn't even say anything, that he would invite her inside with a hand on her back and then – and then—

'I was at the hospital today,' she says.

She's only a step away from him. She can smell the cigarette he's just had, the tea.

'I know. Did it go OK?'

'Fine.' She shrugs.

He puts a hand on her arm and her shoulders loosen. He pulls her into him and hugs her and she clutches at his t-shirt, feeling the solid warmth of him, the scratch of his stubble on her neck, the planes of his chest and stomach. Does he feel the press of her breasts? If she pushed further, if her hips met his, would she feel something there?

'It was awful,' she says, intending to be cool and wry but sounding warbly and pathetic.

'It must be horrible to be back there,' he says, smoothing a hand down her hair.

'It is, it was. It's like I'm just a thing,' she says into the meat of his shoulder, feeling her tears catch in her mouth and bleed into the cotton. 'The lights and all those tests. And the doctor had cold hands,' she says, wanting in some perverse way for Stuart to think of her there, being touched by the doctor.

'I bet they tell you you're brave, that you're stronger for it, hmm?' he says, tilting her head back so he can look at her.

What a mess she must look like. A tearful, wounded girl. But she never promised him she was anything else.

She clutches his t-shirt tighter. His hand slides behind her head, thumb in the hollow behind her ear.

'Please,' she says without breaking his gaze, and she loves him more for not needing any other invitation but that, for not making her beg, as he kisses her.

She's only had a handful of messy early teenage kisses and she doesn't remember what to do now, forgets to open her mouth, scrapes his lip with her teeth. The rub of his facial hair is new, the taste of tobacco, but it's his harsh breath she

likes most, feeling it hot on her skin, like some beast, and his
hands, his hands on her – cradling her head, wrapping around
her back, curving over her hip, tugging her dress up and up
as she lifts her arms.

When it's being pulled over her head, tangling her hair, she
closes her eyes, keeps them closed once it's discarded, as if
to prolong that muffled darkness. But even blinded she knows
he's looking at her, his eyes glancing over her body, and it
makes her want to smile.

She shivers and then he hoists her up into his arms, sideways
so her feet dangle over his arm as he carries her to the bed.
The coolness of the cotton sheets feels like some wonderful
luxury on her skin. She hears him walk away and then the
lock of the door, and then his footsteps return.

She opens her eyes. At the sight of him standing there, his
heated gaze on her, his swollen lips, she feels a deep clench
inside and makes a sound in her throat.

He likes that, she can tell. He settles next to her. He's still
in his jeans and t-shirt.

'How long will it be until someone comes looking for you?'
he asks, placing his hand on her stomach which jumps under
his touch.

'An hour?'

'Good.' He strokes his hand down. 'Can I?' he asks, as he
touches the band of her underwear.

She looks up at the ceiling, the light streaming in through
the windows, as he takes them off, and when he touches her,
her eyes snap shut.

His hand is there, between her legs, fingertips searching,
dipping in. His loud breath is hot on the side of her face, the
press of the buckle of his jeans, the rough fabric, harsh against
her side. Two fingers slide inside as she gasps and winces,

writhes. He's telling her things, saying things. His large hand cupping her, holding her there. *Maeve*, he says, *look at me*. She shakes her head. She doesn't need him to guide her hips, she's moving by herself now, back bowing as his other hand smooths up her body. *Maeve*, he says.

Afterwards, he props himself up on his elbow, one hand with a cigarette and the other idly roaming her body.

'You're not going to . . .' she asks, meaning his clothes which he still hasn't removed. Maybe he's waiting for her to offer but the thought of *doing* anything to him seems terrifying.

'No, I prefer it this way.'

She has no idea what he means, has no framework for this beyond the few times she has furtively searched for slow-loading porn on the family computer. *Was it good for you?* she wants to ask. *Did I do well?*

She's self-conscious of her body lying here, but not enough to get dressed again just yet. Besides, she's too busy watching him look at her.

Doing this here, less than a minute's walk from her house, when it's late afternoon and she might hear the sound of her father's car on the drive, her mother's call, is reckless. But she doesn't care. After the morning in hospital, she wants something for herself, to steal an afternoon, at least.

'You know, they used to call that the little death,' he says. There's an ironic twist to his mouth, as if he's mocking himself too.

She laughs and curls onto her side. 'Is that why you're still single? Your morbid bedroom talk?'

He clutches his chest. 'She wounds me.'

'Why aren't you married?' Surely she has licence now to ask

him things like that, to learn more about him. He seems to know so much about her, innately, without her even telling him, and it's not fair she can't do the same to him.

'Wives don't like it when their husbands run off to warzones,' he says, reaching behind him to stub out the very last of his cigarette.

I wouldn't mind it, she imagines joking, but she can't joke about being his wife, not after they've done this for the first time, slept together (does it count as sleeping together? It must, she thinks), that would be embarrassing. Instead, she says, 'So it wasn't that some girl broke your heart and you never got over it?'

'Going for the probing questions now, are we?' he says like she delights him, and taps her nose.

'Don't do that,' she says, laughing, and grabs his wrist. Her fingers can't quite meet around it.

'Maybe there was a girl,' he says, more serious now.

'What happened to her?' She moves her grip to his palm but he takes his hand back.

'She left me for someone else.'

'I'm sorry,' she says, even though she isn't. Her mind races with thoughts of this other girl, because that's who she's picturing, a girl, with brown hair – with red? – her ghostly competition.

He sits up, shifts to the edge of the bed. 'It's fine, it was a long time ago.'

She brings her knees up, wraps her arms around them. Has she ruined everything?

He stands up and turns to face her. 'Look at you,' he says, his sadness vanished, 'you're a sight for sore eyes, here, like that. Can I take your photo?'

'Sure.'

Maybe he is grieving for this other girl, but maybe Maeve is good for him as he is good for her, maybe she can be his consolation too.

'How do you want me?' she asks when he comes back, his camera strap looped around his arm, already adjusting the dials and lens.

'You can stay like that. But pull your hair over the front . . .' He kneels onto the bed, brings her hair over both shoulders, arranges it to hide the parts of her chest that her knees don't. 'I might get into trouble otherwise,' he murmurs, close and intimate, 'since you're not eighteen yet. This is just for my private collection though, don't worry,' he says, bringing the camera up to his eye. 'It's just for me.'

She stares into the lens, knowing that his eye isn't directly behind it, hidden in the domed black circle, but thinking it might be, there, watching her, blinking too fast for her to see.

'Here, I'll get your dress,' he says afterwards.

She lifts her arms again for him to dress her, a mirror of his undressing, but it feels like she's a different person now, that she's changed.

'Do I look like I've been out for a walk?' She poses her hands on her hips.

'You look entirely unmolested,' he says, with a coy smile. He unlocks the door and peers out. 'All clear,' he says.

'When can I see you again?' she asks, with one foot over the threshold.

'You see me all the time.' He chucks her under her chin.

She tries to smile.

'Hey, sorry, I was being flippant. You can come see me any time, I'm right here.' He squeezes her arm. 'We still need to take more photos anyway.'

'Photos, yeah,' she drawls.

'Are you mocking my art, Maeve?'

She turns her mouth down like a clown.

'Hey, maybe you can come with me on one of my shoots,' he says. 'If that wouldn't be too boring for you.'

'No, that would be cool. I'd like to see you work.'

'The next house I'm shooting is nearby. I'll mention it at dinner, it's got this famous library and a maze, some connection to a writer, or something.' He waves his hand. 'Ask me questions about it, act interested, and I'll ask if you want to come with me.'

'OK,' she says. *Dinner*, she thinks. Sitting around a table with her parents and Stuart. She feels a kind of sick excitement at the thought, a roiling shame.

Well, you wanted me to grow up, Mother, to stand on my own two feet, she thinks with a hysterical pinch. The hospital this morning and this afternoon with Stuart and then dinner—

'Or not,' he adds, watching her. 'Sorry, it's probably unfair of me to ask you to do that. It's just that it would be nice for us to have some time away from here, together.'

His hand slides up from her shoulder to her neck and she feels her body pulse with pleasure, even as her back tenses. They are on the doorstep, outside; one of her parents could come around the corner of the courtyard at any time and see them.

'It would, and it's fine.'

'I just don't want to corrupt you, turn you into a liar.' He squints and his mouth quirks to one side. She remembers her first impression of him, that strange mixture of bashful and sly.

'Oh, I'm well practised at lying.'

'That's good, because I am too.' He winks at her and then takes her hand. 'But not about this – you and I, Maeve – I promise.'

Chapter Sixteen

Sitting in a hospital waiting room gives you plenty of time to think. You tell yourself you'll use the hours there to read, to do a crossword, even to balance your chequebook – but really what you'll do is sit there and ruminate on your failings, your guilt, while your body tenses at every noise and name called, flinching at every door that creaks open.

*

The day after my life drawing session with Stuart, Joan arrived at my house an hour before breakfast, sweeping into my bedroom and waking me up from a confused panic of a nightmare.

'What are you doing here?' I asked, scratching sleep out of my eyes as I sat up, pulling the sheets around me as if I still needed to protect myself from the onslaught of the dream.

'Just saying hi,' she replied, falling onto the bed next to me with a groan of the mattress springs. 'Just wanted to see if you were OK.'

'Of course I am, why wouldn't I be?'

'No reason.' In the bright light of the morning, her dark hair on my white sheets had an auburn sheen.

'Are *you* OK?'

'Sure,' she said. She was lying, but we had learned that if there was something Joan did not want to tell you, you couldn't hope to prise it from her. 'Where did you go yesterday? You ran off.'

'I had a headache.'

'You get a lot of those,' she said and put a warm hand on my forehead.

I shook her off.

'So it wasn't that you'd fallen out with Camille?' she asked, rolling onto her back.

'No, why would you think that?'

'I don't know.' She shrugged. 'She's just quite intense, isn't she?'

'How so?' I said, trying to sound casual.

'It's just a vibe I get.'

'A vibe.'

She stretched her arms to the ceiling. 'I just don't want anything to mess up our group,' she said. 'You know?' She turned back to me.

'I know. It won't. I'm sorry if I ran off.'

'It's fine.' She got up and sauntered to the door. 'See you at the river,' she pointed a peach fingernail, 'and don't be late.'

I heard her run down the stairs and then the noise as she almost collided with someone. With my father. I sat up and fumbled for my dressing gown, hurrying out of my bedroom.

'Sorry, Mr Sinclair,' I heard her say, 'just making sure Ruth was up bright and early. You know how lazy she can be,' she added, grinning delightedly at me when she saw me stagger down the stairs behind them. Joan stuck her tongue out at me behind his back. 'Good morning!' she called out as she left.

'A strange girl,' my father said, with a hand on the banister. 'Does she want to study art too then?' He looked wary.

'No. She wants to be a secretary,' I said.

'It takes all sorts,' he replied. 'Did she sleep here last night?'

'No.' I shook my head and wrapped my robe tighter. I wasn't used to seeing him in the mornings. He had breakfasts at 6 a.m. and then went into work in the city.

'I hear you've been spending a lot of time with the other girls.' He didn't sound approving.

'And with Stuart too,' I said quickly.

'Well,' he said. 'Will you let me past then?'

'Yes, sorry,' I said, stepping back and to the side so he could continue upstairs.

In the kitchen, Helen was clearing up my father's breakfast and setting my plate, pouring my cereal ready for me. Seeing her doing this, and not just skipping down the stairs to find the bowl and its cereal miraculously ready for me, made me feel a deep burn of shame, of embarrassment.

'I can do that,' I said.

'Oh, you gave me a start,' she replied with a hand on her chest. 'What are you doing up so early then?'

Helen had been with us since I was ten or so; her husband was older than her and had been wounded in the war – not enough to need her to care for him, but enough that he struggled to find work. They had never had children but I had never asked her why. She wasn't motherly and she never sat down with me for tea and a natter – but then, why would she? She had no obligation to me beyond the tasks my father paid her to do, beyond clearing up for me, I thought guiltily.

'I just woke up.'

'Will you be needing a packed lunch then?'

'No, I'm fine,' I said.

'You've been skipping breakfast lately,' she observed as she scrubbed the pan of bacon grease. It was a comment that came from her need to plan ahead, to make sure that no milk was spoiled or cereal wasted, and yet added to my father's question about my friendship with Joan, and Joan's own questions, I felt penned in, surveyed.

I pictured Stuart yesterday, frozen, his body tensed as I observed every sinew, every twitch.

'I'm fine,' I insisted, eating my breakfast so fast I dribbled milk down my chin.

Afterwards, I hurried into my clothes and set off out into the fields, the air bright and thin with the haze of a hot summer's day, small white clouds like cotton balls. I felt calmer the further I went, the high grass closing behind my steps, the steep slope dropping me from view of the gate near the house.

The only thing I had with me was the camera; I had forgotten a flask or my plastic sunglasses, my shoes and hat, and I was parched and dusty by the time I arrived at the river. I was the first one there. I watched the swaying willow branches, the trickling water, as I paced along the bank, seeing the marks in the earth from our feet, the tufts of grass we had torn as we clambered out. There was a pigeon cooing in the woods and another bird with a high twisting sound.

Maybe I could run away and become one of those New Age travellers who went back to nature, I thought, who gave up their worldly trappings and carried all their belongings on their backs, tramping across England and sleeping in hedges and fields, selling carved runes and woven bracelets.

I peeled off my dress, unhooked my bra, and slid down the bank into the river, gasping at the cold burn of the water, at how the shock of it brought me out of my head and back to my body.

Swimming naked, seeing the flash of my pale limbs, feeling the resistance of the water around me, the way it stroked and cradled me, the cold rush of it between my thighs as I widened my legs to kick, I thought it was no wonder that it was once frowned upon for women to swim. How dare we find our own pleasures? How dare we know that our bodies could be touched by something other than groping male hands?

It was strange to be here alone, not to have the others in the water with me or on the bank watching me. I turned my neck, sculled my arms, wondering how long I would need to wait for them, how long I had before I needed to put my dress back on.

The pigeon had grown silent but I heard something else, the snap of a twig, a rustle in the undergrowth. I ducked my body down, peered into the dizzying mosaic of leaves and dappled shadows on the opposite side of the bank. Could someone watch me without my knowing? Was someone there right now?

'Hello?' I called, but there was no answer beyond the shush of wind through the trees.

The water was cold now and I was anxious. I got out of the river, holding an arm across my breasts, hurrying to my dress, my skin mottled and chilled, vulnerable to watching eyes. I tugged it on and then turned round, stared at the other bank with my hands on my hips. I would not be cowed.

Then there was a crack behind me and I whipped around, panicking, wondering how I should defend myself.

'Are you all right?' Camille asked as she came into view, her satchel overflowing with fabric.

'I'm fine,' I said, but my voice was shaky. 'I just thought— I thought there was someone watching me from the other bank. I was swimming and I heard a sound in the woods.'

There was another rustle then, decidedly animal-like, and a pigeon squawked as it flew up and then cooed. It was a bright day, I told myself, not the kind of day for horrors and for people lurking.

'You're here early,' she observed.

'Joan woke me up.'

'Joan?'

She stepped out of a patch of shadow. 'Hey, what happened to you?' I asked. I could see her face properly now and the bruise on her jaw, the graze on her chin. 'Oh my God, are you all right?'

'I fell down the stairs.'

'You fell down the stairs?' I raised a hand towards the wound, touched the edge of it lightly, and she winced. My hands were cold from the water.

'Does it look awful?' she asked curiously.

'It looks like it hurts.' Did it feel hot under my thumb or was that just her skin? 'But you're still as pretty as ever,' I said, feigning a jokey tone that didn't come out that way.

A whistle then, coming down the path, and Linda, Joan and Sarah ran into the clearing, breathless.

'What are you two lovebirds up to?' Joan teased, as I dropped my hand and rocked back nervously.

Camille turned around and the girls gasped and hovered, twisting her to and fro, studying her injuries as I hung back, shivering. 'It's fine,' she said. 'I fell down the stairs.'

'Well, Linda has something that will make you feel better,' Sarah said, unhooking Linda's bag from her shoulder to proudly show off a bottle of gin in one hand and orangeade in the other.

'Where did you get that?'

'It was a present from Geoff,' Linda said with a put-upon sigh. 'Although I know he stole it.'

'Stole it?'

'Don't worry, they'll never know. We'll drink it and send the bottle down the river.'

'With a message inside it?' Sarah asked, lolling back on the grass.

'Yes, to your true love,' Joan said, swooning heavily on top of her so that she squirmed.

'You're already wet – did you take photos already?' Joan asked me, letting Sarah go and tugging at the hem of my dress.

'I just went for a swim.'

Linda was now pouring equal parts orangeade and gin, an unorthodox combination, into the single cup she had brought with her. 'It's a little early for booze, isn't it?' I asked.

'What's the matter with you?' Joan asked. 'You still in a mood from me waking you up?'

I took a few gulps from the cup before passing it to Camille without looking at her, the slide of her fingers against mine making me pull my knees up to sit. 'I had a weird moment earlier, when I was in the water. I thought there was someone watching me from over there.'

'Some creep, you mean?'

'I don't know, I was probably just imagining it.'

'Linda, with me,' Joan ordered, standing up. She stripped off her cardigan and marched towards the water.

'You know, if anyone is in a weird mood today, it's you, Joan!' I called out.

'Maybe!' she called back, hissing as she stepped into the water. 'I just woke up this morning and thought, *fuck it!* Fuck. It.' She lifted her arms. 'We've only got two weeks left and I want to enjoy this summer. To enjoy every day. To have my own life, you know. And if they want to ruin theirs,' she added, with a careless sweep of her hand that didn't fool any of us after another embarrassing display at dinner last night, 'then they can.'

'Hear, hear!' Linda said, following her in her dress.

'I knew you'd get it,' Joan said, and lunged to kiss her on the cheek.

'Oh my God, it's like having a puppy,' Linda said. 'Get in the water with you, cool yourself off.' She pushed her down and the two of them play-fought.

I remembered the camera then and took two blurry pictures of two grappling girls, two competing Ophelias, shrieking and turning the river into a maelstrom.

'We're wasting time,' Joan insisted, spluttering. 'We need to catch whoever's there.'

She tugged Linda towards the other bank and they ran into the woods, deep enough to disappear from our view, hooting and shouting. Telling the intruder to 'Fuck off, will you!' Telling him they were going to get him.

'They're mad, the both of them. And they can't even blame sunstroke,' Sarah said, lying back, smiling like a cat in the warmth.

'You don't want to go and join them?' I asked.

I hadn't looked at Camille straight on since the others had arrived. I kept remembering the feeling of her breath on my palm when I touched her jaw. She had downed the first cup herself and half of another strong one before passing it around. Now the edges of my body were starting to go fuzzy and it was harder and harder not to turn and look at her, not to touch her.

'I'd rather not. What if the madness is catching?' Sarah said, as the two girls in the woods graduated to shrieking, their voices echoing against the trees, as if the wood itself were crying out. 'Do they realize their noise is just going to draw attention? That we'll get some poor local bumbling through trying to find out who's dying? And then they'll see one of us in the water and have a heart attack.'

'That's how rumours and myths start,' Camille said. Her book was propped open over her middle as she stared at the sky, the fingers of one hand gripping the ground. 'A group of girls, shrieks in the woods, damp footprints.'

'Ooh, I just got the shivers,' Sarah said, laughing at herself.

Linda and Joan emerged from the trees. They had leaves sticking to their legs and their hair was snarled, their cheeks pink.

'Here come the wild women,' Sarah intoned.

Linda waded through the water and crawled out towards us, lying down in a sprawl, panting.

'Who's got the camera?' Joan asked, standing in the middle of the river.

'I do,' Camille said, taking it from my limp grip.

I risked a glance at her and she smiled at me, lopsided because of the bruise.

It was too hot; I felt dizzy. I lay back and shut my eyes. The sun turned my eyelids an orange-red, revealed the tiny veins.

I heard a splash. 'Does it matter that I'm smiling?' Joan asked. 'Can I still be tragic and smile?'

'Of course you can. Just ask my mother,' Linda murmured.

'Ouch,' Sarah said.

'You know, if we're copying the painting,' Camille mused, 'Ophelia shouldn't even be looking at the camera, at us. We should be watching her unseen. She shouldn't really be aware that she has an audience. So I don't think it matters. But the flowers,' she continued, 'they should mean something, like in the play.'

Like forget-me-nots, I thought hazily, sitting up on my elbows, blinking at the light.

'What do roses mean?' Linda asked.

'They mean love, obviously,' Joan called out.

'What do all these mean?' Sarah asked, holding up the bunch of flowers we had gathered from the meadow and a few wilted stems stolen from a neighbour's garden. She gave them to Camille who peered closer.

'Carnations mean different things depending on their colour. White for luck, pink for a mother's love, yellow for . . . disappointment.'

I leaned over to pick up the camera she had set down by her feet. I couldn't bear suddenly not to take a picture of her, bruised but still lovely, frowning at the bouquet in her hands, a little unsteady on her feet. She looked down at me as I adjusted the lens. She was standing too close to the sun, I thought, and the picture would be washed out with light, but I didn't want to stop her and make her move and I couldn't move either, my body felt so heavy.

'Knapweeds look like thistles so I'd say they mean loyalty, bravery. Anemones mean . . . forsaken love, death. Sweet Williams mean gallantry, noble heroic love.'

'You should write a book about that, or start a business. Send coded messages through flowers,' Sarah said. 'Everyone's starting a business now, we don't have to work for *the man*. Peter is, something to do with records.' Peter was the third of the boys staying at the cottages.

'Hey, what do buttercups mean?' Linda asked, twirling one around her fingers.

'I don't know.'

'Happiness,' Sarah suggested, 'warm summer days, egg yolks.'

'Did no one bring food?' Joan asked, walking over to us and shaking her head so her wet hair sprayed icy droplets.

'Did you have to bring that up?' Linda asked. 'Now we're all going to get hungry.' She changed into the dress that Camille had brought with her, a gown we had decided was suitably

Elizabethan but was really more peasant sack and which we had all been adding bits to – embroidery around the neck and hem, ribbons and tucks at the sleeve. It had an empire-line waist that made Linda's considerable bust look jealousy-inducing. After her turn, she handed the soaking wet dress to Camille to put on.

I watched her back as she got changed, telling myself I was only looking for any more injuries, or to compare her body to mine as we all did. Her underwear was threadbare and old-fashioned, childish, but it felt mean to notice that. Her hair was thick and straight, swaying against her spine as she moved. She had dimples in her lower back, and the curve of her backside made me feel something obscene.

I looked away and ripped up a clump of grass. 'Any gin left?' I asked.

'Oh, did I not say we have another half-bottle?' Linda said with a nonchalant flick of her hair.

'Linda, you are so cool, you know that?' I said after taking a few gulps of gin neat, feeling the burn of it in my gullet like something necessary.

'I try,' she said.

'Are you going to take Camille's photo?' Joan asked me.

'I'm too dizzy,' I replied, trying to take on some of Linda's casual mien and not reveal my unease that Joan might have sensed something between Camille and me. Even though there was nothing *to* sense, I told myself fizzily.

'I'll do it,' Sarah said.

I heard her directing Camille, and the soft wet sounds of her in the river, and within a minute I gave up on lying down with my eyes closed and went to sit on the bank. This was about art, I told myself stubbornly, about my project. About art school. It wasn't personal.

'Not dizzy any more?' Joan asked.

'No. Back off, will you? You're hovering like a mother today.'

'Ouch, all right,' she said, crossing her arms and returning to Linda's side. 'Someone's PMSing.'

Camille's eyes darted between Sarah holding the camera and me. I wondered what a photo of that would look like, if I could look at that photo and know by her gaze how she felt about me, save it, keep it.

Linda was more attractive, Sarah more womanly and Joan more striking, and yet it was Camille I was drawn to. It didn't make any sense.

'Who are you?' Sarah asked.

'I'm Hero,' Camille said.

'Who?'

She sat up in the water, brushed wet ropes of hair from her face. 'Can I have a sip?'

Linda staggered over to her, holding the cup for her to drink as Camille clasped her hand around hers. I was suddenly viciously jealous.

'Hero and Leander?' Camille said, once Linda had returned to the bank. 'Hero was a priestess who lived in a tower, and her lover Leander would swim across the Hellespont each night to see her, guided by her lamp. But one stormy night the lamp went out and he drowned. When Hero saw his body she jumped to her death to be with him.'

'Oh, to meet a real boy who inspires that kind of devotion,' Sarah said with a sigh.

Camille frowned. Because Sarah was making a joke of it? I couldn't tell. Sometimes I felt I had no idea what Camille was thinking at all, that she was unknowable.

'Do you think she regretted it, when she was falling?' I asked.

I was stuck on the picture of it, of Hero walking all the way up her tower, around and around those worn steps, her trembling hand on the wall, weeping and wailing. Climbing up just so she could jump from it and make her death something spectacular, something that meant more than just swimming out and deciding not to keep afloat. Maybe it was because she knew the gods were watching her, that someone would one day record her story; maybe that was the only way she could tell her *own* story, not being a man who could write it down.

'I don't know,' Camille said and tipped onto her back.

'They say that people who jump do regret it,' Linda said. 'But I heard that drowning doesn't hurt.'

It seems strange to say that until this moment we had never spoken of the actual act of drowning. We had discussed what a drowning girl looked like, why she was there in the water, what she was trying to say, but not the actual drowning, the mechanism of it, of lungs filling up with water.

In most of our images our faces were still above the water, just like in the paintings, because how could we look lovely if you couldn't see us, how could you know without our expressions what our bodies meant? And how could we think about the messy reality of dying when the river gave us back to our bodies, made us feel *embodied*, cradled, held, consoled.

'That's a myth,' Sarah said. 'They used to tell it to sailors' wives to make them feel better.'

'Jesus,' Joan swore.

We were all sitting on the bank now. Were we thinking the same thing looking at Camille floating in the water, her arms gliding in and out so that the dress billowed out into wings, were we imagining her struggling, the water sliding down her gullet, her face turning blue?

'It's just a story,' Camille said, standing up with a rush of water, as if sensing our concern. 'Like all the other stories.'

'I mean, I'd rather drown than, I don't know, stab myself,' Joan said as Camille approached us. She held out her hands and helped Camille up out of the water. 'At least with drowning you don't actually have to *do* it, you just have to stop swimming or put heavy things in your pockets or something.'

It was the moment just before drowning that we tried to record, I thought, the moment when the girl decided to give herself to the river, not the one afterwards when the river had taken her. We didn't know yet that the boundary between the two was treacherous, gossamer, liquid.

'I had an aunt who killed herself,' Sarah said. 'She took pills.'

'Why?' Camille asked, pausing from wringing out her hair.

Sarah shrugged. 'I don't know. It's one of those family secrets. No one talks about it.'

'Right, well. Gin makes us morbid, good to know,' Linda declared, but we were too pensive, too in our own heads, to laugh as we trailed our feet in the cold river water.

Chapter Seventeen

Maeve's parents have an argument in their bedroom before dinner. The shape of the upstairs hall means she can hear every word spoken, the little barbs they fling, in her own bedroom where she lies on the bed with her legs propped up high on the wall.

She's trying to sink herself into the memories of what happened with Stuart, how he touched her and looked at her, how it felt, but the voices keep bringing her out of it, making her limbs restless, making her want to kick at the wall.

'How was I supposed to know you had booked someone to come around to look at it?' her mother is saying to her father. 'Am I psychic?'

'I think you'd like me to be,' he replies. 'You're quiet and moody and then you lash out like this. And I'm supposed to read your mind and know what's wrong.'

'Nothing's wrong.'

'Ruth,' he says firmly, and Maeve pictures him putting his hands on her shoulders, switching to his rational tone of voice. *We're all adults here*, he seems to want to say at these moments. 'I know the hospital this morning brought up a lot of stuff for you, a lot of memories.'

'A lot of guilt.'

'You made the decision not to see your father when he was in hospital, and that's something you'll have to deal with. We all have things we regret.'

'What the *hell*,' her mother states, voice shaking with a rare kind of fury that has Maeve on her feet and deciding to leave her room for somewhere further away. 'Are you saying you didn't agree with me? Because you said nothing of the sort at the time. You told me I was doing the right thing—'

'I was supporting you,' her father begins, as Maeve runs along the hall and into an open door, the junk room, closing it behind her.

She can't hear words any more, just a murmur.

So it was her mother's decision that they were estranged then, not his, Maeve thinks bitterly as she looks around a room filled with her grandfather's old, forgotten things; that the man who gifted her the polished jewellery box with its twirling dancer never had the occasion to buy her any more presents or, more importantly, to spend time with her, to get to know her.

At the beginning of the summer, the thought of leaving home made Maeve want to lie down and never get up again – she hadn't had enough time being a child, she wanted to be looked after, to stay with her parents – but now she feels only an aching desire to leave. At university, she thinks, rifling through an open box of books (biographies of politicians and military leaders mostly), no one would keep tabs on her. No one would care if she met with Stuart. But if the tests come back and she is ill again, if she has to go back to hospital and back to chemo and loses her hair, if they have to ask her brother to donate bone marrow again, as if she's some kind of vampire feeding off her family, consuming them . . .

She's not sure she'll have the strength for that. If it happens again, maybe it's the universe telling her she's not meant to be here, to survive.

She stands at the window, staring through the handprints on its dusty surface to the lawn and the fields beyond, the rise and dip of the land, and thinks about running across it, running away. *But then you can't run away from your body, can you*, she thinks. Georgia certainly couldn't. Georgia who felt like a sister to her, a cleverer, more daring sister, who sat down for the first time next to her in the hospital school and drawled, *So, what are you in for?* and declared at the end of the short school day that they were going to be best friends, *That all right with you?*

Fine, Maeve had replied, bemused and half in love.

And how did Maeve repay her friendship in the end? By telling a nurse that Georgia was making herself sick, vomiting after meals, even though the metabolic disorder that had put her in the children's hospital was doing enough by itself to undermine any nourishment she swallowed down.

They'll put me on a feeding tube, you know that, Georgia had hissed, wounded, vicious, her eyes wide like a trapped animal. *They'll put me on surveillance around the clock, I won't be able to shit without them standing over me. I won't be able to decide anything about my own body. Who are you to do that? Who gave you the right? Just because you like it*, she had spat, *being sick and babied and looked after, letting everyone make all the hard decisions for you. You're a child, a spiteful child.*

It was useless to say that Maeve was only trying to save her friend's life, that Georgia's furred arms were so thin it made her want to weep. To give up control, Georgia believed, was a fate worse than death, even as she careened towards it.

Maeve wants control of her body now; she doesn't want to be ill, though she still wants to be cared for, only not by her parents or doctors. She doesn't want to be sick, to die, and when she thinks of the hospital she feels such a panic inside that her heart rocks loose in her chest.

She opens more of the boxes to distract herself. There are more photos – faded line-ups of schoolboys in cricket gear and with felt caps, besuited young men in front of grand collegiate buildings. And more antiques – oval miniatures, wine-stoppers, medals.

She lifts a box down to get to the one underneath, whose corner has been bashed as if it's been kicked in. She tugs it open, old tape tearing with the force. Inside is a quilt of pale pink flowers and lying atop it is a piece of lace trim curled into a spiral, and a photograph.

Maeve holds the photograph up to the light. It's of the river again, the same one as the photo she found downstairs in his office, but the image is blurry and over-exposed. She can just about see the trees at the other side of the bank, the bleached grass on this side. In the river itself, bright and yellow with sun, there's a hazy outline, a whirling, like the splash from something large thrown into it, or the churn as something breaches, and a thin white shape emerging – a branch stripped of its bark? Or a streak of light on the photo?

The photograph unsettles Maeve. She can't understand it, nor why it has been kept with her grandfather's things, but her mother is out in the hallway calling for her, her voice tight from the argument with her father, so she drops the photo back in the box and leaves the room.

'There you are,' her mother says. She's wearing a large striped jumper even though the evening is warm, and has pulled her hair back into a small ponytail. It's the opposite of how she'll dress when they have company, feminine, dressy. 'What were you doing in there?'

'Just looking.' Maeve shrugs.

'Well, be careful.'

'I'll try not to cut my finger on the edge of a cardboard box,' she retorts.

Her mother's smile is brittle. 'I meant more be careful of your grandfather's things – there's probably some valuable stuff in there.'

'What are you going to do with it all?'

'Have some of it valued, clear the rest away.'

'Wouldn't he have wanted you to keep it?'

Her mother starts moving towards the stairs. 'He's not here, so it's not up to him any more.'

'That's *cruel*.'

Her mother pauses with a hand on the banister. 'Don't talk about things you don't understand, Maeve.' She gathers a breath, softens her expression. 'But if you want anything from that room or the boxes around the house, you can have it, OK? Are you coming for dinner now?'

'Yeah,' Maeve says.

Stuart and her father are already at the dinner table on the patio. Stuart gives her a quick wink while her father is bent over Michael's plate, cutting up his sausages and listening to Iza relate the film they watched with breathless intensity.

'It's just pasta tonight,' her mother declares as she brings out the serving dish.

'That's lovely, Ruth,' Stuart replies.

Maeve feels like she's in some kind of dream; not a nightmare, not exactly, but everything feels woozy, as if the world is filmed with glass, and though her breath is tight, her body feels strangely untethered.

She had sex with the man across from her, an old friend of

her parents' who are sitting around the very same table, this afternoon. She can still *feel* what he did, inside, a slight sting as she shifts in her seat – only this time what's inside her body, what's different about her, isn't an illness to be discovered and displayed on lightboxes and monitors for her doctors and parents to discuss, it's a secret for her to keep.

'Not hungry?' her father asks sometime later, as she drags a spiralled piece of pasta back and forth over her plate. The sauce is made from sundried tomatoes, which Iza declared *tasted funny*, and Maeve stained her fingertips with its bright red oil when she retrieved pasta that she had clumsily spilled onto the table.

'No, I am,' she says, and eats a mouthful she cannot even taste as Stuart meets her eyes, rubbing a thumb at a patch of stubble on his cheek.

As planned, Stuart brings up the house he's visiting next – the library, the terribly nouveau riche swimming pool, the story of the writer who worked in its attic bedroom and used to take midnight strolls across the estate, the folly that the lord had built, and the minor collection of modernist paintings rumoured to be in one of the private family rooms. And as planned, Maeve asks questions about it, acts interested (which isn't hard when the house does genuinely sound like somewhere she'd like to visit), praying her cheeks aren't as red as she thinks they might be.

'I could take her with me,' Stuart says, turning to Ruth as though it's her decision. 'If that wouldn't be too boring for a teenager like yourself,' he adds to Maeve. 'You've probably got better things to do.'

'Sure,' Maeve says with a nod.

'Any opportunity to get away from her parents for a day,' her father says.

'You sure?' her mother checks with her. 'We can visit it another time, you and I?'

'I'd like to see the behind-the-scenes stuff,' she says.

'It won't be a long day, Ruth. My shoot is spread out over three, so I'll bring her back early.'

'I'm really fine, guys, I'm not a child.'

'As long as it's not tomorrow,' her father says, picking up the plates to stack them. 'Tomorrow I'd like you to help me wrangle the twins while your mother has a break.' This is supposed to be a treat for her mother, a favour, but by his tone and the sour atmosphere between them it reads more like a martyred punishment. 'We're going to the farm. Will you come, Maeve?'

'OK,' she says, even though she'd rather not, but she doesn't want to wade into the tension between her parents.

'And then you can come with me on Sunday,' Stuart says.

'Great, I look forward to it,' she says with a smile, and when she sees the pride of her parents at her being so polite and courteous to an adult, to *Stuart*, she has to cough to hide a startled laugh.

After dinner, she plays with the twins in the living room. They have transformed an upturned chair and blanket into a horse-drawn carriage careening through the desert towards an oasis, and she is ordered to be the magical prince they meet once they arrive. They delight in her snooty accent, her declaration that their offering of gold (a plastic truck) is paltry, and the tasks she makes them do to win the jewel (an empty Kinder Egg) from her.

It's late by the time she retreats upstairs. But when she goes back to the junk room to retrieve the photograph, the entire box is gone.

Chapter Eighteen

'So, where do you want me?' Stuart asks after Alex's car drives away, dashing my hopes that he would say he was too busy doing other things today.

'In the shade outside?' A chance to enjoy the garden without supervising the twins, and a less intimate setting than a room.

I drag a dining chair in front of the bench under one of the apple trees where Stuart sits in just his shorts, slouching comfortably as if he's the one who lives here and I'm the visitor. I'm flustered as I try to get comfortable. He smiles at me as I snap the lead of the pencil in the sharpener and drop the rubber in the too-long grass that Alex is yet to trim. 'You know I hate you and Alex for suggesting this,' I say. 'Like a parent giving their child a biscuit and a piece of paper and telling her to draw a little picture. I'm so glad you two have decided that the housewife needs a *hobby*.'

'Are you done?' he laughs. 'I don't see why I'm lumped in with your husband though, you're not my housewife.'

'Thank God,' I say, as I arc my wrist to draw the first line, the curve of his shoulder against the cracked wood of the bench.

'Why, because I'm poorly house-trained? If you recall, I was the only one to ever remember to take the bins out in digs.'

'Maybe it's because you're a bad influence.'

'Oh, really?' He tilts his head.

'Don't move your head.'

'Sorry.'

How many opportunities does a woman have to tell a man how to stand, how to sit, that they must keep still? Maybe I could sell other women on this, have an all-female class with a male model. Although thinking about it, there's a horrible whiff of the Chippendales about that proposal, and really, if the women are middle-aged they might have been up close and personal enough with male bodies not to want to sit and draw one.

Stuart watches me while I draw, having chosen my face as his focal point, and when I look up it's as though he's the one dissecting me, the one turning me into shape and line and shadow. 'So are you going to tell me about them, your scars?' I ask, waving a hand to encompass his chest and arms, the scatter of new marks that my artist self noted as interesting shapes to break up the planes of his muscles.

'Not if I don't have to.'

'Tell me about one of them.'

'I owe you stories as well as my body now? Fine, my shoulder,' he lifts it, 'the gunshot.' He shuts his eyes tightly, like a boy remembering where he has left a favourite stick. 'Kiseljak, Bosnia. We were running on a tip, a photographer friend and I. I hadn't sold anything in a week and I needed the money. We had a fixer with us – he was young, had a full beard even though his voice was hardly broken. They're always young. Fervent, brave, foolish. It's the same in every war. Maybe because older men have more to lose, maybe because when you're young you think you can't possibly die, or maybe that your death will mean something. I don't know.' He scratches his neck and folds his arms, and I let him.

They remind Stuart of himself, these boys, I think. Their sincerity, their youthful daring. Maybe he is as stuck in his teenage past as I am, leashed to it.

'So what happened?'

'Oh, the road we were on was too quiet, and then it wasn't quiet and the bullets were flying through the car, through the both of us.'

'Jesus.'

'It was mayhem. I was trying to tourniquet his arm and he was trying to dig the bullet out of my shoulder. We made a mess of each other,' he says with a snort. 'But we survived, all three of us. A lucky day.'

He returns to his pose. The sun has shifted the shadows and now the bottoms of his legs are bright.

My neck is hot; my legs stick to the seat when I shift them as I draw on, as I make lines and then erase them, as the body in front of me fails to appear on the paper.

I shake out my hand.

'Cramp?'

'I'm not used to this. I hope you're not expecting anything good.'

'You've really never drawn since you were a teenager?'

'Never.' I swat away a lingering wasp.

'I find that remarkable.'

'I was busy doing other things. I'm sure there's things you haven't done since you were a child – played conkers, skipped, I don't know.'

He makes a considering noise. The light dips as the smallest of clouds cross the sun.

'What are your plans for the future anyway?'

'Spoken like a parent.'

'I mean, does photography pay OK?'

He squints at me. 'I do all right. I came into some money last year and bought a flat.'

'From who?'

'That's quite a personal question,' he says, with a smile that creases lines into his cheeks. 'A relative, Ruth. I guess they felt guilty for not doing more for me after my parents died.'

'You know, Alex and I took out life insurance when Maeve got sick, not that we could afford it, really. It just gets to you, the idea that you could die and leave them, the kids.'

'I don't think any broker would have given me life insurance. You can't get any kind of insurance if you go charging into warzones.'

'So why did you?' I set the drawing down. It's terrible. I should have expected it, but a part of me was arrogant enough to assume that any latent artistic ability I once had would re-emerge untouched. 'Why did you risk yourself like that?'

'Because I thought that if I took photos, if I showed people what war was really like, the wars would be shorter. I had given up on anything else, on stopping them before they even began, changing the status quo. Because I was angry. I think that's what drove all of us out there. We were angry – at the world, at ourselves, at other people.'

The pencil sweats in my hand. It's too hot in the sun. 'Were you angry at Alex and me?'

'What?'

'The way you left without telling us, after Maeve was born. Did we do something wrong?'

'Ruth, I mean this in the kindest way possible, but not everything is about you. I didn't run off to war because you'd broken my heart by staying with Alex. Did you really think that? That I was pining after you all these years?' There is something pitying about his smile and I hate it.

'No, of course not. I guess I just felt responsible, guilty.'

'You've got enough guilt already without adding to it.'

My chest goes tight. 'What do you mean?'

'I mean motherhood, isn't guilt a mother's central tenet? A good mother, that is, not mine.'

I feel the sting of adrenaline and of bruised pride. 'Let's have lunch,' I suggest, standing up. 'And a drink, I need a drink after this failure.'

'I wish I had the other one to compare it with, to see how terribly I've aged.' He holds out his hand and I give him the picture. 'I remember looking *slightly* more symmetrical, I think.'

'Fuck off.' I try to take it back.

He gasps. 'Language.'

'You didn't keep the other one then, my drawing of you?'

'Your juvenilia?' he says, putting a hot arm around my shoulder as we walk back. He hasn't put his shirt on and I can smell his sweat, different from Alex, but equally unappealing.

'You need a shower.'

'Do you remember when Alex went on strike that time? When you said unless he showered after rugby he wasn't allowed to share a bed with you, and then he didn't wash for a week.'

'Nine days, he didn't wash for nine days,' I say, as I get a bottle of white wine from the fridge and a tub of fancy, too-expensive olives that Alex brought back from the last farmer's market, to give this the illusion of lunch and not just a drinking session. 'I think it impressed me actually, his quiet stubbornness. Impressed me, and irritated me.' I wince as I turn the tight corkscrew, appreciating that Stuart doesn't offer to do it for me as Alex would have. What a boring life I lead that I can't make comparisons between Alex and anyone except the man sitting across from me, with how little adult company I have these days. I'm trying not to think of all the female company Alex has – on his commute, at work, at after-work drinks, at the sandwich shop.

I take two chilled gulps from the wine as Stuart sniffs his own glass.

'It's all we've got, I'm afraid,' I say.

'Wine is wine,' he says, plucking an olive from the tub. 'Some of the people I came across on my travels were terrible snobs about booze, and food. There was this whole cabal of journalists and cameramen who all went to boarding school and Sandringham and lived in these vast old houses. And talked of *Kin*-ya and *Rhodesia*. They used to get special orders from Fortnum's shipped out, silver cutlery and real Christmas pudding. They'd travel with these big entourages and each time I'd expect a man in a butler's uniform to step out.'

'I bet you took them down a peg.'

'Well, I certainly tried. Funny that you can travel half the world away, and rock up in a village in the Afghan desert and bump into a little English lord.'

'And now you're taking fashion photos and rubbing shoulders with the glamorous set.'

He picks up the bottle and motions to me, and I hold out my glass for him to fill even though I haven't finished yet. 'It pays the bills.'

'This wine is awful.' I pucker my mouth, squash two olives between my teeth, but their sour taste doesn't help.

'Have you got any biscuits?'

'Not crackers. I've got custard creams?' I jokingly offer.

'Perfect,' he declares, and I direct him to the tin. 'Hey,' he says, 'do you remember . . .' He trails off as he peels his biscuit apart and then mashes it back together to eat.

'What?'

'Can I talk about it? That last summer?' He watches me closely.

My mouth feels chalky.

'It's just, the wine,' he says, nodding to the glasses on the table. 'I was remembering one of our dinners. Drinking that terrible stuff, and waiting for you and the girls to come back from the river, and that day you were all already bladdered on gin.'

'I think I remember that,' I say, feigning nonchalance.

He lifts his feet onto the chair next to him, the legs screeching loudly on the flagstones. 'You five running up, pink with sun and booze, in your floral dresses and wild hair.' He sounds wistful.

'I need some more food to sop this up,' I say and go to the fridge. I stand there without looking at anything, the chill air against my front doing nothing for the heat that wraps around my neck.

'You don't mind me mentioning it? It's just, being here again brings up so many memories.'

'Of course not.'

'Have you got any cheese in there?'

I bring out a block of cheddar, hard at the corner because it's not been wrapped properly, and another half-bottle of wine from two weeks ago I meant to throw out. *If I just keep drinking,* I think, with the stubbornness of a teenager, *then the memories will stay murky and I will stay pleasantly numb.*

'I think I was a little in love with all of you,' he says, hacking at the cheese with a table knife. 'Even though none of you would have deigned to give me the time of day—'

'I always talked to you, and I drew you.'

'. . . except Joan Summers actually.'

'What?'

'I had a thing with her that summer.'

'I don't remember that.'

'It was nothing serious.'

Joan and Stuart, I think with confusion, trying to remember any time I might have seen the two of them interact.

'That dinner though,' he says, holding up a finger as he drains his wine, 'when you arrived in a swirl of lace and dresses and girly chatter.'

'Girly chatter.'

'It was like you'd all appeared mysteriously from the woods. As though, after dinner was over, you'd vanish just the same. I remember the adults didn't know what to think. They were doing their hippie thing but here you were, young and properly carefree. They wanted to be like you, I think, they were jealous.'

'They were scared,' I offer, too honest.

'Teenage girls can be very scary. Intense.' He picks up the newest bottle from the fridge. 'Like Camille . . .' he says carefully. My body pulses at her name spoken out loud, a spasm of icy fear. 'When she lectured us that evening, do you remember?'

Sarah's mother had been watching as we cavorted at one end of the jumbled dinner tables, giggling and whispering, lost in our own dizzy worlds, eating with our mouths open, sharing the same cups.

'Why Ophelia anyway?' she had asked, leaning into our space. She tapped her long nails on the table. 'Of all of Shakespeare's women, why her, girls? Why not, I don't know, Lady Macbeth, Beatrice? Someone with bite, someone with more words.'

'She's closest to our age,' Sarah replied, after her mother made no move to sit back in her seat.

The rest of the table had quietened now too. I could feel a bristling pass through us.

'Would you rather we be Juliet?' Joan asked. We had actually played at being Juliet too, but the families only saw the river and our damp dresses, our waterlogged hair, and narrowed us down to one archetype.

'Yeah,' Geoff piped up. 'Why Ophelia? It's a bit pathetic.' Geoff was sitting at the far end of the table, with Stuart and the other boy whose name I always forget – Peter, Peter with the curling blond hair. Geoff was bronzed by the sun, his brown hair feathered down his neck. He was the kind of boy you'd call handsome and he was, I knew, frustrated that us girls were busy with each other and not fawning over him that summer.

'Have you studied *Hamlet* properly? Or just read the back of your book?' Camille said. She leaned forward in her seat. 'When Ophelia steps onto the stage with her flowers, she stops everything.' Her hand cut through the air. 'She ruptures the story. The royal court is silenced, dumbstruck by her, a *girl*. They look at her and they are overcome by grief and shame. That's the power she has, Ophelia.' She blushed then; I could see her breath coming quickly.

'But she's still dead at the end, isn't she?' Geoff said with a little laugh.

'So's Hamlet,' Linda drawled. 'That's the point of Shakespeare, that they all die at the end. That everyone dies.'

'All right, Nostradamus,' he mocked.

'You've got your whole lives ahead of you, girls,' Joan's father called out, 'and take it from me, no boy is going to want a dead girl as his girlfriend.'

One of the men made a muttered joke and they laughed.

'Live a little,' he continued, and Joan mimed vomiting. 'Grow up.'

'You grow up!' Linda told him, with a drunken snort of laughter. 'And get a haircut, you look ridiculous.'

'*Linda*,' her mother said sharply.

'What?' she shrugged, eyes wide.

I held a hand over my mouth to muffle my laugh as Joan pinched my leg.

'That's enough wine,' her mother said, reaching over to snatch the bottle away. It was empty and she rocked back awkwardly.

'Speak for yourself,' Linda said and then stood up quickly, her chair falling with a crash as her mother lunged for her. 'Grow up, *Anne*,' she said to her, dancing back.

One of the fathers clapped his hands loudly. 'All right, all right, calm down, everybody.' Linda's mother was rigid with rage, a strand of her hair stuck to her wine-red mouth. 'And girls, why don't you make yourselves scarce for now, hmm?'

'Gladly,' Joan murmured, hooking her elbow into mine as we left the table, the group of us trailing napkins, a cup strewn on the grass, river weeds and petals fluttering loose from our legs.

Later, in the present, Stuart is peeling our last mandarin over the sink. 'I'm eating you out of house and home, sorry about this.'

'I mean, a contribution to your feeding costs might be welcome,' I say as I fiddle with the latest cork, squeezing it between my fingers.

'Oh shit, you mean that.' He wipes his mouth with his hand. 'Alex was so adamant when I offered him rent for the annexe. I was worried I'd pissed him off enough he wouldn't even let me stay.'

'It wasn't up to him, it was both of our decision. If it had been up to me, I would have swallowed my pride and said sure, if you're solvent then we could do with some help. Does that make me a terrible friend? Have I dashed your opinion of me as host?'

'Depends what the rates are,' he says messily, around the slice of fruit in his mouth.

'Very reasonable.'

'You've always been reasonable.'

'I need a nap.' I stretch my arms, pretending to be dozy and not tense with anxiety, and then carry the detritus of our al fresco meal to the sink.

'Hey, I'll write you a cheque, OK?' He puts a hand on my side. He's still in front of the sink so we jostle against one another as I place my load under the running water. He touches my hair. 'Why'd you cut it and dye it?'

'To cover the grey.' And because I didn't want to look in a mirror and see her, see Ophelia, and what I had begun that summer when I took the first photograph.

'I miss how it used to look,' he says, tugging at the ends. His hand lands heavy on my shoulder.

'You really do need a shower.'

He drops his voice. 'Is that an invitation, Mrs Hawkins?'

'Oh yes, I've sent my husband out for the day so I can have my way with you here in his kitchen.'

This flirting, the drawing session – it would be so easy to take it as an expression of interest and not just boredom, convenience. He doesn't want me, not really, and I don't want him. But it would be so simple to give in, to do something wrong. To observe yourself kissing another man and think, *See, I knew I was a terrible person, I knew I was always rotten inside*.

'No,' he says, pulling my hands away from the plates in the

sink, 'you're not allowed to wash up. I'm the guest, you go outside. Enjoy the garden.'

I do as ordered. I stand on the warm stones of the patio breathing in the lavender, the hot grass, the summer. My head is tight, as if it's been wrung out and left to dry in the heat.

Stuart opens the window above the sink with a squeak of hinges. The pane below, in front of him, catches the light, turns from window to blazing mirror of the sun. I stare at it and blink, searing the image on my eyelids, testing myself like a child with her hand over a candle flame.

'You know, I lied to you,' he calls out suddenly, 'when I said I left because of the money, because war was a young man's game.'

I shift to the side so I can see his face swimming in the blue square in my eyes.

'And it wasn't only the corruption either, that if you dug even shallowly you'd find old British interests, oil, business. It was because it was getting to me, eating away at me. Seeing the worst of humanity. I was starting to care less and less for the people I photographed, giving pieces of my soul away with each shot. It scared me.' I can see his face more clearly now, his dipped head, his rounded shoulders. When did we get so old?

'Maybe it was just a protective instinct,' I say, 'maybe it's just what happens to people.'

'But feelings are never divorced from actions, are they? I worried that my apathy would seep into my decisions – to take a photo or not, to help someone or not, to risk myself or turn my back. Or that it already had. Do you ever feel, Ruth,' he says, putting his hands on the window frame, 'like the boundary between you and some other version of you is paper-thin? Like you'd just have to sneeze – to, I don't know, turn on the spot

– and you'd give in to something you know you shouldn't? That we're all just one decision away from being the worst version of ourselves?'

Yes. 'No, I don't know. I think war throws up so much shit that we regular people don't have to deal with. Human minds, human morals, aren't made for that. And isn't that what a conscience is, thinking you *could* do something bad and then not doing it after all?'

'You might be right.'

He finishes drying up and comes outside, bringing a wine glass. He takes a long sip and then hands it to me. 'Seems mad not to finish the whole bottle.'

'Our third bottle, you mean.'

'Second and a half, technically.'

Why not add to the headache, the hangover? Why not?

'Do you ever think of her?' he asks softly, taking his cigarettes from his pocket. 'Camille?'

'Occasionally.' I stare at the back of the garden, the leaves a dizzying distraction, the puffs of flower blooms and darting butterflies. I could cry now, I think. I pick at the dry skin of my lips, tasting blood.

'Do you think it was just her getting carried away, just a teenager messing around?'

'I think . . . I think we were playing with fire. Don't you? That it was inevitable. That's what some people said.'

'You were just kids. *We* were just kids.'

Kids weaving flowers in our hair, sewing wedding dresses and princess gowns and mourning veils.

'You were beautiful. As, like, a collective. Not just in a teenage-boy-fancies-girls-in-pretty-dresses way, but ethereal, mythical. I was jealous of you,' he says, lighting a cigarette. 'You were making art, you know, you had an aesthetic vision.

Maybe that's one way you're like your father.' He waves a hand back at the house to encompass the prints and antiques and wallpaper.

'Was I responsible for your career then?' I tease.

'What, the photography?' he laughs. 'No, I fell into that by accident. Travelled out, picked up a camera, learned it as I went.'

I wrap my arms around my shoulders. 'Yeah, I guess our photos and yours couldn't be more different.'

He blows smoke in a thin stream away from him, but I can still smell it and know that it will settle into my clothes and hair.

'We were young. I think of that now when I look at Maeve,' I say, 'that we weren't as grown up as we imagined. Hindsight, one of the few perks of adulthood.'

'Twins though,' he says, after a pause. 'I bet your dad was pleased. Have you got one of those classic photos of him holding one in each arm?'

'I don't. We didn't— We fell out, my father and I.'

He shields his face from the sun with his hand. 'I know you weren't that close but I didn't know it got that bad.'

'You looked up to him, you two had a bond' – does my voice still sound jealous when I say that? – 'but as a father, he was . . . difficult.'

'I bet he didn't thrash you with a belt though, or knock your teeth out.'

I think of what Stuart said about anger and a boy running away to the mayhem of war, choosing to live surrounded by such violence, of the scars I saw on his body.

I put my hand on his shoulder and slide my fingers across the fabric of his t-shirt as he stares at me, close, my eyes catching the nicks and silvered stubble of his face in the afternoon light, the uncertain twitch of his mouth. I trace the scar I drew. 'Brave boy,' I murmur. 'Brave, foolhardy boy.'

He looks away and covers my hand with his, and I feel the pulse of his heartbeat beneath my palm, the tight clutch of his fingers over mine.

I remember one summer afternoon back then, sitting next to him on the front lawn, close enough to smell boy sweat above the smoke from his father's bonfire out back, and how I had pondered it, our possible future. Of marrying this boy who my father seemed to prefer as a son to me as a daughter, of having his approval, the two of us moving into the house behind us later, filling it with grandchildren for him. It made me go cold, it made my stomach shake. I didn't want it.

Is Stuart jealous of Alex? Not because he still holds a torch for me but because of the house? He doesn't treat him with quite the same fondness as he did at university. But are any of us that free any more with our affections?

'Why are you doing this?' I ask, slipping my arm from him. My lips feel swollen with wine.

'What?'

'Being friends again, acting like—' I shake my head. 'When you leave again, will you even pick up the phone?'

'Of course I will.'

I miss friends, I miss companions who aren't co-parents, but I don't know if I can trust him.

'You know, you're not stuck here, Ruth. You act like you're shut away but you'll be back to work this autumn, you'll find a job again, won't you?'

'Yeah.' I nod, the sun wincingly bright through my eyelids.

'No one's ever totally stuck, there's always a way out.'

Chapter Nineteen

At the farm with her dad and the twins, Maeve drags her feet through the stalls of sheep and cows, the petting pen of rabbits and guinea pigs. She has worn a watch for the first time in months and is checking it obsessively, counting down in increments of five minutes to the time when she'll be home and can see Stuart.

'Are we boring you, Maeve?' her dad asks, as she leans over a fence to the side of the sandpit where the twins play.

'I'm just tired.'

'You know when you go off to university, you'll miss them growing up. You'll come home for holidays and they'll have shot up. You should soak up all the time you get with them,' he says. 'Just my advice,' he adds mildly.

'Do you feel the same way with you working all the time?' she retorts.

'Maeve.'

'What? It's a genuine question. Do you miss us when you're away?'

'Fine, I'll take it at face value then. But you're becoming rude recently, Maeve, and it's not an attractive thing.'

'*Attractive?*' she repeats incredulously.

'Come on, a figure of speech.'

'Would you tell that to a boy, to Michael when he grows up? That he mustn't be rude because it would make him *unattractive*?'

'This is exactly what I'm talking about,' he says, digging in. 'You, lashing out. Your mother and I aren't the enemy, Maeve. The world isn't your enemy.'

'Who said it was?'

He sighs wearily and she hates him.

'I'm going for a walk,' she spits out.

Right now, she thinks as she strides across the too-soft bark pathway, what she'd really like is to smoke, to have something to do with her hands that isn't punching a wall. Or to jump into a cold pool and scream underwater, to thrash her limbs.

If only she had a phone and could call Stuart to pick her up. Maybe she could ask him to buy her one and that way they can talk whenever they want? But then she'd have to hide it somewhere her parents wouldn't find it.

She lingers at the back of the reptile hut as long as she can, until she's had enough of parents peering at her, a lone sullen teenager, like she's something dangerous. Returning towards the sandpit, she sees her dad leaning on the fence just as she was. He glances at his watch as if he's trying to calculate how much longer he'll have to stay here, and she snorts. Then she sees him look up and watch a woman, a mother, walk past, his eyes sliding down her body and back up before he turns around to face the twins again.

Maeve feels a little sick. Does he always do this? Check out other women? Is she only noticing it now? He's a hypocrite, she thinks; he talks about family but all the while he throws himself into his work, his business trips, and perves on women who aren't his wife.

'I was just about to go looking for you, Maeve,' he says when she approaches.

'Can we go yet?' she asks, loud enough for Iza and Michael – who have escaped from the pen – to hear.

He checks his watch again. 'Yes, I think we've given her long enough.' Long enough, as if it's his job to parcel it out, as if they're all on his schedule. 'Are you feeling better now?'

'Yeah, my headache's gone,' she says with a sarcastic smile. But he's looking down at the twins and misses it.

'Good.'

'Can we get a toy?' Iza asks as they leave by the gift shop.

'Please, Dad?' Michael begs.

'No,' he says, peering to find the car in the car park.

It's just where you left it, Maeve wants to say. 'They deserve a toy for being good today.'

'They already have enough toys. Come on, you two.'

'Not even a pencil or something?' Maeve asks. 'You always used to let me buy a pencil.'

'We're tightening our belts at the moment. Come on, you two,' he repeats, as the thunderous look on Iza's face threatens a tantrum.

'Why? Is something wrong with your job?' Maeve asks as they weave through the cars.

'No,' he says, frowning. 'The house is expensive to run, Maeve. And your mother isn't working at the moment.'

'That's not her fault. She stayed home for me.'

'I didn't say it was anyone's fault,' he says, as he leans into the back seat to help Iza pick up a book from the floor.

Yeah, right, she thinks, getting into the front passenger seat.

'You'll be gone to university soon anyway, one less mouth to feed,' he jokes, as he starts the car.

She stares blankly out of the window and picks at a shard of fingernail. When she was sick she knew she was a burden; that was part of the pain, the guilt. And when he talked earlier of the hours he missed of the twins when he was at work, didn't he also mean the hours he missed with them when he was looking after her? The hours her parents couldn't spend together because they needed to be split between the children? If her parents' marriage is in trouble – and even thinking that makes her heart kick with panic – then isn't she to blame?

Her mother and Stuart are in the kitchen making dinner when they get back.

'Did you have a nice time?' Ruth asks the twins as they crowd round her.

'Daddy didn't let us buy a toy, even though we were good,' Iza says, betrayed.

'You're a big girl now, you don't need a toy just for being good,' she replies.

Maeve stands there, awkward, but Stuart seems nonchalant, his voice entirely neutral when he asks if she wants a slice of the melon he's just cut up.

'Sure,' she replies, feeling like she's on a stage as she crosses the room. She takes the slice from the knife he holds out, meets his eyes for one hot moment as she slips the melon into her mouth.

Behave, he mouths, and she hides her smile behind her hand.

'Is there any for me?' her father asks then and, flustered, Maeve mumbles something and leaves for her bedroom.

She begs off dinner early too, agitated by her parents, the wasps dive-bombing her plate, and the blinding evening sun. At sitting there pretending everything is normal.

She can hear the murmur of dinner conversation from her bedroom where she's closed the curtains but not the windows, so that the fabric billows out with the breeze, tickles her face where she lies on the carpet with the top of her head hard against the wall. Her body feels like it's fizzing. She wants to touch herself, to slide a hand into her shorts, to listen to Stuart's voice and remember yesterday, but she can't isolate his voice and even she isn't so sick as to do it right now.

This morning she had woken early and lain in bed for two hours as her room heated up with the sun just thinking about it, thinking of what happens next and thinking of what she looked like to him, whether she would look changed in that photograph he took, beautiful and *post-coital*, and not just flustered and out of her depth. He'll look at it again, that photo, when he's by himself, she thinks, rolling onto her front, pressing her pelvis into the carpet before the touch of the curtain on the back of her neck makes her jump up to sit.

She hears Stuart say his goodbyes for the night and checks her watch, calculating how much longer she'll have to wait for her parents to go to bed so she can go to him.

'So was it good today?' she hears her father ask.

'Yes, thank you.'

'Do we have another Picasso in our midst?' he asks, nonsensically. Maeve wonders what he means.

'I know that's a joke but it lands a little harshly,' her mother replies.

'Come on, Ruth,' he sighs.

'I'm just being truthful. How was your day? How was Maeve?'

Maeve stills, grabs hold of the edge of the curtain so it stops moving.

'It's funny you should ask. She's in a mood with me too – I seem to have hurt her unforgivably in some unexplained fashion, just like you.'

'That's not fair. She's just a child. She's been through so

much. Any normal teenage angst is to be expected, to be welcomed if you think about her only a year ago. She was like a wraith, it was like she had faded away. I didn't know if we'd get her back, our daughter and not just a shell.'

Maeve is barely breathing, her eyes stinging. She hears the glug of wine being poured and a few moments later, an empty glass being set down.

'She looks at me sometimes like she knows,' her father says, his voice low.

'Knows what?'

'That I gave her up,' he says with a huff of breath, a tone of self-loathing. 'That those years were too much for me. That sometimes when I left the hospital or I got on a plane for a business trip, I gave her up. I thought, that's not my daughter, my daughter isn't sick, she isn't dying. I pushed her aside, made her disappear.' He snaps his fingers.

'You don't mean it like that,' her mother says softly. 'It was a coping mechanism – your love for her was just hidden, you pushed those feelings deeper.'

'Is that what your therapist would have said? No,' he says firmly, with a hollow certainty, 'I know what I did and she does too.'

'So that night you called me, the one-night stand,' her mother recites with a brittle amusement, 'that wasn't because you were grieving?'

'Oh, it *is* that,' he exclaims. 'It's *that* that you're so pissed off about. Still.'

'Still?'

'You'll be pushing me into another one soon, you know.'

'You're drunk,' she states, 'and this conversation isn't going anywhere.'

'Oh, I think it's getting to the crux of things—'

'Alex,' she says firmly.

'Oh, I forgot, you're in control, sorry,' he says sardonically.

'We can talk about this, just not now when we're both tired.'

Maeve hears the clinking sound of plates being stacked, her mother moving things inside.

The smell of cigarette smoke drifts through the window as Maeve sits with her back to her bed, the edge of the base digging sharply into her spine. She's rubbing the heels of her feet back and forth over the carpet, her skin beginning to burn with the friction.

Her father had an affair. Her parents' disagreements, their discord, run deep and bitter, and her illness, her failing body, is a large part of it. And when she thinks about what her father said, about forgetting her, she feels her chin crumple, her mouth twist.

She waits, listening to her mother come upstairs, the muffled sounds of her washing her face and brushing her teeth, a drawer being opened and closed as she gets changed, and then the light being switched off. She waits for her father to leave the patio and come inside, for him to lock the front and back doors and come upstairs, for him to use the bathroom and then join her mother in the dark of their bedroom. But an hour later he hasn't come. It's past midnight and Stuart's probably gone to bed now too. Besides, if Maeve went to him now, she knows that the minute he opens the door she'll start crying.

In the end, she's half dozing when she hears her father come up the stairs. She drifts the rest of the way, wondering how you can have a conversation laced with such cruelty and then share a bed straight afterwards. If that's what marriage is then she doesn't want it.

———————

Inevitably, the moment Stuart's car leaves their drive the next day, after an awkward charade of nonchalance from both of them, and her mother cheerily waving her off, Maeve bursts into tears.

'Oh God, what's wrong?' Stuart asks, stricken, stopping the car on the path, reaching over to her.

'It's fine, please keep driving,' she says through her tears, 'please keep driving.'

'I will, but you're not fine,' he says, releasing the brake. 'Please tell me what's wrong? Do you want to go back?'

'I'm fine,' she repeats, still crying, as he takes the exit from the hamlet and turns onto the country lane.

'You're not, someone's upset you.' He glances over, checks his wing mirror. 'I'll pull in somewhere, just wait a moment,' he says, reaching for her hand and squeezing it.

He speeds up with a jolt, follows the bend of the lane, and then crosses into a driveway with a rotten gate in front of them and high hedges on either side.

The car stops with a deafening quiet. The engine ticks; the driver's seat creaks as he shifts around.

'Oh, Maeve, darling,' he says, looking at her.

'We'll be late,' she says, wiping at her eyes with her fingers.

'We're not going anywhere with you in this state. And besides, I'm the photographer, the artist, I can arrive whenever I want.'

'Really?'

'Who would argue with this face? Please, tell me what's wrong. Is it me?' He looks out of the windscreen. 'Have I made you uncomfortable?'

'No, of course not. It's just my parents. God, I know that makes me sound like a child,' she says, her breath hitching, her voice messy and high-pitched. 'They're fighting all the time and I don't know if they'll stay together, and what happens if they get a divorce? My dad had an affair, a one-night stand, and he was so mean to my mum and she's so cruel to him sometimes. And it's my fault, because me being in hospital was just like this – like this bomb going off,' she cries, splaying her hands. 'And it's ruined everything, it's ruined me, I think, I'm fucked up. And I'm worried my dad hates me, and he keeps asking me about university like he wishes I would just fuck off.'

'Hey, it's not your fault, hey,' he says, stroking her hair. 'Come here,' he says, pulling her onto her knees so she can lean forward into his hug. 'You're not ruined,' he murmurs, 'don't be ridiculous.'

'I'm sorry, I know my dad is your friend—'

'He *was* my friend; I'm not sure I know him any more.'

'You don't?'

'I don't think he treats you carefully enough.'

He rubs a hand down her back, strokes the nape of her neck. She trembles and shifts on her knees because the gear-stick is digging into her stomach. It's getting hot in the car without the air, and the sky outside is hazed. *There's a heatwave starting today*, her dad had declared, toast in mouth, as he left this morning.

'I'm sorry I ruined your day.'

'You haven't ruined anything.' He reaches into the back seat for a bottle of water that he drops in her lap. 'C'mon, that's fatalistic talk. You're heartbreaking when you cry, you know that?' he adds, framing her face with his hands, brushing away her tears.

'I'm ugly when I cry.'

He shakes his head.

'You're lying.' Her voice is gummy. She sits back and gulps down the water. 'When did you last cry?'

He starts the car, sets his hands on the wheel. 'I think I cried when I got drunk with a photographer friend of mine – we were toasting to the friends we'd lost.'

'I'd like to see you drunk, properly drunk.'

'Would you?' He smiles. 'Are you good to go now, you all right?'

'Yup,' she nods.

'Good girl,' he says, kissing her on the top of her head. He reverses out of the lane and she wipes at her sticky cheeks. 'It's only an hour's drive. I'm surprised you haven't been to visit it already.'

'Forty-five minutes in the car is Iza's threshold before she gets carsick. And my parents have been busy with the house.'

'I imagine it needs a lot of work.'

'I don't think they have the money for it. I don't think I'm supposed to know that. Not for the house and school for the twins.'

'They're not paying for your school?' Stuart asks. He glances over at her. There's something so masculine about his driving to Maeve, every small motion – checking the mirror, turning the wheel with one hand – so thoughtlessly at ease as to be mesmerizing.

'The local sixth-form college is meant to be good,' she says with a shrug. Is it uncomfortable for him to hear her talk of school, to be reminded of her age? If it is, he doesn't show it.

'I'm lucky with property upkeep,' he says. 'I only have a flat so it's a bit easier to look after.'

'In London, right?' She hasn't even asked him where he lives normally. It's as if he didn't exist before he arrived on their doorstep.

'Yeah, Richmond, near the river. It's nice.'

'I'd like to see it.'

'Maybe you will.' He smiles shyly and she grins.

He puts his arm around her shoulder and she leans back into it. To the cars passing they must look like any couple, off for a day trip in the sun. She in a summer dress and he in his olive-green t-shirt. 'I feel like I've been remiss in asking you any questions, like there's so much I don't know about you.'

'*Remiss*,' he teases. 'And ask away, I'm an open book. Truth or dare me.'

'Really? OK, truth or dare?'

'Dare.'

She taps a finger on her chin. 'I dare you . . . to roll down the window and sing "Happy Birthday" as loud as you can.'

He snorts. 'That's a small-time dare. Here you go,' he says, rolling down the window. 'Ready?' he asks her.

'Wait, I want to get a photo of you doing it, where's your camera?'

'I've got one in the back, a point and shoot.'

She takes it from the seat and pulls off the cap, positions it in front of her eyes. 'Ready,' she says, and he bellows out a raucous rendition of 'Happy Birthday' as the car slows down at a crossing, and she tries to hold the camera steady despite her laughter. 'You'll have to send me this photo. It's only fair that I get to keep one of you.'

'Done. Now, your go, truth or dare?'

'Truth.'

'OK . . .' He taps his fingers. 'Truth, did you fancy me the first time you saw me?'

'What makes you think I fancy you at all?'

'Oh, you're a tough nut, sweetheart,' he drawls.

She bites at the flesh of her thumb. 'I was surprised when I saw you – you weren't who I had expected.'

'I was more handsome, you mean.'

'Maybe. Truth or dare?'

'Truth.'

'Did you? Fancy me when you first saw me?'

'You know I did. When I saw you it was like getting kicked in the stomach. You with your hair and your big eyes. Truth or dare?'

'Truth.'

'Hmm . . . have you ever told a secret you swore you'd keep?'

'Yes. Hasn't everyone?' she says, curling a lock of hair tight around her finger.

'What was it?'

'It's not your turn. Truth or dare?'

'Truth.'

'Where's the riskiest place you've ever had sex?'

He laughs, rubs a hand across his mouth. 'Does a hotel under gunfire count?'

He's had a whole other life, other *lives*. How can she compare with some daring blonde photographer he shagged in a warzone? 'I guess so.' She picks at her nails. The air is so warm now that her fingers are throbbing. 'What's the worst thing you've ever done?'

'Oof, that's a big question. Going for the jugular.' His hands flex on the wheel. 'I mean, take your pick. I've stolen. I stole a jeep from the army once, in Afghanistan, nicked it so I could get where the fighting was, and who knows what knock-on effect that might have had. I've watched people do terrible things without intervening. Terrible things,' he says hollowly. 'I think I can confidently say I've seen the very worst of humanity. I've lied too, I've cheated. Some people might say that this,' he looks at her, 'what I'm doing with you is wrong.'

He's trying to scare her off. But she knows how kind he is,

how thoughtful, and it was her who pushed him into doing something more than just taking photographs. 'Why? It's legal.'

He sucks in a breath. 'Oh, legal doesn't always mean it's right.' They make a sharp right turning onto another lane, past the blur of a long red Volvo stuffed with children, and a village green opens out before them, cricket nets portioning out the sky, grass neatly clipped. 'What's the worst thing you've ever done?'

'I've stolen too. My mum's lipsticks, the twins' toys once when I felt jealous of them, five pounds from my dad's wallet to buy sweets that made me feel sick. I've lied.' She flips down the sunshade as the sun flashes through high trees. 'I've lied about you. I betrayed a friend once, in hospital. I told the nurses she was making herself sick and they sent her away to another clinic, put a feeding tube in her. She hated me for it, *loathed* me,' she says, trying out a word she's only read before.

'Sometimes people don't see that we have to hurt them to help them. Tough love, you know. Meanwhile, don't think I didn't notice you skipped two turns. Truth or dare, Maeve?'

'Dare,' she concedes.

'I dare you to take your knickers off, right now.'

Pervert, she thinks with a thrill, as the mood in the car turns. 'Only if you don't watch,' she says primly.

'I'll keep my eyes on the road, Scout's honour.'

'Were you ever in the Scouts?' she asks as she reaches under her dress, wriggles her hips to pull them down without flashing him.

'No, couldn't afford it, didn't have parents who cared either way. But I did spend lots of time starting fires in the woods and making dens.'

'In our woods?'

'Spoken like a lady of the big house,' he says and holds out his hand, raises his eyebrows.

She puts them in his hand, feeling a shivering, queasy rush as he stores them on the seat by his leg. A flash of pink against denim and worn car seat.

'I set a few fires in there, yeah. It's a good place to hide when you're a moody teenager, a good place to get up to mischief.'

'Maybe we should visit. Hey, there's a river there, right?'

'There is indeed. You read my mind – we can do a shoot there.'

'You still want to take photos of me?'

'Why? You think I've got what I wanted now?' Something like pity crosses his face. 'Oh, Maeve. Someone's done a number on you if you don't see how much more you have to offer.'

She's flustered when they arrive at their destination, not least because she only realizes they're there once the car has passed through the gates, and then she has to hurriedly put her underwear back on while ducking her body down and swearing at Stuart, who laughs at her. When the car comes to a stop, she tugs on the cardigan her mother insisted she bring despite it being blazing hot outside.

The house is grand, red-bricked – four soaring storeys with turrets and a hundred windows looking out onto the grand circular drive – and surrounded by gardens with strict hedges that stretch into the distance. Stuart shakes hands with the smart woman in a white linen suit and sunglasses who comes to greet them as Maeve picks her way carefully across the shingle in her flimsy sandals.

'The owners are occupied elsewhere today, but you informed us that you'd like to do the other pictures first,' the woman says.

'Yes, I'll do the house and get started with the staff today. You've told them about the project, yes? Handed out release forms?'

'I have.' The woman looks politely uncertain. 'And—' The woman looks between Maeve and Stuart.

'Oh,' Stuart says, clasping her shoulder. 'I brought my daughter along for the day, is that all right? Just to watch.'

'That's fine.' The woman smiles as Maeve freezes, holding her skirt down even though there isn't a hint of breeze.

The heat, and the lie, the unfamiliar setting, remind her suddenly of being on holiday, of the feeling that you have slipped sideways out of your life into another one, that all the normal rules have melted like ice cream in the sun, and soon the flagstones around the swimming pool will be so hot you'll have to make a burning run for it.

His daughter, she thinks, as they are led off and the woman glances back at them, *is that what we look like?* Any normal person would have corrected him, would be biding their time to tell him off, but Maeve isn't. Maybe it's the punishing heat of the day that seems to flatten any impulse to be indignant. Or maybe she is coming to like the way Stuart presses against the boundaries of right and wrong, how he folds her into his worlds of make-believe. She can be Ophelia or Persephone for him, his teenage lover, his daughter.

If Stuart owned this house, she imagines, as they slip inside the cool marble-floored hallway, past bronze lamps and antique umbrella stands, towards the stairs carpeted a lush red, she might have been his ward. She would be given a velveted tower all her own with a schoolroom, and in her seventeenth year she would be brought to him by her tutor on a hot summer's day in a froth of white and tightly laced boots to be told that she was promised to marry him, silly little fool that she was, and she would swoon, overcome with a snarl of so many emotions, of horror and trembling hope, Maeve thinks, as she clutches the polished banister and tips her head back.

She looks up to see Stuart standing at the top of the stairs with his camera, and the two versions of her – real and imaginary – seem to shimmer as he takes a quick photo of the grand staircase, and of her, before dropping the camera around his neck and turning back to their guide, and her crisp vowels and kitten heels.

Chapter Twenty

This morning I woke gasping for water, not air, choking on a hot, dry cough. It was late and I could hear Alex downstairs picking up his keys, putting on his shoes, the quiet snick of the front door closing behind him and then his car up the drive.

After Maeve and Stuart leave, I feel out of sorts. The twins wave away my offer to take them for a walk, or play a board game together, and when I sit down on the sofa in the living room they turn around – with one of those synchronized twin-movements that make your eyes feel like they've glitched – to tell me that they want to play alone, that I'm ruining their game.

It's the heat, I tell myself; that's why I have a headache, why I feel like a visitor in someone else's home. I take out the post, the bills and paperwork, trying to make sense of the detritus of my father's life, of the bills we have to pay. The sink and the water glass I left by it feel too far away from my seat at the kitchen table so I sit and sweat, letting my lips go dry, my headache worsen. I know what Alex's base salary is but not what his bonus might be this year, if he gets one at all, and it's hard to compare energy bills from the past, when my father was the only permanent resident, to a wasteful family of five.

Every time I try and make a budget, like the ones we kept to so strictly in London, I seem to add more and more expenses, my handwriting becoming smaller as though, if I could keep the list on only one page, the cost will be less too: new school uniforms for the three of them, stationery, sports clothes, all the extra classes that add up, the dentist, the two cars, the train season ticket, groceries, toiletries, insurance; the house – the oil for the Aga, the gas for the heating, the electricity, the pipes and the water, the ivy digging into the walls, the rotten windows, the roof—

Oh, to be a girl again, I think. To have no responsibilities except to dream, to brush your hair, to do your homework now and then.

I've picked up one of Iza's discarded crayons and am shading in the bottom of a piece of paper I realize belatedly is the drawing I made of Stuart. I drag it out from under my pile of paperwork.

Is there any talent to be found in it? I reach to pick up the red crayon and rest the point of it hard against the paper, near the line of his leg against the bench, thinking about scribbling in the whole thing, erasing it like a frustrated child. But it's the only art I've made in twenty-four years.

I've shaded the bottom blue and green now, a child's impression of an expanse of water. I'm embarrassed for myself as I take up my HB pencil and sketch a tiny figure of a girl standing in it, the water up to her thighs. It's easy to draw a dress, easier than drawing a man sitting on a bench with one leg crossed over the other, just a soft A-shape and floaty sleeves like elongated bells. I twiddle the end of my pencil to make flowers, dot the fabric with purple and yellow crayon points, the wax residue giving it texture. Faces are the hardest part, like Stuart's above; a wonky nose, the jaw out of alignment, shading instead of eyes because I lost my nerve. I draw the girl's hair instead, long and to one side, as if there's a wind blowing through her. Orange and then shaded with brown to make it look less like Pippi Longstocking. But now I've gone too far and it looks auburn, hazel, the colour of brown hair under dappled summer sun.

*

Another drunken afternoon at the river, or was it the same afternoon as the one with gin and orangeade? It's difficult to pin the days down, impossible to say which picture of us was taken on which day, or sometimes which girl was in the picture; we shared dresses, flowers, ribbons tied around our waists, we shared the river.

Linda was singing a folk song she had learned for an exam, something about a man lying in his bed on a windy night and the sound of his lover knocking on the window. Joan was making small plaits in Camille's hair, and Sarah and I were looking through a stack of Polaroids. The film had run out and there wouldn't be time to get another one this summer. It felt like things were all coming to an end, that I could already feel the cold breath of autumn, that the dry leaves on the trees were twitching, ready to fall.

'Do we have enough?' I asked Sarah. By which I meant, were these pictures enough to last us until next summer, or some future point when we were no longer girls and needed to look at them to know how lovely we once were. 'Do you think we achieved what we set out to do?'

'You're a perfectionist,' she replied, laying out a top row of pictures, close-ups: white fabric billowing in the water, hands curled in the cold of it, petals flecking the surface, flashes of pale skin and wet hair stuck to cheeks and chin. 'We started the summer with nothing and look at what we made.'

'How are we going to divide them?' Linda asked, stopping her song, her voice out of breath.

'What do you mean?' Sarah replied.

'I mean, who takes which ones home with them?'

'Hasn't the summer only just started?' Camille said plaintively.

'We've still got time,' I said to the group, but I meant it as a reply to Camille.

'We've only got a week,' Linda said, passing her cigarette to Joan and sliding her orange sunglasses back up her nose with the jaded insouciance of someone who has had many a teenage summer.

'School,' Joan said mournfully, 'and boys.'

'Like you're not dying for male company,' Linda said. 'You're fizzing with frustration.'

'I'm fine with the sisterhood, thank you very much.'

I raked my hand in the grass to my side and focused on the photo in the corner, one I had taken of Sarah on dry land, her hands clutched in the skirt of her dress, water dripping from her bare legs onto the earth. A week was not enough. I looked up to see Camille watching me from beneath her fringe, the bruise on her jaw still the same. I looked back down and flushed.

'I just think you've got to be realistic about things coming to an end,' Linda said.

'Who died and made you our mother?' Joan replied. There was anger simmering beneath her teasing – had something happened between her and Linda away from the river?

Linda arched an eyebrow above her sunglasses, crossed one leg over the other. She was wearing a miniskirt today and a crocheted top with straps shaped like daisies.

'If you're so keen for summer to end, to go to *university*,'

Joan said, with a singsong tone, 'then why be down here at the river at all? The boys are up at the house, and the interesting adults too.'

'It's you who's boy-crazy.'

'I mean, isn't that natural?' Joan said with a mean laugh. They seemed to be arguing from the same point of view, arguing against themselves.

'Joan is angry at me because she has a thing for Geoff,' Linda announced.

'Geoff?' I asked, baffled. In my head, any time we didn't spend with each other was time spent alone, or asleep, but what did I know about the other girls' lives when I wasn't with them?

'I do not,' Joan spat, rising up on her knees, hands in fists at her sides.

'And Geoff has a thing for me.'

'He has a thing for your tits.'

'Hey!' Sarah called out. 'No arguing at the river.'

'We're not arguing,' Joan said, and walked across the clearing to the old oak tree. She jumped up to grab the lowest thick branch. 'Linda is just being a bitch,' she added, hoisting herself onto it.

'She's so childish,' Linda muttered.

'I thought you said Geoff was a twat?' I was making a pile of the Polaroids in my hand, the shallow depth of them like a measurement of the summer.

'He's not bad when you get to know him.'

'What about your boyfriend back home?' Sarah asked.

'What about him,' Linda retorted.

'Is Geoff boyfriend material?'

What did that even mean? I pondered. I had been on some dates, group ones mostly, had kissed and been kissed, been felt up in the back of a cinema, and been sent several slapdash Valentine's cards. But I didn't want more than that; I didn't want a boy looking at me soft and hopeful, being tied to someone like that.

Linda shrugged.

I rolled onto my back, feeling irritated, stung, as if she had disappointed me personally. I flicked my eyes near the sun, winced when they hurt.

'You'll roll on top of them,' Sarah said, tugging a few photos from my side.

'Do we have more booze?' I asked.

'Yes, do we, Linda?' Joan asked, and then I heard the thud of her jumping down from the tree. She sauntered over, twisting her hips so that her feet met in a perfect line ahead of her, holding her arms out like she was on a tightrope. 'She has more, but she was saving it for a cosy date with Geoff.'

'I wasn't. I just didn't think it was a good idea for us to get drunk down here. I didn't want to carry any of you lot up the hill.'

It was a steep hill back to the hamlet, and nearly every time we climbed it one of us would groan and stop and say, *God, do we have to go back?* and be tempted to lie in the soft grass, to make a mattress from it.

'Hand it over then,' Sarah demanded. She poured a cup's worth of neat gin because we had no more mixer; the only liquid we had was the river water that we scooped out or bent over to drink from when we got thirsty in the sun. She moved towards the river. 'Are you coming?'

I slipped into the water behind her, glad for the distraction, for the pull and tug of the river, the burn of the cold on my skin, on my warm scalp as I dipped my head back. Camille followed too but Linda and Joan were still in a standoff, lying in the sun ignoring each other.

'Maybe the water will help your bruise,' Sarah said to Camille, holding the cup above the surface as she treaded water. She passed it to me and I took a sip, wincing at the taste and sipping river water afterwards as a chaser.

'Maybe,' she said. She sank under the water fully, her outline hazy and green, a few bubbles rising above her. I paddled closer, waiting with the cup, grabbing onto her arm when she emerged with a splutter.

'Here,' I said, and Camille drank the rest of it. Our legs met under the water, her toenails sharp on my calf. I looked over my shoulder at Sarah, who was floating with her eyes closed, and then back at Camille.

In the golden light of the sun on the water, I could see every freckle and blemish on her face, the flecks of light in her brown eyes. It wasn't fair.

Our legs tangled up again. I touched her waist to get my balance.

On the bank of the river, Joan was sitting up and watching us. I ducked under the water again. But my body was too buoyant, awkward in my attempts to swim away from Camille, kicking her accidentally and then popping up hardly a foot away.

'Sorry,' I said, and then swam in a backwards crawl that splashed Sarah and had her complaining.

Camille reached from the bank to get the cup refilled, gulping the whole thing down and then handing it to Linda when she grumbled that she was going to finish the bottle all by herself. When Camille slipped back into the river, she watched me, calm and intent, as I kneeled on the bottom of the river and felt the surface trickle past my chin, burble against my lips, brackish and metallic. The reflected sun was almost violent this close to the water, flashing into my eyes.

She swam across to me with an awkward paddle. I told myself not to look over at Joan, not to worry if she was watching us. We weren't doing anything out of the ordinary. I had swum topless with the others, had undressed them and done up the buttons of their dresses when their hands had curled into cold claws or their fingers pruned. I had brushed their hair and plaited it, spread suntan lotion onto burned backs and shoulders and noses, shared clothes with them, photographed them. All Camille and I were doing was floating alongside one another.

We stayed there until we were shivering. Not talking to one another, just floating, swimming, ducking under the surface or lying back and looking at the sky, joining in the conversation between Sarah and Joan, and Sarah and Linda.

It's the memory of that afternoon I remember most, viscerally – the bump of our legs, the slide of our arms, the way even when we weren't touching I could feel the swell of the water from her moving limbs, the crest of her strokes lapping against me. Sometimes even now I can feel phantom presses against my skin, frozen spots, a trembling in my flesh, as though the world is a large vat of water and the cold echoes of her kicks are still rippling out towards me.

Chapter Twenty-One

They tour through the rooms of the house, Stuart and their female guide, with Maeve trailing after them, touching the edges of polished tables and chairs, the fringe of curtains and embossed wallpapers, snatching her hand back innocently each time the woman looks over her shoulder with a polite smile.

She's keen on Stuart, Maeve can tell. The way she sways towards him, catches her fingertips on his chest when he makes her laugh.

'I'm at your disposal today,' she tells him as they cross the upstairs hall, past a tall marble table topped by an extravagant vase of dried flowers.

Stuart smiles back at Maeve and then she watches as the way he holds himself, his expression, change. 'You're too kind,' he tells the woman, his voice taking on a lilt, becoming ever so slightly camp. 'Now tell me,' he says, coming to a stop. 'Is that Chanel?' He points to the suit the woman is wearing.

'No, it isn't,' she replies, her smile dimming.

'It's just a great look,' Stuart says intimately, dipping his head.

'Mmm,' she says, her eyes darting out of the window. 'Do you need my help with anything right now or shall we check in later?'

'Later is good. I've got my assistant with me, after all.' He winks at Maeve.

'I'll be in the office if you need me.'

'Thank you, and thank you for the marvellous tour,' he says, and he and Maeve are left alone in the mother of pearl room, its ceiling-high cabinets inlaid with milky hexagons.

'You made her think that you were—'

'No, I didn't. I said a few things, let her draw her own conclusions.'

That didn't account for the way he had changed his body, his self, like slipping into a different skin, she thinks.

'Otherwise, she'd be following us around all day and we wouldn't get any peace.' He clears his throat. 'Sorry about my lie earlier, I couldn't think of a different excuse,' he says carefully.

She doesn't say that he could have just told the truth, that she was a friend of his parents'. He looks like he expects her to be angry with him so she only says, 'You're a good liar.'

'I told you I was. Now, let's continue on our tour, shall we?'

'I thought your project was about ruins?' she asks, her flip-flops slapping against the fine polished floor.

'If you talked to the owners of this house, they'd tell you that it was crumbling and that's why they desperately needed funds. It will be crumbling in parts. There'll be mould in corners of the ceiling, and the roof probably leaks and pipes have burst. But these are just the public rooms open to visitors. If we duck beneath the red ropes and go through the closed doors' – he opens a door that has been built flush to the wall and patterned with the same greying wallpaper – 'we might find some juicy secrets, or maybe just mice.'

'Don't say that,' she says, clutching the back of his t-shirt as they shuffle into the narrow panelled corridor.

He loops his arm back around her, gathers her in close. They enter a small room covered with dust sheets and Maeve watches as he takes preliminary photos, checking the light with his handheld light detector.

'Stand by the window a sec?' he asks.

She peels off her cardigan. 'Looking at you or with my back to you?' It feels so natural now to be photographed by him, she can't believe she was once so nervous and unsure.

'Look over your shoulder at me, yes, like that. You look forlorn and wonderful,' he murmurs as the shutter clicks in quick succession. He comes up behind her, putting his hands either side of hers on the dusty windowsill. The view outside is dusty too and the air is hot. He kisses the top of her head and presses closer. The muscles deep inside her abdomen spasm as he slides a hand over her waist.

'Here?' she asks as he kisses her neck.

'Hmm, you're right, we need somewhere more picturesque. C'mon.'

He grabs her by the hand and leads her out of the room, quickly along the corridor and then up a poky spiral staircase. They emerge into a carpeted hallway with dark low beams. He tugs her onwards, and they hurry past a dated bathroom and a bedroom wallpapered with a football pattern and an odd vestibule, and then he pushes open a double set of doors to bring them into a master bedroom. The room has rich pink and gold wallpaper, a four-poster bed, and a bay window looking out over the gardens. It also has a stained carpet, the detritus of the owner's life sprawled over it and the other dusty surfaces – dressing table, faded bench at the bottom of the bed – and clothes bulging out of the walnut wardrobe with a door off its hinges, a dying houseplant that litters the windowsill with its dry petals, used cups and glasses, a bin overflowing with tissues, and a chewed-up dog toy that Stuart kicks to the side of the room.

'Rich people are the worst slobs,' he says, shoving a dressing gown and a tray with a chipped mug off the bed.

The covers are crisp broderie anglaise at least, Maeve thinks, twisting her dress between her fingers.

He pushes open one of the windows with a creak.

'Someone will see that open.'

'We better be quick then,' he says, coming to stand before her, taking her hips in his hands. He nudges her backwards until her legs hit the bed and she falls back on it. He's blocking the sunlight so that she's in shadow and can't quite see his face. 'All right?' he asks.

She nods. He squats down and she lifts a hand to shield her eyes. His hands are on her ankles. He tugs her forward and her dress rucks up. She stares at the dark folds of the bed canopy, flexing her other hand in the sheet. His fingers slide up her thighs as her legs dangle over the end.

'Can I?' he asks.

'Yeah,' she says, feeling dizzy, feeling a squirm of horrified arousal when he helps her wriggle out of her underwear and she realizes she's already wet. She knows that teenage boys are the ones who are supposed to be obsessed with sex, but since Stuart arrived she thinks about it all the time, her body always thrumming, liquid.

He widens her thighs, curls his hands round them to grip. She hopes she looks all right there, that she doesn't look weird. She tries to shift her hips but he's caught her tightly, and somehow she likes that best of all. *Fuck.*

His mouth on her there, his tongue, the muscle of it obscene. His hot breath, the bones of his face hard against her pubic bone, pressing her downwards, his whole body between her thighs. She's making embarrassing noises, whimpers that increase every time she hears him grunt and every time she thinks of what they must look like; she caught and splayed on someone else's bed with the window and the door open, he with his hand in his shorts, the jerk of his shoulder rubbing against her leg as she throws an arm across her face.

Later, sitting on the grass outside the house eating a sandwich from the coolbag her mother gifted them, she watches hazily as Stuart directs two of the groundskeepers who are standing in front of their ramshackle shed with the silhouette of the main house behind them. In the blast of the heatwave, she feels daring, giddy, a buzz in her stomach each time Stuart glances back at her. She could feel ashamed, she could let herself tumble into an anxious slide, but, she thinks, justifying herself to an imaginary authority figure – a therapist, a doctor with a kind, pitying face – how could she feel ashamed when Stuart had made all the decisions, when he was the one who pushed her down on the bed, who took control?

The light has lengthened now, it's late afternoon, but it hasn't got any cooler. Inside, after Stuart took pictures of the maid in her cramped cupboard, carrying in two lamps to light it properly, he had taken pictures of the foreign cook and her help in the narrow kitchen while Maeve sat against the wall outside.

Maeve imagines accompanying him on all his shoots, driving across the country, trawling through stately home after stately home, poking into their back rooms, having picnics in the gardens. *How is this a real job?* she thinks, leaning back in the grass and tipping her face to the blazing sun. And how is she going to go back to normal once Stuart goes in a couple of weeks' time and she's left alone with her family?

'Did you not bring your own sunglasses?' Stuart asks her after putting his camera and bags in the car, sprawling next to her on the grass with his sandwich. 'Here.' He gives her his, and she holds them against her nose to stop them sliding down. 'You look fetching. The prettiest assistant I've ever had.'

'I can't believe we did that in their bedroom,' she whispers, giving up the sunglasses and holding her warm water bottle against her cheek. 'If someone had walked in . . .'

He snaps open the Coke he's pilfered from the kitchens. 'They would have thought me a brute,' he raises an eyebrow over the can, 'torn me off you to defend your honour.'

'Wouldn't they tell people? Wouldn't it ruin your project?'

'You'd be worth it,' he says, with an earnest shrug.

To inspire such devotion feels like walking across a very tall path, terrifying and thrilling and something Maeve will never be able to capture again once she's on solid ground.

'You said there was a swimming pool here, right?' she asks, brushing the crumbs off her dress and standing up.

'I did.' He squints uncertainly.

'Well?'

'I've created a monster.'

'I was promised a swimming pool – those were the terms of the offer,' she says tartly.

'Spoken like the granddaughter of a lawyer.'

They make their way through the gardens, asking one of the gardeners for directions and then following the slight tang of chlorine past a walled garden and through a pathway lined with fir trees, the dark pines incongruous on a heatwave day.

The pool is surrounded on three sides by brick walls with the fourth open to the view of the picturesque fields beyond. The pool cover has been rolled back already, the water a perfect still mirror reflecting the blue sky. Looking at it, Maeve can imagine the soft tickle of the lip of the water on her skin, the surface breaking and then re-forming seamlessly as she slips underneath.

'Did you even bring a swimming costume?' Stuart asks as she kicks off her flip-flops.

'Nope.' The flagstones are burning hot under her feet, the air dry, her head throbbing with the heat of the day. She stares at him as she peels the straps of her dress down and then shimmies it around her waist, pushes it all the way to her feet.

'Jesus Christ.'

His approval has a tremor of apprehension that thrills her. She saunters over to the edge of the pool in her underwear, glancing back to check that he's watching her, and then she dives in.

She twists her body under the water, kicks to swim deep, the bubbles from her mouth stroking down her sides, streaming past her legs. Her chest is burning by the time she skims over the shallow floor of the far side and pops up with a heaving gasp, grasping onto the edge.

'You're a natural in the water,' he calls out.

'I used to go swimming for my rehab.'

Her mum used to take her to the local leisure centre in London, its water soupy with chlorine, churned up by flashy male swimmers or rocked by the careful strokes of groups of elderly female friends straining their necks to keep their hair above the water. Ruth would watch from the spectator seats while Maeve did laps, wearing thick goggles that steamed up and left her blind and knocking into other bodies, flinching and grimacing at the wet slap of flesh, at the stray hairs that tickled her legs, the chewed-up floats that bobbed against the corners. Ruth couldn't swim well, or she hated the feeling of being in the water, some combination of the two that meant she would only ever dip her feet in when they were on holiday, no matter how much her children cajoled her, and stubbornly took poolside showers to cool down from the heat instead.

'You should come in too,' Maeve says, and turns onto her back, swimming towards the deeper end as the sunlight melts in silvery contours around her body. Stuart follows her on dry land.

'I'd have to come in naked, and I think being found like that might be pushing it.' He checks behind him again. 'You should probably get out soon,' he says, 'before someone really does find us.'

She shakes her head and ducks under the water, letting her air out in gusts of bubbles, sinking further to the floor until she sits on it. Looking up at the surface makes her dizzy, the sway and flicker of it like being in the sea. She pictures Stuart peering uncertainly into the depths, getting more worried the longer she is under the water. She feels the pressure in her throat, a squeeze in her head, and then she kicks upwards and bursts out.

Stuart is crouched at the edge, his sunglasses on the top of his head. 'Are you done?' he asks.

'I don't think so,' she says and dives deep again, spiralling her body in the water, kicking out wide, scything through the water. She breaks the surface just to gasp in another breath and then swims deep again, cheeks hurting from smiling. If she refused to leave, would he jump in and drag her out?

'Maeve,' he says again when she pops up close to him, 'c'mon now, I really don't think you'd like to be caught like this.'

She wouldn't, but the gardens are so big and the day is so hot – who's going to bother coming all this way? She bobs in the water, hiding her smile.

Her joints, her muscles, are starting to burn now so she

grasps for the edge, but she misses it and then sinks further under in a disorientating rush of water. She reaches up for it again and her feet scrabble uselessly against the side.

Two tight bands clamp around her forearms and then she is being lifted up out of the water, spluttering with shocked laughter as Stuart rocks back on his heels and steadies her to stand, her fingers gripped tight in his t-shirt.

'All right?' he asks, pushing her hair from her face. 'This is becoming a habit. You, drowning. Me, saving you.'

'I could dive in again,' she says, jolting her body.

He grabs her. 'Don't you dare. You're all slippery, it's like I've caught a mermaid. A mermaid with see-through under-wear,' he notes, hand skimming down her chest before he lets her go.

'You know the mermaid story, the original one, was darker?' Maeve says as he picks up her dress for her. She lifts her arms for him to help her on with it. The version of her from a few weeks ago, the girl who used to get changed in a cocoon of towels, would die at flashing her chest for the long few moments it takes him to tug the dress down. 'She dies at the end, no happy Disney ending for her.'

'I think I might have heard that before, but my memory is like a sieve.'

She twists the water out of her hair and it splatters over their feet. 'When you get older, do you forget more? Like, is there a finite limit to the mind's memory?'

'Maybe? For me, it's my youth I remember most now, vividly, in tiny detail. And certain moments abroad, but sometimes the rest of it's a blur.'

'So your memory's getting worse with age, you mean?'

'Are you calling me old?' he asks, as he guides her towards the gate. 'Are you worried I won't remember this? You, Maeve?

Because I can tell you right now that I'm going to remember everything.'

She stops him in the fir tree passage. 'You say that like there's going to be an end, like this is temporary.'

'You'll grow up, you'll meet someone your age.'

'I don't want someone my age. I want you.'

'For now.'

'I'm not going to change my mind.'

'I'd like to think you won't, but I'm just trying to prepare myself.' He strokes his thumb on her cheek, kisses her before she can reply.

On the way back through the house they run into the woman with her clipboard.

'What time should I come tomorrow to photograph the family?' Stuart asks.

'Any time after nine.'

'Excellent, I'll see you then.'

It's dark in the hall, but as they leave the doors and are hit with the full light of the sun, Maeve wonders if she can see the damp patches Maeve left on Stuart's t-shirt, the wet twist of her clutching hands.

The car is scorching hot; the seats make her yelp as she slides inside.

'So, home now?' he asks.

She rests her shins against the burning dashboard, her head on her knees. The air that blasts out of the vents is warm and stale, but she'd rather stay here in the car, rather cramp her limbs inside it, than go back home.

'Or . . . shall we stop off somewhere on the way?' He turns the car round in the circular drive. 'A pub maybe? Sit in the garden there and have a drink? You can blame me if we're late, I'll tell your parents I lost track of time or got lost.'

'Yes, please.'

'As my lady commands.'

She pushes the tape into the stereo and the whine of an electric guitar, the throb of a drum machine, fill the car underneath the noise of the road and the wind whipping through the open window where her elbow rests. At a stoplight he reaches back to retrieve his camera, takes a quick picture of her and then drops the heavy camera into her lap. She thinks about scenes from films, of what couples do in cars, and wonders if he'll dare her to get undressed again. It's enough to think of it, to watch him and listen to his music, and to imagine the road will keep unfurling in front of them.

He doesn't introduce her to anyone at the pub as his daughter, just stands at the bar with an arm around her and orders a gin and tonic for her and a beer for him, leading her out of the back door with a hand low on her hip.

'If you keep looking at me like that,' he murmurs close to her ear as the dark of the garden, lit only by weak strings of lights, envelops them, 'I'm going to get arrested for public indecency.'

'Have you ever been arrested?' she asks when they take their seats side by side at a picnic table, turning her legs to rest on his lap.

'Maybe,' he says, lighting a cigarette.

'Can I try?' She holds out her hand.

'Nope,' he says, blowing his smoke away from her.

She sips at the fizz of her drink and smiles. *See, Mum*, she thinks of saying, *he looks after me, he's not that bad of an influence*.

Her parents would be horrified if they knew what he had done, what she had agreed to, and that horror might be thrilling in a reckless kind of way, a *so-there* sticking up of her fingers, but only for a moment; then everything would implode.

But why should it? She's legal, they know him, he's their friend. She'll be at university anyway next year, and she's always hearing about students having affairs with their teachers.

He's curling locks of her hair around his fingers, dropping his hand to stroke down her back, to brush his knuckle down her arm. If he goes, all these little tendernesses of his go with him and she'll be all alone again.

'What happens at the end of the summer?' She stops his hand and he turns his wrist and laces their fingers together, the cramped fit of his knuckles painful. 'Tell me?'

'At the end of the summer – in about two weeks' time – I'll go back to London, and you'll go back to school.'

He sounds resigned and she feels a tickle at the back of her throat, her voice gets thick. 'I don't want to.'

'Maeve.'

'I won't survive without you, I know I won't. I can't bear staying with my parents.'

He kisses the top of her head, and she feels the press of his chin against her crown as he says, 'Maybe you could come live with me.'

'My parents would kill me, and you.'

'Well, it's your choice ultimately – you're seventeen, aren't you, they can't drag you back. If you want to, you can.'

'You don't really want me to though,' she says, 'not really.' Her heart is beating very fast.

'I do.'

'It would be a mess, there would be drama and gossip, my parents would hate you.'

'You'd be worth it.'

'Did you fall out with them?' she asks, tracing his knuckles where his hands are in her lap, curled around the hem of her dress. 'Is that why you never visited or called?'

'If I had visited and you had grown up with me as an uncle, I'm not sure this would have happened, do you?'

'You didn't answer the question.'

'We outgrew each other,' he says, his beer glass knocking gently against her head as he drinks.

She's sitting in his lap now, enveloped, safe.

'Groups of three never last long. There's always one person on the outside. They had each other and what did I have?'

'What about the girl, the one who left you?'

'Oh . . . that was before university. But don't worry, I had lots of girlfriends afterwards, I haven't been a monk,' he says, tickling at her side.

'Any redheads?'

'Mmm, nope. Just you.'

Just her, she likes that. 'I feel like I should ask you questions about what my parents were like before they had me—'

'For blackmail?'

'No!' she says with a laugh. 'Why? Do you know something bad?' she asks, twisting round and peering at his face in the dark.

'I'll have to think about that,' he says, and then takes a sip of his beer with a smack of his lips. 'I can't believe it's still so hot at this hour. It's like we're in the Mediterranean or something. Like we could walk to the end of the path,' he points his arm, 'and the beach would be right there. We should go on holiday, you and I. Where would you like to go?'

She sighs and stretches her toes. 'Florence? Venice?'

'Good choices. For a start,' he says, and then he tells her all the places he will take her, the villages and beaches, the temples and museums and art galleries where he will take her picture in front of gorgeous backdrops, the hotels they will sleep in and the campsites they will rock up to at midnight, the food he'll cook over a fire, or the restaurant where he'll ply her with so much wine and ice cream he'll have to carry her home.

In the car she feels achingly sad, gripping the edge of the seat with her fingers as if she can slow them down.

'Was I an accident?' she asks, resting her cheek on her knees again. 'Mum getting pregnant with me?' Her parents had pushed her grandfather away and Stuart, and now they're pushing each other away too. Maybe they only ever stayed together because of Maeve.

'If you were, it was a happy one. They were devoted to you. Your mother didn't want kids when she was a teenager, but then lots of people think that when they're young.'

'It's ironic,' she says, 'because I can't have children.' Tears leak from her cheeks onto her legs.

'Are the doctors sure?'

'Very sure.' She wipes her eyes with the back of her wrists. One of Stuart's hands is woven in her hair. 'It's fine if you're a boy, a man, you can freeze stuff. But there wasn't enough time to take my eggs. I don't even *want* children.' She's still a child herself, she feels, still wants to be looked after. 'I just feel like this is the end, this drive, this day with you,' she sobs, 'I feel like everything is going to disappear and be *over*.'

He jerks the car to a stop that rocks her forward, her knees and palms hitting the dashboard hard. They're on a quiet countryside lane but another car could drive behind them at any time.

'The car—'

'I'll start it again when you believe me that I'm not going to leave you, that we'll figure something out. Even if we have to wait until you're eighteen. OK?'

'OK.' She nods quickly.

'Sorry,' he says, as he starts the car again. 'Shit, sorry.' He rubs one hand over her knee, glances back and forth between her and the road.

She circles her sore wrists. 'It's fine, I'm fine.'

'I'm sorry if I scared you.'

'You didn't.'

'You were scaring *me*, you sounded so hollow and sad. I hate the thought that I've ruined this summer for you, made you upset.'

'You haven't.'

'God, I'm sorry,' he says. 'You were crying this morning in my car and again now. Maybe we'll just take trains from now on, it'll be safer.'

'I'm only crying because of them,' she says, waving her hands at the dark outside the window, the beams of the lights low and mesmerizing, as if the road is rushing towards them as the car weaves around tight corners. 'Not because of you.'

On the lane to the hamlet, he brings the car to a stop again, slowly this time, turning in his seat to take her face in his hands and kiss her for so long she finds it hard to catch her breath, her lips feel bruised and swollen, her tongue sore.

'Better?' he asks.

'Yeah,' she says with a laugh. 'Thoroughly mauled.'

'Right, let's compose ourselves.' He straightens his shoulders, cracks open a pack of gum and hands her a piece. 'Good to go?'

'Good to go.'

Her mother is a silhouette in the doorway as they approach the house. When Stuart leaves the car he doesn't look back at Maeve or put an arm around her, and even though Maeve knows he can't now, she misses it, blames her mother for it.

'I was going to send out a search party,' Ruth says. She looks anxious, peeved.

'So sorry, Ruth,' Stuart says, hoisting his heavy bag back on his shoulder. 'It was my fault – I got caught up in my work and then we had to stop at a petrol station on the way back and I got completely turned around. Maeve here was a faultless navigator though, it was all me.'

'Did you have a good time?' Ruth asks her, reaching out to cup the back of her head.

'Yeah.'

'I'm not sure I've seduced her to the dark side of a job in the arts yet, but I'm working on it,' Stuart says, and Maeve chokes on a cough.

'Well, you're the first ones home – Alex is still at work, apparently,' her mother says with a tight smile. 'Thought I was going to be left to raise the twins myself,' she adds as they follow her into the kitchen. 'It's a cold dinner, I'm afraid, I just didn't know what time anyone would be back.'

'It's fine, Mum—'

'That's fine, Ruth—'

They share a look as her mother sighs in front of the open fridge.

'So, tell me all about it, darling,' she says, brightening her face. 'How was the maze, did it have a maze? I can't remember, sorry.'

'It had a folly,' Maeve said, 'but we didn't walk that far in the heat.'

Stuart slips away to take his camera bags back to the annexe and Maeve tells her mother what she did that day, besides the obvious. She's a good liar, she thinks, or maybe her mother is just too distracted to see that she's lying. Ruth keeps checking her watch and peering out at the dark of the garden as though it might tell her something about her husband's journey back from London.

Maeve humours her mother right up until the point when she remembers that her father had an affair, that he's *late from work*. Then she feels anxious, a bitter twist to her gut that she had to return here at all, to have to be a spectator to the charade of her parents' marriage.

But she doesn't have to stay here, she reminds herself – as she rolls a bruised apple from the fruit bowl noisily back and forth across the table until her mother tells her to stop, that she's got a headache – because Stuart is going to take her away from here, help her start again somewhere new, be someone new.

Chapter Twenty-Two

Three days into the heatwave and the twins have turned feral. Running around the garden in their underwear, demanding the sprinkler be turned on and that they be given enough ice lollies to turn their tongues blue, lying in warm piles and bemoaning that they are *too hot, Mummy, too hot*, like little aristocratic lords sojourning in the jungles.

'It's hot for everyone,' I tell them, as they moan, 'everyone experiences the same weather.' But they are unconvinced; their pain and discomfort are unique.

Every teenager thinks their angst is unique too, and though it's true there are variations and gradations, youths who are beaten, who live in appalling poverty, who are severely unwell, I tell myself that underneath, what Maeve is going through is just a flavour of the norm. I tell myself this to try and understand her, this sullen almost-adult who looks so much like me from the corner of my eye, with her red hair and floral summer dresses, that it makes me nervous.

Yesterday, the doctor called with the good news, that her results were all clear, that she was still in remission.

I wanted to run and hug her, to spin her around in my arms like I did when she was little, before she got ill, but her bedroom door was closed and she kept saying she would be *just a minute, Mum,* so I had to tell her the news through the door and wait for her to shuffle out and stand there awkwardly while I hugged her.

'It's good news,' I said. 'I'll phone your dad and tell him too, he'll be delighted.'

Her smile was strained and it frustrated me.

'What's wrong? I don't understand.'

'Nothing's wrong.'

'Are you sad you're not ill, is that it?' I said. It was a joke but I meant it too. Children who have been invalids can get stuck, the family therapist we consulted said. They fear the unknown, even if the unknown is good health and a future without a dark shadow over it.

'No.'

'You have your whole life ahead of you, your whole life. You can choose anything, go anywhere, be anyone. You can meet someone, get married—'

'I can't have children though,' Maeve replied. It felt like she was trying to hurt me; there was something about the bitter edge to her voice that seemed like a dig.

'There's lots of ways to have children, remember what the doctors told you? There's surrogates and adoption.'

'I just want to rest.'

'You've been resting all summer!' I had become one of those mothers I hate, the ones with bright voices and chivvying smiles.

'Can I go back in my room now?' she asked.

'Sure. We'll celebrate the news at dinner, OK? I can make the chocolate torte for you, or maybe some wine?'

'Fine,' she said, and closed the door slowly.

My smile dropped. Maybe this was why my father parented at one remove, maybe any rejection hurts less then. I rubbed a hand across my forehead and felt the smarting of my eyes, before the twins called for me and I returned to the kitchen, finding them splattering water from the sink onto the floor because they couldn't fit their bucket under the tap.

'There's a tap outside,' I snapped, as I grabbed for something to mop up the water and got down on my knees. 'You used it this morning.'

Is there anything that makes a person want to cry more than spilled liquid? The way it creeps slow and yet faster than you can react to, rolling along a sloped floor or slopping down a table, soaking into tea towels and your shorts and ruining everything.

I let myself have a short cry, a few sobs, a pitiful sniff, there on my knees in the kitchen while the tap outside made the pipes under the sink bang and hiss and I counted down the hours until dinner, until bed.

Stuart left yesterday afternoon for a week, called away on a favour for a friend, and the house is quieter. I miss him and dislike him for missing him, for coming back and offering a friendship that somehow doesn't feel equal, and for our last conversation which left me feeling sore.

The twins certainly missed his usual tricks last night at dinner, the juggling he does with the cork mats and the stories he makes up about the fantastical beasts he's seen on his travels, and had to be shouted at to sit still. It felt awkward between me and Alex too, with no other adult to look to, no one to smooth the sharp edges of our conversation – when Alex eventually came home, that is. He has an important project, he says, and he'll be needed late at work for the next little while. *Is the important project a brunette in a tight blouse?* I want to ask, but I know that would just start another fight.

'Do you think Alex hates me?' I asked Stuart two nights ago, when we sat at the bottom of the garden with the sherries I had poured from my dad's old stash. Alex had gone to bed at eleven but I didn't want to lie awake for an hour next to him, feeling the yawning cavern of things not said.

'Ruth,' he admonished sadly, putting an arm around my shoulder. 'Alex doesn't hate you.'

It felt good to be held. How long had it been since Alex and I had touched one another so easily?

'Marriage is hard,' Stuart declared.

'How would you know?'

'Relationships are hard and marriages are only long relationships with some extra legalities. Why do you think I'm still single? Staying with one person, growing at different speeds, hoping that your feelings will stay the same through time. Impossible.'

'You're supposed to be encouraging me.'

'Am I?' he asked a little pointedly. He took his cigarette pack out of his pocket and I drew back.

'Of course you are.' I wrapped my arms around my shoulders.

'At dinner,' he said, putting his cigarette behind his ear, 'you said you didn't swim.'

We had been talking about holidays. Alex had been musing about our next destination and how there was no point in getting a villa because I couldn't swim. Then I said that it was silly to think about holidays anyway, when the upkeep on this house meant we wouldn't be able to afford one in the near future.

'I *don't* swim, I didn't say I *can't*.' When I turned my head towards him I felt dizzy. Too much sun, too many drinks.

'Because of what happened?' he asked.

'Yes,' I said. 'But do you want to know a secret?' I added, as if we were children again and testing our friendship by the stories we spilled – and ignoring the part of me that remarked that Stuart had only really shared the one story with me, that long day when I drew him, that I seemed to be the only one giving parts of myself away.

'Always,' he said and tucked my hair behind my ear, and I felt reassured.

If I had married Stuart, would things be different now? Would he be devoted to me or would he have run away from me when I couldn't give him what he wanted, my devotion in return?

'In London, Alex made me get a therapist,' I confessed. 'Well, he didn't make me, but he was worried, he felt helpless and got frustrated with it. You know how he is with things, how he wants a rational answer. I was struggling too; Maeve was so ill and the twins were such a handful. So I called up some woman and booked an initial appointment, a consultation. She was in Hampstead – I don't know why I didn't go with someone closer, I must have been given a recommendation from someone, I don't know. Anyway,' I continued. Stuart was watching me closely, bent over with his hands clasped in his lap, mirroring my forward hunch, my arms thrust through the hollow of my thighs like I was a girl again. 'I got to her house and stood outside looking at her front garden, looking at her front door. I was picturing the whole thing. Saying *Hi*, walking in, polite chit-chat and then us sitting down so I could spill everything out, so I could sob in a beige-carpeted room in some stranger's house.'

'You didn't go.'

'I didn't go. I went to the Heath instead. It was late spring,

a warm day but not a summer's day, not yet. I realized I was
following someone walking through the wooded path, matching
my stride to theirs, and then they arrived at the ponds, holding
the gate open so I could follow them. The swimming ponds,
you know. Have you heard of them?'

'I have, yeah. Never been.'

'I didn't have a swimming costume but the lifeguard must
have seen how desperate I was, must have wanted to soothe
this crazy lady who just turned up with her handbag, and said
there was a spare in lost property. So I got changed and then
I stood at the top of the ladder, staring down at the murky
water, wondering what the hell I was doing. It was icy cold,
I've never felt something that cold. I slipped off one of the
rungs of the ladder and went under and it was like – like a
hundred icy needles in my skull, like I had thrown myself into
a fire. When I breached the surface I was gasping and laughing.
It was incredible.' I shook my head.

'Cold water shock.'

'Yeah. I only managed five minutes or so that day and my
hands were still claws when I got out. My skin was humming
for the rest of the day, I had this glorious shivering feeling in my
chest. I went back once a week, sometimes more, built up my
exposure as the water got warmer, swam full lengths, got stronger.
It was my little slice of paradise, my hour snatched from the
world. I kept waiting for someone to notice. I had to keep my
swimsuit hanging on the balcony where Alex never went, but I
still thought he'd notice that I smelled like pond, that my hair
was damp, that I had leaves from the park stuck to my shoes.'

'Why didn't you tell him? Why don't you tell him now that
you can swim?'

'I lied to him for too long, it would sound so strange. He would
be hurt.' Maybe when you tell one lie, hide one truth, you get

used to it, it becomes a habit. I clinked the lip of the sherry glass against my teeth, wishing I had brought the bottle with us too.

'He still doesn't know about the girls, does he?'

'No.'

'Jesus.' I heard the rasp of his hand across his chin.

'I'm sure he doesn't tell me everything about his childhood.'

'I'm sure he'd tell you if he was there when someone drowned in front of him.'

My breath caught. The garden around us felt very still, bright somehow, hyper-real. 'Don't—'

'What? Don't say it?'

'You've never talked about it either, you never mentioned it to me.'

'Because I knew it would make you upset.'

'It does, so don't.'

He scoffed. 'So we can only talk about what you want to talk about?'

'That's not what I said.'

'I was there too, you know. I dream of it, don't you?'

'Don't—' I shook my head.

'Fine, whatever you want,' he said, and got up and left.

The gate to the annexe creaked in the thin air and a bird skittered away unseen in the sky.

*

Maybe the river has dried up in the heat, or will do soon, if it doesn't rain again. Maybe it will never rain again.

In my memories of that summer, it's always hot – blazing perfect summer days – but if I think hard I can remember the rainy days too, the overcast skies that turned the river pale with cloud, dulled the dizzy sparkle of its surface, how we got cold so quickly in the water and then huddled for warmth with a blanket if we remembered or a scarf, elbows linked tightly together and legs jammed up against one another. Because our cameras were cheap and over-sensitive, the photographs we took on cloudy days had more detail in them – ribbon trim, the floral pattern of a dress, the shade of eye colour and the sheen of lipstick – whereas the ones taken on sunny days were often bleached by it, or came out almost black if the strong shadow of the trees hit the river right.

It was sunny, but not hot, that afternoon when Linda and Joan had their argument, when Camille and I had swum beside one another for so long our skin went blue and the skin on the bottoms of our feet furrowed, our fingerprints lost inside pale topography. It was sunny even when we left the river, and in the woods the light broke through the leaves and shone irregular shapes before us.

The other girls had gone on ahead, Joan and Linda still ignoring each other, and by some unspoken agreement, Camille and I had been slow to get out of the river and dry ourselves with a scarf and a jumper, slow to shake out our legs so we had enough feeling to walk from the clearing as the sounds of the others drifted away.

'I'm going to miss the river,' I said, reaching out to touch a low-hanging branch, cupping the leaves, careful not to pull any off.

'Me too.'

The empty camera was slung around my neck; I had almost forgotten it. I wished that I had just one more film, that I could lift up my camera and stare at her through the lens, that I could record every change of her expression, every angle of her face.

'Thank you for the silk nightgown and the tea dress,' she said, stepping over a root, 'I still haven't paid you back.'

'They were a gift.'

'But I didn't get you anything.'

'Did you really fall down the stairs?' I asked, watching the way the dappled light hid and then revealed the mark on her face. 'You can tell me.' There was something forlorn about Camille even with her quiet strength, something she held back.

She studied my face, opened her mouth and then closed it, looked away. 'I really did. I was reading a book and I missed a step.'

'I don't like to see you hurt,' I said. I felt chivalrous towards her, protective. In the woods with my hair tucked into my hat I thought of *A Midsummer Night's Dream*, of *Twelfth Night*, of a girl played by a youth and a boy playing a girl playing a boy.

'I've always been clumsy,' she said, and then proved her point by tripping over her own feet.

I caught her hands as she threw them out and we broke into laughter, our bodies loose with it, with the afternoon's alcohol, and she wobbled again. We stumbled sideways off the path past a dry prickly bush that sheltered us from the rest of the woods. I pressed her shoulders back against a broad tree trunk for balance, my diaphragm aching.

'Ouch,' she said, gasping for breath and touching her face. 'It hurts my jaw to laugh.'

'You're sure it isn't broken?' I touched my thumb to it, felt the heat of her skin again, the softness.

She shook her head and my thumb slipped along her jaw. I kissed it, the bruise, a soft peck. And then kissed the edge of it, closer to her mouth. I let the corner of my mouth meet the opposite corner of hers, feeling her quick exhale searing hot on my chin. Then she pulled me towards her by my neck, knocking my hat off, and kissed me properly.

I was shaking as her hands roamed over me. Everything was so much, every touch and sound and taste. This was awful, I thought, and wonderful, and I wanted her so much I felt my jaw go tight, knocked my teeth against hers as we kissed. I slid a hand down her back, the bark of the tree rough against my knuckles, and then across her backside, tugging her hips towards mine. Her fingernail caught on my stomach as she fumbled for the button of the jeans I had cut up to make shorts. The fabric of her skirt pleated in my hands, slipped away from her skin so that I could feel the short hairs of her thighs against my palm. My hands went inside her knickers; I felt the first touch of her, like dipping a finger into the molten centre of a candle, and I jerked back and turned away.

It was bright suddenly and I was frozen. I watched the wind rattle a dry twig along the ground, refusing to look at her, to see the disorder of her hair that I had tumbled out of place, to see her – blame me? To see her look at me as if I had *done* this to her?

'Your hat,' she said and bent to pick it up, dusting it off. She held it out to me.

'Thanks,' I said but it took me a moment, a sharp breath, to reach out my hand, to glance up as I took it back.

There was a fervour in her eyes that terrified me. 'I knew you felt the same,' she said. Was this worse or better than her hatred? Her lips were swollen, looked soft.

'It's nothing,' I insisted, moving away. 'It's just the gin, just a game.'

'OK,' Camille said. But I could tell she didn't believe me.

It's just the booze, the sun, the heat, the river, I told myself. *It's just a moment of madness that won't ever happen again.*

*

Four days into the heatwave and the air feels like an oven, the leaves in the garden are crisping yellow, the nights never cool down and I can't get any sleep – I feel as though my breath might evaporate, that the hot air might rush into my mouth and muffle me as I lie in bed with all the windows wide open and the curtains perfectly still.

Alex says the trains are hellish, that by the time they reach London the tension has boiled to fever-pitch and arguments kick off at the turnstiles. The twins are simmering with frustration; the sprinklers aren't enough for them, the cool baths I give them make them cry, they don't want to eat dinner. Maeve doesn't want dinner either; she stays in her room with the door closed, and when I call through and say that she needs to let the air flow in, that it's cooler downstairs, there is either no reply or later I see her slipping down the stairs and out of the door in a short sundress and no shoes and returning hours later, her cheeks so red from the heat they looked slapped. She skips lunch and refused to come down for dinner yesterday, and I would be worried about her following her friend Georgia except that when I open the fridge or the bin the next morning I see evidence of her late-night feasts.

'She's just being a teenager,' Alex says, his voice slow with exhaustion when I tell him I'm worried.

Alex arrives home hours late for dinner and the act of saving him leftovers, heaping them up on a plate so he doesn't even have to serve himself, makes me feel that I am some 1950s wife and exactly what I swore I'd never be.

I keep thinking of what the girls would think if they saw me now, what *Camille* would think, and it makes me feel a trembling pinch of shame. I picture them following me around the house, leaving wet footprints on the carpet, trailing damp hands on the wallpaper, peering at me with an insolent sneer, or worse, a deep sadness, as I pick up dirty clothes and make beds and wash dishes and scrub the bathroom.

One morning, overheated, jumpy and dry-mouthed from lack of sleep, I imagine that the dripping sound isn't from the broken tap but from a wet plait swung over a shoulder or soaked curls heavy on a shivering girl's back, and I turn around expecting to see a younger version of myself among the ghosts, looking at me in horror, as if I am the spectral presence haunting her.

Chapter Twenty-Three

Maeve had two blissful nights with Stuart, slipping out into the warm breath of the night air and across the path to the annexe, the moon her only witness. Inside, the space was lit by a lamp that Stuart moved to the bedside table when he took her to bed, and the blue dial of the radio that crackled and hummed, Stuart turning it up to share a song with her and then Maeve padding across naked to turn it back down when the distracting voices of the DJs returned, turning to find Stuart watching her. After she left the annexe, she pulled her hair across her face to smell the scent of cigarettes and aftershave, wondering if he was doing the same with his hands.

But then Stuart said he had to leave for a week.

'It's a favour for an old friend, he's got some horrible virus and he needs me to cover his shoot,' Stuart told her at the bottom of the garden as the overgrown grass throbbed with crickets. He had ventured upstairs in the house to find her, knocking on her door so softly she knew it was him, telling her to find him in the garden in a few minutes' time.

'Can't you say no?'

'Only if I want to burn bridges, and besides, it pays more than double what I usually get, money that we can use, you and I, in London.'

'It feels like you're leaving me.'

'Oh, Maeve. It's just a week. And you can call me. I have my mobile phone with me, I'll give you my number. You can call me anytime. Here.' He tore a piece of paper off his notebook from his bag and wrote a string of numbers. She hadn't seen his handwriting before; maybe she had seen his notes but she had been too distracted to focus. There are so many things she has left to learn about him – habits, stories, skills. Perhaps he feels the same way about her.

He leaves her with his number, with five photographs of her, and with a kiss stolen against the back wall of the house, just out of view of the windows, the bricks scraping her shoulder through her t-shirt.

At first it's fine, the ache of missing him, the anticipation of his return, its own kind of pleasure. She goes to the annexe, rifles through the things he left behind in his haste. Notes about photography, the settings on his camera and for the developer – numbers and strange symbols. To be able to look at an image and know how to make it better – brighter, darker, louder, quieter, more beautiful – would be a wonderful skill to have. She avoids his books of photographs, all those images of destruction and death; it doesn't seem right to scoop them into her self-indulgence. She puts on one of his t-shirts and shoves her feet in the pair of shoes he left, marvelling at how much larger they are than hers, and then she lies on the bed whose sheets smell of sweat and – she can tell the scent now – sex, and pictures them here as they were, feeling mildly, recklessly regretful that he didn't take any photos of that.

She's brought the photos of her with her from her room. He didn't leave any in the annexe and not just because he doesn't want them to be found, it's because he's covetous of them, of her. She looks at them – at herself in the field and submerged in the bath. The colours of the bath photos are washed with blue, or is it that the blue already there has been pulled to the surface? She doesn't know what it's called but the whites are bruised, there's a bluish blush in the shadows of her neck and collarbone, and she can see a vein on her temple and on her throat. The ones in the field glow an orangey yellow, her hair brighter than it is in real life, the grass brassier. In one of the photographs in the bath his hand is touching her jaw, his skin darker than hers, his knuckles gnarled. She thinks of how one night he took her hand and traced the scars on his body with her limp fingertips. *Aren't you going to tell me the stories behind them?* she whispered. *Not yet*, he said, *we've got time*, and then he put his own hand on her breastbone, over her heart, and she thought it was like he was a surgeon; if he pushed his palm, he could crack open her ribs tenderly and grip her heart in his fist.

It's difficult to use the phone without her mother seeing or hearing; the signal isn't strong enough to take it further into the gardens. She risks it the first day, swaddling herself in the blankets of her bed as her mother helps the twins with lunch, catching Stuart as he is walking down the street in London. *Are you being good without me?* he teases. *Are you?* she replies, and hides her grin at his laugh in the back of her hand like it might give her away. Returning the phone to its cradle in the hall without being seen is stressful. It's easier to call him that night, when her parents are finally asleep, taking the phone into the living room, lying on the couch in the darkness.

There is an intimacy to talking on the phone that she hadn't noticed before. The gust of his breath, the clearing of his throat, his rich laughter, seem to travel straight into her mind, bypassing her ears. It makes her stomach twitch, her toes curl.

I like your voice, she says into the dark of the room.

Do you? he replies.

There's things that she feels she can't say over the phone, words and expressions that might be whispered to him inside a room with a proper lock or hidden in the fields, but not here in the house where she keeps her other ear cocked for noise, for intruding footsteps.

Maeve is tired the next day and has a headache that the heat only worsens. She lies in the bath, watching the way the water rocks up and down the channel between her breasts, inspecting her body, pointing her feet and imagining that her photograph is being taken like some coy Hollywood starlet, hair gathered in a clip on her head, bubbles hiding her nakedness.

She slips under the water, trying to make it so her nose and mouth are the only parts of her face above the surface, but the water keeps sloshing up over her chin. Her hair feels like a cape around her shoulders, luxuriously soft in the water. A muffled sound becomes an insistent knock on the door when she lifts up her head. 'Don't use all the water,' her mother calls. 'The twins need a bath today too.'

She knocks again and calls out her name until Maeve replies, 'All right!'

Maeve waits a good ten minutes and then rises from the bath, the sudden shift in gravity, the weight of her body in the air, making her dizzy for a moment. She watches as the water glugs down the plughole, sucking against the sides, and wraps herself in a towel.

Her mother is in the hall, rifling through the cupboard, and turns when the door squeaks open. 'Are you OK?' she asks.

'Yeah,' Maeve replies.

Her mother pauses with one hand on the shelf. 'Are those bruises on your knees?'

'I tripped.'

'Looks painful.'

'You know I bruise easily.' Her hair is dripping down her back but she's still warm. 'It's too hot.'

Her mother smiles. 'You sound like the twins. Hey, wait,' she adds as Maeve opens her bedroom door. 'Can you try these shirts on, see if they fit for school?'

Maeve sighs, wishing she had never got out of the bath.

'It's not that big a chore, is it? Trying on a few shirts? You try on half your wardrobe every morning,' her mum teases. 'And don't stay in your room all day, it gets too hot in there.'

That afternoon, while going through a box of things from London she had yet to unpack, Maeve finds an old card from her mother that went with a present of a pair of pearl earrings. She gave it to Maeve when she had completed her chemo and before the complications that sent her back to hospital. *We're so proud of you*, her mother wrote, although her dad had only signed the card, not composed the message. *We're so proud of you, you're the bravest person we know, our warrior.*

Reading the message, seeing her mum's love and hope, her jangling nerves, makes Maeve cry silently, her mouth an ugly grimace, her head throbbing as she wipes her cheeks. There is something about knowing that after this card Maeve got more ill than she had been before, so ill she would have welcomed death. She wasn't a warrior then, just a tired girl.

There is something too about the love of her mother set against the way Maeve feels irritated with her now, frustrated, scornful. Her parents do love her, but Maeve can't stay their little girl and she can't stay here with their fighting, her mother's stifling attention. Leaving with Stuart might be an acceleration of things, an abrupt rupture, but it's only natural that she grows up.

On the second night, she creeps down at 1 a.m. to phone him. The twins were awake late with the heat, and her parents argued about whether Alex should bring an electric fan back from London. *To spend that much for only one week in a blue moon is ridiculous*, her mother had said.

We can't afford to buy a fan? You're being over-dramatic, he had replied.

In the afternoon, Maeve had picked a rose from the garden and stroked its petals until her fingertips felt buzzy and over-sensitive, but when she tried to plait it into her hair the brambles only snagged and scratched at her neck. She's plucked the petals off now, is cupping them in her spare hand as she dials him.

How was your day? she asks, the teasing 'darling' implied.

Swell, he says, *long. I got through it by knowing I'd be speaking to you tonight. How was yours?*

A little sad.

Sad?

I don't know.

Are you looking forward to the river photoshoot when I'm back?

We're still doing that?

Of course we are, Maeve.

On the third night, Stuart takes twelve rings to answer and he has to shout to be heard over the noise. He's at a party, he says, he'll go outside, *Call me back in a moment.*

She holds the phone to her chest and counts to a hundred, staring at the dark ceiling, feeling a shiver despite the heat of the night.

Am I selfish? she asks him after the opening pleasantries are over. Every bad thought about herself is swirling in close now he isn't here for her to focus on, to tell her she's OK, that she's good.

You are, but I like it that way.

Sex, he's talking about sex and the way they are together. *You can tell me, you know*, she says, dropping her voice to a whisper, bringing the phone tight to her mouth, *what you want me to do.*

Yeah?

She likes that it feels daring, a little wrong, but afterwards she seems even more aware of her loneliness, the quiet of the house, all the empty rooms, her family fast asleep. Her body feels so small, unanchored.

You are my one good thing, do you know that? Stuart says. He's been drinking; she can tell by the shape of his words, the rise and fall in volume.

I am?

Yes. I went through so much shit, you don't even know the half of it. I walked through hell and then I come back home, tail between my legs, and there you are, waiting for me, and you're perfect.

On the fourth night he doesn't answer. The automated voice tells her that his number is *unavailable.* She calls four times but the answer is the same.

Back upstairs, she can't sleep; her body feels hotter than ever, her breath tight. She hates the night, and the house, and her room.

She locks herself in the bathroom and gets in the shower without turning on the light, fiddling with the controls to make it too cold and then too hot. *Tell me you love me*, she thinks of saying to him the next time they speak. *Tell me you won't leave me, promise.*

In the morning she wakes with the sheet kicked off and her t-shirt rucked up to her waist. She curls onto her side to stare at the postcards on her wall; the models and muses, the mythic heroines, the perfume adverts.

If she put her own pictures up there, would they fit?

Will Stuart's project go on display one day, and where? She can only be so many heroines with red hair – Ophelia, Persephone, the Lady of Shalott – even with wigs she's not sure his project can just have one model. Who will the others be? Has he already met them or will he in the future? Will they be as young as her? Or cool, composed, knowing?

Eventually she gets too hungry, too hot, to stay in bed, and picks up an apple and a pot of the twins' Petits Filous from the fridge to eat with her fingers, hurrying through the front door before she's seen.

The sun outside hits her like a clap but she keeps moving, across the gravel and through the disorientating shade of the tall bushes and trees either side of the gate, until she reaches the bright field and slips into the overgrown, yellowing grasses. She pauses at the top of the field and bites into the apple, which was once crisp but is now soft and lukewarm on her tongue. It's impossible not to think of what she looks like right now, not to be both inside herself and outside, watching. With her loose hair and short purple dress, long bare legs and apple held in one pale hand, she would make a good picture. *Click*, she thinks, blinking her eyes and imagining Stuart is somewhere further below.

She trains her gaze on the woods and wonders if it's any cooler inside them, what the river will feel like when she wades into it and lies down in the water, and, with a numb kind of curiosity, what will happen to her, what she will do, if Stuart doesn't return.

Chapter Twenty-Four

There are muffled voices in the night – they drag me out of dreams of drowning, they rise and fall like the lap of water against stone – but by the time I am thinking straight and have heaved myself upright in the solid heat of the air, I'm unsure if they were only a dream, if the sound I catch snatches of is only the breathing of the house, the crackle of the fridge.

Sometimes I only remember them the next day as I wash my dry eyes, hold my wrists under the tap to cool them, and tilt my head as if I could catch the hazy memory.

'Were you on the phone last night?' I ask Alex one morning, when he wakes early for work and gets dressed with silent efficiency.

He looks at me over his shoulder. 'I didn't know you were awake. And no, I wasn't. Are you having funny dreams again?'

'I'm hardly sleeping. Didn't you notice me tossing and turning?'

'You know I sleep heavy.'

'Well, I hope you have a good day at work.'

'What's that supposed to mean?'

'Nothing! It was just small talk.'

I was trying to get things back to normal but I was too tired to make my voice sound anything but weary, and for weary read accusative. In a marriage with children, you can't ever say you're tired and have it mean only that. 'I'm tired' becomes part of a competition or a recrimination, a result of something the other parent didn't do.

'I hope you have a relaxing day at home,' he replies, doing up his tie.

'Now you're just being a dick.'

'I meant it nicely. Have you seen the glorious weather outside?' He tugs open the curtains and I wince. 'What I wouldn't do to sit out in the garden and not on the train or in an office without air-conditioning until 7 p.m., I mean, God.'

'It's too hot.'

He shakes his head in disbelief as he takes his wallet out of the bedside table. 'When did you get so negative, Ruth? All your children are healthy now, you have the summer off from work, you live in this wonderful house. Why is your life so hard?' He closes the drawer sharply. 'Sorry, I'm just—' He throws up his hands in quiet defeat. 'I'm just trying to figure out how we got here, you know?' He stops at the door with his back to me. 'They say contempt is the sign that a marriage is really over, and I look at us and I think . . .' He trails off, taps his knuckles on the doorframe and leaves.

I stare at the ceiling, my eyes burning, my body still. He deserves a better wife than me, and my children deserve a parent who doesn't snap at them, who has the energy to play and not just nag.

Four nights into the heatwave, I hear it again. One voice, maybe two, and girlish laughter.

Is it the twins talking in their sleep?

I stand overheated at their open doorway but their bodies are still, quiet. I stand at Maeve's closed bedroom door and hear nothing either. If Alex wasn't still asleep in bed I would think it was him, phoning up some late-night lover.

I try to doze back to sleep, but I keep getting distracted by the shushing of Alex's breaths which turn into waves in my mind, my body twitching like some unfortunate beached creature.

There. A feminine voice, a laugh. I grasp for the wall, the door, as I stagger out of the bedroom, blind from standing up too quickly. The world outside my head comes into view again and I wait, hand on clammy chest. The voices have stopped but there is a creak downstairs, the sound of something living.

I walk down the stairs, hand tight on the banister, and when I reach the bottom and look to my left my lungs spasm with panic.

'Hello?' I ask in a choked voice.

The dark shape moves and I make an awful moan, and then I realize that it's only Maeve wearing a large t-shirt, her pale legs sticking out of the gloom.

'What are you doing?' I whisper.

'Nothing,' she replies.

The phone is missing from its cradle on the hallway table. 'Were you talking to someone on the phone?' Who would she be talking to? A friend? She hasn't called any friends all summer. 'Is something wrong?'

She puts the phone in her hand back with a soft beep. 'No.'

'Maeve.'

'You're going to think this is silly . . . but I was phoning the speaking clock.'

'What?'

'I woke up and my watch doesn't work and I wanted to know

the time. I remember someone mentioning it at hospital once, that you could call at any hour of day.'

'You could have checked the clock in the kitchen.'

'I told you it was silly.'

'It's fine. I just heard a noise.'

'Sorry to wake you up,' she says, as she climbs past me on the stairs.

I wait for the soft sound of her door closing before I take the phone and bring up the previous number dialled. Sure enough, it's the clock. *At the third stroke, it will be two thirty-two precisely.*

I think about her late-night call the next day, as I struggle to open some of the windows on the second floor, their hinges rusted, the paint littering the carpet beneath them and only giving me more work to do. Was it because she woke up from a nightmare, or because she felt alone in the middle of the night? There is something horrible about the thought that she might be so desperate for comfort that she calls an automated voice.

Something isn't right with her, I know it, and I'm not going to miss it again, to ignore it, like I did the pain she felt before I finally took her to the doctor's.

I knock on her bedroom door, dumping my armful of laundry on the carpet. There's no answer so I knock again, call her name, and then lean my hot ear to the wood. Hearing no signs of life, I open it carefully and walk inside, expecting to see something wildly out of place, something that explains what's wrong.

Messy piles of clothes, tissues stained with smeared lipstick, the shine of CDs strewn near a Discman. Dusty soft toys at the bottom of her bed, unmade sheets that smell stale, air several degrees hotter than the rest of the house because the

windows haven't been opened. There's a jewellery box on her
desk that I don't recognize, and when I lift the lid a ballerina
spins to the brassy music. I snap it shut.

Does she still read? I wonder, looking at her shelves, at all
the cracked spines, their colours soft and faded. When did I
last see her with a book? What does she do all day, what world
does she disappear off to?

I run my fingers along the books, so many too young for her
now. Noel Streatfeild and Roald Dahl, the set of Narnia books
that Alex and I used to read to her when she was quite little.
I remember he and I had an earnest discussion about whether
she should read the last book in the series, the one where
everyone dies and turns up in a strange hallucinogenic heaven,
and how it turned out to be her favourite. When I asked her
why, she said it was because it was comforting that no one
was left behind, that they all went to the same place. Ridiculous
in hindsight to try and protect her from death when she would
come so close to it. Sick children make it hard to believe in
any kind of merciful god.

I thumb through its pages and a spray of pink petals, dozens
of them, falls out over my hands, onto the floor.

I stumble back, a cold flood around my heart.

They're still soft, the petals, not yet crispy and dry, just like
the ones I saw on her floor earlier this summer and hadn't
been able to find the plant they came from.

I pick up another book a few along and flick through it.
More petals join the pile on the floor, yellow this time, so
flimsy they flutter slowly down to the old carpet. The same
carpet that I had as a child.

I stride to the other end of the shelf and take another book
with trembling hands, shaking it out roughly by its spine as
though I'm shaking out dust from a cloth. White confetti falls,

dozens and dozens of petals so thin that when I bend down to touch one, the barest smear of my fingertip tears it into nothing.

Another book conceals the same secret, and another one, and again. Small daisies and blue cornflowers and orange dahlias. So many petals, so many flowers, all hiding here innocuous in her books, hiding beneath the faded covers, and now the air smells of them, of bouquets held in sweaty hands, of drooping fistfuls of flowers and garlands gone limp in the sun—

'Mum!' a voice screams, and I am being pushed away from the shelf by Maeve. 'Get out of my room! What are you doing?' She scrabbles at the petals on the floor. 'You've ruined them! Why would you do that? You've ruined them,' she says, sobbing. 'I hate you!' she swears.

'I'll get you more, I promise, I'm sorry.'

'You can't,' she says. 'Just get out! Get out!'

I back up towards the door, hands raised as if to ward off a wild animal. 'I'm so sorry.'

She never said where she got the flowers from; but where did we get our flowers from? My garden, other people's gardens, the florist. Has she been walking all the way to the village? Cycling there?

I stop in the doorway. 'Maeve, I just have to say—'

'Get out!'

'If you're cycling to the village on the road or you're walking there, it's just too dangerous; there's blind spots on the lanes, you could be run over.'

'I'm not going to the village.'

'Please, Maeve.'

She slams the door shut in my face and I flinch back, wanting to cry myself.

———

The heat makes alcohol hit your body harder, at least that's what it feels like to me. I'm sitting on the patio two glasses of sherry down and my head feels like cotton wool, the muscles in my face treacle-slow. The twins are watching yet another video, I've failed as a mother, and I am cursing this hellish heatwave that shows no sign of ending, the yellowing grass in front of me a marker of shame. I've brought the phone out with me in case it rings with one of the handymen Alex said was going to call, and so he can't complain at me for not answering, and sure enough, right when I think my face is probably beginning to burn despite the sun lotion, it rings.

It takes me a few moments to identify the caller because he sounds equally surprised to be calling.

'Stuart?'

'. . . Ruth? Hello there.'

'What are you calling for?'

'To check you hadn't chucked my things out of the annexe yet, of course.'

'Oh yes, we've got guests lining up for the five-star luxury here. Do you know,' I say, reaching for the bottle and sitting up so I can get my hand around it properly and bring it towards me, 'the black mould in our utility room is growing – it's on the ceiling now and I think it'll spread upstairs soon, I noticed it this morning. Do you think that it's bad to breathe in? I think it is. It's lucky the twins don't have any in their room. This house is a death trap,' I grunt as I pull out the sticky bottle topper.

'Put Alex on it – he should get his hands dirty, do some good honest work.'

I laugh. 'What's wrong with the chemical business?'

'Oh, where to start.'

I sip the sour bubbles of the sherry, vile stuff. 'We miss you,

you know.' It's easy to forget our last terse conversation, easy
to feel hungry for his friendship again.

'I miss you too.'

'I doubt that somehow. Where are you now? Is that a party
in the background, at' – I twist my empty wrist – 'whatever
o'clock it is.'

'No, just city noise.'

'I miss that too. Hold up the phone for me.'

'Ruth.'

'Go on.'

He does as asked. I close my eyes and press the phone
tighter to my ear, so hard the cartilage of my ear hurts, but I
can't make out the sound of traffic on the road or beeping
traffic lights, heels on pavement or laughter ringing down an
alleyway, snatches of conversations as people hurry past. Just
a muffled hum and a few horns.

'You got it?' he asks.

'Sure. Sorry, I've been rambling on, what did you want?'

'I think I might have meant to phone someone else actually?'
he says, sounding baffled. I picture his squint, the tilt of his
head, how he'll smile like he's making fun of himself.

'I'm glad you called, I was going stir-crazy here. This heatwave . . .'

'Tell me about it. At least my hotel has a pool.'

'Git,' I swear.

'I'm joking. How is everyone? The twins? Maeve?'

'My children are turning feral in this heat. Maeve is cycling
through her missed teenage years at lightning speed.'

'Mad dogs and Englishmen. Where are you right now?' he
asks.

'On the patio, looking at the overgrown lawn.'

'I can picture you there,' he says, and I think that I don't want anyone to picture me as I am now; old, sweaty, burnt, halfway to drunk. 'Actually, Ruth, I've been thinking about something.' The background noise has dipped as though he's sheltering in a doorway. I hear his breath against the receiver – does he hear mine too? 'You lied to me about the ponds, didn't you?'

'No? I lied to Alex about going to them.'

'Ruth.' He sounds disappointed in me. Kind, but disappointed. I want to tell him to piss off. I want to tell him, to trust him.

'I don't know what you're talking about.' I stand up carefully, each movement precise despite my dizziness, despite the queasy knot in my stomach, pulling out the chair and pushing it back in with a quiet scrape of the patio stone.

'That figure you mentioned following,' he says as I look for shade in the garden – there's only bushes inside the walls of the back garden, the fruit trees are outside it, the larger trees are on the boundaries of the property or at the front of the house, and I can't exactly lie down next to a bush. 'It was a woman, wasn't it?' Some of the branches of an apple tree shade part of the bench at the back, and that is where I sit, the dry wood scraping my bare thighs, my feet white in the sun. 'You went to the ponds once a week to swim with a woman; you went for her,' he says.

'I don't know what you're talking about,' I repeat. Could I hear the twins from here if they called for me? I stand up on my tiptoes but the flower beds, the lavender bushes, the azalea and rhododendrons are too tall. Too tall to see over but not tall enough to shelter behind.

'You can tell me, you know, like I told you last time. I'd never judge you.'

Like he told me last time. I shake my head, the phone dangling from my hand. *Like he told me last time.*

'Ruth? Are you still there?'

'I'm here.'

'Was it because of Alex's fling?'

'When did I tell you about that?'

'I overheard you arguing.'

'I don't see why any of this is your business,' I note, standing up and stepping into the sun.

'It isn't, you're right. I guess I just assumed you might not have anyone understanding to talk to, someone who knows Alex, who knows *you*.'

'Do you think we're still the same as we were back then? Don't you think people change?' I tug at a bunch of lavender and the whole bush shakes, two white butterflies flee.

Her name was Sylvia, the woman at the ponds, a pretty name for a handsome woman who wore her hair short and black and had the mahogany lipstick of someone who worked in the media, who was artsy, serious. *Lipstick lesbian*, I had thought the first time I saw her, having read such a phrase a few years ago, in an article about how it was now *hip to be gay*. She was the one I had followed through the park and the one who I swam with once a week when I was pretending to be at therapy. It was she who had befriended me, but it was me who never told her about my husband and children, hiding my wedding ring in the pocket of my jacket, never mentioning that I had come from the hospital where Maeve was seriously ill and that after I left the ponds or the cafe in Hampstead where we went for tea and cake, still smelling of pondwater, of weeds and damp cold things, I would be returning there too, or hurrying home to pick up the twins from their minder.

Why lie to her? Why cheat on my husband and my children like that?

Nothing happened with Sylvia, except her finding out the

truth in one awkward phone call to our flat when Alex had
handed me the phone and I had to say *my husband* in response
to her question of who she had just spoken to, and tell Alex
that it was just a mother I had had coffee with, while inside
I was dying, pickled in the worst kind of shame and burning
regret. Our friendship had been teetering at the threshold of
being something more and I had spent our time apart
daydreaming, picturing her and me and an impossible life
together, all the gut-wrenchingly embarrassing minutiae of it
that makes me sweat now to remember. The perversity of
imagining such a cosy *married* life with someone other than
my husband.

That was the night when it rained and I stole into the park,
walking through the dark like I wanted to be swallowed by it,
as if I were daring all those seedy strangers who were supposed
to live in parks eager to prey on women taking shortcuts to
come and get me, gasping at every shift of tree in the wind,
every crack of branch in the undergrowth, too far gone to cry.
I climbed the locked gate, shed my clothes and slipped naked
into the black pool of the water, so dark it seemed like my
limbs had been neatly erased, that I was only my head, my
thoughts. But there was nothing to be found there, no answers,
no relief, just the muscles of my body burning, my feet dragging through the silty water and a chill that made me despair,
at both the boundless cruelties of nature and at myself for
performing such an empty ritual. Grown up now, I could no
longer sink into a picturesque story, an imagining, when I
dipped my body into water, couldn't see the beauty in my
tragedy, only the embarrassment.

'I'm late for something, I need to go,' Stuart says on the
phone.

'Me too.'

I return to the house, carrying the bottle inside from the patio and returning it to the high shelf above the fridge. The twins sit around the kitchen table as I make dinner, chicken in a white wine sauce. I sip from a glass of the cooking wine as I listen to their impassioned review of the film, as I answer their questions about why people don't have swords any more, how they could make a magic potion and if there are any poisonous flowers in our garden, all the while feeling as if I am floating above myself or, when I catch sight of my hands and the murky reflection of my face in the windows as it turns dark outside, feeling that I have retreated so far inside myself that there is only a facsimile of me left, a dry husk.

'Have you got everything in for tomorrow?' Alex asks when he's home, as he opens the fridge.

He hasn't noticed my turmoil. Perhaps a paper cut-out of myself is all anyone in this family needs. Perhaps the answer is to give up any lingering echo of my own desires. 'What?'

'The lunch?'

'I forgot about it.'

'Ruth,' he sighs, like I have disappointed him, like a disappointed father. 'But you've had time to finish the wine, I see.'

'I used it for dinner.'

'The sherry too?' He nods to the shelf above the sink.

'I'll rustle something up from what we already have.'

'Great,' he says, unwrapping the dish of chicken.

'Great,' I repeat.

'The last big meal of the summer, I imagine,' he adds.

The evening of the last dinner party of the summer of '73 ended with two bodies being pulled from the water of the river.

But no one needs to know that, no one needs to remember, least of all myself as I stand in the kitchen of my childhood home, and hear the drip-drip-drip of the kitchen tap and the rock forward of Alex's chair that sounds for a moment like the knock of knuckles on the doorframe.

Are you coming to dinner, slowpoke? Joan says in my memory, standing at the door where I stare now. *The sooner we eat, the sooner we can go to the river.*

She winks and turns on the spot, pale petals drifting down from the garland on her head, skirt billowing out, and I want to freeze her there, to freeze myself too, young and hopeful and free.

Chapter Twenty-Five

The petals Maeve collected from the flowers Stuart had posed around the bath were ruined yesterday when her mother snooped in her room. Maeve tried to pick them up one by one, to lay them back in between the pages, but they stuck to her sweating hands, they folded over and tore. She cried onto the books and the petals, and the salt in her tears made her cheeks feel hotter, her mouth sore. Why couldn't her mother leave her alone? she thought. Why did she have to ruin everything?

At lunchtime the next day, returning sun-dazed from the field, the smeared remains of the petals are still there, rotting now in the heat. She thinks of telling Stuart about what happened, how he will offer to buy her a dozen new bouquets, pick the flowers himself if he has to. *It's not the same*, she'll tell him, and he will understand and that's why they fit each other, why he is right for her.

She's not going to go downstairs for lunch, no matter how many times Ruth calls up. Maybe she'll refuse to join her family for any meal, sneak things from the fridge and the pantry, eat in her room or outside. What can they do about it, anyway? There's no way to punish her worse than how she feels.

She slips into the junk room and rifles through the boxes carefully so that nothing falls or makes a noise. She's looking for more photographs of that summer, of Stuart; even though she doesn't have an emotional connection to the younger version of him, a blurry image is better than none.

The twins are outside the window on the front lawn; they're ratty today, contrary, shrieking, she could hear them earlier from her room. But it means that Ruth will have to supervise them, that she won't have time to snoop, to dog Maeve's steps. She's been asking Maeve how she is, if she's looking forward to school, if she's growing gills spending so much time in the bath, using a bright nervous voice and looking at her with widened eyes. Her mother feels like she's losing her, like Maeve is slipping her grasp. She doesn't know that Maeve is already gone.

A knock on the door of the junk room, and the cricket ball Maeve has been squeezing in her fist falls to the floor.

'Can I come in?' her mother asks.

Maeve looks out of the window and sees the white hair of Mrs Quinn with her hand shading her eyes, watching Iza and Michael.

Her mother knocks again and pushes the door open slowly, without, Maeve thinks viciously, actually waiting for an answer.

'Are you looking for something?' Ruth asks.

'No,' Maeve replies and then she changes her mind, her irritation at being found catching into anger. 'Have you even looked in them? His boxes? They're all dusty.'

'I haven't had the time.'

'Like you didn't have the time to visit him when he was ill?'

A flash of anger, of hurt, across her mother's face. Ruth taps her fingers on the shelf next to her, opens her mouth to speak and then combs her other hand through her hair. 'My relationship with your grandfather was complicated.'

She's going to tell her something now, Maeve thinks. A small kind part of her wants to say, *You don't have to spill your secrets to me because you think you're losing me*, but the other part is only hungry.

Ruth crosses her arms. 'Your grandfather could be cold . . . callous. He wasn't supportive like your dad is with you. Once I was eight or so, he left me alone to raise myself. It was a different time back then, I know, but still—' She rubs a thumb over her wrist. 'He didn't like me, Maeve,' she says carefully, 'and I'm so glad you'll never grow up like that, with a parent who dislikes you, who often seems to hate you.'

'Why? Why did he hate you?'

'I don't know.'

'There must be a reason.'

'If there is, I don't know what it is. Except that I couldn't compare to my mother in his memory.'

'Do you look like her?'

'I look more like him.'

'If he was so horrible, why did we see him at all?' she presses, unsatisfied with her mother's vagueness.

'He wasn't horrible to you. He was a good grandfather, he adored you . . . When he held you and watched you, I used to think, *Oh, is this what he was like with me, after my mother died, when I was small?*' Her smile is pained. 'I thought maybe being a grandfather had mellowed him out, even if he was still off with me, still cold. I thought we could put the past behind us. But then we were both at an event in London – it was an art opening, I didn't know he would be there, I think he was with a client.' Her eyes lose focus as she remembers. 'I had just found out that I was pregnant with the twins. I ran into a friend at the event and I remember she was congratulating me, touching the bump, when I noticed him across the room,

watching me. He looked . . . disturbed to see me, *horrified*.'
She shakes her head. 'I don't know how to describe it. He left
the room, but I followed and caught up with him outside. He
wouldn't look me in the eye. He just kept asking me, *What
are you doing here?* as if I had sneaked into his own private
party or something.

'I remember wondering whether he was there with someone
he didn't want me to see him with, a woman, a sensitive client,
I don't know. I'd never seen him like that, so flustered. Maybe
I should have waited to tell him, phoned him up, but I thought
he'd be happy to hear he was going to be a grandfather again.'

'He wasn't?' Maeve asks as her mother's voice trails off.

'No,' Ruth says dully, and then rubs her hand on her neck.
'It's such a mess, that conversation, I don't even . . . He called
me selfish, I remember that. He asked how I could do that to
Alex, that if he had to raise children without me it wouldn't
be fair. *Do you want your daughter to be motherless?* he hissed
at one point. *Do you know what damage that would do?* I told
him I wasn't leaving Alex, that I didn't know what he meant.
Why would my children be motherless? Did he think something
was going to happen to me like my mother?'

Maeve knew that her grandmother had died in birth but
had considered it only as an abstract, a family curiosity or a
quiet absence, until she was hospitalized herself and started
to think of her at odd times. This woman who went into
hospital and never came out again, whose body carried her
mother's body inside her safe for nine months before failing.
I've never liked hospitals, her mother had said near the beginning of Maeve's stay. *Who does?* Maeve had retorted in her
mind before remembering. The echoes of her mother's grief
scare her, the trace of the lost little girl in her voice, then as
well as now.

'I said it was fine,' Ruth continues. 'That I knew twins could be more dangerous but that I was fine, I was healthy, everything would be all right. He was so agitated though, so scornful, that I just let him go. He couldn't hear anything I was saying.'

'Maybe he was just shocked,' Maeve says as her mother shakes her head.

'It didn't seem like shock, or like he was drunk, or, I don't know . . .' She opens her hands. 'People don't make sense,' she insists with a tired, bitter bite to her words, with a resonance that Maeve doesn't understand. 'If there's one thing I could tell you, it's that people don't make sense, Maeve. They let you down, they have their own . . . dogmas. They keep secrets, they do things that don't make sense.'

Does she know? Maeve thinks with a horrible clench in her chest, as her mother's eyes dance over her face. Does she know what Stuart's done, what she has done? 'Did you try to talk to him again?' she asks quickly, to distract her mother from any suspicions.

'Yes, I tried to call him but he didn't answer. I told Alex what happened and he couldn't understand either, and asked me if I had remembered the argument right,' she adds sorely. 'He was worried about me, and the midwife was too, because I was so distressed about it. I kept thinking, OK, my father has some bad connotations with pregnancy that are coming out, terrible memories, delayed grief, but when he hears that the birth has gone fine, that we're all fine, he'll get over it. But he didn't. When he finally answered his phone, he told me in a calm, reasonable voice that he didn't want to see me, that I wasn't welcome at home but he would still like to see his grandchildren, as if I were superfluous. I could drop you off, he said, and pick you up from the end of the drive, but that was it.'

'You could have done that,' Maeve says and her mother winces.

'Well, call me selfish, but I didn't want him telling you horrible things about me, things that he made up. Besides, I couldn't trust that he wouldn't do that to you, turn on you. I kept picturing you staying there and him being suddenly cold, mean. I couldn't trust him with you, Maeve, especially not when you became ill – I couldn't bear it if he upset you.'

'You said he adored me.'

'Maeve.'

'It's all about you. It's you and what *you* want, and who cares about anyone else.' It's all about Ruth, Ruth and her father, Ruth and Alex, and Maeve is just a thing to be used and argued over.

'Maeve!' her mother calls, as Maeve shoulders her aside and runs along the hall.

She skids down the stairs and then flees to the annexe, where no one will look for her. With the door shut behind her, she shoves the pillows off the bed, throws one at the wall and feels stupid doing it, melodramatic, hollow.

It isn't even that she blames her mother exactly or that she feels a longing for her grandfather any more, for what the cards and presents promised, after her mother's story, the picture of an erratic man. It's just that there's nothing that's *hers*, Maeve's, except Stuart, and he's not *here*.

She lies down on the floor beside the bed. It feels only right for the stone of the floor to be so hard against her head, for her spine to ache.

People keep secrets, she thinks once her breathing has slowed. If she is Stuart's secret, something she has been happy to be up until now, if she is something cherished, if what they have is precious, does he have others? It's only fun being a secret when he's there too, when she knows he isn't with someone else.

Why didn't he answer last night? Why didn't he call her or send a message through her parents somehow? *Lie*, he was supposed to be good at that. Won't he know how worried she feels?

Is this what being abandoned feels like? she wonders some time later, when she has left the annexe for the unbearable heat of the field, prodding at the bruise inside her, trying to grasp the story she now inhabits. Has she been used and discarded?

She doesn't try to phone Stuart that night; she doesn't want to hear that message again if he's too busy for her. And if he is waiting for her call, she wants him to wait, to feel her worry. She's not above being petty, she's not perfect. But she's not that strong either, she can't be cool and confident. There's a tremble in her ribcage, her heart fumbles its beats, and she bites at the skin around her nails until it comes apart in sore strips.

Georgia used to dabble in Wicca; she had a spell book for modern witches that she showed Maeve. It was all rubbish, of course, Georgia said, but Maeve knew she didn't think that – as with other things, Georgia liked the idea of control. When they read through the book side by side, they skipped over the healing section by mutual silent agreement – they weren't that delusional – but everything else seemed fair game. Spells for protection, spells to find something you have lost, spells to make someone love you, spells to bring someone back . . .

Georgia had smuggled in a candle from somewhere, but

their first and only attempt to do a spell – one for luck maybe? Or protection? Maeve can't remember – set off the sensitive fire alarm and caused a whole drama. The book was confiscated, along with the candle. *Don't worry*, Georgia said to the ward sister with a wicked smile, *I memorized the curses.*

It's too hot now to think about candles and fire, but there are other kinds of spells, ones that come to Maeve instinctively.

Like plucking petals from daisies – *Does he love me? Does he love me not?*

Like running baths so full that when she enters them the lip breaks over the side and water floods on the bathroom floor until she makes her body still, so still that the only ripple of the surface is from the throb of her pulse in her neck – *If no more water overflows, if she can make her spine float off the bottom of the bath so she's weightless—*

—If she dresses exactly the same as the first day she met him, or the last—

—If she makes her curls neat or wild, if she puts blusher on and lip-gloss and then scrapes it off—

—If she touches herself lying on the bed in the annexe, if she doesn't touch herself and makes the bed neatly instead—

—If she runs another bath and gets in fully clothed, with the flowers she picked from the garden and the meadow, and arranges them around her, like her, like Ophelia, like the girl he wants her to be . . .

Chapter Twenty-Six

'Meet me at the river,' Camille said to me that last day, as the families milled around the garden of one of the cottages, waiting for all the dishes, the plates and cups and wine bottles for dinner, to be brought out. 'Tonight,' she said, clutching my hand, her voice hushed but fervent. 'I need to tell you something.'

'All right,' I replied, feeling a quiver through my body at the touch of her hand.

We had been at the river that afternoon with the others but I had ignored her, or tried to, ducking my head, turning my body from her, chattering to Linda and Joan and Sarah. I had barely slept last night, veering from giddiness to fear, my skin hot and tight as if I had been in saltwater. *I won't do it again*, I told myself and then, turning my face into the pillow, would picture Camille laid out before me, would imagine her hands in my hair, pushing me down her body.

'Promise?'

There was a simmering vulnerability to Camille that was both enchanting and terrifying, like standing too close to a fire. 'I will, I'll meet you there,' I promised.

We sat at opposite ends of the tables; I couldn't even see her during dinner unless I tipped my chair far back to catch a glimpse of her long hair, or leaned over my plate. But I thought of her as I ate, without tasting anything at all, as I talked to the girls near me, and as we drank our glasses of wine, which were refilled and refilled again on the urging of one of the fathers, who would be driving back to London tonight and wanted us all to finish the copious spare bottles of hessian-cradled wine he had brought with him.

Was Camille lying about needing to tell me something, was it just an excuse? Maybe she was going to tell me she loved me. But what would I say in return? *I'm sorry, I don't feel that way. I'm sorry, you're mistaken. How do you imagine this will work? What kind of world do you think we live in? I'm sorry, but I don't know what you mean. It's just girls being girls, it's just the summer madness, it's the river and the stories, we're only confused.*

I wanted dinner to go on forever and I wanted it to be over as quickly as possible. It was so strange to me that no one other than me knew how tortured my mind was, how whirling my thoughts were. I must have been a good actress, I thought. At least it distracted me from the tug of war between Joan and Linda, and Geoff who sat between them lapping it up with an appearance of nonchalance. Every time I looked over he irritated me; his artfully furrowed brow, the way he held his cigarette as though he were a rebel and not just a teacher's son, the way he leered at both girls like they were only meat.

As we ate yoghurt for dessert, freshly made by Joan's mother, with help from Linda's father, he announced, someone brought out a record player and the twang and thumping shake of a Rolling Stones record filled the air — or was it Led Zeppelin? Does it really matter who the band was? — and people started to sing and dance in their seats, to get up and dance too.

Linda leapt up, drunk and laughing, grabbing onto the hands

of some of the fathers, making them spin her around until her short dress showed her knickers. I caught Joan looking at her with loathing but she started dancing too, winding her arms through the air, the curl of her body like a snake's charm meant to catch Geoff who leaned back in his chair and smoked, watching them, watching the whole crowd of us.

'Come up and dance,' Stuart asked me, tugging me from my chair.

'I'm a bad dancer,' I said, as he shimmied his shoulders and moved me by my waist. *Is Camille watching me?* I thought, flipping my sweating curls over my shoulder. *Is she watching me and wanting me?*

Stuart trailed a hand down my arm and I plucked it off, held it in mine instead, pushed him out to spin and return as he laughed. I knew that he was as beautiful as a boy could be, narrow-hipped, blue-eyed, curly-haired – yet I felt nothing for him but sisterly fondness.

We were out of breath. I slumped against the tree, panting as he leaned an arm next to me. 'Liar,' he said, 'you are a good dancer.'

'You just think that because you're drunk,' I said, nudging his shoulder so he stumbled.

I finally looked over at Camille. She was sitting in her seat, one of only a few who still were. She had her glass in both hands and was frowning, her lips so red with wine they looked blue. *Look at me*, I thought, and she did, her eyes glancing up, her face filling with light.

'Hey,' Stuart said then, quiet, thoughtful.

'Yeah?'

'You're not—' I turned to see him squint in the blue dusk light. 'You and Camille . . . You're not a lezza, are you?'

'*No!* What?' I rocked forward off the tree as if I had been stabbed from behind. 'Why would you think that? That's disgusting.'

'You can talk to me about it. I mean, I promise I wouldn't tell anyone if you were, if you and Camille—'

'We're friends, that's *all*.' My heart was in my throat – I don't think I understood that phrase until then. I felt like I was choking, like my lungs were being squeezed.

He shrugged and reached into his tight pocket for his cigarettes. 'But it would be fine if you were. It's the seventies, everything is fine. Everything is cool.' He glanced over at the table and I followed his gaze.

Camille stood up, clutching the table when she swayed. She motioned her head at me and I turned mine away, scraping a hand down the rough tree bark.

There was no way now that I was going to slip away from the group, that Stuart was going to see me leave. I would not meet her at the river, I couldn't.

I drank to stop thinking about it – my shame and the terror of Stuart knowing something about me, of anyone thinking I was like that, perverse, *wrong*.

I drank to forget about Camille waiting there for me in the dark next to the velvet river, brimming with a hope that would soon flood away.

*

Drinking didn't work then and it doesn't work now, and yet in the evenings, in the afternoons, at lunch, I keep reaching for a glass of wine, sherry, gin, for anything else that's left in my father's well-stocked cellar. It's summer anyway and you're supposed to enjoy a drink in the sun, to have a fridge crowded with bottles of white wine so slick to the touch you have to lift them out carefully in case they slip to the floor and smash;

to scrabble for ice cubes across the kitchen countertop once you've fought them out of the tray – when you remember to fill the trays again, that is, when the tepid water even gets a chance to freeze in this endless heat.

When the air is this hot, it feels like you're breathing in someone else's breath. It feels – when you're in bed in an unrestful doze, fighting the urge for another cold shower, kicking down the thin sheet from your itching legs – like someone might be leaning over you, like the whisper of hot breeze from the wide-open windows might be a gust of breath, a disappointed sigh. That you might open your eyes and see her bending over you, that she might steal the very breath from you and leave you choking.

I wait to hear the whistle of Alex's snore before I get up, hand sweeping through the dark in front of me as if I am looking for a wall, or a person, something solid to help keep me from slipping back into my dream that wasn't a dream because my eyes are dry as sand and my head is spinning.

Parts of the carpet in the hall feel wet, chilled, but I tell myself it's only my hot feet being confused by the texture change. Hot can sometimes feel cold, can't it? And dry, wet.

I remind myself at the top of the stairs that there is a large mirror opposite, that as I descend I will see a murky figure descend at the same pace as me, move with the same dream-like motions.

In the kitchen, though, I find a true ghost from my past, and she doesn't disappear when I blink; when I screw my eyes tight and then open them, my heart twitching, my stomach heaving. She doesn't disappear when she makes a noise, and my hand touches her shoulder and comes away wet as she flinches back.

A girl in a soaked summer dress, dripping water from her

hair, from her fingertips onto the floor, a pool around her feet. Her skin shaded blue by the moonlight, by the dark leaching every colour but that.

It's Maeve, I tell myself, but turn on the light anyway because I'm also convinced it's her, Camille, or maybe me, that time has looped, that all of us are still trapped inside this house, that everything is repeating.

'Mum,' she says, holding up an arm against the light.

I wince too; my legs wobble as though my last drink was only half an hour ago. 'What's going on? Are you all right?'

'I'm *fine*.'

'You're all wet.'

'I took a shower. It's *too hot*.'

'In your dress?'

'Mum, leave me alone.'

I see her silver footsteps on the flagstones when she leaves. Am I asleep? I pinch my arm, hard, then pinch it again.

Even though I saw her, the minute I turn off the light again, I'm not sure. Why was she wet? Where had she been?

There are flowers in the sink that she left behind, meadow flowers whose stems are starting to rot. Flowers again. Flowers held in damp fists, woven in hair floating in a river.

I knock on Maeve's bedroom door but it's locked, so I bang on it. Alex wakes up. Maeve finally emerges.

'Mum's going mad,' she tells him over my shoulder as I search her face.

'Are you drunk?' I ask.

She bats away my hand and pushes me back. 'You're scaring me!' she says.

'What the hell, Ruth?' Alex tugs me and I go easily with him, my limbs dreamlike and useless. He turns on the hall light to check my own face, my eyes. 'What's going on?'

'I thought something was wrong with her,' I say, looking at Maeve silhouetted in her doorway with the dark of her room beyond. 'She was walking around the house in a wet dress. There were flowers in the sink, *flowers*,' I stress.

'You're not making any sense.' He puts his palm on my head. 'You're hot. Are you ill? Is this sunstroke?'

'I'm fine,' I say between gritted teeth but I'm not, I can taste tears.

'Have you got a fever? What happened?' He looks to Maeve as if she did something.

'She's crazy,' Maeve says, her voice shaky and young.

'She's not, she's just got sunstroke. Sunstroke and too many gin and tonics last night, all right?' Alex says, his voice calm and reassuring. He's a better parent than I am, a saner one.

Back in bed and both of us are awake now, the hot air tight with silence.

'Is this the menopause? Your night sweats and this craziness?' Alex asks. 'Is this what I have to look forward to?'

'It's just sunstroke.'

'Jesus, Ruth.' He takes my hand, squeezes it, and I make myself squeeze back. 'Are you going to be all right for lunch?'

'I'm fine, I'm fine.'

'You're spooking Maeve. What would you have done if the twins woke up as well? Get yourself together, Ruth.'

'It's this heatwave. Why won't it stop?' I grimace to hold off my tears.

'I'll stay home in the morning instead of going on my ride, keep the twins busy while you rest.'

'I'm fine, you hate to miss your rides.'

'Ruth—'

'Look, wake me up in the morning and you'll see I'm fine.

It's the sun, and a bad dream, and Maeve wandering about the place. Something's wrong with her.' I turn towards him, touch his chest.

'Worry about yourself first.'

'Don't you think something's wrong with her?'

'You were so strong when she was sick. Don't fall apart on me now, Ruth, OK?'

'We just need some rain,' I murmur, licking my dry lips.

As promised, I am more coherent the next day, back to normal, bright and chipper. I apologize to Alex; I apologize to Maeve, who is rightfully wary and won't be fobbed off by the chocolates I was saving as a treat for her first day back at school. Everything is fine, it's just the heat and the heat is something to get through, and once I get through it and get used to this house I'll be fine. I am in control. If bad memories are triggered here, it's because I'm letting them be triggered. I am an adult, I am in control.

After breakfast, the twins and I make potato prints and I water down poster paints so they can print their stars and circles, their misshapen creatures, onto paper, pinning them up above the Aga to dry. They help me wash the lettuce for lunch, taking it in turns to twirl around with the salad spinner outside as I stand on the patio with a cooling coffee and watch. For their mid-morning snack, I hull strawberries and scoop out dollops of yoghurt to go on top, licking my tart fingers, washing everything clean in the sink.

Iza wants to play a game in the garden afterwards, and hide and seek won't do. Neither will 'It' or a treasure hunt or kicking around a ball. *How about badminton?* I offer, thinking of the old racquets I spotted in the cellar last time

I was down there for gin. *What's badminton?* they ask and I explain. They wait in the garden while I go to retrieve them, thinking that I probably should have checked there were shuttlecocks first. *It might be cooler down there anyway*, I think as I open the door, *I might get a moment to breathe, a respite from this heat.*

Is it cooler down here? I feel my way down the stairs. It's darker certainly. The switch is on the far wall, because whoever put the electrics in before my father bought the place was an idiot.

Darker, cooler. The flagstones of the floor are cooler too. No, not cooler, wetter. I switch on the light. The floor is a slick sheen, a pool an inch thick.

The cellar is flooded.

Am I going mad? I ponder, leg shaking as I lean over the Yellow Pages opened on the hall table, one hand balanced on the cool shine of the mirror and the other flipping through the pages.

How does a house on a hill flood during a heatwave when it hasn't rained for weeks? How can the earth still hold that much water?

I can hear the thwap of the damp shuttlecock I gave the twins, and their delight in their new game, as I ring a plumber. Each time I close my eyes, I see it, the stretch of water across the floor, the splash as I walked through it, feel the spray of droplets up my bare legs.

The first plumber who actually answers says it's probably a burst pipe, or that there's a problem with the groundwater and the foundations. *Is there a well nearby?* he asks. *There used to be*, I say. He is busy for the next two weeks. *Is it safe to leave it that long?* He makes a noise; a laugh? A sigh? *I mean, will the foundations rot? Is the house in danger? I couldn't say*, he says. *Great*, I say. *Great. And your price? Well, now, that will depend. Of course. An estimate? OK*, I reply. *Sure*, I think. We have that money spare, of course we do. Should we take it out of the roof fund or the pipe fund or the heating fund or the school fund?

I return to the cellar because I don't believe my memory; I don't quite believe I had that call either, that I could be polite and coherent while this house and my mind are both falling apart.

It's supposed to be a late lunch; that was how Alex pitched it to the couples on the phone and the family who have children at the twins' new school, one younger than the twins and one in the same year, a chance for them to make friends before term starts. A late lunch and some gentle games in the garden and maybe some white wine.

I spill the wine over the recipe, the one I wrote out from one of the weekend supplements a month ago. *Perfect for a summer's lunch, perfect to share, goes well with white wine.* I can't picture the woman, the wife, the mother, who wrote this waterlogged recipe down. The handwriting is mine but I don't know.

'Everything all right, Ruth?' Alex asks, opening the fridge.

'Fine,' I say, tearing the prosciutto. 'I'm fine.'

The sound of a car down the drive. 'They're early,' Alex says, with a frown and a double check to the kitchen clock. Alex likes things to be orderly, to make sense. I wish things could make sense.

I join him at the front door, wipe my hands on the ratty apron that used to belong to Helen, doing my best to appear like a person who will host an excellent late lunch. But I needn't have worried because it's not one of the guests, and I feel a prod of relief as the banged-up car comes to a stop.

'You're a sight for sore eyes,' I call, finding my voice as Stuart gets out and stretches, looking up at the house.

He slots his sunglasses over his t-shirt, holding up the wine in his other hand. Pink, rosé, so much better than white. 'It's good to be back,' he says.

Chapter Twenty-Seven

Maeve doesn't hear his car because she's been in the bathroom, showering for what feels like half an hour, standing in front of the mirror watching individual droplets course down her skin, fingers tracing her collarbone, her neck, thinking of his hands, of her reflection as a photographic image. *Forlorn and wonderful*, she remembers him saying.

It's when she leaves the bathroom, swathed in steam, that she hears his voice downstairs and stops in the hall, clutching her towel.

In her bedroom her hands shake as she gets dressed. A summer dress, her shortest one to show off the legs he likes, the knees whose bruises have faded to a slight yellow wash if you look closely enough, her toenails painted a peachy pink, an innocent pink. She knows that part of his attraction to her is her innocence; he skates up against it when they're together, thinks of himself as both corruptor and preserver.

For a moment when she sees him in the kitchen, she's disappointed, in a way she can't quite explain. It's only that he looks so ordinary, so his age. But then he glances up at her and she feels it, the hum of excitement, connection. The warmth of being looked at, seen.

The lunch guests have already arrived; they're milling out on the patio in the back garden in the dry heat.

'Can someone do something with these?' her mother says, a tightness in her voice as she sets a vase down forcefully next to the flowers one of the guests has brought. 'Thank God the others brought wine,' she adds, waving the bottle at Stuart before leaving by the back door again.

Maeve twists on one foot. 'Hi,' she says.

'Hi,' Stuart replies, biting his lip in a giddy smile.

'Can we—' she begins.

'Are you the photographer?' one of the wives asks, slipping into the kitchen carrying an almost empty plate.

'Yes,' Stuart replies, and then looks over the woman's head at Maeve. 'What did your mother say I needed to get from upstairs?'

'I'll show you,' Maeve says, feeling her pulse thrum in her ears. It's too busy, there's too many people, and Stuart is here.

She climbs the stairs without looking back but she can feel him there, the weight of his body and gaze making her spine feel molten. The noise from the garden recedes to an echo.

'Is your dad out there?' Stuart whispers. 'I didn't check.'

'I think so,' she says.

'You *think* so,' he repeats with a mocking twist, and then his hand meets her waist and she spins around and lets herself be pushed into her bedroom, holding a palm over her mouth to muffle her own gasping laugh.

'I missed you,' he says, without closing the door.

She tilts her chin. 'Did you?'

The tracks his eyes make up and down her figure, her face, his wistful hunger, make her feel powerful again. He's here in front of her, not a distant voice on a phone living a more vibrant life without her.

'I'm sorry we didn't speak for the last few days. I dropped my phone down the stairs and it shattered. I tried to call the landline with my new number but Ruth answered. You're not mad at me, are you?'

How far can she push him, she wonders, staying mute.

'You are, aren't you. I'll make it up to you.'

'I thought you weren't coming back,' she says finally, thinking of every unspoken ritual, every spell she made.

'Oh, sweetheart.' He kisses her cheek, sets his hands on her shoulders.

His thumbs play with the thin straps of her dress and she glances at the open door behind him. 'Is this a good idea?'

'No.'

The curl of his smile and then the taste of tobacco in her mouth, the rasp of his stubble on her chin like dozens of tiny needles and his fingers clutching tight at her waist.

'Maeve?' her mother's voice calls. From downstairs? Or from the stairs themselves?

Stuart swears under his breath and strides towards the door.

'Hi, Ruth,' she hears him say from the hall. Stupid of him not to just hide, Maeve thinks hysterically. For someone who's survived wars he has a terrible sense of self-preservation.

'Have you seen Maeve?'

'I'm coming, Mum!' she calls.

A moment to check her reflection, to see the red rub around her mouth that she can't do anything about.

'Everyone's waiting,' her mother says as Maeve walks down the stairs. 'What were you doing?' She looks at Maeve and then at Stuart.

Is this the moment when she realizes? Maeve wonders with a flicker of panic, the scene in front of her bright and vivid – the dust motes streaming down past her, the reflection of the three of them in the hall mirror, the shine of the banister under her hand. Is this it, the rupture?

'I was looking in the junk room,' Stuart says. 'Poking about, you know me.'

Her mother's smile looks strained. She looks worn out, old and tired. Maeve feels a little guilty as she follows her to the kitchen but it's quickly dampened when Stuart reaches back to tug at her dress, throwing a smile over his shoulder and then asking Ruth if there's anything he should bring out to the table.

'Just you,' her mother replies. 'Penny is dying to meet you properly,' she adds.

Maeve repeats her mother's sentence in her head as she sits down at the table, smiling politely at the adults who shift in their seats to see her as if they don't know what to do with a teenage girl. *Don't worry, you won't have to put up with me for long*, she thinks, sneaking looks at Stuart and ignoring Penny, who is blonde but old, too old for Stuart's tastes.

'Can I have some wine?' Maeve asks, because she's barricaded by the twins on one side and three more children on her other side.

'It's good for children to start drinking at home,' one of the husbands opines without looking at her, 'better than having your first taste at university. I had a friend whose parents were deathly teetotal, Presbyterian, you know, and he had to get his stomach pumped in his first week.'

'It's always the boys that happens to, haven't you noticed,' a woman – his wife? – notes.

'Girls just hide their wildness better,' Penny says.

Maeve rolls her eyes.

'Don't you agree, Ruth?'

'What?' Ruth replies distractedly.

Her mother's hair is flat, Maeve notes; her polo shirt looks tomboyish next to the other women in their summer tops and cardigans.

'Girls are wilder.'

'They can be, yes,' Ruth replies and reaches for the wine bottle.

'It's like Diana,' one of the husbands says. 'There she was, meek as a schoolgirl, and you had no idea what was lurking beneath. Her and the Harrods heir.'

'It is a little hard to stay sympathetic when she's busy playing up for the cameras and swanning about on yachts in tiny swimsuits.'

'Oh, are they tiny? I hadn't noticed,' the first man jokes.

'I don't think she's playing up for the cameras,' Ruth interjects. 'They'd be photographing her whatever she does. I think she's just living, enjoying her freedom.'

'As a photographer, what do you think?' Penny asks Stuart.

Iza is kicking Maeve in the shin but she's too busy watching Stuart to pay attention to her. It's hard enough to remember to eat and the wine has already gone to her head.

'What do you mean?'

'Does she know the camera is there?'

He shrugs. 'I don't really keep up with the royals.'

Penny snorts. 'And yet there you were in *Harper's* last month in the society pages. Ruth showed me.' She nods.

'Ruth,' Stuart teases, 'am I in your scrapbook?'

'You're avoiding the question,' Ruth answers, smiling over the rim of her glass of wine.

Stuart is wearing a similar smile now and Maeve feels a twang of uneasiness. It's so bright today and the grass is dry and harsh under their feet, the wood of the table so parched that splinters stick up.

'Photography is about power,' he muses. 'The people I photograph think they're powerful, that I'm there to witness their
greatness. But I have the power; I choose what pictures to
take and which versions of them to preserve.'

'What about photos of you?' Ruth counters.

'What's the story with you two anyway,' Penny interjects,
taking off her cardigan. 'You and Stuart.'

'Stuart went to university with Alex and me, we shared digs.'

'A love triangle, was it?'

'No.'

'She doth protest. I have a nose for this kind of thing. I
think there was something between you two.'

She looks over to Alex, who clicks his tongue and points his
wine glass at Penny.

'Oh, do I have the right of it, then?' Penny laughs delightedly.
'Second best, were you, Alex dear?'

Maeve feels sick. Her gut roils, an iciness throbs from her
heart. Her eyes flick back and forth between her parents and
Stuart. They're joking, surely? Just one of those horrible bawdy
jokes that adults make when they drink and think that they're
teenagers again, forgetting that they're supposed to be grown-ups
now, parents.

The table is talking about Diana again, about some tabloid
gossip. Stuart isn't looking at her; he's concentrating on the
salmon on his plate, eating with neat movements. Did he eat
like that in wartime? she thinks nonsensically. Did he eat with
a silver knife and fork off an unbroken china plate while bombs
careened outside, while dust was blown in through the
windows?

The shock of the conversation dulls to a queasy shiver. Her
horror turns to anger at her parents for playing along, for being
so cosy with Stuart. Why do they have to ruin everything?

And yet, at the end of lunch, nauseous with the sun and everything else, Maeve can't help but ask her father, as she helps him clear the table while the other guests, including Stuart, linger further in the garden, what he had meant.

'What did Penny mean? About you and Mum and Stuart?'

A neighbour's cat has ventured into the garden and now everyone, adults and red-cheeked children, are cooing at it, marvelling as it cautiously picks its way across the lawn.

Her father stacks the glasses, catches one when it slips with a squeak in his hand. 'Stuart was your mother's first boyfriend,' he says. 'One of the summers here before university.'

'She never said that,' Maeve replies, voice cracking, making her father stop to look at her. *Stuart* never said.

'You know your mother and I dated other people before we met – it doesn't mean anything, Maeve. We're allowed to have lives apart from one another.'

'Like your one-night stand,' she spits out, waiting until she sees his shocked reaction before she turns and runs, heels sore on the hard ground, sobs jolting out with each stride.

Chapter Twenty-Eight

In my dreams each night, I am in the river and so are the girls, a shoal of us, limbs sliding over limbs, hair tangled together, toes kicking up pebbles that roll underneath us, that tumble, joining with rocks and branches, creating a wave that grows in power, that spills over the banks. In my dreams we leave the river, laughing, to find a flooded landscape, and as we wade through it our high spirits recede. We trip over submerged obstacles, we lose all sense of direction. We start to cry. Staggering through the cold water, searching for something familiar to guide our way.

The lunch is done. Food has been eaten, wine drunk, a good show of normalness put on. I am serene. Or am I numb? Maybe they're both the same thing.

'Thanks,' Alex says, as I enter the house looking for more wine to top up our guests' glasses.

'For what?'

He looks at me and I can't read him. 'For lunch.'

'Sorry, I've been a bit in my head. I guess it's the heat.' It's funny that despite not having a mother myself, I seem to have picked up the natural maternal tendency to apologize. *Sorry*

about dinner, sorry about my hair, sorry I'm not dressed up, sorry
I haven't done enough today, sorry that I'm *not enough.*

'Maeve is in a huff,' he notes, opening the fridge. 'She asked
me about Stuart and you, and I told her you had a history. I
think she has a crush on him.'

'We hardly have a history.'

'Sure,' he says, and drains the last splash of wine from his
glass.

'Stuart and I were never an item, what do you mean?'

'Where do you get off telling her my private business, our
private business?' He presses his glass to his chest. 'You told
her about what happened on my business trip – what the hell,
Ruth?'

'Of course I didn't tell her! She must have overheard.'

He shakes his head.

'I feel like you're blaming me.'

'You're never to blame, are you?'

'That's not true, not at all.'

He tears a chunk from the loaf on the bread board. 'Stuart
used to talk about you, back in university before I met you.
There's always been something between you anyway, you've
always been weird about him. There's this tension there, I
mean, come on.'

'He had a crush on me when we were younger, that was all.
You know you were my first boyfriend. And why are we even
talking about this? I don't—' I hold up my hands, drop them
at my sides. 'Is Maeve in her room?'

Alex leans against the kitchen counter, bending his upper
body towards me. 'You used to show off for him when we all
lived together. You loved that he had a thing for you.'

Sometimes, when Stuart saw Alex and me together there
was a part of me that wanted to say, *See, you were wrong about*

me, I am normal; to prove myself to him. No one else had noticed my interest in women except for him and it worried me, drew a thread between us, perhaps was even a reason why I kept him close. One night, drunk and high after my second-year exams, I had become convinced that Stuart was out in the hall watching us have sex through the crack in the door, and it was a notion, an imagined threat, a kind of twisted fantasy, that stuck with me as time went on, even though I hated myself for it. I overcompensated during sex, performed for an audience in my head, trying so hard to convince us both that I was straight and that my feelings for Camille had just been a phase, that I believed it. After all, why else would I think about him watching me if it wasn't that I was interested in him doing so, if it wasn't that I was interested in men? I didn't know then that fear – of being found out, of someone watching me and *knowing* – and anxiety could be identical to arousal to a body, lighting up the same nerve endings. It was the way Alex and I were when Maeve was ill that clued me into it, that made me see. How the stress of it all made me feel as if I was desperate for sex, my body fizzing like a live wire, but that I never felt any satisfaction and barely ever climaxed, just stayed awake afterwards, agitated and aching, feeling a queasy sickness in my gut.

How long has it been since I've had sex without thinking about what I look like from the outside, what someone might see if they look at me? How long have I used some disapproving figure to make my body tight with nerves and ignored what I actually want?

'I know you—'

No, you don't, I want to say. *I barely know me.*

'—and to be honest, it did come into my mind when he talked about needing somewhere to stay. More fool me,' he barks a laugh, 'but I thought that maybe it would help rekindle things between us.' He waves at the physical distance between us, the kitchen table with its detritus. 'Or at least that you might take the out.'

'Take the out,' I repeat. I can feel my jaw trembling. 'You think I'd have an affair with him? I don't want him, I never did.'

'Well, you don't want me, either. What do you want?'

I shake my head and then stop, catching the hazy scene out in the garden, the happy families talking and drinking and watching their little darlings tumble across the lawn. Iza and Michael are there, sitting next to one another on a rug. I can see them, I can tell it's them, even though I can't make out their faces. I would know the shape of them anywhere, their gait, their gestures, their voices, the smell of them when they were warm babies reaching their arms towards me. 'I can't do this right now. I don't know what you want from me.'

'I want to separate,' he states.

'I need to find Maeve.'

'Ruth, did you hear me?'

I pause on the threshold.

'Ruth, did you hear me? I want to separate.'

'They'll need you in the garden, they'll need wine top-ups,' I say, leaving without looking back.

*

I stayed with Stuart that last evening of summer when I should have followed Camille away from the table and the crowd. I was nodding along to what he was saying, acting like he was the only person I was thinking about, touching my hand to his arm, his chest, watching the effect of my feigned interest, the way his eyes got softer and he tugged on his hair with a nervous, excited twitch of his shoulders.

I couldn't tell you what he was saying, what was supposed to have me so riveted. I only remember the heat of him under my hand, that it felt wrong, that I knew it wasn't the body I wanted to touch, that the smell of him – sweat and the joint that one of the boys had handed him – was wrong. I drank from the glasses I was handed as the other teenagers gathered close, took a few pulls from joints and cigarettes, watched as Linda and Joan lingered by Geoff, twirling their hair, pouting their lip-glossed lips, looking up through their eyelashes. They looked ridiculous; they looked meek compared to their river selves, to the beautiful, enchanting girls I had photographed.

'Here,' Stuart said at some point, 'you're not doing it right.' He took the sloppily rolled joint from my hand and inhaled deeply, and then he took my face in his hands and his lips met mine and he exhaled. I breathed in the smoke, dry, harsh, sore in my parched throat, and then I coughed it out, pushing him back.

'That's how it's done,' Geoff crowed, clapping a hand on my shoulder, and I shrugged him off too. My feet were unsteady, my head was swimming from all the wine.

'Let's go to the river,' someone said. A girl's voice but I don't remember whose.

'Oh, are we allowed now? You don't want to keep it a *girls only* space?' Geoff mocked.

We made a vow, I thought, my tongue too slow to speak, my face tingling.

But no one was thinking of that now; they were only thinking that this was one of the last nights of summer, a last opportunity to *do* something, to have something to tell the others back at school, a story for social currency. After all, we couldn't tell other people about the photographs, about the Ophelia girls – the magic would vanish when we were back in our grey pinafores and tight ties, back in a rainy quadrangle waiting for the bell to ring for lessons and sitting in rows behind cramped desks.

I didn't want to go but I went anyway, tumbling down the hill of the meadow as the light waned, the giddiness of the crowd of us making my heart race, my head spin. I was laughing at one point, I remember that, and Stuart tugged me up by my hand when I tripped over. Sarah was singing and so was the other boy whose name I can't remember, singing so loudly it sounded like squawking, kicking at the grass in front of them. Geoff was giving Joan a piggyback, her head swaying in the air in front of me, her black hair waving like a flag. The sky was pink and a colder breeze made me shiver, made me wish I was in bed, but my bed was so far away. It was only when we entered the woods, the whoops and shouts echoing strangely off the trees, that I thought Camille might still be waiting here for me, that we would find her there, lonely and pitiful with flowers braided in her long hair. I moved ahead, pushing my hand against tree trunks, stumbling as I tried to get there first so that no one else saw her like that, so vulnerable. The undergrowth, the bushes and roots and felled branches, were scratching at my legs even though I took the same route as usual, but I kept moving, unsteady and dizzy, as though if I stopped I might fall head first.

She wasn't there. In the dim dusk light, the bank and the river in front of me were both empty, untouched, calm, and then the noise of the others grew like thunder and a crowd gathered, blocking my sight of the water. The alcohol hit then, and I lost some time. I was leaning against a tree; Stuart was standing in front of me talking again, talking about his plans, about law, about something to do with my father. I could see figures on the other side of the bank. A girl resting against a tree just like me, a girl with black hair and pale legs sticking out of her skirt that was being pushed up by the boy in front of her. I saw her arms shove him away feebly and then fall, I saw her head loll to the side and heard her slurred words and then, so quick I reached towards Stuart for balance, as though the whole world were tipping, he was tugged off by Linda who was shouting, shoving at Geoff's chest, pushing him back. He laughed, and then she pushed him again and he leaned too far back, falling and falling and hitting the water awkwardly, loudly.

I slumped to the ground, my legs giving out, and Stuart tried to help me up.

Geoff was thrashing in the water, calling out, and a girl was being sick on the bank. There was noise and movement and then it was quiet. Then Stuart was gone, jumping into the river along with everyone else, and Geoff was being dragged back up the bank, and Joan was crying and Sarah was too, and someone was hunched over him, shaking him, pushing at his chest.

He coughed and spluttered, groaned but wouldn't sit up.

'He's fine,' someone said, as a girl called out for someone to run to the house and get a parent, an adult, to help. 'You're fine, aren't you, Geoff,' they said. Was it Linda?

Geoff coughed again, turning on his side.

People were arguing. A whirl of drunken motion in front of me, the dark of the night pulsing, the forest breathing.

By the time the bobbing of torches heralded the arrival of the adults from the cottages, the mood on the riverbank had calmed, my head was clearer and I was on my feet again. Most of the parents had come, although not my father of course, and not Camille's parents either. Someone had brought a blanket that they wrapped around Geoff as he stood shivering, shell-shocked. Linda and Joan were holding hands, inseparable once again, and I remember thinking jealously that it was all right for them, that they could touch and have it mean nothing but friendship, sisterhood.

'There's always an excitement near the end of the holiday,' one of the fathers was saying.

'We told you not to mess about in the river,' Joan's mother said crossly, arms around herself against the chill, the night's cold sinking down through the trees towards us.

'It was his fault,' Linda replied with a shiver, her voice mulish. 'None of us were going to go for a swim, he just wanted to show off.'

One of the torches slipped from a hand, and the light speared across our feet before it blinked out. Stuart picked it up and turned it back on, sweeping the beam across the black water of the river.

It was Stuart who spotted her first, even though it should have been me, even though I should have looked for her, should have known.

It was Stuart who spotted her, the waterlogged figure snagged on the root of a tree far down one riverbank, but it was a girl who screamed first; maybe it was me.

Chapter Twenty-Nine

Maeve's dad had been lying, of course, she thinks tearfully, desperately. He just wanted to hurt her or maybe he was just trying to warn her off. He was just teasing, just being mean. She pushes the door of the annexe open with a bang and it creaks as it shuts behind her. She sniffs and wipes her nose with a shaking hand.

She picks up Stuart's leather satchel from the table and upends it, shaking out the contents – film canisters rolling across the dusty floor, spines of notebooks landing with a clap, the flutter of so many photos. She scrabbles through them, looking at the evidence of where he's been this week. The Amazonian models, all leg, all arched collarbone and proud profile, draped over concrete architecture. Harsh shadows and red-taloned nails and stiletto heels stabbing into the ground. Is this what he likes? Is this what he's into?

She pushes them away, opens a second envelope and finds pictures of her. Softly focused, with flyaway hair, freckles painting her cheeks in the light. Her bluing skin showing through damp lace, her open mouth, plaintive eyes. His hand on her thigh, fabric crushed in his fist. She holds the evidence of his desire in her own hands. *See*, she tells herself, wiping her chin on her shoulder. *See, pictures can't lie.* She flicks through the notebook, searching for something – a sign, a note addressed to her – but it's just business, just boring scribbles. Her name isn't in here. Another envelope of pictures. Black-and-white shots of war and devastation. Her knees hurt on the floor.

The jumble of furniture, the whitewashed walls of the room, look tired, not romantic as they had when she was here with him. The dust of the bare stone floor makes her cough in the dry heat and a bee is flying at the window, its light body making a sound larger than she thought it could. She made the bed for him earlier; it's neat, with no depression in the pillows from their heads, no imprint of his fist in the mattress from when he was holding himself up over her.

When she gets to her feet, the motion makes something skid away. She reaches for it, the last envelope, not plastic like the others but paper, old, fraying, edges rubbed red from the lining of his bag.

There are five faded Polaroids inside. At first, she thinks that the top two are of her, and even when she realizes that the girl in them is floating in a river and not a bath she still thinks it's her. Red hair frizzed golden by the sun, a pale dress moulded to her skin by the water. A blurry face that looks like hers. The girl in one of the other photos can't be her because her hair is darker, but it could be. That could be her looking up at the camera with an arm draped over her head and a ribbon around her neck. The next, of a girl leaning against a willow tree with the river behind her, her long dress cinched in under her breasts, her hand holding a bouquet of flowers. That could be her. And the last photo, of a girl standing up to her waist in the water squinting at the sun, a white veil covering her hair, that could be her too.

She lines them up in front of her with shaking hands,

crouches down again. Did that happen? Did he take her down
to the river but she forgot?

It must be the heat that makes her stupid, and slow. Or
that it is so long since she saw a picture of her mother as a
child, before she lopped off her hair and dyed it blonde.

Stuart was your mother's first boyfriend, her father had said.

Footsteps on the gravel and the door swings open.

'Maeve?' Stuart calls out.

She doesn't answer him. Her legs are weak and sore crouched
down, and she slumps to sit.

He touches a hand to her hair.

'What are these?' she asks, and looks up with a thready hope
that he might be able to fix this.

'They're old,' he says.

'Is this my mother?' she asks, holding up the Polaroid. It
feels liquid in her hands; it feels as though, if she squeezed
it hard between thumb and forefinger, ink would come spurting
out and stain her.

'Yes.'

'You're supposed to lie to me,' she says and stands up. Her
breath is hitching and here she is, a useless weeping girl
again. 'So, what? I'm just a do-over, a second best? You
fucked her first and then thought you'd have a go at her
daughter too?' Thinking it is one thing but saying the words
makes her feel like something is breaking inside her, or rising
inside her, horrible and vile. 'I hate you!' she says and shoves
him. She was never his Ophelia, she was a cheap copy, one
in a long line.

'I wasn't with her,' he says, holding up his hands. 'I was
never with her, I didn't touch her. We were friends. I didn't
even take this picture,' he says, picking up the Polaroids.

'Liar.'

'I didn't, I swear it. You can ask her.'

'I don't want to speak to her ever again, I won't!' she swears and then stamps her feet, pushing him again with a wailing, angry noise.

'Calm down,' he says, reaching for her. 'Hey, Maeve, you'll hurt yourself.'

'Get off me.' She pushes him again and then flees through the door. Her vision is black at the edges, her head roaring, but she can still hear her footsteps on the gravel and then the grass, and his own behind her, his jogging breath.

She hates him, she hates how everything has been ruined – her summer, her life. She feels so small, so pathetic and foolish and stupid. She hates him. But as the meadow grass whips past her legs, dried yellow and sharp, she can't help but listen hard to check that he is still following, that he is chasing after her. Like a child who wants their tantrum, their crying, to be witnessed, because otherwise it wouldn't really exist, she doesn't want to be alone.

'Wait,' he calls, 'wait, you've got it wrong, please.'

Her legs are tiring now; the ground is hillocked and hard like rock, and it's difficult to imagine she could have lain down in it only a few weeks ago and imagined it some fairytale bower. When her foot falters over a tight knot of grass she comes to a stumbling stop.

'How can I prove it to you?' he pants. 'I'll take you down to the river now, I'll get my camera.'

'No, just go away. I hate you.'

'Oh, Maeve,' he says, hand cupping her face. He looks as tortured as she feels. She soaks it in, his concern, and wants to spit it right back at him, to make him feel worse. He looks at her and she wonders, spitefully, yearningly, what picture she makes now, whether she is still lovely to him.

'Leave me alone, go away,' she says, hitting his chest with her palm.

'Let me explain.'

He grabs her arm. His grip spans the width of it.

'Let go.' She pushes him weakly with the other hand but he doesn't even rock on his feet. He smells like garlic and wine. 'Let me go.'

'No, I won't. Listen,' he says, squeezing his fingers.

He's not going to let her go. Perhaps she doesn't want him to.

The sun is behind him, still so bright she can't see his face properly. A bead of sweat drips down her spine.

Chapter Thirty

Maeve is the only thing I'm concerned with now. Finding her and comforting her if she is upset. A crush is a minor drama for a teenager, I tell myself without the least bit of irony, and with the application of ice cream and a few soppy films she will be fine. I was, after all, wasn't I? I finished the last year of school without a blip on a report card or an eating disorder, just a few drunken nights when I pilfered my father's healthy booze stash in the cellar and vomited all over myself, but what teenager doesn't drink a little too much? And then I was fine at university, totally fine, working hard and playing hard. Alex said I was the coolest girl he'd ever met, drama-free, easy.

Maeve isn't in her room, she isn't in the junk room, the two spare rooms, the twins' room, the two upstairs bathrooms or my room. She isn't in the kitchen, the utility room, the dining room, the lounge, the drawing room, and she isn't sandwiched inside the glass doors of the flower room. She isn't in the walled garden and she's not on the front lawn. She could be in the field, she could be in the woods, or she could be some-where else.

I don't wait for an answer to my knock on the annexe door before entering but there's no sign of her here. There's a mess on the floor though, papers, photographs, books, as if a pile has been knocked down in a hurry. I lean over and pick up the photograph nearest to me, turning it the right way up.

Yellowing grassland and a woman's sandal discarded on the ground.

I reach for another; it's the right way up this time but shadowed by the table above it.

White rumpled sheets and red locks of hair that trail out of view.

Sometimes a body knows something before a mind does. Sometimes your diaphragm can spasm, your head sink under a rush of blood up through your neck, and your ears crackle as if they are about to let in all the hidden noises of the world.

I make a stack of pictures in my trembling hands and flick through them, these pretty pictures of a terrible crime. Her bare legs, his weathered hands, her in a dress in the field, in a dress in a bath surrounded by flowers. So many flowers. I feel my chin dimple, my eyes grow hot. I force myself to look through them, to see what I was too blind to see. Her bare back, her long hair, her body submerged as though she is drowning. And worst of all, her face. Looking at him as if he is some kind of saviour. Looking at him with the brittle confidence of youth that I know is so easily shattered.

I leave the annexe, photographs, evidence, in hand. Where is he?

Alex is by the front door when I pass, frowning and drying his hands on a tea towel.

'Did you know the cellar was flooded?' he asks.

'Where's Stuart?'

'I saw him running after Maeve,' he says, nodding across the lawn to the gate to the fields. 'I guess he found out why she was upset, although I'm not sure he's the right person to talk to her, she's probably embarrassed. Did you hear me about the cellar?'

'I called someone for quotes,' I say distractedly, shielding my eyes to look across the lawn.

'You didn't think of telling me about it? You've had all afternoon, Ruth. This is what I'm talking about. *Ruth.* Are you OK?'

'I'm fine.' I don't need to tell him yet, I don't need to tell him at all – Stuart can do that himself. (Or maybe there's an excuse, a pitiful voice in my head wonders, maybe these photos don't mean what they mean.)

'OK,' he replies, and someone calls from the house. 'I just don't need this fuss today,' he mutters, and returns inside as I set my sights on the gate, the hot meadow beyond too bright to make out.

Chapter Thirty-One

'Listen,' he says.

'I love you,' he says.

'And what we had – have – has nothing to do with your mother, you know that, right?'

'I don't know that,' Maeve says as the sun gets caught, refracted sharp and white, in her eyes.

'You're special, Maeve,' he says, thumb touching her cheek, wiping the tear away. 'And we fit, you and I, don't we? Who we are, what we want.'

She thinks of them together; of his hands on her, of how they fitted around her hips as he pulled her up to sit on his chest, her twitching thighs either side of his head. She thinks of the noises she made and it's like they're hanging in the thin air around them, a stabbing humiliation.

'I didn't take these photos,' he says of the Polaroids in his hand, 'your mother and her friends took them of each other. I was never her boyfriend, I had a bit of a crush, that's all. Like all your teenage crushes. You don't think I'm jealous of them too?'

'It's not the same.'

'It wouldn't have worked, trust me.' He tugs a piece of Maeve's hair and she bats his hand away. He looks at the landscape over her shoulder. 'Your mother's not like that, anyway.'

'Like what?'

'Well . . .' He draws out the word. 'She wouldn't have let me take her photograph, for one. You think those pictures I took of you mean nothing? These are just girls posing for each other, holiday snaps.'

Maeve bites the inside of her lip, looks at him, wonders if she can believe him. 'You said you didn't want to hurt me, but you have.'

'I'm sorry, I'm sorry I never told you. I'll explain more, we'll have a long talk. Later, all right? We need to get back now though.' He cranes his neck to look back at the gate.

'I'm not going back.'

'Come on, Maeve.'

'I don't want to talk to them again, *ever*,' she swears.

'Someone will see us out here,' he says. An anxious twitch of his shoulder.

'Why can't they see us?' she retorts.

'Maeve.'

'We can go to the woods, like you said. Hide in there.'

'Forever?'

'What are you scared of?' She feels a fizzing petulance, a giddy heat, at his discomfort.

'You're just being contrary now, Maeve. We've talked about this, about London and the future. Do you want your dad to come down here and see us? For your parents to find out?'

'Come to the woods with me.'

'I can't, they'll be looking for you. We can go tonight, if you really want to.'

'Now. You said you would.'

'Maeve.'

'*Liar,*' she says. She shifts on her feet. The tufts of dying wildflowers stroke the backs of her legs. 'I'm going, you should follow me.'

'Maeve.'

She backs away from him.

'What am I supposed to tell your parents about where you are?'

'Lie. Or tell them you've broken my heart and I'm off to drown myself in the river.'

'Maeve!' he calls out but she's already gone, running down the hill, whipping past tall grass, feeling the thud of each step in her ribcage, juddering up her spine.

In her mind's eye there is a camera at the level of her knees, capturing flashes of light, pale legs, brief snatches of the hem of her dress. There is music too, a suitable soundtrack to the scene. A girl running, her panting breaths loud as if they've been recorded later, breathed right into a microphone.

The only green in the landscape before her is the woods ahead; the rest is yellow, white, dead, bright. But the sky is blue and running down a hill makes it look larger, a pool she wants to dive into.

It's too hot, even in motion, the air dry, her mouth sore.

She pushes on.

Running, she thinks, only feels triumphant if there's somewhere to go, if you're heading for somewhere good, otherwise it feels like running away, like fleeing.

Picture something nice, the nurses told her when they needed to take blood, inject medication, hook up IVs. Picture a beach, a sweet shop, a princess tower.

Picture the woods, the river?

Follow me, she thinks, but she doesn't need to turn her head to know that this time he isn't. She's on her own.

A stitch in her hip. She stumbles on a bramble and a panicked breath bursts from her mouth. She could fall so easily, fall and bruise and break; her body is that fragile, all bodies are. She hasn't run in years and it hurts her lungs. It makes her think of other hurts, of real wounds.

Pick me up, carry me, she thinks, legs heavy and unsteady as she continues on.

Now each sharp blade of grass that pricks her ankles is a lance and her righteous fury is oozing out, leaving familiar, ordinary, unbearable sadness behind.

The grass falls away from her as she approaches the woods, the ground harder, roots like knuckles. The shade of the trees reaches out and she hurries the last few steps, bursts past trunks and branches and then stops, gasping for air.

Chapter Thirty-Two

As I approach the gate to the field, Stuart approaches it too from the other side, looking ordinary, looking unbothered. Lifting a hand in hello.

'Have you seen Maeve?' I ask in a reasonable facsimile of my ordinary voice. I can't see anything in the field beyond him but grass.

'No, I don't think so.'

'You're such a liar, *God*.'

He stops a step away from the gate, startled. 'What?'

'Alex said he saw you running after Maeve.' I'm so furious that my hands are clawed, my jaw is shaking. 'Oh yeah, and I found these.' I hold up the stack of photos, watch his face go blank.

'Yeah,' he says, nervous tongue swiping across his top lip.

'Tell me you didn't touch her.'

'It was just a photoshoot, I knew you'd get weird about it. It's an art project.'

'An *art* project! You lie like breathing.'

'So do you,' he retorts, as if we are children again and only bickering.

'I can't believe you, I can't— You knew it was wrong, you kept it secret, you sneaked around. How could you do this?'

'I didn't do anything to her. She modelled for some photos, that's all.'

'Am I supposed to believe you? You think that's convincing?' I shriek. It's only a matter of time before someone comes to see what's going on, before all the guests tumble out of the house, their late lunch ruined. Me ruined. Maeve ruined.

He turns his head, rubs a palm over his mouth. 'You ignore her, you know – Maeve.'

'Don't say her name.' His horrible eyes and his calm mouth and his aged skin. His hands on her. 'God, and there I was sympathetic to you, listening to you talk about wanting a family. *Jesus Christ*. You're a predator.'

'She's seventeen.'

'And you're old enough to be her father, talking absolute shit about loneliness—'

'You do ignore her,' he barrels ahead. 'You and Alex. She's hurting, she's struggling, and you turn a blind eye. She needed someone.'

'That's a great story.'

'It's true.' He moves closer, his hand clutching the top of the gate.

'I have a better one. That you were obsessed with me, the younger me. That you saw her and thought you'd have another chance.'

He shakes his head. 'Not everything is about you.'

'You dressed her up as *Ophelia*.'

'Among other Pre-Raphaelite paintings.'

I make an incredulous sound. 'How fucked up are you? To do this after what happened?' I shove at his shoulder and the gate groans loudly as he rocks back. 'How could you do this? We opened our *home* to you! All your overtures of friendship, talking to me like you cared.' I should have trusted myself, I should have known not to trust him, *God.*

'I did care, I do care about you, Ruth. I can't help it if I fell in love.'

'*Love—*'

'Like you never fell in love with a girl.'

'When *I* was a girl too.'

'Are you going to tell Alex?'

'You're worried about that now? Where the hell is Maeve?'

'She ran down the hill, she was upset,' he says, with an intimacy in his voice that outrages me. 'You should go after her—'

'Don't fucking tell me what to do! You don't know anything about my daughter. She's my daughter, I know how to comfort her. Get away from the fucking gate—' My fingers miss the catch on the gate and I yell and kick it and then manage on my second try, shoving it open as the hinge squeaks.

'Can I have them back, the pictures?' he asks, standing back like I might claw at his face. I might just.

'Can you have the pictures back,' I repeat. He's so small, pathetic, that's what makes it worse.

'I'll switch?' he says, holding something out.

'Polaroids too?' I spit. '*Jesus Christ . . .*' But my voice trails off as I see the top picture.

A girl with black hair. A sun-dappled river. A familiar face.

'I need to tell you something,' he says.

As if in a trance, I snatch them from him, the other photos slipping from my hands. Greedy and unnerved, I stare at the square images.

'It's something I should have told you a long time ago,' Stuart continues.

I had forgotten how young we looked. Joan, Linda. There I

am with my long hair, my wide grin. Did I ever smile that
bright after that summer? Was I ever so hopeful?

And there she is, Camille, reaching towards me across time.
A vision of girlhood, frozen. Sinking me right back, pulling me
under.

One photograph, and I remember a dozen things I had
forgotten. Her laugh, her crooked front tooth, how she beat
us all whenever we played cards on the riverbank. That she
liked to eat the whole core of her apples, seeds and all. That
the fine hairs on her thighs caught on mine when we swam
next to one another in the river. How small her body looked
when it was pulled from the water.

'Where did you get these pictures? Do you have more?'
Everything feels very slow now, my mouth, my words. The
wine and shock a sludge in my limbs.

'No.'

'I thought I burned them all.'

A private bonfire in the bathroom the day after the night
before, once all the families had fled, cutting their holidays
short. A pile of pictures in the sink and a whole box of matches
needed to turn them into ash because the thin drip of the
leaky tap kept putting out the flames. Then I had opened the
tap all the way, let the water curl the mess down the plughole,
leaving a black smear behind that I wiped at frantically with
my hands, terrified of someone finding it, scrabbling with black
fingers in the sink, rubbing my hands raw against each other
to try to get them clean.

'It's about Camille.'

'What?' I ask, forgetting he was there, forgetting that she
isn't.

'She was pregnant. When she died.'

'You're lying again.'

He shakes his head, looks pitying. 'No, I heard your father talking to the police. She was about three months gone. They assumed she had been with someone at school, a boy or a teacher or something.'

'This is a sick joke.'

'You can read her files, ask the police. I'm sorry I didn't tell you.'

I shake my head and peer closer at the image of her, her blouse loose, her skirt long. I close my eyes, remember her body pressing against mine, tugging her towards me, the round flesh of her hips.

'It's why she did it,' he says. He just keeps *talking*.

'No. She would have told us, told *me*. And if it is true, she didn't know, she was . . . naive, neglected by her parents.' The threadbare clothes, her parents' nonchalance, her surprise at our offers of friendship; clues I only learned how to read later.

But how many other clues had I missed?

The day with the storm, the way she gulped down neat spirits, her talk of stealing a summer, of a secret she needed to tell me—

'She threw herself down the stairs, don't you remember? She had bruises,' he says.

'She *tripped*.'

'I know you had feelings for her, but there's lots that people keep secret. You only knew her a few weeks.'

'Shut up, just *shut up*. You were jealous of her, you . . . Why did you never tell me?' I grab his t-shirt and he tries to break my grip, the veins in his neck standing out as we tussle. 'You wanted me to blame myself for what happened, didn't you? You wanted me to feel guilty.'

'No, I just didn't know how to tell you,' he insists. 'I just didn't know how to talk about any of it. That night, her body. You didn't want to talk about it either.'

'My fault again then.' I laugh acerbically, pushing him away. My stomach heaves and my throat is sharp with acid. What am I doing wasting my time with him? 'Fuck off, Stuart, fuck off and get out of my house before I call the police and have you arrested.'

I hurry away from him, swat him away from my thoughts. Easy when there's a mental refrain getting louder and louder, a sick guilt rising inside me. *It's my fault.* It *was* my fault. Camille had wanted to tell me something, she had been waiting for me, she needed me.

And this, *Maeve.* I failed as a mother, failed again, was blind.

Of course she's gone to the woods, of course she has. Where else could she be, I think as I sprint down the hill, my hand clutching my roiling stomach and my breath sour. Where else could she be but the woods and the river?

In the corners of my mind, memories are creeping forth, rolling forward as though the glasses that held them have been knocked over by an errant elbow, an accidental kick.

My father, what he said at the gallery, the implication that I had a death wish, that I got pregnant with the twins to tempt fate, to follow my mother. I didn't, I swear that's not true. But it's true that I did think of her, I did when I was in labour, when Maeve entered the world blue and I felt myself struggle for breath too, the midwives crowding around me and her, blocking my view of her, this strange blue creature I had called into being. I did think for that too-long minute before the oxygen did its work on her, and she breathed her first dry-land breath, that my mother's curse had found me and her, that it was a foolish thing to imagine I could be a mother when I had killed my own.

I'm not a good mother, I'm not a good wife. Alex will divorce me and we'll have to sell the house. Iza and Michael will be inconsolable without the garden and the fields where they can run and play, the family home where their parents are together. I did this, no one else. I let Stuart come here, let him hurt Maeve.

I've entered the woods now. I call out her name and it echoes back towards me. It's still light, the night isn't encroaching yet. The last time I was here it was dark. It was dark and they carried her out, head lolled back, her wet hair like ropes in the air, her pale wrist dangling down. They crowded around her, and couldn't they tell that she wouldn't be able to breathe with them there like that? Didn't they know to step back and let her have space? *Let her have some space*, I said, walking over and pushing at shoulders. *Let her breathe, you're crowding her.*

Everything else of that night is flashes, sounds. Weeping and torches flickering. Barking voices, the smell of vomit. Standing in the kitchen of my house while someone in uniform asked us questions. And then the dawn creeping in, blue. The summer birds. The grass tracked in through the house. The cups I washed so that every visitor could get a drink. It only felt real, I remember, when I saw my own reflection for the first time, catching it in the bathroom mirror and coming to a jolting stop. It was only real when I saw an image of myself, when I knew that I was real and so was she.

I'm at the river now, in the present, older, here. I've been calling but she isn't answering. It doesn't look the same; the bank isn't smooth with grass and moss but gnarled by weeds and low bushes, roots and fallen branches. The water level is lower too, murkier.

The heatwave has dried it up. Or maybe it's been drying up for years. Maybe it was never that deep and we just misre-membered. Maybe when we floated in it, our backs were always grinding against the pebbles of the riverbed, bruising our spines. Maybe when it looked like we were treading water we were really crouched down with our knees hard against rocks, their imprints dug into our kneecaps.

I slide down and into it, cold on my feet, slick against my knees, flowing past my thighs. I had forgotten the current, the way the water is never still but travels. How had we never been curious about where the river came from or where it went? A river isn't static like a pond or a bath; it flows, it moves. A river goes on and on and on.

Was she really pregnant, like he said she was? And if she was, could I have helped her? Did she love me? Did I her? Does love ever not hurt, does my love, or lack of it, never not hurt people?

I call her name again and turn around and around, scanning the banks, peering into the trees. I pace up the river, the muscles of my legs burning against the flow, the weight of it, until I reach the part where it slips into the undergrowth, where the trees crowd too close for me to squeeze between and then I walk back down, down and down, the water pushing me, tugging me forward.

Then I slip on rocks, of course I do, and fall, bashing my ankle on something sharp, inhaling a mouthful of water.

I'm in the river and it tastes of metal and moss. It tastes of stone and mud.

I am in the river again. Did I ever leave? Was everything just a dream? The bright sky hurts my eyes and the cold of the water hurts my skin, the bump of the ground, the pebbles, painful on my hips.

Every mother knows that a child can drown in the shallowest of water – a bath, a pond. I made my father dry up the pond in the garden so that Maeve couldn't accidentally fall in. I ferried all three to swimming lessons even when they cried and complained. I haven't brought the twins to the woods; they don't know the river is even here. You can drown with a tablespoon of water in your lungs, isn't that what they warn? And pneumonia can make you drown even though you're nowhere near the water. Even though you're in a hospital bed and your mother is standing in the hall while doctors try to save your life, make you breathe again. *Breathe, Maeve*, I told her as her face went blue, as her chest heaved. *Breathe*.

I'm tired. My body is awkward now in the water, sinking, not floating, and the river is washing over my face. Up into my nose, across my mouth.

I duck under where it's loud and the light is green, where each of my movements kicks up silt and stones. It hurts to hold a breath. The pain starts in your sinuses, in your mouth, and then spreads outwards; you can feel the inside of your skull, your lungs, and every hope you have turns to panic. Holding a breath underwater feels like being buried alive.

There's someone else here, I think, as my head roars. Someone else in the water. I can feel the wake of their movements, can see something, a pale shape coming towards me.

And then a hand, small and cold, grabs me by the shoulder and tugs me up, and I breach the surface with a deafening gasp, breathing in and in, my limbs flailing as I cough, as someone shouts at me and tries to prop me up.

'What are you doing?' she demands, righteous and tearful. 'Mum, what are you doing?!'

'Sorry,' I say, wiping my eyes. 'Sorry.'

Maeve tugs me again and I get my feet under me and look at her, properly. Pale and frightened, and too young for any of this.

'It's all right,' I tell her. 'I just slipped. I was looking for you and I slipped.'

'No, you weren't.' She shakes her head.

'Are you all right? Stuart said you'd run off to the woods. I saw the photographs, Maeve. Did he hurt you?'

'He never hurt me.'

'Maeve.'

'I'm fine.'

I wade over to the bank and clamber out, Maeve following. I reach out my hand for her but she doesn't take it, the line of her mouth hard, her eyes wide in their sockets.

'It's my fault, I'm sorry,' I tell her. 'I invited him to stay. I shouldn't have.'

She doesn't reply.

We're both soaked now, river water flooding onto the ground behind us as we trudge away from it.

My teeth are chattering. The heat of the day is drying the top of my head already.

'I'm not keeping this a secret,' Maeve says, her voice cracking.

She walks ahead of me up through the field. The dust and grass are sticking to my damp clothes, my skin. A cut on the bottom of my foot makes each step hurt.

'I'm telling Dad,' she insists, and when she glances back the devastation on her face makes me feel sick. 'You need help, Mum.'

No more treading water, Ruth. No more solo late-night swims, in dreams or otherwise. No more drowning, enough.

Chapter Thirty-Three

At the gate, Maeve gestures her mother forward and follows her sodden footsteps from the field. Ruth is shivering, her teeth clinking together like a shaking hand lifting a china cup from its saucer.

Stuart's car is gone. Maeve stands where it was, in front of the house, as Ruth vomits next to the flower pot outside the front door.

'Mum's ill,' Maeve says to her father when he comes to see what's happening.

'Jesus Christ,' he says, 'Jesus Christ.'

He looks frightened in a way that Maeve remembers from hospital, pale-faced, mouth thin, as he helps Ruth upstairs to bed.

'How much wine did you have at lunch?' he asks Ruth, when Maeve carries the bucket that he told her to get into the bedroom.

'Not much,' Ruth groans.

'Not much.'

'She was drinking in the morning,' Maeve interjects.

'Your clothes are soaked,' he says to Ruth, 'what the hell happened?'

Ruth closes her eyes.

'Where's Stuart?' Maeve asks.

'I don't know, Maeve,' he says, as if she's asked something unreasonable. 'He packed up and left, said he had an urgent job.'

'Mum was in the river.'

'What river?'

'In the woods.'

'The river in the woods,' he repeats. He blows out a breath. 'Just – just watch her for a moment, OK,' he tells Maeve.

Maeve stands just inside the door of the room while Alex says goodbye to the guests downstairs.

'Is Mum going to die?' Michael asks from the hall.

'No, don't be silly,' Ruth replies croakily, lifting her head with a wan smile. 'I'm just feeling a bit poorly this afternoon. I'll be fine, don't worry.'

Michael's question, the matter-of-factness of his voice, cracks open a new seam of loathing inside Maeve.

'C'mon,' Maeve says, 'let's play some Lego,' and she leaves the room, and her mother, and sits cross-legged on the floor of the twins' bedroom, building houses with them, trawling through the tub of bricks so that Iza's walls can all match.

The heatwave doesn't break for another week, but even when it does, the days feel heat-hazed, bleached out. Visitors come – a doctor, a lawyer, an aunt and uncle – and boxes pile up in the hall. Diana dies on the news. Maeve breaks her Discman, throwing it on the floor. Iza loses another tooth. Ruth leaves for a treatment centre.

Her parents are divorcing and selling the house; the family is moving back to London.

'It'll be good for us,' her father tells her, rifling through papers in the kitchen, in the same tone he used to tell her that the move here, to the countryside, would be good for them. 'Do you have to do that, Maeve?' he snaps, as she crunches on the ice cubes she's just scooped out of the tray.

She started eating ice cubes after the ice cream in the freezer ran out and now she craves them all the time. The painful crack between her teeth, holding them on her tongue until it feels bruised, the cold slick of water running down her chin.

Her father hasn't mentioned what happened between her and Stuart but his discomfort is clear, he can barely look at her some days. When she's feeling particularly sour, she thinks of asking him why what she did is in any way worse than what he did, cheating on Ruth.

'You'll be good when we get to London, won't you,' he says wearily.

'Good,' she repeats, thinking of what Stuart meant when he called her *good*, and what her parents mean. Whether she will ever *feel* good again, feel anything but hollow.

'You know what I mean. The twins need you to set an example for them – they need you, Maeve.'

'They need Mum.'

'Well, she can't be with them right now. She needs to get better. It's only going to be a couple of months. Then things will go back to normal.'

No, they won't, she thinks of replying, pointing out that their divorce, and being shuttled between two homes, are unlikely to feel normal to the twins. But, as sullen and contrary as she feels, even she has limits when she sees how tired her dad looks, when she knows how much her mother has scared him.

On her last night in the house, Maeve stays awake until the small hours, listening. To the wind that scratches the early fallen leaves across the gravel of the drive, to the creaks of floorboards that she can imagine might be footsteps, to the sudden rain shower that splashes drops through her open window which reach as far as her pillow, and to the silence of the phone.

It takes her a few days to unpack her things in London, and she thinks it will take her quite a bit longer to work out what to put on the walls of her room in the attic of her dad's new rented house, what to do with the stacks of postcards and prints of art, the five photos of her that are all she has left of the summer, of him.

Now she's set up her radio, and with the soundproofing of the eaves, she can play music late. If she stands on her bed she can swing open the skylight and lean her elbows on the window-sill, look out across London. The tinny beat from the radio, the soaring vocals of the song, can mix with the shunt of a late-night train, warring cats on a street nearby, the hum of traffic.

The air feels thicker here, sour-sweet with hot rubbish and tarmac, and the sky glows above the rooftops and tower build-ings dotted with red airplane warning lights, blots out the stars.

London is so vast she can never hold the shape of it in her head, and she only knows such a small part of it, even after a childhood here. But she's not a child any more. She can go to bars and parties, stay out late. She can smoke, drink, dance up close to someone in a club, dizzy with strobe. People she meets now won't know that she's been ill, and she can't decide if that is unnerving or thrilling.

You could become someone new here, she thinks, playing her fingers in the warm breeze, *lose yourself, find yourself. You could run into anyone here.*

Chapter Thirty-Four

This is a dry facility, they told me when I was admitted, and I admit that I laughed out loud. Not the best first impression to make when you've been trying to convince everyone around you that you don't need their help.

It was voluntary, my coming here, I wasn't dragged or forced, and when I saw the face of the kind consultant who interviewed me go still when I mentioned the river, I was the one who quickly said, *I think I need something residential, just for a little while.*

Yes, she said, *I'll get the forms you need*, and I clasped my hands in my lap tightly and looked at the floor.

My time here is being paid for from the money we had set aside for private schooling for the twins, more guilt to add to the load, even though Alex, logical as ever, had brought out the stats to show that the state schools the twins could go to back in London were just as good. Still, when I'm in the twice-weekly art therapy sessions – which sometimes feel like the only things that are keeping me sane here – it does feel wrong and topsy-turvy, selfish, to be messing about with paints while Alex is stuck with our children, dealing with the mess I've left behind.

Alex is reluctant to come to joint therapy sessions while I'm here, or later. *What's the point of rehashing everything?* he says, without irony. *I know we can parent civilly together. You just need to get your head down and get through your time there, learn your triggers and some new coping mechanisms* – terms he's cribbed from a book and will now repeat ad infinitum as though he is the one who coined them, but at least he's trying in his own way – *and then go back to work and everything will be fine. You'll be fine, Ruth.*

He knows about the girls now – the drowned ones, the Ophelia girls – but doesn't really understand why they're important. He doesn't know about the women yet. I'm not ready for that; I don't want him to hate me more than he already does, and besides, I don't actually know who I am, I don't know what I want.

Maybe I'm just confused, I tell the therapist I see here, and she tilts her head to the side and asks, *Do you believe that?*

Well, if you know what I believe then why don't you just tell me? I think of saying.

We talk about my mother in therapy. We talk about my father. We talk about how, when I left home as a teenager, I thought I had left them there too, without realizing that I had taken them with me, coiled and barbed inside.

Maeve won't talk to me. I hear her telling Alex to fuck off when he asks her to take the phone and have to tell him not to get too frustrated at her. *She's being childish*, he says, *and rude. You're her mother.*

Things are fraught between them. She's not his little girl any more and he doesn't know how to deal with that.

'You wanted her to be a normal teenager,' I tell him during our latest call. 'Teenagers are supposed to be moody and difficult.'

'Is what she did normal? She crossed the line this summer. Sorry, I know Stuart took advantage but it's not like she isn't responsible at all, she's not a child.'

'Do you tell her that? Alex—'

'Of course I don't talk to her about it, I don't even want to think about it. Come on, Ruth.'

'I can come home if she needs me, I'm doing better. I mean, I'm fine, really.'

I listen to the muffled scrape of the phone across his face as he turns his head to call the twins for tea. I'm sitting at the empty desk in my bedroom, running my palm across the groove some past resident has made with a pen. In the group meeting earlier I told a room full of strangers about how, when Maeve had just got ill and I was trying to juggle hospital appointments with the twins being unreasonable toddlers, I used to pour a shot – or two – of whiskey into my mid-morning coffee, *just to keep me going.*

'I don't think that would help,' Alex says kindly. 'I think the best thing you can do is to get better. The kids have to get used to living in separate houses anyway. We have to get used to a new normal.'

It doesn't escape my notice that Maeve and I have swapped places, that I am now institutionalized and under the care of medical professionals, that she was the one who pulled me out of the river. In worrying that I was a terrible mother, I became one, made her grow up too quick, burdened her.

So much of my time here is spent being asked to ruminate on the past. The past is where my hurts are, but my therapist wants me to reach back and rummage in all the boxes, lay each piece out on the ground for us to study. Stuart is one of those pieces, one of the shards that hurts when I pick it up. What he did, the secrets he kept.

Do you think I should call him up? I asked my therapist, half jokingly, *try and get some answers from him? Do you think that would help?*

What do you think? she replied with irritating sincerity. *What do you want to do?*

It's a sunny afternoon as I linger in the empty rec room, with its dry houseplants and table strewn with old magazines. I have the phone in my hand, a queasy tremor working its way through my chest.

'It's Ruth,' I say when he answers.

'How are you?' he asks, after silence has stretched across the line.

I tongue the inside of my cheek, marvelling at his even tone. 'As well as can be expected, I suppose.'

'I was going to ask if you wanted me to drop over some contraband, a good Chianti maybe.'

I bark a laugh. 'You would. You don't think I have a drinking problem?'

'No more than he did, your dad.'

'Dear old Dad.'

'Mm.'

I flick at the curled edges of the magazines, folding and unfolding the tips of the pages, before walking to the window overlooking the gardens. I can feel my pulse in my wrists, my hot face. I don't know how to start this conversation. Trying to reconcile our shared past with what he did this summer makes me feel dizzy. 'You got the better deal there, you know, from him.'

'Yeah,' he says and then clears his throat. 'Did you ever

wonder why I never went back there in the holidays to see my
dad, or yours? Why I stopped talking about law?'

'I mean, I knew your dad was a bully,' I say, 'I wouldn't
imagine you would be keen to see him.'

Outside, a bird hops across the wet lawn. I track it with my
finger pressed hard to the glass.

'You'd be right about that,' he says. 'He beat the shit out of
me at the end of that summer. He broke my nose, and a couple
of ribs. You didn't see me because I got the first train to my
mum's the next morning. I still had a black eye my first week
at Cambridge.'

'You never said.'

'I should have said, I think that now. I regret not telling you
about it, and about your father.'

'What about him?'

'Well. Your father took a shine to me, you know that part at
least.' There's a noise in the background of the call; a tap
turning on and off. 'And he had all the things I dared to hope
for as a boy with a violent, thick father and a useless mother . . .
the nice things, the house, the power and connections, you
know. He told me I was idealistic, and foolish. That wanting
to go into human rights law, although it wasn't called that back
then of course, was a stupid thing. But it was a gentle mockery,
it was paternal. He didn't stop letting me read his notes or
talking to him about his cases. I loved sitting in his office,
leaning against his shelves, and all those thick leather books.
You remember what it smelled like in there? The cigars and
the ink?'

'Yeah.'

He takes a sip of his drink, sucks his teeth. 'I thought he
wanted a surrogate son. Then I realized that wasn't all he
wanted, or it wasn't what he wanted at all.'

The rec room feels quiet, clinical, in a way it didn't five minutes ago in the streaming sun. I rest the crown of my head on the glass and close my eyes.

'The books about ancient Greece, the prints of classical statues, were one thing,' Stuart continues, 'but the way he looked at me, Ruth, the way he'd sit back in his chair and let his eyes wander up and down. He was a connoisseur, after all, he liked to be surrounded with nice things and I was one of them. Do you remember the fashions back then? The tight jeans, the tiny shorts? It was easy to tell when a man was looking, and I gave him a lot to look at. I thought about what I'd do when he finally made a move on me. I thought, *Yeah, sure. I'll do what he wants, what's it to me, why is it worse than anything else?* I was used to it anyway, I know how I looked back then. You know too, you drew me.'

I picture him with his lighter in his hand, flicking it round and round. It's dizzying.

'It was a fortnight after what happened with Camille – I guess in hindsight maybe my head wasn't quite right. You were back at school but I wasn't due at Cambridge until late September. I thought he might like the drawing – I mean, it wasn't a bad portrait,' he laughs, 'it got the gist across anyway. So the next time I was in his office, propped up against his desk in my tight shorts, on display, I let the drawing slip from a pile of books. And he looked at it and then at me. I could see everything on his face. His desire, his fear and horror, his anger.

'I've had a lot of time to think about it, Ruth, about why he reacted the way he did. It was fine when it was something unspoken, when he had the power, when he watched me and I let myself be watched, pretended not to know he would have happily bent me over his desk, but the picture, and my presentation of it, the way I broke the unspoken rules, *his* rules – it was like I had sunk down on my knees for him, it was that obscene.'

Someone walks past the closed door behind me and I feel my neck spasm. In the garden, two smokers share a light, cupping their hands against the breeze that scuttles leaves around their feet.

'Then he got control of himself again,' Stuart recounts, 'and turned his smile cold, contemptuous. You know how he could be, you know that more than me. *I'm not going to recommend you to any law firms*, he said. *In fact, I'm going to write to the law department at Cambridge myself to dissuade them from taking you too.*

'*Why?* I demanded, and I remember,' Stuart makes a sound in his throat, 'I remember my voice broke when I said that. And I remember your father's voice was so even when he replied, so . . . detached. *Because of your politics, because you think you can worm your way into my family through my daughter, because someone like you doesn't belong in law.* Because he felt like I had exposed him, Ruth, because he *could* do all of that. And that was bad enough, being told I was blacklisted for nothing I had done, for a drawing *you* made. But he also said something to my father, made an implication, and that's when he kicked the shit out of me. It would have been pointless to tell Dad I wasn't like that; I could have fucked a girl in front of him and he wouldn't care. I was soft, I had long hair and floppy clothes, I wanted to be an academic, I wanted to save the world.'

'My dad didn't have that kind of power, he couldn't have really blacklisted you,' I say, as if I don't care about what else he's told me, as if I'm not sweating and dry-mouthed, feverishly flicking through memories in my mind like an old flip-book, trying to put the story together in reverse.

'It was an old boys' club back then, everything was. It was hard enough getting them to switch my subject at the last minute before your father had a chance to do what he promised he would, I had to beg the college for it. University was a joke, it was all about who you knew and who your daddy was, what job they could get you in the city. Power, old money, new money pretending to be old money.'

'I didn't know.'

'You never suspected? Not once?'

'No.'

'How did you fall out, you and him?'

'I – I saw him at a party in London, an event at a gallery, when I was pregnant with the twins. He didn't want to see me there.' Or for me to see him? That's what I had suspected. 'We argued, he said some horrible things about my pregnancy.'

'Was he with someone?'

'No, I don't know. A client. An older client, not *that*.'

'Were you with someone?'

'Alex was at home with Maeve.'

'That wasn't what I meant.'

'I know what you meant,' I spit back, thinking of everything Stuart knows about me, what I've told, what I've given away. 'I was there by myself.'

'I saw him watching you at Maeve's christening, your dad,' Stuart says. '*I* was watching you at Maeve's christening.'

'What's that supposed to mean?'

'Sometimes, when you talk to women, you light up, you . . . flirt. Repression and shame are powerful things. When we hate something about ourselves we throw it on someone else, we make an enemy, an other.'

The friend I had run into at the gallery. My father looking over and seeing us together. The way he talked about me leaving Alex. I squeeze my eyes shut and try to remember. Did I only assume he was upset about the pregnancy, did I put those words in his mouth? Was that moment just a catalyst for everything to come to a head – the way he had treated me for so many years, his coldness, the scorn that sometimes looked like fear?

He had been so happy at my wedding, I remember that. *Your mother would be proud of you*, he had said at the reception, his cheeks flushed red with wine. I had set aside two bottles of the best just for him.

'I think that might be why he hated you,' Stuart says, after a pause. 'Because he thought you were the same.'

'I'm hardly the same as him. If anyone's preying on teenagers it's *you*.'

'I mean that neither of you are straight, are you?'

'It's you who's like him, taking advantage—'

'It's been painful for me – it *was* painful for me, to see you lie to yourself like that, to see those similarities between you both.'

'And that's why you left? That's what you're trying to say?' I scoff, frantically batting aside his accusations. 'No, if I had any small part to do with you deciding to go gallivanting round the world, it was because you knew I'd never want you the way you wanted me. And you know what else? I used to think we were close at university because I trusted you, but I think it might have been fear' – or shame, but the two go hand in hand, don't they – 'and I suspect you found ways of stoking it. I was afraid you would tell someone, that you knew about me, and that's why I kept you close – how did you know, anyway?'

'I saw you two in the woods, you and Camille. But Ruth—'

'Of course, a voyeur from the start.' I push myself away from the windowsill and shake my head at my reflection. 'I think you think I should *thank* you for telling me this about my dad, and for blowing up my family like you did this summer.'

'Ruth—'

'I'm not finished. What I was going to say is that I think you got lost out there, that you're too used to war and destruction. The world doesn't look right to you unless it's been torn apart.'

'No.'

'Like Maeve. You saw how good she was and you wanted to ruin that, to bring her down with you.'

'It's the opposite actually. What I've been through – seen – has made me search for beauty, appreciate goodness where I find it. What Maeve and I had—'

'Jesus Christ, listen to yourself. You talk of love, *love*, but all you've done is mess her around, and take what you want. You have no idea the damage you've done to her and you never will.' I turn my back to the window. 'I guess I should thank you though for making it clear today that it wasn't about love at all, but some kind of sick revenge. The sins of the father being visited on the daughter.'

'That's not— That's ridiculous, Ruth, you have to see that. You were the one who offered the annexe, I didn't invite myself.'

'Alex did.'

He mutters something under his breath, but I'm done with this, with him.

'You didn't have to take him up on it, you didn't have to do any of it,' I say. 'All these things that have been done to you. Your father, my father. It doesn't matter, you're in control, you *chose* to do what you did. I called because I wanted answers but you're just giving excuses. I never want to speak to you again, Stuart, ever.' I hang up the phone.

This is a dry facility, but some days I'm fucking parched for a drink. Just one. A small one. A sherry, a few sips of white wine, the dregs of a bottle of gin.

I am in control. The past shapes me – my flaws, the patterns of my mistakes – but I'm the one who can make choices now, to learn from it or not, to change or don't.

Fine words.

Do I believe them?

I'll try to. Because there's no soothing depths to drown in here, to get wilfully lost in, no pool of water to float in, weightless, untethered. Just my own squat body and the ground, just me.

Perhaps – like the clay from my art classes that I press my thumbs into, that I knead and roll and shape – there's a chance for me still to mould myself into something better, something stronger. Perhaps.

Epilogue

I go back and back to him to have his fingers [. . .]
clothe me in his dress of water, this garment that drenches
me, its slithering odour, its capacity for drowning
                              – Angela Carter, *The Erl-King*

2004

It's warm on the train south. The dry landscape through the
dusty windows looks sepia-toned, looks the same as it did
seven years ago. Maeve hasn't explored much of England; she's
been swallowed up by London, and has only left for weekend
trips to European cities and summers in French villas and
Italian hotels. Summers of hot nights and bitter mornings,
summers which, until two years ago, were documented artfully
by a camera that caught her looking lovely and sullen, burnt
and sun-fevered, drunk and tired.

When she first went on holiday without him, she found it
strange. To spend the day at the beach without thinking about
how she was posed, what story a picture of her might tell. To
not think of herself at one remove, a figure with a backdrop.
Even now, she can feel herself slipping into it, gazing out of
the window unseeing, wondering what she looks like to the
woman inching down the aisle of the train with her hands full
of shopping bags, the image she makes: curly red hair over

one shoulder, sandaled feet propped on the empty opposite seat, crumpled stonewash jeans, and a green men's t-shirt tied in a knot at her waist. Maeve had briefly considered wearing a sundress for this excursion, dressing for the part, for the scene, but couldn't muster the energy this morning to try one on, to shave her legs properly. Or is that a lie? Is her apparent dishevelment artful too? This is the problem with being alone sometimes, she thinks wryly, it gives you too much time to think.

This morning, she had slipped out of the house before her flatmates were awake, breathing in the thin summer's day, zipping up her jacket against the breeze as she walked to the tube, taking note of passersby with lazy interest, smiling at the sausage dog being walked by his yawning owner. She likes her life in London, the rented Victorian terrace, her small circle of friends who don't demand of her more than she's willing to give, or probe her for things she doesn't want to talk about. She likes the job at the art charity – even if she has to schmooze rich idiots, even if sometimes when she reviews a guest list she holds her breath just to check that he isn't included. It would be fine if he was, she tells herself; he's not going to cause a scene and neither is she. It might hurt a little, a pinch to the gut, a wave of shame, but she'll get over it, she'll survive. She's good at that, after all.

When the train stops at the station closest to her mother's old house, her grandfather's old house, she feels her breath tighten. She takes her feet down and crosses her legs, staring at the platform with a nonchalance she doesn't feel. She hasn't been back here since they sold the house and moved to London. It was hellish, moving weekly between her father's house and her mother's small flat that last year before university. But then any location, any setting, would probably have been hellish after dragging her mother from the river, and after her parents had found out how Maeve had spent the summer, what their houseguest had done.

As the train moves on, she shuts her eyes and remembers. Her father looking at her as though she were a stranger, his mouth twisting awkwardly, unable to cope with her not being a girl any more. Her mother treating her as if what had happened were a punishment for herself. All the silences and sighs and pained looks. All the attempts to get her to 'talk'. *You don't really want to know about it*, she told her mother, for the brief satisfaction of seeing her hurt again, *you don't really want to know about all the sordid details.*

They only wanted it to be over, for Maeve to put the past behind her, to move on, to become an ordinary teenage girl again. *But what teenage girl is ordinary?* Maeve thinks now, and – having heard some of the stories, given in crumbs and drunken outbursts, hinted at by her friends – why would getting drunk with girls her age and staggering out of clubs have been any better? There are dangers everywhere for young women and they come in so many shapes and sizes, forms, ages.

It was supposed to be the end that day, after Stuart's revelation that he had, at the least, had feelings for her mother when they were teenagers, and after he ran away and left her. With her broken heart, she felt like she was back to floating around inside the shell of her body, an invalid, her limbs trembling at intervals, her breath catching on jagged dry sobs at any odd time of the day. All she were her thoughts and her memories of the summer, her memories of him and what he told her in the field and every other moment they had shared. She believed him when he said it was different between them, that they suited one another, that Maeve was special. She *wanted* to believe it. She didn't want to be alone, to be stuck with her parents or with her peers, to be dragged back to those first few months out of hospital when living seemed like the hardest thing she'd have to do, when she didn't know how she would go on.

She didn't even have to do the work of reaching out herself, although she imagines she would have, soon enough. It was only a month after they had moved to London that Stuart called her at her father's house on the listed home number, told her to phone him again sometime and gave her his London address, said he wanted to see her, and that was that. No further seduction was needed. She was easy pickings.

It's not fair to think of herself like that, she reminds herself, as she drinks from the water bottle she bought from the cart, the plastic crinkling under her hand; she should have more compassion.

Easy, foolish, blind, young. She was young, but she felt old, maybe all sick children do. She struggled to muster enthusiasm for school, for people her age, finding it easier just to hunker down in his flat and let herself be cared for, subsumed. When her parents found out where she was going after school and on weekends, they tried to stop her but she wouldn't let them, and they could hardly lock her up and throw away the key. If they had, she would have only thrown down her hair and he would have climbed up to get her. And at the end of her first year of university, she gave up pretending and moved in with him full-time.

Young, Stuart liked that she was young. The prospect of her growing older, evolving beyond him, terrified him. She remembers one evening when she came home from an event she had attended without him.

'Nice lipstick,' he had said in the kitchen as she gulped
down the water he had poured, 'don't you look all grown up.'

He had seen her wearing make-up before. She had worn it
for him sometimes; red lipstick, pink, and wings of dark
eyeliner, thick mascara. But she wasn't wearing it for him now.

'Should I not want to grow up?'

He smiled tightly. She imagined him reaching out to smear
it across her cheek with his thumb. But that wasn't his style.
'All grown up,' he said again, and leaned back against the
countertop, and she felt humiliated just the same.

'You've ruined me, you know,' she told him once, kneeling
over him in bed, looking at all the lines in his face, the patches
of stubble, the folds of his neck. She wanted him to feel
remorse, to see what he'd done to her, but not enough remorse,
maybe, to regret it either.

'Don't be ridiculous,' he laughed, 'don't you know that it's
you who's ruined me? You've got your whole life ahead of you
– what have I got but growing old and grey and useless?'

'What has you being *old* got to do with me?' she said, to
make him flinch.

'You can be a cruel little girl, you know that, sweetheart.'

I'm what you made me, she wanted to reply, even though
that wasn't true. She wasn't some blank page before he arrived
that summer, an empty vessel for him to pour his fantasies
into. She was hungry, ravenous, filled up to the brim with
stories that he was only too willing to act out. Yes, he had
moulded her – bought her clothes, guided her tastes in food
and drink and culture (tripping down the street with him after
seeing a play at the Southbank, sitting underneath his heavy
arm in the back row of a slow arthouse film, falling into a taxi
after a party in Hackney and starting an argument with him
that ended in tears), influenced her opinions, her behaviour

– but she thought that she had done the same to him too. He had been guided by her own desires, changed himself into what she wanted. *I've always been eager to please*, he joked once, without realizing it was a confession. The child of an alcoholic mother, he liked to be wanted, to feel useful, needed. And who could need him more than a waifish teenage girl who wanted to be scooped up and taken away from her life, from living? She had taken from him greedily – time, money, attention, love – just as he had stolen things from her that she would never ever get back.

Her mother had seen a villain and she a saviour. But in the end he was just a man. Kind, mercurial, complicated, cruel, charismatic, damaged. Still, untangling herself from him was the work of years. Moving out, moving back in. Leaving him, calling him up at 2 a.m. to save her. Telling him that she had slept with someone else, listening to him tell her she had only done it to make a point to him and knowing he was telling the truth. Changing her number, leaving pleading text messages unsent.

She can smell the sea before the train pulls into the last station and hear the raucous call of seagulls overhead. The town feels familiar, even though she's never been here before. Fading, whitewashed, with narrow streets and a wind that whips in from the thin strip of the sandy beach. It's three weeks after the exhibition opened and a weekday morning; she might even have the gallery to herself, she thinks, as she arrives outside the unassuming building, which doesn't have a poster hanging outside as she feared it would.

The invitation in the post, inside the envelope addressed in familiar handwriting, only had one image on it, a hand in water with a white ribbon threaded around its fingers. Her hand.

She wasn't surprised, only that it had taken him so long to put the exhibition together. She knew that she'd have to reckon with the images someday; she had signed a release form years ago, after all. A younger version of her might think that he arranged the whole thing as a message to her, a way to win her back. Perhaps part of her does think that, the part that still sighs over myths and stories, that dresses up sometimes only to stand in front of her bedroom mirror and mouth along with the crooning of a sad song.

Photography has never been her favourite artform, to his chagrin, and to her mother's relief. Maeve and her mother have monthly trips to galleries and museums now, meeting at weekends when Iza and Michael are busy with their friends. The rift between them has eased; Maeve has forgiven her, or at least come to realize that her parents are both fallible adults, their own people, and not just the possessions of their children. Over lunch, her mother talks about her work, about the twins and their teenage dramas. Maeve talks about her job and her friends and the health niggles that crop up now and then, her fears of what the future effects of such strong doses of chemotherapy drugs might have on her body. The only thing she and her mother don't talk about is dating – the women that Ruth sees, or Maeve's current lack of it – but she can tell that Ruth is happier, more settled, and she's quietly relieved each time her mother hands back the drinks menu and asks only for water.

Maeve is waved ahead by the bored attendant and enters the first room, her sandals slapping on the concrete floor. As she gazes around she lets out a laughing breath. She isn't here – not her face or her body.

The first image is of the bath near the annexe, flowers floating in a shape that suggests a girl might have been lying there before she vanished. The second is of her sodden dress in its heap on the floor, the coil of the black ribbon peeking out from the lace. The third: her wet footprints on flagstones. The fourth: a hairbrush with wisps of red hair. The fifth: the back of her head on the pillow, a water glass on the table in the foreground next to a posy of flowers. The sixth: the field, the depression in the grass made when she lay down for that first photoshoot, the echo of her body.

Two young women who look like art students enter from the second room and take a last glance around.

'Ana Mendieta did it better,' one of them says dryly to the other.

'I was going to say,' her friend replies as Maeve hides a smile. 'I'm almost offended, but not really, because it's so derivative. Typical man to think he's doing something new when really he's just copying second-wave women artists.'

Maeve will wait to see the other rooms before drawing her opinion, but right now, she agrees. She thinks of the Polaroids she saw in that snatched moment, the ones of her mother and the other girls. She's sure that no picture Stuart took could be better than theirs. Stranger, purer, angrier, more unsettling, lovelier. A perfect snapshot of girlhood. Even the accidental blur in those shots was artful, the river a suggestion of light, their outlines glowing.

The light is dimmer in the second room of the gallery, the photographs picked out by spotlights. She feels her face get warmer as she circles the images in this room, her shoulders hunching, aware of the two other gallery visitors standing studiously in front of photographs of her that aren't quite PG. Close-ups of her body in the bath, in the shower, lying by the side of the pool – shoulder, leg, chest, hip. Always clothed, but then wet dresses and slips and t-shirts don't hide much of the shape underneath. *They're about colour and form, line and shadow*, she hears him explain in her head. *They're about vulnerability*, she thinks in counterpoint, *voyeurism, a camera consuming its subject. Sex.*

Maeve had tried to read a biography of Lizzie Siddal once, thinking that she might find herself in there, that it might help her understand. But she never got past the first dry paragraph. What she wanted to know was how Lizzie felt when the water got cold, when her body started shivering. Did she feel there was no point in leaving the water, that she had made her choice already? Did she just want to please him, to be beautiful for him, and would have accepted any discomfort that might be owed for that? Or did she want to be beautiful for herself, to be immortalized, young and lovely? Or was she thinking of nothing much at all, stoic, doing as she had been told? Or thinking of dinner, humming a song in her head, cursing the man whose brush flicked back and forth across the canvas?

She enters the third and last room. In contrast to the smaller size of the pictures in the others, the image here covers a whole wall and is impossible to ignore: Maeve, head to toe, in her white dress in the bath, clutching flowers in a loose grip and looking up at the camera, the jeans of the photographer's legs two dark shapes against the paleness of her skin, the cream of the enamel. Of course he had to include himself in this image, she thinks with an inward scoff, as she considers it, tilting her head. Considers herself, looking younger than she thought she had been.

The girl in the picture isn't looking at Stuart at all, she realizes, but through him, at the viewer and beyond them. She's looking at herself, this future self. Asking her to be a witness. *I see you*, she wants to say. *I see your hunger and your sadness, the things you don't think you should let yourself want. I see how scared you are of living, of leaving girlhood behind.*

Someone walks through from the previous room, another young student, with a camera hanging around his neck. He comes to stand beside Maeve, looking at the picture and then at her and back to the image.

'Excuse me,' he says, clearing his throat, 'do you mind if I take a picture of you in front of that? It's just, your hair—'

Does he realize that she and the model are the same girl, or does he think they're close enough to look interesting?

'No, sorry,' she says, and studies herself as he walks away.

Acknowledgements

Parts of this novel have lived in my head for fifteen years or more and writing it felt like the most wonderful hazy fever dream of an experience; I loved it from the very first words of that first draft, and all the way through edits and copyedits and final read-throughs, so thank you to this novel (if one can thank one's own novel) for bringing me so much satisfaction and joy, and to the characters for keeping me company into the small hours at my desk as I unknotted their plots and wove together their stories.

Thank you to all of those who made the book you hold in your hands possible:

The women and girls whose self-portraits of Ophelia inspired this novel and whose photos seemed to haunt me wherever I went on the internet.

Maggie Bridge, for an electrifying conversation on a bench by the lake in Regent's Park five years ago that made me think this novel might have a readership; and for your enthusiastic response to an early draft.

Hayley Steed, for your warmth and your shrewdness, for championing this book from the beginning and for being the best agent a girl could wish for. Liane-Louise Smith and everyone at the Madeline Milburn Agency for your indefatigable energy.

Sam Humphreys, for the clarity of your editorial vision and for your wisdom, kindness, and encouragement. Alice Gray, for your galvanising enthusiasm, for encouraging me to delve deeper into the parts I had set aside for being 'too much', and for the care you've taken with my novel at every stage. Rosie Wilson, Neil Lang, Charlotte Wright, and everyone at Mantle and Pan Macmillan.

Nicole Angeloro, for your generous and insightful feedback which unearthed new threads of imagery and meaning for me in this novel, and for your support and enthusiasm. Lisa Glover, Liz Anderson, Emma Gordon, Martha Kennedy, and everyone at Houghton Mifflin Harcourt.

My first novel (and Hetty, Lucy, Heloise, Mary, and all the animals), for everything you taught me about writing and editing.

Fellow authors, for your comradery. Booksellers, book bloggers, reviewers, and publishing people for your support. Waterstones, for championing my first novel. The independent bookshops of Edinburgh for being the best bookshops in the land—Lighthouse Bookshop (thank you for giving me the first launch of my dreams!), Edinburgh Bookshop, Portobello Bookshop and Golden Hare Books.

Abbie Greaves, for the gossip/emotional scaffolding/laughter. Molly Aitken, for your sisterhood, for the hours and hours we've spent talking about the dark delights of storytelling, and for your immaculate taste.

My friends, who travelled to the launch of my first novel and checked in on me when I was editing my second. Among them: Iza Vermesi, Leah Hazard, Ursula Burger, Imogen

Lambert, Aude Claret, Nadine Aisha Jassat, Katherine Harding, and Sally Brammall.

Andy and Madeline (and Jack) for being legends. My parents for the fathomless depths of your love and support.

And those of you along the way who taught me how to swim.

A Note from the Author

Dear Reader,

I don't remember the first time I saw Millais's infamous painting of Ophelia and whether it was before or after I had come across the echoes, the ripples, of that image in art and fashion, movies and photography. As a girl, when I floated on my back in a body of water, I sometimes imagined I was her, wondering what I might look like from dry land.

This novel sprang from my fascination with the proliferation of self-portraits of women and girls posing as Ophelia, clutching bouquets of flowers in rivers, lakes, and, more often than not, a humble bathtub—self-portraits that have haunted me across image-sharing sites since I was a teenager myself. Where does that impulse come from, to pose as a beautiful, dying, girl, I wondered, and what does it say about the experience of girlhood?

I wrote this novel in a fever dream of late nights, drawing from memories of my own hazy summers exploring the fields, the woods, and the cold waters of the river near my childhood home. I loved writing it, and I hope you enjoyed reading it.

—Jane Healey

A Discussion Guide

1. Who are the Ophelia girls and how did they get their name?
    What are some of the personas they take on, and what do
    these figures have in common? How do their parents feel
    about their behavior and why did Ruth ultimately "run from
    that summer" and "tr[y] to forget it" (2)? What do you think
    she meant when she said that the Ophelia girls' "inspiration
    had been more primal, innate, as if a drowning girl lived
    inside each of [them]" (15)?

2. Evaluate voice and narration. Why do you think that the
    author chose to write the story in alternating first-person
    and third-person narratives? Why might the author have
    chosen to let Ruth tell her own story, while Maeve's is
    observed from a distance? How do these alternating story
    lines shed light on girlhood and the transition to woman-
    hood, with both how they are lived and remembered
    working in tandem to provide perspective?

3. How was Maeve affected by her experience of illness, and
    how did she feel after coming "back from the brink" (4)?
    What does Maeve crave once she is in a period of remis-
    sion? Maeve's parents say repeatedly that they want her to

be a "normal" teenage girl now that her illness is in remission, but what does the book reveal about what is "normal" or common about the experience of girlhood during these years?

4. Explore the theme of desire—particularly illicit desire. What is "one thing about girlhood" Ruth forgets? What does she say that she and her friends were "desperate . . . to be told" (140)?

   What—or whom—do the characters in the book desire, and how does this influence their choices? Why do they feel that they must keep these desires secret? Do any of the characters ever get what they desire? If so, what are the effects or consequences of this?

5. Discuss setting and imagery. How do they underscore the major themes and motifs of the novel? For example, why does the author have Ruth reflect often on the condition of the grand home they are living in? How do descriptions of the outdoor setting reflect the period of life that Ruth and her friends or Maeve find themselves in and their mindsets? How does the author use water as both symbol and motif to lend insight into the emotional lives of the characters and to build suspense?

6. How does the author work with secrets as a motif of the novel? What are some of the secrets that the characters keep, and why do they feel that they must keep these things private? How do their secrets shed light on social norms and what is—or was—considered taboo? While the novel takes place in the 1970s and the 1990s, how might these situations be viewed today? Has much changed? Explain.

7. How does the book create a conversation around memory and trauma? What are some of the memories that Ruth and Maeve carry with them into the present, and how do these memories affect them and their relationships? Does the book suggest how they might best deal with these difficult memories and heal from these traumas?

8. What daydream does Maeve tell Stuart that she had when she was ill? What does this dream reveal about the common stories that girls grow up with and their influence on girls' experiences, hopes, desires, and expectations for their future? How does this compare to the stories appropriated by Ruth and the Ophelia girls? What does this suggest about the power and influence of art and storytelling and the significance of dominant narratives or canon, for better or worse?

9. Consider the various parent-child relationships depicted in the story. What is Maeve's relationship like with her mother Ruth? How does Ruth feel about being a mother? Why was Ruth estranged from her own father, and how did her understanding of this change by the book's conclusion? What does the novel ultimately reveal about parenthood? What does Maeve say in the book's conclusion that she has learned about her parents, and how does this change her way of understanding them?

10. How does the author take on the subject of the gaze in order to explore issues of vulnerability, power, and control? What does the book suggest about the male gaze in particular, and its effect on those who are the subject of this gaze? How do the Ophelia girls and Maeve change

their behavior based on who is looking at them? "Photography is about power," Stuart says (302), but what does he mean by this? How does the book create a larger conversation about what it means to see and be seen?

11. Were you surprised by the conclusion of the book? Why do you think that Maeve made the choices that she did? Why might she have decided to attend the exhibition with her photographs, and why do you think that she declines to be photographed at the story's end? What might her choice be symbolic of? How do her perspectives on desire, power, and her own sense of self seem to have shifted by the story's end?

Read on for an excerpt from
Jane Healey's first novel,

The Animals at Lockwood Manor

In August 1939, thirty-year-old Hetty Cartwright arrives at Lockwood Manor to oversee a natural history museum collection that has been taken out of London for safekeeping. She is unprepared for the scale of her duties: protecting her charges from party guests, wild animals, the elements, the tyrannical Major Lockwood, and Luftwaffe bombs. Most of all, she is unprepared for the beautiful and haunted Lucy Lockwood, who has spent much of her life cloistered at Lockwood suffering from bad nerves. The arrival of the collection brings new freedom for Lucy, but it also resurfaces her nightmares and memories of her late mother. When the animals appear to have moved overnight and exhibits go missing, it is not only Hetty's future employment that is in danger, but her sanity too. There's something, or someone, in the house. Someone stalking her through its darkened corridors . . .

Prologue

Large houses are difficult to keep an eye on, to control, my mother used to tell me, looking fraught and harried, before bustling out of the room to find the housekeeper or the butler or the tweeny maid to demand a full reckoning of what was happening in the far corners of the house. Lockwood Manor had four floors, six sets of stairs, and ninety-two rooms, and she wanted to know what was happening in each of them, at all times.

It was the not knowing that seemed to concern her most, but she had a long list of specific fears too: mold that squatted behind large pieces of furniture; rotten window frames that let in an unwholesome breeze; mice that had gnawed a home in a sofa; loose floorboards whose nails had pricked their way free in the heat or the cold; wires that sparked and spat; birds that had nested in a wardrobe in some forgotten servant's room, scratching the walls with their claws; damp that had bled through a gap in the roof tiling; a carpet that was being feasted upon by hungry moths; pipes that rattled their way to bursting; and a silt flood that slithered ever closer to the basement.

For my grandmother, who had grown up in the time when every task had a servant assigned to it, when calling for tea necessitated the maneuvering of a veritable regiment, it was the servants she suspected. They were lazy, slapdash in their work, prone to stealing; they spent their time idling and daydreaming and making mischief. She wore a vast selection of pale gloves, neatly pressed by her own personal maid, ever ready to sweep a pointed finger along a mantelpiece or a shelf, and if she found the merest whisper of dust she would summon the housekeeper. Because my grandmother was also of an age where the lady of the house did not deign to speak to any servants but the housekeeper, the poor woman was forever being called away from her tasks to rush through the back corridors of the house and appear in front of Lady Lockwood as if from the ether.

There was thus relief felt among the servants when my mother and grandmother died a few months back in a single awful motorcar accident, and I did not begrudge them it; I knew what harsh taskmasters these two women had been, and besides, I had seen the servants weep dearly at their funeral, so I knew they also cared. I swore that I would not share my relatives' habit of making impossible demands on the servants, and yet my mother and grandmother's role—that of keeping an eye on the house, that of keeping it in mind—was one that I reluctantly took on my own shoulders, like the fur coats I was also left; scratchy, heavy things that bristled with the claws and teeth of the beasts that had been skinned to make them, and swamped my form completely.

Ever since I was a young child, I had suffered from attacks of nerves and a wild imagination that made sleep hard to come by. It was my favorite governess, the one who used to sing lullabies to me when I was a few years too old for them, who taught me a way of tricking my mind into sleep: I should picture myself walking through Lockwood Manor, she said, gliding through the rooms one by one, and count them as if I was counting sheep— and before I could finish even one floor, I would be asleep. It was a method that worked just as she said, although it did not succeed in removing the monstrous nightmares I suffered once I had fallen asleep—dreams of a beast hunting me and, sometimes, of a desperate search through the corridors of my home for a blue room in which I knew some horrible creature was trapped and scratching at the walls, a search which baffled me when I woke up, knowing that there was no such room at Lockwood.

But after my mother and grandmother passed away, it no longer felt like a simple counting game, a trick to help my mind ease into sleep; it took on a new and frantic urgency. I could not sleep until my mind had completed a full tour of the house, and if I made a mistake—if I forgot the buttery, or the bathroom on the second floor with its sink ripped out, or the housekeeper's bedroom with the narrow eaves—then everything was ruined and I was compelled to start again from the very beginning, my heart rabbiting in my chest, my back prickling with sweat.

Sometimes, though it was mad to think so, I felt that if I did not concentrate, if I did not count all the rooms and hold them all in my mind, everything that my mother had feared would occur, and more; that the very edges of the house would spin apart, that the walls would crack and crumble, that something truly terrible, something I could not even fathom, would happen.

Lockwood had too many empty rooms. They sat there, hushed and gaping, waiting for my mind to fill them with horrors— specters and shadows and strange creeping creatures. And sometimes what was already there was frightening enough: empty chairs; the hulk of a hollow wardrobe; a painting that slid off the wall of its own accord and shattered on the floor; the billowing of a curtain in a stray gust of wind; a lightbulb that flickered like a message from the beyond. Empty rooms hold the possibility of people lurking inside them—truants, intruders, spirits. And when there is enough space for one's mind to wander, one can imagine that loved ones are not dead, but only waiting in a room *out of the way, a room you forgot you had, and the urge to search for them, to haunt the corridors and the rooms of your house until you find them, becomes overwhelming.*

But there was respite on the horizon, because the house would not be empty for long, and myself and my father and the servants—not that we had many by this stage, for we seemed to find them hard to keep—would soon have company. For it was August, and trucks were on their way from London, evacuees from the coming war looking for shelter within the walls of Lockwood. A population feathered, furred, beaked, hooved, ruffed, clawed, and taloned would soon lodge here, and when the rooms were occupied again, when they had a purpose, and were full to bursting, my mind would settle again, and the house would settle again. No more empty, echoing rooms; no more bad nerves; no more ghosts. I was sure of it.